The Essays

CHICANA & CHICANO
VISIONS OF THE AMÉRICAS

Series Editor

Robert Con Davis-Undiano

Editorial Board

Rudolfo Anaya

Denise Chávez

David Draper Clark

María Amparo Escandón

María Herrera-Sobek

Rolando Hinojosa-Smith

Demetria Martínez

Carlos Monsiváis

Rafael Pérez-Torres

Leroy V. Quintana

José Davíd Saldívar

Ramón Saldívar

The Essays

Rudolfo Anaya

Foreword by Robert Con Davis-Undiano

UNIVERSITY OF OKLAHOMA PRESS : NORMAN

The Essays is Volume 7 in the Chicana & Chicano Visions of the Américas series.

Library of Congress Cataloging-in-Publication Data

Anaya, Rudolfo A.
[Essays. Selections]
The essays / Rudolfo Anaya ; foreword by Robert Con Davis-Undiano.
    p. cm. — (Chicana & Chicano visions of the Américas ; v. 7)
Includes bibliographical references.
ISBN 978-0-8061-4023-0 (alk. paper)
I. Title.
PS3551.N27A6 2009
814'.54—dc22

                                                                    2008045200

The paper in this book meets the guidelines for permanence and durability of the committee on Production Guidelines for Book Longevity of the Council on Library Resources, Inc. ∞

1 2 3 4 5 6 7 8 9 10

I dedicate this collection to the writers, artists, teachers, students, community activists, politicians, and all who have worked purposefully and diligently to achieve social and political justice for the Mexican American community.

Our civil rights movement of the 1960s and 1970s included an outpouring of artistic work. We called our efforts el Movimiento Chicano, the Chicano Movement. We marched and demanded equality in all fields of endeavor from the mainstream society.

I presented many of these essays and lectures at state and national teachers' conferences. I read them at community gatherings and in university settings. One of my objectives was achieving equal educational opportunities for Mexican Americans. Looking back, Chicanos and Chicanas involved in the Chicano Movement can say we did make a difference. In many positive ways we influenced this country's relationship to our community. Old prejudices began to fall away as many heard our call and joined the struggle.

Some of my compatriots from those years are dead; some are still working and contributing. We fought for justice, not only for our community, but for all people. Now it's up to new generations to work at making this a better world. Much remains to be done.

ALSO BY RUDOLFO ANAYA

Bless Me, Ultima
Heart of Aztlan
Tortuga
The Silence of the Llano
The Legend of La Llorona
A Chicano In China
Lord of the Dawn: The Legend of Quetzalcóatl
Alburquerque
The Anaya Reader
Zia Summer
Jalamanta: A Message from the Desert
Rio Grande Fall
Shaman Winter
Serafina's Stories
Jemez Spring
Curse of the ChupaCabra
The Man Who Could Fly and Other Stories
ChupaCabra and the Roswell UFO

CHILDREN'S BOOKS

The Adventures of Juan Chicaspatas
The Farolitos of Christmas: A New Mexico Christmas Story
Maya's Children: The Story of La Llorona
Farolitos for Abuelo
My Land Sings: Stories from the Rio Grande
Elegy on the Death of César Chávez
Roadrunner's Dance
The Santero's Miracle: A Bilingual Story
The First Tortilla: A Bilingual Story
Juan and the Jackalope: A Children's Book in Verse

Contents

Part IV. Culture and Art of the Southwest

Part V. Literature of the Southwest

Part VI. Modern Ethnic Literature and Culture

Series Editor's Foreword

The Essays by Rudolfo Anaya presents a fresh view of this major writer by bringing together in one volume for the first time all fifty-two of his essays. For almost forty years, the world has known Rudolfo Anaya as an important novelist who wrote the classics *Bless Me, Ultima* (1972), *Heart of Aztlan* (1973), *Tortuga* (1976), the Sonny Baca novels, and many other successful novels, short stories, and plays. With this volume of essays, readers will discover the full range of Anaya's formidable powers as an essayist, his poignant and still timely observations, his wit, and his sure touch as a writer of nonfiction prose. These essays also establish his status as a shrewd commentator on the world around us—about literature's ability to probe the deep myths underlying our culture, the workings of censorship, land-use policy, the value of tradition and the past, Chicano literature and art, the sense of place in literature, and respect for the environment, among other vital topics.

With this volume people will learn that Anaya is a major essayist as well as a major novelist. Why don't more people know that fact already? One answer is that he is well defined by his reputation as a novelist, but it is also true that essays get published once in magazines and newspapers and then typically are "lost." This fact is a hazard for essayists, as over time there is no convenient way for readers to locate previously published essays, while novels and even short stories often are excerpted and otherwise kept in print. Even the most brilliant essays flash like meteors in the dark sky and then disappear—that is, unless they are gathered and published in a single volume like this one.

The publication of these fifty-two essays—four of them published for the first time—is an important literary event, as an almost lost side of Anaya's work is being unearthed for general and scholarly readers to enjoy. The moment is especially timely for highlighting Anaya as the public intellectual these essays show him to be. The current debate on "green" policies and the environment touching almost every aspect of our lives draws attention to the ideas that were always visionary and ahead of their time in Anaya's essays. Current discussions, in other words, need the insights that Anaya provides, especially concerning our sacred relationship with the earth.

This volume shows that his essays deserve an even larger audience than they found the first time around. For nearly forty years he has shared his insights on the clash of traditional values and the forces of modern commerce and unbridled land development. He explores as few others do the value of cultural traditions and embracing a relationship with the sacred, and no one has so fully analyzed, as Anaya has done, the devastation that may occur when communities lose touch with their pasts and their origins.

Literary scholars will need to consult the corpus of Anaya's essays for the light they shed on his other work. The early career struggle to get published, his commitment to his "New World" vision, and his broad reading in European and American literature are all clarified in these essays. The freshness of these essays, however, makes an especially strong case for making them widely available for a general reader. The foremost Latino writer of his time, Anaya probes the myths, especially in his essays of the 1980s and 1990s, underlying cultural and social values and choices for how we live, and especially the relationships between people and the land they inhabit. That relationship points to critical ethical decisions in relation to land and the sustainability of communities. He discussed this broad range of social and cultural choices before such questions became fashionable and "green." Public intellectuals like Anaya, especially when not originally *from* the mainstream, can see the dominant culture aslant and, in so doing, can make connections otherwise unavailable and can even see ahead to points where present issues intersect with future possibilities.

Anaya's essays address a rich array of topics in literature, art, society, and culture. Most importantly, they highlight a large-scale reorientation currently taking place in America. In dramatic fashion, and with rare effectiveness, Anaya foretells a massive shift in the way we understand American culture. He argues for shifting to a new focus with a north/south axis of orientation to the Americas that links the United States to Latin America—what he calls a "New World" perspective. In this view, the U.S. is no longer the isolated "exception" to culture but an active participant in a five-hundred-year historical and cultural drama taking place in our own backyard. This hemispheric view of the U.S. focuses less on Dutch and English settlement and more on the great variety of developments taking place in the Americas during this time.

His promotion of a north/south orientation competes directly with the traditional east/west orientation emphasizing American exceptionalism and westward expansion. Anaya and a few others—especially Genaro M. Padilla, Ramón Gutiérrez, and María Herrera Sobek—effectively addressed these issues in the second half of the twentieth century, and others have followed suit. Even now, however, not every cultural historian working in this area wants to emphasize the U.S. from the "north/south" viewpoint that Anaya emphasizes, a lack owing surely to the influence of "official" histories oriented toward the east coast and the east/west perspective over the last two hundred years.

In this "New World" perspective, the diversity inherent to U.S. national culture reflects the influence of life in the Americas and says little about Dutch and British colonization. The traditional view focused on the eastern seaboard belies the rich traditions of the ancient peoples of the New World and extensive Spanish settlement before the British arrived. David J. Weber and other historians have discussed this perspective on cultural development over the whole of North and South America (see especially *The Spanish Frontier in North America*, Yale University Press, 1992).

Anaya's essays tell this big story about modern America's need to rediscover itself within the diverse cultures and rich traditions of this hemisphere—regarding trade routes, shared religions, wars, marriages, and other New World developments contributing to the growth of the mestizo (mixed heritage) cultures of the New World. This dramatic shift of perspective to a north/south orientation is happening at a time when Latinos are ascending to economic, political, and cultural power in the U.S. Globalization is also revealing the cross-cultural ties that already exist and the long-standing internationalism evident in so much of the United States. The limited history that highlighted European immigration, westward expansion, and domination of Native cultures is passing and giving way to a hemispheric view of cultural and social history.

Anaya attempts to focus this more expansive view by demonstrating at close range how the world looks when books, people, land, and art are viewed from the New World perspective. This perspective is partially empowered by the rise in Latino populations and economic growth and also by the work of writers like Anaya. The commentary in his essays about life and culture in the Americas, and his reframing of "American" culture within the larger context of Latin America and its history in the New World, is not about promoting a tribe or recognition of Native sovereignty. His more expansive view promotes a permanent shift of perspective that begins with the assumption that Latin America is the proper stage for understanding culture in our hemisphere over the past five hundred years.

Anaya details this hemispheric, cultural context in the essay "Aztlán: A Homeland without Boundaries." This essay shows that Mexican folklore long ago identified the American Southwest as a sacred site of origin for Aztec culture. Whether this claim is historically accurate or not, it has long been said that Mexico City provided the staging for mythical/historical acts and dramas that possibly began in New Mexico, particularly in Santa Fe. In "The New World Man" he asserts that "the indigenous American perspective, or New World view . . . is at the core of my search." The story that emerges from both essays tells about a large stage upon which the Spanish and the English step briefly. He emphasizes the cultural drama of glimpsing the larger view of Spanish and native peoples, a view that was previously foreclosed as "western expansion" focused on Anglo culture and its impact. "We must know more of the synthesis of our Spanish and Indian natures," he writes, "and [also] know more of the multiple heritages of the Americas" ("The New World Man").

The New World as Anaya defines it is grounded in the rich mix of the multiple heritages that actually make up our area of the world. Anaya's articulation of this emergent perspective foregrounds Native culture but includes all that has happened to make the New World an incredibly rich sphere of cultural possibilities.

This revolutionary perspective informs all of Anaya's work, his essays and fiction, from his earliest through his most recent work. In effect, any cultural event, book, person, or theme that Anaya writes about promotes an understanding of the New World perspective that he defined and embodies. Each of his essays stages an encounter of this perspective in relation to an issue that can be used to clarify a little more about life in the Americas. How would a particular book, artist, commercial practice, or cultural event such as censorship, the loss of a historic land grant, or the emergence of the Chicano tradition be understood in the perspective that Anaya advances? Each of his essays answers this question anew, and each essay conveys the New World inflection in everything it says.

The vision of Anaya's essays can be seen as well in his novels, short stories, and plays. He argues that the totality of America's sense of itself—what it has been and what it will become—needs to incorporate a vision that arises from indigenous traditions in the Americas. A vision of this magnitude, challenging and potentially disruptive to received notions of the hemisphere, could get deliberately suppressed, marginalized, or simply ignored. Truly challenging ideas commonly get such treatment. Anaya succeeds in publishing many essays that are challenging in this way—I would argue—because they are exceptionally engaging and are kept below the culture's radar by being published in academic magazines and journals.

Two characteristics of his essay writing—pertinent to the classical tradition of the essay—help to explain this success. First is the voice of Anaya himself. In essays like "Requiem for a Lowrider," "The Journal of a Chicano in China," "Shaman of Words," and "Take the Tortillas out of Your Poetry," he has mastered the art of speaking in an unassuming and personal voice. He does this by drawing examples from personal experience (as with the story of his friend Jessie in "Requiem for a Lowrider" and his travel to China in "The Journal of a Chicano in China"), and he lets these stories speak as stories (without extensive analysis) to establish their own authority. He could cite statistical trends or sociological literature that would be relevant to the contemporary scene, but he uses stories to let his readers participate in the cultural perspective he is trying to foreground. In so doing, Anaya establishes the authority of his argument not in an external source but in the reader's assessment and experience of the essay.

"Voice" in Anaya's essays is a constructed effect created by the persistence of certain patterns of diction and examples and references from the U.S. Southwest, as well as values that seem to arise from life in the Southwest. Anaya makes frequent use of the eastern New Mexico setting and the famous llano (plains) that are also common points of reference in his fiction. He grounds his own spiritual and ecological commitments in relation to New Mexico culture and geography. We see this when he encourages readers to associate great energy and discovery in eastern New Mexico with the llano and placidity and nurture over time with the mountains nearby and the agrarian life at their base. His "voice" in these essays comes from the totality of choices he makes—cultural and geographic references and language range (diction) and also how he frames his values within those details. Readers come to value these references as belonging to Anaya's voice and his worldview.

Adopting this voice also means using accessible and non-specialized language. He has a good ear for reproducing working-class speech and creates the impression of using the "plain" language of local communities instead of sociological insider talk. Anaya's essay about lowriders and Chicano youth who need to stay in school could easily fall into professional "education speak" and sociological jargon about latchkey children, demographic trends, and parental responsibility. Anaya never chooses to go in that direction. Readers may not be immediately familiar with New Mexico culture, but Anaya's repeated use of that setting creates familiarity. In other words, the voice in Anaya's work comes from his choices to avoid specialized language, to stay within a geographical frame, but also to take the time to effectively orient his readers to his material.

The second characteristic occurs when he makes his essays a response to a recent event, an occasion for writing the essay in the first place. In "Return to the Mountains," Anaya uses the death of Frank Waters, the acclaimed scholar of Mexico cosmologies and observer of Southwest culture and geography, as an occasion to address the need to remain open to experience and to continue to reopen oneself to the world. In "Model Cities/Model Chicano/Norma Jean," Anaya references the opening of the "South Broadway Cultural Center" in Albuquerque and describes this community center as raised from a "model cities library," the product of a defunct program started by President Lyndon B. Johnson in the 1960s. This same event becomes the occasion for reflecting on the nature of community and communal health.

This practice of referencing public and cultural events has a strong pull for readers, reminding them that serious thought exists to illuminate and bring about effective change in the world. Anaya invites readers to step with him into the world of serious reflection and potential action and to begin to do the work of improving the world. Not surprisingly, there is often a sense of urgency in his essays, as they attempt to create a bridge into the world with the potential of renewed, effective action. His personable tone in response to crises often suggests that people need to take responsibility for their world and act to advance the good, one of the major themes, by the way, articulated by Ultima in Anaya's first novel, *Bless Me, Ultima.*

While Anaya's approach to the culture of the Americas is visionary and could lead to fundamental change, his essay writing, however, is a classic version of the essay form. His style derives from the Western essay tradition of open and lively writing. The essay as a genre, dating to Michel de Montaigne's *Essais* in 1580 and Francis Bacon's *Essays* later in the sixteenth century, treats weighty topics, as Anaya's essays do, but also shuns technical language. The traditional essay, also consistent with Anaya's work, responds to an event in a personal manner.

Historian of the essay Claire de Obaldia describes the traditional attitude of the essay as the "essayistic spirit," the willingness to be personal and rational at the same time. The classical essay makes sense of an event or issue for a nonspecialist reader, and the essay's loose form, as described by Montaigne (the Renaissance originator of the genre), projects exactly this sentiment and approach—the invitation to take a serious look at something of importance in concert with other well meaning people who are not experts either. One adopts the essayistic perspective at a moment of encountering an occasion in which to make discriminations on behalf of someone or something of value. Essays typically do not give a definitive answer to a question but emphasize the particularity of perspective, often a personal perspective, and a non-specialized exploration of an occasion that has given rise to a pressing question. The traditional essay has this strong degree of worldly connectedness and the commitment to ethical responsibility.

Along with Anaya, the modern essayists who practice this tradition are a "Who's Who" of essay writing and are generally the nonfiction prose masters of the West. Think of the essays written in this manner by Ralph Waldo Emerson, Aldous Huxley, Virginia Woolf, E. B. White, Joan Didion, and Susan Sontag, and you have identified many of the great modern essayists. Like Anaya's essays, their essays advance a discussion through non-specialized language that is inclusive and engaging. It is this classic form of the essay that Anaya writes with great skill and loyalty to the requirements of the form.

This volume would not exist without the support of Charles Rankin, John Drayton, Jay Dew, Julie Shilling, Kimberly Wiar, and Byron Price of the University of Oklahoma Press. Their belief in Rudolfo Anaya's work speaks volumes about the University of Oklahoma Press and its place in scholarly and humanistic publishing. Early in this project, John T. Allen, an OU student and intern working for me, established many of the texts for the essays in this volume. Julie M. Davis made valuable contributions at every stage. Staff members at *World Literature Today* at the University of Oklahoma—Marla F. Johnson, Daniel Simon, Terri D. Stubblefield, Victoria Vaughn, Laura M. Johnson, and Merleyn Bell—also supported this project in various ways. I thank all of these friends for helping to bring Rudolfo Anaya's work to the University of Oklahoma Press.

On behalf of the University of Oklahoma Press and all at the University of Oklahoma who contributed to this project, I would like to thank the author Rudolfo Anaya for his fierce investment over a forty-year career in bringing to light truth and beauty and for the incredible essays that convey that commitment on every page. We were all honored to work on this project and to make available his large and masterful body of work.

Robert Con Davis-Undiano

PART ONE
Living Chicano

I'm the King
The Macho Image

The word "macho" has one of the shortest definitions in the Spanish language dictionary, and yet the cult of macho behavior (machismo) is as ambiguous and misunderstood as any aspect of Hispanic/Latino culture. To be macho is to be male, that's simple, but when the term is applied to Hispanic male behavior, then the particulars of the role are defined according to the particular culture. From Spain to Latin America, from Mexico to the USA Chicano communities, one gets a slightly different definition of the macho image at every turn.

Being macho is essentially a learned behavior; as such it is a conditioned behavior. We males learn to act manly from other males around us; the macho behavior that preceded us was learned from the cultures from which it evolved. Many forces impinge on the Hispanic/Latino cultures, so throughout history, machismo—or the conditioning of male behavior—has attracted all sorts of positive and negative elements.

Many cultural forces (from literature and religion to the latest musical fad, movies, MTV, or car styles) play a role in promoting the behavior of the macho, and these influences are the issue here. Still, beneath the conditioned behavior, the essence of what maleness means remains largely unchanged across time. We can describe conditioning and its effects; it is more difficult to describe the essence of maleness, especially today, when males seem to be retreating from describing, or laying claim to, a positive macho image.

Drunkenness, abusing women, raising hell (all elements of la vida loca) are some mistaken conceptions of what macho means. And yet the uninformed often point to such behavior and call it machismo. In fact, much of this negative behavior is often aped by a new generation,

Originally published in *Muy Macho: Latino Men Confront Their Manhood*, ed. Ray González (New York: Anchor Books, 1996), 57–73.

because as young men they are not aware that they are being conditioned. Young men acting contrary to the good of their community have not yet learned the real essence of maleness.

Sex

Our generation passes on to the next its ideals and rituals, and also behavior patterns that have to do with our sexuality. People have always composed games around sexuality. In this respect, the macho image has a history. The cock-of-the-walk behavior is game playing. Games and sex go hand in hand.

The game can be spontaneous and fun, reflecting the courtship and mating we see in the natural world. Part of the purpose of gender games is to reflect nature's dance of life, evolution playing itself out in each new encounter. Animals, insects—high and low organisms—engage in this dance of life. We are caught up in "nature's game," this vast and beautiful dance that is part of the awe of life. We feel love in the harmonious flow of nature, the movement of birth and death, and we take meaning from our sexual natures.

But the game has taken on a manipulative aspect. The assertion of one person over another is part of our conditioning. The game has turned ugly in many ways, and we are numbed by the outcome of the conditioning factors. But we can still be in charge of the game and change the negative aspects of the game. We can choose not to play a power game that hurts and demeans women.

Macho behavior, in large part, revolves around the acting out of sex roles. The games the macho plays may be part of nature's dance, with the goal of procreation imprinted on the cells long ago, but the power to subjugate is also inherent in out relationships. When the male gets caught up in superficial power plays that have to do with sex, he is acting against his community. It's time to analyze the social forces that condition negative behavior and toss out the ones that destroy family, friendship, and community.

For the Chicano, the roots of the idea of maleness extend not only into the Mediterranean world but also into the Native American world. We still act out patterns of male behavior emerging from those historic streams. To fully understand our behavior requires a knowledge of those literary and cultural histories. The Don Juan image and how it sets the tone for a pattern of behavior from the Mediterranean Spain of the past to the present day is only one aspect of a behavioral legacy. We need to know the role of the Native American warrior and how he cares for the community. The Chicano is a synthesis of these, and many more, streams of influence.

"I Can Piss the Farthest"

Little boys like to brag about the length of their penises, or they have contests to see who can piss the farthest. Acting out "I'm bigger, I'm better," the game begins to have its built-in power aspect. Later, boys will brag about having scored with a girl, and in the boast is contained a hint of the power they have exercised. Those who haven't yet scored have less power. They're virgins in the game. Those who don't see girls as the goal to be conquered have even less power. A hierarchy of needs and behavior begins to define the male role and the power inherent in it. The truer essence of male and female doesn't need this hierarchy, for hierarchy implies the use of power over others. And why should that which is most natural to our nature, our sexuality, require us to deal with others as objects?

Macho needs partners, not objects.

Until my father's generation, the men of the Mexican culture of the southwest United States could continue to speak Spanish and interact within the parameters of their history. That is, they set the code of behavior, one that was communal and focused on survival in an often harsh land. As Anglo-Americans moved into the territory, a wrenching of male relationships took place. The language of domination shifted from Spanish to English. Anglo-American law came to New Mexico in the mid-nineteenth century, but the rule of law in daily life and most communal enterprises remained Spanish. It was not until after World War II that the ways of my ancestors were overwhelmed. And therein lies an epic tragedy.

My father's generation *had* to adjust to the new language, the new man in town, the new laws. To be a man under Anglo domination was difficult if you didn't have the tools. I saw men broken by the new time, the new space. If they didn't adjust to the new language, they were demeaned. I now better understand my father's behavior, why he gave up. He didn't have the language, the tool with which to protect his own dignity, his own concept of macho. An excellent example of this meeting of cultures is shown in the movie *The Ballad of Gregorio Cortez*, a film that takes its story from a real corrido.

In some areas the males did absorb one another's concept of maleness. For example, the New Mexican land owners, lawyers, and politicians (those generally known as los ricos or los patrones) quickly learned to work with their Anglo counterparts. The Mexican vaqueros taught the Anglo cowboys the trade, so there existed some camaraderie on a macho level in those endeavors. But overall, the power of law and language was too vast and overwhelming. The Anglos could dictate roles; they could piss farthest, so to speak.

"I'm the King"

"Sigo siendo el Rey." "I'm the King" are the lyrics from a popular Chicano rap song I hear on the radio. The words and rhythm are catchy. I listen to the song and find myself repeating the lines.

Macho behavior is instilled in us as children. Both father and mother want their boys to grow up to be manly. Usually, the more traditional the rules of behavior are for the macho, the stricter the behavior the child learns. When he becomes a man the child sings, "I'm the king. I rule the family, like my father before me, and what I say goes." The child is the father to the man. But fathers at home are more and more rare. The child turns to the gang in the streets. A new style of being king is learned.

My parents knew a wonderful couple, old friends who came to visit. My mother and her comadre would cook up big meals, my father and his compadre would buy the wine. It was fiesta time. The old man would have a few glasses of wine and start acting like the king. "Yo mando," he would tell his wife, and the teasing about who ruled, the man or the woman, would go on. Visiting across the kitchen table and drinking wine, they were caught up in discussing the roles of man and woman.

It has always been so. In that space of the family fiesta in the small kitchen, they could define and redefine their roles. The mask of gaiety put on for the fiesta allowed them to speak freely. But beneath the surface a real dialogue was going on, defining and refining the roles of the men and the women. Do we have that dialogue about machismo going on in our community today, or have we accepted old roles conditioned by forces beyond our control? Are we too programmed to see the light?

The male child observes and learns to be the king, how to act as número uno, how to act around men and women. In a community that is poor and often oppressed there is much suffering, so he is taught aguantar: to grin and bear it. "Aguántate," the men around him say. A macho doesn't cry in front of men. A macho doesn't show weakness.

Grit your teeth, take the pain, bear it alone. Be tough. You feel like letting it out? Well, then let's get drunk with our compadres, and with the grito that comes from within, we can express our emotions. Lots of essays could be written on aguantar. The women also learn aguantar: Bearing it crosses the gender boundary. How women express the floodwaters of the aguanto is now being documented by Chicana writers.

The macho learns many games while learning to be número uno. Drinking buddies who have a contest to see who can consume the most beer, or the most shots of tequila, are trying to prove their maleness. From the pissing contest to drinking, the wish to prove his manliness becomes antisocial, dangerous. The drunk macho driving home from the contest he won can become a murderer.

The car in our society has become an extension of his manhood for the macho. The young male hungers for the most customized, flashiest car. It replicates him. It is power. The car is used in the mating ritual. As in our small villages generations ago the young vaqueros came into town to show off their horses and their horsemanship, the young now parade the boulevard showing off their cars. The dance is the same; the prize is the same.

To other males, the vato with the best car is saying, "I'm bigger, I'm better, I'm the king." Exactly the lyrics to the rap song. "Sigo siendo el Rey," he sings, "I continue being the king." The song describes one goal of the macho, to be king, to be número uno, to answer to no one. The message is aimed not only at other males, it is also for the female of the species.

Outside Influences

But guns have entered the game. Perhaps they've always been there, because certainly the Mexican charro and the cowboy of the movies both carried pistols, both fought it out with the bad guys, and the fastest draw won. In the rural areas hunting is most often male behavior. The gun extends the power and the sexuality of the young men. Now you can strike farther and deadlier.

It is time to call that behavior that is good, good. And that which is negative to the self and the community, not good. To be unkind and violent is not macho. The vato in the song who wants to be the king needs to find positive ways of acting for his community.

In my generation the "attitude" of James Dean influenced young male behavior, as did that of black musicians and black talk. Today, parents worry about the violent influence of the movies. The characters portrayed by Arnold Schwarzenegger (and other such exaggerated macho images) and the Power Rangers have become the symbols of violence in our society. Machos seem to solve problems only through violence, and quickly. Discourse and problem solving, which take time, are not honored in such movies. Parents worry about the influence such media are having on the young. Macho has really gotten out of hand; in fact, it's been perverted by those who use a false ideal of manliness to achieve their goals. We need to stand up and say loudly and clearly, that violence and oppression are not macho.

As more Chicano families become single-parent families, the traditional role of the father and of males in the extended family will not be as influential in shaping the behavior of boys. The boys are being conditioned instead by the behavior they see on TV, in movies and music videos. Boys loose in the hood are being shaped by the gang instead of the father.

La ganga shapes behavior, provides initiation, belonging. (Life in the gang—whether it's a neighborhood group of boys; an athletic fraternity, "the jocks"; or a gang that is into la vida loca, cruising, drinking, drugs, and guns—is a subject that requires a book to itself.) In the traditional culture, we didn't practice drive-by shooting as initiation into maleness. Young Chicanos moving into the maleness of the gang now practice a more violent form of initiation.

Young Chicano males learn from the past generations (drinking is often learned from brothers or close relatives), and such behavior is greatly influenced by the mainstream society. The influence of the Anglo-American culture on the Chicano culture cannot be overlooked. We can no longer speak of a continuum of learned behavior that is solely Mexican macho, because young males are greatly influenced by the totality of the culture around them. MTV, music, movies, television, and the behavior of other cultural groups *all* influence the behavior of the young Chicano male. To truly understand himself, and his maleness, the young male *must* ask himself: "Who is affecting me?" "What do they want of me?" "How can I take charge of my own life?"

There is a lesson to be learned here. Let us *not* repeat the loss of the prior generation, a loss we see today in the streets. Let us *not* be "powerless" as men. Let us *not* act out negative behaviors. We have within us the power to change. We have the future of our community at stake, so macho behavior has to be used positively for the community.

Los Chucos

Each generation becomes a new link in the group's tradition, but also transforms behavior. My adolescent years saw the advent of the pachuco, a radical departure in the male behavior of the small New Mexican town I knew. Who were esos vatos locos imitating in the forties when they invented the pachuco argot, the dress, sexual liberation in attitude and action, use of drugs, use of cars, and so on? Was there a continuous line of macho behavior in which the chucos were a link? Or was the behavior so spontaneous and new that the pachucos initiated a new definition of what it meant to be macho? After all, being macho does mean to defend the territory, and the chucos did defend their barrios against mainstream encroachment. Were the pachucos a reaction to the growing oppression by Anglo America? Partly, but once the warriors defined themselves, they spent as much time fighting each other as they did fighting the enemy, el gabacho.

The pachuco became a new model of behavior, breaking with the past, and yet in his role vis-à-vis la chuca, the male-female dance contained the same old elements embedded in the Mexicano culture. The power play was definitely at work. La chuca, as liberated as she was from her contemporary "square" sister who remained a "nice" girl, was still subservient. The pachuco loved to show off *his* baby doll.

This makes us question if breaks with the past are really radical, or does only the surface dress of the macho change? Beneath the zoot suit of the pachuco, old cultural forces and conditioned behavior continued to define the relationship between the macho and his woman. "Esta es mi ruca," he said proudly, introducing the woman as property in which he was pleased.

The pachuco practicing la vida loca continued to influence the definition of macho behavior in the nineties. They were the early lowriders. They spawned the baby chooks and those Chicano males who today are acting out roles, sometimes unknowingly, with roots in the pachuco lifestyle. (The Chicano rapper borrows from the Black rapper, but in his barrio and in his strut and talk, he is borrowing as much from the old veteranos.) This role of an "unconscious energy" in the community is something we can't measure, but it's there. History is passed on not only in stories and books, but by osmosis.

It makes us ask: Is behavior only learned? Or is there real maleness, a golden rule not only in the blood but in the myths? I look at the young machos parading down the street, acting out their roles, and I wonder how much of their behavior comes from that unconscious influence, something inherent in maleness itself. There is something in that dignity of maleness we don't want to give up. But what is it? We know those negative forces that condition us have to be repudiated. But we also yearn to be noble men, and to act in a noble fashion for our families.

La Familia

The pachuco macho behavior, while very visible in the barrio (and introduced to a larger audience by the U.S. Navy anti-pachuco, anti-Mexican riots during the early forties in Los Angeles, and made more visible through the Valdez "Zoot Suit" film), was not the only model of maleness in the community. A far greater percentage of the men of the barrios went about their work, raising families, trying to do the best they could for them. Macho means taking care of la familia. Perhaps this is the most important definition of macho, the real, positive meaning of the word. And yet it is often given short shrift. Critics often look at the negative behavior of the macho and forget the positive.

In the villages and barrios of New Mexico when I was growing up, being manly (hombrote) meant having a sense of honor. The intangible of the macho image is that sense of honor. A man must be honorable, for himself and for his family. There is honor in the family name. Hombrote also means providing for the family. Men of honor were able to work with the other men in communal enterprises. They took care of the politics of the village, law and order, the church, the acequia, and the old people.

The greatest compliment I could receive as a child when I did a job well was to be called hombrote. I was acting like an hombre, a man. This compliment came from both males and females in the family and in the extended family. By the way, this compliment is also given to the girls. They can be hombrotas, as well as muy mujerotas, very womanly. Either way, the creation of male and female roles are rewarded with the appropriate language, and the language is male centered.

Much is now written about male bonding, how the father and other males in the community shape the macho image. In Hispanic culture the role of the compadres is such a role. (The compadres are the godfathers, for lack of a more thorough definition.) The compadres bond at marriages, baptisms, or other family celebrations. Their goal is to ensure the welfare of the child that one of the compadres has baptized or confirmed. The best man at the wedding becomes a compadre. Compadrazgo has a very positive role to play. The compadres act manly toward one another, and the children of the compadres learn male behavior through those interactions.

Still, it's not just the males that are in charge of shaping the macho image. Women play an important role.

The Woman Creates the Macho

Talking about being macho also means talking about the role of women in our lives. In a traditional setting, the Mexican mother raises the male child and has a great influence on the learned macho behavior of the child. We learn a lot about the sexual behavior from the males of the clan, but the mother, if she does the raising of the male child, is a most crucial ingredient in the evolving macho role.

Food, warmth, protection, the first sounds, and all that has to do with the tactile sense of the first years on earth are provided by the mother. In our culture the mother is the first confidant of the male child. The mother imprints her femininity on the child, and the child's response to that feminine aura is formed in the womb. No wonder mothers exclaim at birth, "I have created."

In her novel, *Face of an Angel,* Denise Chávez explores the role of women in the formation of macho. By exploring the lives of women in the culture, she gives us an excellent, uninhibited view of the woman's influence on the life of the male. Other Chicanas are also doing this in their writings. Ana Castillo in her essay on machismo (in *Massacre of the Dreamers: Essays on Xicanisma,* University of New Mexico Press, 1994) has much to tell us of the history of the macho image. We need to listen to the ideas of such writers as the role of the macho is transformed. By us, by them.

Oedipal complexes and fears aside, we are our mother's creation, and so early macho behavior will be shaped actively and by nuance by the mother. Perhaps this is what we recognize when we attribute great value to the family. A mother who is active in shaping the maleness of her child will produce a more integrated man; if the mother is not there or if her behavior has been conditioned by an oppressive patriarchy, a more dysfunctional child will emerge. (This role of the woman who has historically been controlled by the demands of a male-oriented society has been amply analyzed by Castillo.)

Chicano males brought up in a positive atmosphere do not hesitate to say they love their mothers. Embracing (el abrazo) is as common for the mother as for the father. A continuing relationship with the mother as a guide who provides warmth, love, strength, and direction is integral to the culture. Our community did not traditionally initiate a cutoff age when the young male had to leave the household, that is, leave his mother's side. Both father and mother remain confidants—thus a description of the closeness of the family. Only recently, as we copy Anglo-American behavior and as the status of the culture has changed from rural to urban, do some Chicanos begin to practice readying the child to be more independent of family.

As we grow we begin to leave the mother's side. I learned about the male's role in the family and society from my father and his compadres, men who worked and drank with him. And I was fortunate to have brothers who were around long enough in my adolescent years to allow me to learn from them. I learned from my boyhood friends. Playing together we created and acted out the mythology of boyhood. Sexuality played an important part in those years of definition.

We learn not only how to talk, act, respond, and think like men from the intimate clan of males in which we are raised, we also learn an attitude toward life. We learn those intangibles that lie beneath behavior. Part of that essence is how we carry ourselves as men, the dignity and honor we exude. Men who don't have this dignity are sinvergüenzas, men without shame. They have a tough time holding their heads high, a tough time being macho. We learn to carry ourselves as men in our families, in the community, and in respect to women and men. And because we are members of a different cultural group living within the boundary of Anglo America, we learn to carry ourselves in respect to the Other, in this case, other white males.

Myth and Macho: La Llorona

There are deeper currents to wade in when we speak of our maleness. For me, myths and their inherent messages are integral to a definition of our humanity. Myth and legend shine in our folklore; folklore is a reflection of myth when there is no written text. The stories of the people also define our maleness. Let me propose a few areas of interest that don't have their history in a Eurocentric past. For example, let's look at one of our most persistent legends, which I believe also describes the macho image.

Part of the underpinning of our worldview, our values, is indigenous. The indigenous myths are part of our inheritance, working most often quietly in the cells, in memory, in dreams, and appearing as stories in the folklore. Our male relationship to the female can be better understood if we understand such pervasive legends as that of la Llorona.

Every Chicano I know has heard of la Llorona. Some have had experiences with the wailing woman, that is, they claim to have met her. (Who knows how many times we have met her in our dreams and our pesadillas, but contemporary psychologists have not been trained to listen to our mythology. They have not paid attention to that body of work and therefore lack interpretations intimately useful to us.)

Briefly, la Llorona is a young woman who is taken advantage of by a man. She has a child (generally out of wedlock) by the man. But the man does not stay home; he goes off seeking a new adventure (and usually a new woman). The young mother goes insane, or into a jealous rage. To get revenge on the man who has jilted her, she kills the child (or children) and throws the body in the river, into a pond or lake. She is returning the flesh to the primordial water, the ooze of primal creation.

This is not the replaying of the Medea tragedy. It has closer kinship in myth to the pre-Greek, Mediterranean world. When the Egyptian Osiris is killed by his brother, it is Isis, Osiris's sister, who wanders along the Nile, collecting the pieces of the dismembered body to "reconstitute" Osiris. (She symbolically gives birth to her brother, that is, the virgin has delivered the male child who will be God.)

La Llorona of our legend also seeks the pieces of the (male) child she has murdered. Or sacrificed? To date, the legend has been too narrowly analyzed. Has la Llorona really sacrificed the child to re-create him in the waters of the river (the earth womb) and thus raise him symbolically to the status of god? Perhaps la Llorona realizes the child has to die to be reborn a better male. That is, the consciousness of the child has to be reshaped to fit the time. Consciousness is evolving, and in this case the mother (la Llorona) is a key player in that new consciousness. Put another way, la Llorona is creating a new humanity.

Another interpretation would question if it is la Llorana who really kills the child. In the Osiris myth, Osiris is killed by his brother, a male. It seems to me that feminist Chicana critics need to dig deeper into this paradigm. In my novel *Zia Summer*, my main character, Sonny Baca, a thirty-year-old trying to understand his maleness (and his cultural identity), is told the story of la Llorona by his grandmother. In the grandmother's story, it is a man who kills la Llorona's child.

What if it is the man who kills la Llorona's child, a child she would raise to a new consciousness, thus defeating the father's old macho ways? The woman has the power to create the new male, not Nietzsche's Superman, but a child more closely aligned to the feminine sensibility, which is the mother's inheritance. The man kills the male child not because he fears an Oedipal ending (after all, in the legend the father is going off searching after a new woman), but because he fears the status quo, and his macho role in it will be supplanted by the son. Therein lies new hope. We can constantly re-create the child, raise the child in a new way, so the macho image of yesterday need not be a prison to us, especially its dysfunctional aspects. La Llorona knows this, and so like Isis she searches along the river's bank, the lake, the sacred springs of myth in search of the pieces of the child she can bring back to life. What incredible power lies in this woman of legend that we have dismissed as a "boogey woman" of the river. We've used her to frighten children, when we should be using her to raise them—the new children of a new era who understand that each one carries the hope of the future.

Children, both male and female, can put aside old, destructive ways of behavior and define maleness in a new way. La Llorona, the mother of the sacred lake, can play a role in describing the new macho. (The lake image represents the unconscious, that creative energy from whence rise new images.) In our time, the greatest change taking place in the macho image and its behavior is the influence of a new generation of liberated Chicanas. Their cry is not a cry of despair, but voices insisting that they are taking a greater role in defining male-female relationships, and so they *are* redefining macho. These contemporary Lloronas can be liberating mothers creating new concepts and behaviors by which to live. Or they can be shortsighted and engage in old gender accusations that don't move us toward the definition of a new paradigm. A lot rides on their thoughts, their stories, their actions.

So, la Llorana has pre-Greek, Egyptian, Semitic roots. Roots in ancient civilizations. Blame men, the pillars of the morality of the community, if she has been given a bad rap. Blame ourselves if we do not reinterpret the old myths and give them new meaning for our violent time. There's hope in new interpretations, a hope that will bring new understanding to our roles as men and women. We don't have to be stuck with old stereotypic roles of behavior that define dysfunctional machos.

La Virgen

La Virgen de Guadalupe is another mother figure. She is the Aztec goddess Tonantzin, the indigenous New World answer to the goddess religions that were destroyed during the Neolithic Age around the fringes of the Mediterranean world. La Virgen de Guadalupe exists because

Quetzalcóatl (the feathered serpent god who can fly and is of the heavens) could not erase the goddess worship in indigenous America. Perhaps the cult of Quetzalcóatl chose not to erase the goddess cult, after all, Quetzalcóatl was not like the Yahweh of the Old Testament. He was not a thundering god of vengeance, he was a god of the fields and civilization.

Quetzalcóatl and the cult of goddess worship went hand in hand. But Quetzalcóatl flew too high. One reason for his banishment is that he mated with his "sister," a heavenly sister of the starry skies. The feathered energy of his nature drew him toward the heavens and thus separated him from the earth energy, the intuitive energy wound up in procreation and nurturing. He should have mated with the Earth goddess and thus preserved his serpent earth energy and procreative powers. Or at least he should have kept the energy of these polarities in balance, in harmony, able to wed the intuitive with the rational, the earth-creative with the aspirations to the spiritual. In a sense, Quetzalcóatl deserted the fields, the earth, and his people, and as such, except for the words of a few Chicano writers and poets, he passed out of our consciousness. In Mesoamerica he was easily replaced by the Catholic Cristo. But not the earth goddess Tonantzin. She lives on in la Virgen de Guadalupe.

Quetzalcóatl was banished. He traveled east to be absorbed into flames, into Venus as the morning star, into the sunlight of dawn. Tonantzin, the earth goddess, did not flee, nor was she banished from the hearts of her people. The Spanish friars knew they could not destroy the adoration of the goddess. The ties to earth were too deep in the ancient Mexicans. The church could stamp out Quetzalcóatl (after all, the god had already forsaken his people just before the arrival of the Europeans), and so Cristo did not have the competition of a strong, indigenous male god. But the natives would not let go of the goddess of the earth. She is incorporated into the pantheon of the Catholic Church as la Virgen de Guadalupe. The smartest move the Church ever made in the Americas was not to fight this syncretic impulse.

The female goddess was imprinted in the psyche of the people of the Americas. The goddess created, nurtured, provided. She is seen in corn, the sustenance of much of the New World. She spoke to the god of rain on behalf of the farmers. All attributes of la Virgen. And so the female (anima) of the human psyche remains represented as an active force in our lives. Take whatever route you like to the past, you will discover the prototypes of la Virgen. Her role remains the feminine sensibility with which we identify. For the male she is a living presence of the anima within, the female within.

Is being macho *only* learned behavior? Well, mostly, but what of this stream of myth? What part of this inheritance describes the history of our blood? What whispers do we hear from the collective memory, and how can it describe a new way of being macho? Perhaps the old macho image has to die when it does not engender the community. The essence of maleness doesn't have to die, it merely has to be understood and created anew. To re-create is evolution's role. We can take an active role in it, but to do so we have to know the history of false behavioral conditioning.

Nature dictates much. The chemicals, hormones, and elements in the blood and in the psyche are elements she needs for the job of procreation of the species. But she also provides a fantastic interplay of forces within the essence of the human, within the soul. The soul exists as a motivating, energizing force within. We can transform ourselves, and in that transcendent encounter, or epiphany, we become more than the humans whose feet are bogged down in the mud.

To do that we need to pay full attention to the forces within. We are not all male at any given time, nor are we all female. We need to find balance and harmony in the deep currents of our nature. Macho need not be all male, puro hombre. Nothing is pure one thing or the other, especially when we speak of human nature. The old dictates of the fathers have to be transformed to create a new macho, and for that we need to listen to the feminine sensibility. To listen within.

Requiem for a Lowrider

I'd like to tell those of you who are graduating from high school a story about my graduation. In 1956 I stumbled up to the stage and received that piece of paper that said, You did it, you finally graduated from high school! It was a time for feeling high, and I don't mean just from the elation of receiving my diploma.

We already had a week of partying under our belts, and there were more parties to come on commencement night. During that final week of school, we felt as if we owned the world. Very few of us were worrying about the really heavy concerns, like getting a job, planning our future, deciding on more education, or whether to get married or wait a while—the same important decisions facing graduates today.

Graduating classes today and mine in 1956 are two generations apart, and yet we still have a lot in common. I have been asking myself, what is our common ground? What is it that we can talk about across this span of time? We were the generation of the fifties, of bebop, rock 'n' roll, sock hops, *Leave It to Beaver*, Marilyn Monroe, and Joe DiMaggio. A decade of innocence, it has been called.

A lot of Chicanos living in the United Sates were poor and undereducated, but no one cared about the ethnic communities of this country then. My family couldn't afford to send me to college, but I enrolled anyway, paying for tuition and books by taking part-time jobs. In literature classes I fell in love with reading and the wealth of ideas literature presented. Around us, the beatnik poets were reforming the way we

Originally presented at the graduation ceremonies of Albuquerque High School, New Mexico (June 1978); and subsequently published in *Albuquerque News* (28 June 1978, A1, A7); and published in slightly different form in *The Anaya Reader* (New York: Warner Books, 1995), 263–71.

thought of poetry, drug use, being on the road to nirvana, social values, and the so-called alternative cultures that would change the way we looked at things in the sixties.

I ask myself: What is the culture of high school students like today? How do the music, movies, and television that shape you express who you are? What books are you reading and what ideas are you discussing? What is the vision of your future?

What is the *one* thing that can help us communicate with each other? I keep asking myself that question, and my mind keeps coming back to Jessie. He was my friend; we started Albuquerque High School together. He was a great guy, a real easygoing vato loco, but he didn't graduate. He was one of the original lowriders, a crazy cruiser with a customized '48 Ford. He spent more time cruising around the school on Broadway and Central than in it.

He was one of the kindest and brightest persons I've ever known, and in thinking of him I think I discovered the one element we have in common. In different times, you and I are a generation of lowriders. In the fifties we spent four years in high school, cruising. The fifties saw lowriding and cruising developed to an art. The pachucos, the grand-daddies of all the Chicano rebels, not only dressed "cool," they drove cool ranflas.

And thank heaven for cruisers and lowriders! Just think how many lowriders it has taken to make this country what it is today. Christopher Columbus was one of the original lowriders! That's right, I think old Chris was just kicking back, cruising around the Atlantic, and by accident he happened to bump into the Americas. And most of us wouldn't be here today if he hadn't gone cruising that Sunday.

Yeah, just think for a moment what came out of that Columbus cruise.

But what is cruising all about?

When you say, "Hey, Dad," or "Oye, Jefito, I'm going cruising," the typical response is: "Where are you going?"

And the typical answer is: "I don't know, just cruising."

Just cruising, huh? That's the question that keeps turning in my mind when I think about Jessie.

"We have a big assignment in history," I'd say to him, "let's go hit the books at the library."

And he would smile and put his arm around my shoulder and say, "Hey, let's go cruising, man. You only live once. You take life too seriously . . . Just cool it . . . "

Cool it. In the fifties, it meant kick back, take it easy. That's another thing I've discovered as I compare our generations: the words change, language fads come and go, but deep down inside we all still have to deal with the real gut issues that life presents us. Today you have to make choices. You have to think about cruising as I have.

What is it that we're looking for when we go cruising? Let me suggest to you that we are looking for excitement to put in our lives. We go cruising to meet a friend, we hope that that special someone we like is also out there, just cruising. We turn up streets randomly, we follow the crowd. If there's a wreck, a fight, or a party, everybody shows up, looking for the action, looking for some excitement. In short, we're all waiting for an accident to happen.

That's what Jessie was doing. I know now. He was dissatisfied. He cruised around waiting for something to happen. In a roundabout way he taught me that life requires a little more planning than goes into just cruising.

Oh, everybody loved Jessie. Ducktail, baggy pants, hair slick with pomade, swinging like a pachuco, he'd come dancing down the hall, snapping his fingers, looking the girls over. He was Mr. Cool! He acted crazy, but he treated everybody with respect. Even the teachers liked him—that is, when he was in class long enough for them to get to know him.

"Hey, Rudy!" he used to say. "Let's go cruise around before class. We can smoke a few tokes and be back in time for third period."

Life was easy for him when he was cruising and smoking up, looking for that excitement he needed.

By his senior year he was beyond just drinking beer and smoking mota. I still remember the first night I saw him loaded with heroin. We were going to a dance at the Heights Center, and he came to pick me up. He was really high, and I knew it was on heavy stuff. Carga, horse, smack, call it what you want; the words change, the junk remains the same beneath.

I cried, "Hey, Jessie, what are you doing to yourself? Do you know what you're getting into?"

I don't want to sound moralistic. I had done a lot of the crazy things he had done. We were young men and we were growing up. Bumping into accidents and new excitement every day was a part of our lives. All I tried to tell him was that there was other excitement to life. I tried to tell him that sometimes I got my high from some of the books I was reading, and that, yes, even some of the ideas the teachers kicked around in class were exciting. It wasn't all sheer boredom. I didn't give him a lecture, I talked to him as a friend. I was concerned for him because I loved him as a friend, and I knew he was on the wrong road. "Easy, Rudy, easy, Daddy-O," he said. "I'm okay . . . I know what I'm doing, hey, this is a great high. I can handle it. Come on, Let's go dancing!"

And he was a great dancer. The girls loved him. We all loved him. The only people who couldn't have cared less about him were the ones he had run into while cruising, the ones who sold him the junk. After a while his habit was daily. He dropped out of school. We drifted apart . . . went our separate ways. I stayed in school, hoping there was something there that would help me solve the complexity of my own life. Jessie began to run with a new crowd, but he was no longer the happy-go-lucky lowrider I once knew. He was running scared.

We talked once, but it didn't do any good. "You take life too serious," he told me. "It's only a slow cruise, so take it easy. Look, I'm not busting my ass on books, and I've got a car, plenty of bread, everything I need." And he smiled.

But we both knew it wasn't Jessie who had those things, it was the monkey on his back who owned everything, and the monkey was growing, sitting by Jessie as they cruised up and down the barrio streets.

The last time I saw him was graduation night. I remember it as if it were yesterday. I was graduating; he wasn't. I wanted him to be with me and share whatever this small accomplishment meant. "I wouldn't miss it for the world," he said. "I may not be getting my little piece of paper, but I'm glad you're getting yours. Hey, you keep getting those things and you're going to be a big vato someday!" We laughed.

How could any of us be mad at him? He was a lovable guy. We could only hurt for him. There was a gang of us, friends from the barrio, who had gone through high school together, and Jessie was the only one not graduating.

But he was there to wish us luck, and he came to the party afterwards. And for a few moments we were all happy and things seemed to be the way they used to be. We joked, laughed, and talked about what we were going to do now that we owned the world.

I could go on to tell you how each one of us, each member of that small gang, went on to develop his potential and live a worthwhile life. But this is not our story. It's Jessie's story.

He was really high that night, and he was desperate. He mentioned once that he needed money, that he had big debts to pay, and then the party got loud and crowded and I lost track of him for a while. Later, when I asked for him, somebody told me that some of his "new" friends had taken him outside. I ran outside, but his car was gone. Jessie had gone on his last ride.

The following morning his brother called me and told me Jessie was dead. They had dumped him down by the river that night. He had paid his debt. When I got to the mortuary, his family was already there. It was a sad time. Nothing to say or do. I could only promise him that someday I'd tell his story, that maybe it would make sense to someone. And now I'm telling it to you. This is Jessie's story, it's my requiem for a lowrider.

And why have I told you this story now, when graduation should be a time of rejoicing for you and for your families who have helped you through school? It's a time of celebration for the teachers and the counselors who have helped. Now you've made it, and it's your time. It's also a proper time to remember the help you received, the encouragement when you were down, the love when you thought things were hopeless. And because we share our lives with many brothers and sisters, it's also a time to remember that we, too, can give help. Maybe we didn't give Jessie enough help, maybe we didn't give him enough love, maybe we saw too late that he was drifting into an accident from which there was no return.

I sincerely believe that there is a time in life for drifting. There is a time for sitting back and getting in touch with yourself. Some of our most interesting illuminations and ideas will come when we take time to reflect, time to kick back and cruise a while.

But there's also a time for planning, a time for looking into the future, a time for more active participation in life. You can't cruise forever. The gas is running out, you're older and at a new stage of life. Your lives will be very complex, and there will be many friends like Jessie who will need your help. So I ask you, engage life actively! Embrace it and love it! And help make it a fulfilling adventure, not a dead end where we have to write more requiems for friends like Jessie.

On the Education of Hispanic Children

Hispanics in the United States are well aware that attaining a good education is crucial to the future of our children. In the Southwest, where large communities of Mexican Americans make their homes, the debate is not over how much education we want for our children—since every parent wants the best quality education available—the question is what form that education should take.

We know the public schools in our country are failing in offering a top-notch educational curriculum to a high percentage of students, especially the Mexican American youth. Recent reports document an atrocious dropout rate, and reports on the quality of our schools indicate students graduating with little or no reading skills. Many of us continue to ask if there is something in the environment of the school that turns off the Mexican American child. Why have our children become the objects of these alarming dropout statistics?

We know not only that our future as cultural group is threatened if our children are not educated but that our role in the future of this country is also threatened. The education of our children should be the concern of all of us.

As a lifelong educator, I have argued for years that education must take into account the culture of the individual child. No one can develop his full potential in an uncomfortable environment; one only learns to escape from an uncomfortable environment as quickly as possible.

The first task of the school is to make the child feel secure and safe in the learning environment. This means that the language and cultural

Originally published as "Shaming Hispanic Students Best Way to Teach Dropping Out," in *Albuquerque Journal* (12 May 1991, B3); and reprinted with revisions as "On the Education of Hispanic Children" in *The Anaya Reader* (New York: Warner Books, 1995), 399–403.

background that the child brings to the school should be reflected in the school curriculum and setting. Children should not have to give up their history to partake in a solid education that will prepare them for the future. It is important for parents and grandparents who speak only Spanish to be welcomed to the school so the children can take pride in their affiliation with that school. These parents, who may not yet be as pragmatic as their Anglo-American counterparts, and who possess their own inherent cultural values, are as hopeful as other parents that their children will succeed in school.

My generation was often made to feel ashamed of our language, food, and other cultural values because those values were not reflected in the schoolroom or curriculum. Many still tell me stories of the torment school became for them as recently as the 1950s. That is one reason so many of my generation dropped out. We felt we didn't belong in the school, and I believe that feeling of *not* belonging affects many of our children today.

The educational system has never committed itself to a curriculum that puts an emphasis on learning foreign languages. (Many of us remember being reprimanded for speaking Spanish on the school grounds.) This country has, in a very narrow-minded way, insisted on the monolingual approach in creating its national identity. It has refused to see the value of being multilingual. Students whose native tongue is not English are still told that the monolingual way is best and that they must give up their native tongue in order to succeed. The English-only movement is an effort that encourages children to discount the language of their parents.

We must reverse that narrow and damaging perception of language. Languages are the core of identity and creativity, and they are important to better world understanding. If we build on the native language the child brings to school, we can not only educate the child in English but sustain the mother language. It is simply better to create multilingual rather than monolingual students. We must commit our schools to the importance of language study. Every other country in the world does this.

Those who fear diversity in education, and fear that the canon of Western civilization is under attack, continue to belittle efforts to include different languages and histories in the school curriculum. Hispanic/Latino efforts to participate in the school systems have been demeaned, and it is our children who have suffered. Children know when they're not respected, and when they feel they have lost self-respect they leave the schools.

In our Spanish-speaking culture, to lose one's self-respect is to be "sin vergüenza." Many of my generation were made to feel shame or vergüenza in school because we were different. The burden of feeling shame is very heavy; it makes the individual feel worthless. The schools must respect the cultural background of the children, for otherwise they create a climate of shame which drives the child away.

We want our children to learn English and study Western civilization, but we also see the value in learning many languages and our own history. As Mexican Americans, we are heirs to those many languages and worldviews that connect us not only to Western civilization but to the civilizations of the Americas.

We must not allow our children to feel shame simply because of their cultural background. It is not shameful to be different, rather it is part of the beauty of the cultural diversity of this country. We must insist that quality education for our children in this country include a reflection of their language and history.

I have taught and lectured at many schools and universities. I know children love to learn, and when they feel secure in the learning environment, there are no limits. We know this, and yet Mexican Americans continue to leave schools at alarming rates; our community cannot afford another generation of dropouts.

We are now engaged in a struggle of immense importance to our future and to the future of the country. Each one of us must make a commitment to that struggle. We understand the power inherent in the educational process, and we know that personal fulfillment is the birthright of our children. Those who understand that every individual is worthy of fulfilling his or her potential will join us. Ours is a battle of liberation against old oppressions.

We ask educators and parents to join us in this struggle. We will educate our children; that is our commitment. Everyone must be actively engaged in the educational process, as surely as everyone will be affected by the consequences if we continue to allow the horrendous drop-out rate of our children.

I now understand why I felt shame for so many years while I was in school. I was told too many times that I didn't belong. I was made to feel that my language and my parents didn't belong. Even as a graduate student, I still felt shame, because I was constantly reminded I was not like the other students, I did not come to school with an Anglo-American background.

I had to battle that feeling of vergüenza every step of the way. My family helped me in my struggle, and writing novels and stories reflecting my cultural ways helped me find the pride I needed to continue my education. I knew that many of our traditions were beautiful and my history was as important as any other. Finally, I realized that shame was not something I was born with, it was a negative feeling put on me by those with prejudice.

Education is liberation. For Hispanics in this country, the next decades must be ones of educational enhancement and advancement. We must open the doors to the schools and insist not only that the resources be made available to our children, but that the sense of shame they are made to feel should be expunged. Discrimination against ethnic groups—that insidious discrimination that creates shame in the child—must be eradicated forever.

We need our language and our history taught in the schools, and we need important role models with which the children can identify. We need more parents involved in the schools. We know our literature, language, and history will enrich the curriculum and help provide a positive environment in which learning can take place.

Foreword to *Growing Up Chicano*

Growing up is one of the universal themes in literature. It is during the childhood years that our values are formed by family and community. It is also a time when we acquire many of the basic skills we will use later in life. For the child or the teenager, growing up is a series of new experiences, emotions, relationships, and the awareness of sexuality. Everything about growing up is extremely intense and heartfelt.

Writers often need to describe the world of their childhood. We believe that by writing about growing up we can give meaning to those tumultuous years. That is how I felt when I wrote my first novel, *Bless Me, Ultima*. It was important to capture in a story the swirl of emotions and experiences that shaped my growing-up years.

Our growing-up stories provide a history of our past, and in so doing they illuminate the present. *The Adventures of Huckleberry Finn* and *Tom Sawyer* are classics not only because of the wonderful characters, but also because they provide a history of the times and thus inform us of the world of the author.

It is important for each generation to read the growing-up stories of previous generations, and thus gain a touchstone to help chart a course for the future. Each one of us remembers the stories, written or in the oral tradition, that affected us as children. Those stories fired our imagination, filled us with wonder, and allowed us to understand our place in the world. Those stories also taught us that each one of us is a storyteller, each one of us is a creative human being.

Storytelling is very important in the Chicano community. Listening to or reading stories leads one to become a storyteller, and in writing a story one can re-create one's life. For the more than eighteen million

Originally published as the foreword to *Growing Up Chicana/o: An Anthology*, by Tiffany Ana López (New York: W. Morrow, 1993), 5–10.

Mexican Americans living in the United States, the growing-up years have been a mixture of joy, frustration, pain, and a search for identity. Our history, language, literature, and the Chicano Movement of the 1960s are important elements that make us a distinct community.

It was during the Chicano Movement of the 1960s that many Mexican Americans decided to call themselves Chicanos. By naming themselves they took on a new awareness of their place in society. Chicanos began to take pride in their mestizo heritage, pride in both their European and Indian history. It became important during those years to preserve the Spanish language and many of the traditions that were being lost as the force of assimilation led more and more into the mainstream culture.

During the sixties and seventies, the Chicano community struggled for more civil rights and equality. We looked back on our history and reminded the world that our European ancestors had been in the southwest United States since 1540 when Coronado marched into what is now New Mexico. During those important explorations the language of commerce and education in the region became Spanish. Spanish has been spoken in the area of the present-day United States since long before the first permanent English settlement, Jamestown, was founded in 1607.

From Texas to California, the rich mother heritage that is Mexican in origin has spawned the culture we call Chicano today. It is a Hispanic culture because of the language, and even though there are many regional differences, elements such as history, language, religion, food, fiestas, and other ceremonies keep the core of the culture intact. Whether our ancestors were the first Españoles and Mexicanos who settled the Southwest or are the newly arrived immigrants from Mexico, we all are heirs to the same common history.

Unfortunately, the history we read in school has often not included the Chicano community of the Southwest, and it has certainly not portrayed those who have sought work in the migrant streams that took them up into the Midwest and the Northwest where they, too, have founded branches of the Chicano community. The family of Mexican Americans has grown, it has spread to many places, and yet everywhere the common elements still exist.

Why have we been left out of the history books? For me, history includes the daily life of people, and it is written in their stories, poems, songs, and corridos and in the everyday communication of the people. Historians have often not looked at these sources, or their narrow prejudices have kept them from taking note of the important contributions Mexican Americans have made to this land.

Chicano writers and historians are setting the record straight. In the stories that Tiffany Ana López has collected in *Growing Up Chicana/o*, you will find a special slice of Chicano history. It is a creative history, told in the form of stories that deal with that special time of youth. Enjoy the stories for what they are, creative works, but keep in mind they also allow you a view into the Chicano world.

We know from the stories we read in school, from newspapers, magazines, television, radio, and even from the advertising media, what it means to grow up in white America. For many Chicanos in this country, those experiences of growing up were a fantasy. They did not speak directly to our experience.

It is fair to say that as long as our literature was not available to white America, this country did not really know the life of the Chicano community. A book like *Growing Up Chicana/o* helps open a window to a part of the life of Chicanos. You may be surprised to learn that the same issues that concern the Chicano writers concern all readers. The stories are about growing up, encountering love, school life, life in the barrio, making friends.

You will also find attention given to the family; la familia and all the relationships involved therein are very important in Chicano literature. The relationship with the elders in a family provides a valuable learning context for our younger generation. The elders are the roots of our cultural ways. An important theme is the theme of identity. We know who we are and we know our history, but belonging to an ethnic group within the confines of the wider society makes it necessary for us constantly to affirm this identity. This push and pull between the world of our own culture and the larger Anglo-American world provides our literature with important subject matter.

How we relate to each other in this multicultural society is a theme in the stories. As members of a minority ethnic group within the mainstream society, Chicano writers have important things to say about the experience. Racial or ethnic prejudices and bigotry do affect our community!

The voice of the woman writer in these stories should draw special attention. Chicano culture is patriarchal in orientation, and as more and more Chicanas write, they influence not only the content of the literature but also the culture itself. If literature is a liberating experience, then the voice of the Chicana writer in our culture is one of the most influential in helping to shape and change the cultural ways.

Language, like history, is at the heart of these stories. For Chicanos, one community within the larger Spanish-speaking world of the Americas, Spanish is the mother tongue. Our ancestors spoke Spanish, and so the language became the unifying element of our culture. Today, many of the young people are not keeping up the practice of speaking Spanish, and yet they are still historically connected to the language.

A contemporary question for the Chicano writers has been whether to write in Spanish or English. We know that in order to be published in this country, Chicano writers have to write in English. There is a big audience of Spanish readers in this country, but very little effort by publishers to publish for those readers. There are also other forces at work that have dictated that Chicano writers write in English.

More and more the language used at home is English. Survival at school and in the workplace dictates that one must speak English. Many of the stories told by Chicano writers take place in a Spanish-speaking setting, for example, at home or in the barrio, but the story is told in English. This has created unique problems for Chicano writers.

Some writers use a technique called code-switching, a bilingual approach to the story. The story is largely written in English, but at appropriate times Spanish is used. This technique reminds the reader the world of the Chicano is bilingual, shifting back and forth between Spanish and English. I have heard some readers complain that the bilingual use of language in stories interferes with the reading of the story; I suggest this technique is a creative use of language that enhances the stories.

The setting and ambience of the stories also remind the reader they are in a barrio or in a Chicano home. At times the stories enter into a realm that critics have labeled magical realism. The entering of this magical plane has been common in the style and content of Latin American literature, and it is common to Chicano writers.

Storytelling is communication. In this anthology by López you will learn how Chicanos feel about their world; you will also learn how they relate to the Anglo-American world. If Chicanos and Anglo Americans are to understand each other better, then these stories are one way toward that eventual understanding.

Cultural groups that live next to each other affect each other. Since the war between the United States and Mexico ended in 1848, the

Spanish-speaking Mexican community and Anglo Americans have occupied the same land. This theme is woven into the stories. Perhaps learning how we "can all get along" is one of the most important functions of literature.

Contemporary Chicano literature has come a long way since the first poets and writers joined César Chávez in the fields of California to protest the unequal treatment Chicano and other workers received. In the short span of a quarter century, Chicano literature has blossomed. Written in English, it now assumes a place in the literature of the United States. With its historical relationship to Mexico and its grounding in the Southwest, Chicano literature speaks to the Latino world south of Mexico. It is the bridge across la frontera, joining Anglo America to Latin America.

The writers in the collection of stories in *Growing Up Chicana/o* represent that bridge. You will continue to hear from them, for they are professionals dedicated to their art. Their voices and their works will continue to grow in clarity and expression. Their reputations will grow, as will the body of Chicano literature.

The Journal of a Chicano in China

In May 1984, I embarked on a journey to China, a pilgrimage that turned out to be one of the most incredible journeys I have ever taken. I had traveled abroad before, but there was something singular about China, something special that prompted me to keep a journal of my daily impressions.

My response to China was highly personal. I felt that important answers would be revealed to me. What answers? I did not know exactly. But I would be a traveler in search of symbols that could speak the language of my soul. I would be a traveler in a country that was the birthplace of the Asiatic people who, thousands of years ago, wandered over the Bering Strait into the Americas. What were the symbols of those people? And what do they communicate to me across the millennia?

I call my notes the *Journal of a Chicano in China* for specific reasons. First, I am a native son of the Mexican community of the United States, and I proudly identify with that community. And, second, as a Chicano, I also take pride in that part of me that is a Native American. I seek out the history and thought of the Americas, because by understanding that past I understand better my present.

My trip to China was sponsored by the W. K. Kellogg Foundation. The foundation fellowships encourage growth in new and multidisciplinary ways. Certainly, travel is one of the ways in which we gain knowledge about the integrated earth on which we live. So in mid-May, nineteen Kellogg fellows—some of us accompanied by our spouses—set out for China. Our Chinese sponsor was the Chinese Athletic Association. Why the association? Our group was such a diverse mixture of scholars that it was the only agency that dared to sponsor us.

Originally published in *IMPACT, Albuquerque Journal Magazine* (16 April 1985), 4–9, 14–15.

In China, I visited the holy mountains and temples, I prayed at ancient shrines, I walked the polluted streets of the cities, I mixed with the people, I pulled them into my dream. I walked in their factories, prisons, and hospitals; I toured their markets, and I sat in their homes. I went to communicate, and these are my impressions of that communication.

May 11

I am going to China today. Where do I find the beginning, the desire for this pilgrimage? A family story whispers that our grandfather, when he was a young man, visited China. I asked my mother, "Did Grampa go to China?"

She rapped my head. "Mind your manners, Boy. Don't speak ill of the dead. Yes, your grandfather could speak Chinese when he had a cup or two, but he never went to China."

So, I am going to China for Grampa and for myself. A visit to the origin. The origin that does not belong to Spain. I go to find an understanding of that other half of my nature.

My wife, Patricia, and I spend the day in San Francisco. All trips to China should begin in San Francisco, city of the Orient, city that gazes into the setting sun. The Spaniards came into your bay in the sixteenth century. But Chinese voices had lingered in your air centuries before. In Portsmouth's Square Park, the old Chinese men of the neighborhood gather to take the sun (as I imagine today in some village in northern New Mexico, the old men gather in the chill of a spring morning to take the sun). The Chinese gentlemen play cards, gamble, play dominoes. Feisty old men. Brown like me. Wrinkled. In heaven, Grampa plays checkers with old Chinese gentlemen.

May 14

¡El Tercer Mundo! He llegado, con una canción en mi carazón. Peking, land of my grandfather's dreams. I rush to embrace the Chinese. Brown brothers, Raza! Can you imagine a billion new souls for La Raza? We could rule the world.

Peking/Beijing does not surprise me. On the bus ride into the city, I have a vague feeling I have been here before. The streets are busy with construction, a new subway. It's like Mexico City, but with less color, fewer cars, more people. We pass the shops that line Beijing University, the gates of the Summer Palace, the Empress's Pagoda on the hill and come to rest in northwest Beijing. Our hotel is a beautiful one in the foothills. The Fragrant Hills Hotel. A fitting name.

Our room has bathroom marble, a sliding glass door that looks down on a pond of golden carp, grass, Chinese pine trees. There is a swimming pool where the hardy of the group swim before dinner. I drink Five-Star Beijing beer, make friends with the old pine trees outside my window, and sleep. At night, the full moon of New Mexico peeks over the garden. The breeze through the open door is cool. The golden carp in the pool sleep.

May 15

Today we will tour the city, camera in hand. We are ready to see China. We are ready to see the reality of El Tercer Mundo.

The ride into Beijing is bucolic, with a hard edge. People on the way to work fill the narrow streets. Peach tree orchards line the roads. There are fields of tomatoes, onions, vegetables. Rice paddies. Farmers are at work everywhere, Grampa's folks. An occasional fisherman sits by the side of the canal, bamboo pole over the water. Lots of trucks are on the road. Chinese trucks loaded for work.

Our destination is the Forbidden City, the old imperial city of the Ming and Qing Dynasties, now a museum. Gold Chinese roofs, pastel red walls. The crowds are thick. The Chinese do not smile. And yet, there is an air of gaiety. Workers, families with their children, have come to see the glory of the old dynasties, the ancients who created such opulence and glory. This is an old civilization. Perhaps the oldest on earth. No wonder they have called outsiders barbarians. No wonder, throughout their history, they have been wary of the West. Modernism has just come to China.

In the palace grounds, the dragon abounds, carved into roofs, carved into bronze. Something about the vast courtyards between buildings reminds me of Teotihuacan in Mexico. The walls, the smell, the sprigs of grass and weeds on the grounds. The dragon is everywhere, the flaming Quetzalcóatl of Mexico. The face of the fierce dragon looks out at me from walls, from gargoyles, from decorative pieces, almost exactly as the serpent head in the pyramids of Mexico. This is my first clue. This is the door I seek.

The dragon means supreme power, the emperor's wisdom. Quetzalcóatl means supreme power. In what dream in Asia, millions of years ago, did he have his beginning?

In the faces of the people is written the migrations from Asia across the Bering Strait, down into the Americas, bringing their dragon dreams. On the face of our guide, Mrs. Wang, I see a woman from Laguna Pueblo.

I am reminded this is the Chinese Year of the Rat. The rat is well liked for its witty, crafty character. To be born under its sign is propitious. Rats are also a delicacy. The rats, like the cucarachas of the Southwest, will survive. In the narrow street, surrounded by a billion brown faces lost in a rippling sea of Chinese bicyclists, I sing to my brothers, "La Cucaracha, la Cucaracha, ya no quiere caminar."

May 16

A Chinese magpie lives in an old pine tree near our window. Early in the morning he awakens me with his complaints. He is a beautiful bird, large with shining black feathers and spots of white. He brings the gossip from the village below: The people do not know what to make of the members of our group who jog in the morning. These men with hairy legs are the barbarians of old. The women joggers: ladies of little decorum.

In the morning, our group tours a market where farmers sell their excess crops. It is nothing more than a good old-fashioned Mexican mercado. Patricia and I smile. We have probably been in every mercado in Mexico. I buy a small print of a buck and doe from an artist. Patricia also buys a print. Chinese themes for adobe walls in New Mexico.

Later, we tour Haichain, a neighborhood on the outskirts of Beijing. A wonderful place, quiet, clean. We see people at work, small shop owners, a woman carrying mail on a bike, the local women washing clothes at the neighborhood water pump. If you have ever walked in a colonia in a Mexican city or a poor man's barrio in the southwest, you know what a typical neighborhood in Beijing is like. Clean, swept barrio streets, some vendors, lots of people, a horse-drawn cart. Only the language is different.

In the afternoon, we tour the Summer Palace. There is a lake, and I imagine the old emperors in their colorful garb walking the breezeway along the lake, escorting their concubines. Outside the masses toiled. Of such things are revolutions made. One empress, the Empress Suchi, spent a fortune building a marble boat. The boat still sits on the lake. It goes nowhere. Tourists clamber aboard.

During the Chicano Movement of the sixties, a few of the more radical Chicanos thought they would go to war against the United States to make their grievances known. In California, a group of activists formed the Royal Chicano Air Force and built airplanes of adobe. With these we would attack. The rains came and washed the adobe away. The Royal Chicano Navy submarine, when launched into the flood-swollen Chavez Ravine in Los Angeles, also sank. Adobe submarines. Let that be a lesson to you, Raza! Next time, we build the fleet of marble.

May 20

When I was a child in school in Santa Rosa, we studied China. We read about the Great Wall of China. We looked at the huge globe of the world Mr. Gold had in his room. We knew that China was on the other side of the world. Later, in the dusty playground of the school, I scooped out a small hole. Better watch out, somebody said, you'll fall into China.

Each village here is composed of communes. So was the village of Puerto de Luna, my grandfather's home. In Puerto de Luna, the farmers owned their land, they nourished their families from the earth, they sold their produce, but they led a communal life. At the heart of the village was the family, but at the heart of the commune was the church. Other aspects of village life created the sense of community. The system of irrigation that the farmers used, for example. The main irrigation ditch, la acequia madre, brought water from the river. Caring for that ditch was a communal responsibility. The most friendly feelings of community and the most vociferous arguments took place around the delegation of cleaning crews and the choosing of the ditch rider, el mayordomo. Was el mayordomo the cadre's leader? A leader in the commune, a man on horseback who rode the ditch and saw that the source of life was kept clean. He assigned watering days. The men of the village gathered in the evening or around the post office and made rules for governing themselves and decided who to give power to. How simple it is for me to relate to these brown men and women I see here, bent over rice fields or vegetable gardens. I have seen them before, there where I began to dig my hole to China.

Today, on the road north to the Great Wall, we pass through farmland. Small ditches are everywhere, carrying water from the main canal. Water pumps rush the water to the fields. Men and women stand by the pumps, working and talking. Mayordomos of the water. The life spirit of the commune flows into the fields, and all around us, as far as I can see in the haze, the farmers work the valley.

About an hour and a half north of Beijing, we come to the Great Wall, the tourist part of the Great Wall. I feel awe at my first sight of the massive wall. Built on the back of a mountain slope, it is like a serpent that crawls up and down the hogbacks.

I am reminded that when the Anglo-Americans first swept into New Mexico, the Great Wall of Resistance was the Hispanic culture they found there. That wall of culture has been battered and bruised, but it's still in place. Will it disappear or will it always be there, like the Great Wall of China?

A month ago, President Reagan was at the Great Wall, our guide says. He promised to build ten nuclear plants in China. Will they become the new symbols of China? Dragon breath, dragon fire. Does the new dragon feed on plutonium U32? Along the wall, Chinese families pause to eat their lunches: boiled eggs, bread, cakes, soft drinks, and beer. In the future, will Chinese families visit the nuclear reactors? Will they sit in the shade of the nuclear power plants to eat their picnic lunches?

May 21

This morning, Patricia and I do not join our tour. One group is going to the site where Peking Man was discovered, the other to a steel factory. But my bones are still weary from yesterday's excursion. I sleep, and in my fitful sleep, a dragon enters my body. China is entering me. The dragon settles itself in me, its eyes breathing fire through my eyes, its breath the life in my lungs, its serpentine body settled along my spine and heart and liver and stomach. The tail of the dragon spreads to my feet. Finally, it has entered me completely. Finally, I have made my peace with this giant country and its billion people.

When I awaken, I feel refreshed, a new man. A dragon man. Or a man carrying the potential of the dragon within. The yin and yang. The opposites, the polar forces waiting for me to use them as I wish. Patricia serves me hot Chinese tea. I say something in Chinese, a language I do not understand. My Chinese eyes look out the window. The pine trees are wet. It is raining again. Looking at the pines, I do not know whether I am in the western hills of Beijing or in Taos. Some of my happier moments have been spent in Taos.

I had a friend at Taos Pueblo, the commune of the Taos Indians. Cruz, an old man, taught me to hunt. Cruz, old man of the pueblo, governor, hunter, farmer, communal man, man of power. Now I know the power he carried within him. He was a dragon man. He knew how to balance his energies. Those thousands of years separated from the Orient, thousands of years since the migration from Asia, and still he carried the supreme sense of the dragon in his soul.

Now, I hear him call from the forest. He calls in the language of Taos Pueblo, but to me, it sounds like Chinese. So now I have Cruz and my grandfather to guide through China. I am a new man. A Chicano Chinaman.

May 22

This evening is our last in Beijing. Earlier in the day, we visited the Mao Dedong Memorial, the central prison at Beijing, and Beijing University. Now, we gather at a hotel restaurant for a feast of Peking duck. What a fiesta. Mai tais flow freely. Toasts are made. Patricia toasts Chairman Mao. I toast my grandfather. We all toast the beautiful Chinese people. Peking duck is broiled whole, then sliced. The slices are put into thick, round, rice tortillas, garnished with plum sauce and green onions. Delicious. Peking Duck Taco. I could make a million dollars selling them at sidewalk stands in Albuquerque. Forgive me, Mao.

May 24

Our first day in Xi'an, the countryside is bewitching. Fields of rice spread into the morning mists. The country is alive with people. There is color to their dress. There are small shops, family operations. Mercados. A sense of excitement. How unlike Beijing. Policemen wear white jackets and salute smartly. The dull blues and grays of Beijing have disappeared.

Before dinner, I set out alone to walk the streets of Xi'an. The boulevard is packed with people. My walk up the street is rewarded. I discover the small shops. Here a man sits in a cubbyhole and mends shoes. The bicycle repair shops are numerous. There is a toilet and plumbing-supply shop, groceries, clothes. Most are hole-in-the-wall entrepreneurs, but happy and thriving. All greet me with awkward stares and some surprise. I pause to talk to a man at work repairing a bike. He speaks Chinese. I speak the Spanish of New Mexico. We part on good terms.

I disappear in the crowd, I flow, become one with the crowd, dare to lose my identity. I join the flow of the masses and, for a while, I am no longer a Chicano in China, I am no longer American. I am a dark man walking in twilight in the streets of Xi'an. No lights, no garish neon, no loud music blasting, there is only the sound of the people. China is people. A sea of people, a sea rippling against the shore of the world, a wave bursting with energy on our dreams. I start—become me again, find myself again—leave the sea, a strange piece of driftwood from the llano of New Mexico, cast on the shore of Xi'an. The faces smile again, watch as I pass, do double takes; I am a Chicano in China again. Alone.

May 25

This afternoon we visit a commune with about 20,000 members. It is larger than most of the towns I know in New Mexico. We visit a small factory and a nursery, where the children sing songs for us. But the real treat is being taken to the house of a woman who has volunteered to speak to us. Her courtyard is small, but spotless; plain, but cool. Two trees shade it. She invites us into her house. The floor is brick. Sprinkled and swept, it resembles a packed-dirt floor of the old village homes of New Mexico. She lives with her son and daughter, takes care of the grandchild. She has a television set and a sewing machine. Her early life was full of poverty and suffering; so she now praises the liberation of 1949. I look at the wrinkled face of the woman and feel at home. I am back in my childhood and the woman is a neighbor who has come to visit my mother. Only this woman's kitchen is different. A clay oven with two hot plates for cooking. Comales. Plain and primitive. I remember the cast-iron, wood-burning stoves of the ranches I knew as a child. Tortillas browning on the comales.

May 16

Our plane to Chengdu is an old prop model, a dragon sans jet power, but smooth and reliable. Below us spreads the most fertile valley in China, the rice bowl of the country. From the air we can see miles of rice paddies.

Each new region produces surprises. On the ride into town, we see the peasants winnowing wheat along the road. They use the pavement to beat the wheat. Then they stack the dry wheat stalks, all cut by hand, by the sides of the road. I see my first water buffalo, a huge animal used to plow the rice fields. Everywhere the farmers are at work, planting new fields, knee-deep in water and muck.

The Chengdu Hotel is new, the young attendants eager. We taste our first Szechuan food, hot and spicy rice, pork tongue, cucumbers baked in a spicy sauce, seaweed soup, other tidbits. For the first time in weeks, my tongue burns. "More chile," I say, a pleasant smile on my face, my forehead sweating.

After dinner, Patricia and I walk down the street to a free market to buy oranges. The crowds turn to watch us walk by. Everywhere we go, we draw the attention of the people. After all, how many Chicanos have walked the streets of Chengdu on a May evening? How many have argued over the price of six oranges? The salesman calls the price in Chinese, and I answer in Spanish, then in English, enjoying the bartering. The old women at the gate of the hotel smile at the barbarians who enter the Chengdu Hotel carrying a bag full of oranges.

May 28

Chengdu, city of 2.5 million people, a sprawling city, polluted city. Today the smog hangs like a thick dirty gauze over the skyline. The factory smokestacks belch like dragons of industry. Buses and trucks rattle back and forth, and, as always, the constant stream of people fills the streets.

After dinner we attend the Chengdu opera. In a back street, midst the hole-in-the-wall shops and homes, stands the opera house. The play tonight is a comedy. The greatest comedy for me is to watch the people. Attendance at the opera is an informal event. Men come in undershirts. This is really operetta for the masses, a kind of entertainment that might have taken place in the Old West a hundred years ago in the Red Dog Saloon. A famous opera star from the East comes to town, the miners and cowboys and Mexicans pack the hall. Opera in the provinces.

The Chinese have a habit of clearing their throats and their noses. They have developed this ritual into an art form. What a cacophony of sound begins when the first man clears his throat and spits into the aisle or in front of him. Then another follows suit until it seems the entire theater is busy clearing their throats and spitting into the row in front of them. Nauseating to some of our more sensitive Western foreigners, quite natural to the Chinese operagoer.

May 30

In the afternoon, we drive to the train station. Hundreds of people are there, but foreigners are whisked into the first-class facilities. The train to Chongqing (or Chung-king) is on time. It is a pleasant ride in the night. It rains.

On the train, our Chinese guide, Mrs. Wang, reveals part of her history. Her father was a rich man. He sided against Chang Kai-shek and was killed. When the Japanese invaded in 1939, Mrs. Wang, then a girl of eighteen, escaped by walking across three provinces of China. She lived with the peasants, a life of extreme poverty and brutality. The old feudal warlords and the old village bureaucrats kept the people enslaved. The rich got richer and the poor were treated like animals. An intelligent, young woman who had studied English in Hong Kong, Mrs. Wang saw the reality of China. She wanted to help her people and so she joined the Communist Party. It offered hope where there was no hope. Today, people complain, "There is no free thought." But the masses still remember the conditions before 1949, and they know they are better off now.

May 31

I awaken to greet the sun and to sing his song so the day may dawn. I look outside the train window. The train has stopped on a bridge that spans a river. All is silence. Below us, the river rushes, mad and raging. It has rained all night, the mist and clouds hang close to the green hills, the yellow, muddied water rushes down to the river. We are suspended in space—suspended in time. I forget I have to go to the bathroom and sit by the train window, drinking in the beauty of the wet morning. The train jerks forward. I awaken.

"Grampa," I say, "where am I?"

"You are where I always thought you would be," my grandfather answers. "In the center of your heart."

Chongqing train station. Gray. Dirty. I have seen many like it. Chongqing, city of Chiang Kai-shek. Capital. You are gray and dirty. I do not like you. City of the Yangtze, you spew smoke from your factories.

Now, I admit to myself, I am tired of China, I am sick of China. I only wish to return to my land, my earth. I wish to ride to Taos and see the mountains. I wish to see the Sangre de Cristo of northern New Mexico. I want to fish in the small, blue stream of the Sangre de Cristo mountains. I do not wish to fish the raging waters of the brown, powerful Yangtze.

There is no privacy in China, no beauty, no creative imagination to be engendered and nourished and made to produce. Only the dull gray of the people, the streets, the polluted sky, the grime that hangs everywhere.

Yet there is one redeeming feature to Chongqing. We have arrived at the Yangtze River. Through the fine mist of the morning rain, we catch our first glimpse of the dragon river, the center of China. It is boiling and muddy, full of spring runoff. The third largest river in the world, it cuts from the mountains of Tibet to empty into the Sea of China at Shanghai. Here at Chongqing we will board a river boat for a three-day journey to Wuhan.

I remember growing up in Santa Rosa and playing every day along the banks of the Pecos River. I grew up along that river. I knew its seasons. In the spring the floods came. Then the quiet river, swollen with water, brought with it sediment and debris—the history of the northern part of the state. We swam in those flooding waters, as Mao once swam the Yangtze. Symbolic endeavors. For us, it was coming of age; for Mao it was a return to the mother river of China, a symbolic act to draw China together. Smart man. Smart politics.

June 1

Early in the morning we board the ship, *The East Is Red No. 45*. Nearly eight hundred Chinese board with us. Intelligent, wise, and traveled professors board together with Chinese peasants who carry their bundles. First class and fourth class. Even in the socialist state, the distinction remains. You get what you pay for.

I have dreamed of sailing down this magic river. Who has not? It is a river of the imagination. It is the blood of China. In the morning light, the water is the color of Chinese chocolate, the same color as the spring water of my childhood river, the same color as the Río Grande. The Yangtze is China's past, present, and future, all in one.

We have begun our journey into the heart of China. For three days, we will live on the river. Mile after mile, we stare at the Chinese in their sailboats, their ancient sampans, the faces of the people, the huts of the slopes of the hills, the meager fields of corn beautifully cultivated on the terrace slopes.

The day is a dream. The people whose pictures we take and wave to on the banks live in another reality, another time. The lesson is that parallel streams of time can exist side by side. I know why I am here: to connect the streams of time, to connect the people. To connect and connect and keep making connections. I did not come to measure or count. I came to make love to China. Today I enter her blood and mix my dreams and thoughts with hers. For the day on the river, my faith in the people is renewed.

We dock at Wanxian for the night. After dinner we go into the city, a city of more than a million people, and yet to us it is only a river city. After the trip to the city, Patricia and I host a party in the lounge of the boat. We break out peanut butter, Kraft cheese spread, crackers, and a bottle of Chinese brandy I bought in the dock in Wanxian, on the Yangtze, in another time in another place.

June 3

Today I stare at the wide Yangtze and remember images of China:

In the middle of the wide river, we pass a small sampan. There is one man rowing, guiding the boat. In the middle of the boat sits an elegant, old woman dressed in black. She holds a bright purple umbrella over her head. She sits as if she is a lady of refinement going to an evening performance.

A Tibetan appears in the thick crowd we have drawn as we board the bus in Chengdu. He is dressed in his traditional dress. I say hello. His eyes are flat, menacing. He wears a long blade under his tunic.

At the Qing terra-cotta exhibition a young woman comes up to me and says hello in a provocative way. All she wants to do is practice her English.

In Beijing a young woman in a bright western suit and red shoes rides her bike in the flow of traffic.

We drink our water from Chinese thermos bottles, large bottles far superior to anything made in the United States.

The Chinese hotels in the provinces have a most civilized custom: The hot water runs only at certain times during the day, usually in the evening. I find it an admirable practice. Think of all the energy saved by stoking up the hot-water heater only once a day and how happy are all the guests splashing away in unison. Of course, very often when the hot water begins to run, the cold water stops. Some consider this an inconvenience, a technical deficiency in the Chinese system. One learns to shrug in China. Paciencia, my grandfather would say.

The face of a little girl who pauses to rest and look up at me. She is carrying a shoulder basket of coal. Its weight is easily seventy pounds. She is to carry it up to the peak of Green Mountain.

Knee-deep in the water of a rice field, a young girl looks at me. She has the most exquisite face I have ever seen.

I have seen only two dogs in China. Extra mouths cannot be fed. There are no flies.

An orange telephone that does not work.

A Chinese spider on a white wall.

A statue of Mao always saluting me.

No ice.

June 4

After dinner, the group hires a bus to take us downtown. Wuhan is really three cities on the banks of the Yangtze; its population is nearly five million. A hotel downtown sells Coca-Colas. Served in a glass with ice. We have not had ice in weeks. No cold soda or beer.

The streets are packed with people. It is a hot and humid evening, and it seems that all the people have poured out into the streets for fresh air. There is no fresh air, but there is a friendly feeling to the masses of people who throng the streets. They sit on stools or chairs in front of their shops or houses. Parents buy popsicles for their children; there is a long line at the soft-drink shop. I buy three oranges and a white hat for

Patricia. Walking the streets is an enjoyable experience. After a day's rest and much needed solitude, one can return to the man-swarm. This is the China I will remember in my future dreams. The hot, humid streets, the masses of people, the quiet, the few neon lights, people at their shops, the well-stocked department stores that we enter in awe, the fires where people are cooking rice, the end of the day, a feeling of community.

June 5

China is not for the weak. Our tour has been strenuous. Today we don't leave for the airport until 10 A.M., an easy morning, but our 12:20 P.M. flight to Shanghai is delayed. For three hours, we sit in an unbearably hot, humid waiting room, packed with Chinese travelers. When we are finally loaded on a bus, we drive out to the runway where three planes sit. We have to wait again in the boiling bus while someone decides which plane will take us to Shanghai. Our plane is an old, converted cargo plane. The smiling hostess hands us fans when we enter. We sit in the boiling sun while the plane is fueled. We say our prayers. The plane can fly, but just barely. It groans. It creaks as I have never heard a plane creak before.

June 6

After a tiring train trip, we arrived in Hangzhou last night. This morning, we drive through the tree-lined streets of Hangzhou to go to West Lake, a huge park within the city. We board a boat and cruise the lake. The breeze is cool. The water of the lake is clear. There are boaters out, even three wind surfers, one on water skis. All is quiet and peaceful, the green park surrounds us. In the distance, the green hills. Chinese families also enjoy the park, a perfect place for lovers. The trees are sculptured, the bushes neatly trimmed, the grass cut, the pavilions placed throughout the walks. Small bridges span the waters.

At the end of our walk, we come to an area on the lake that is full of golden carp. They are swimming on the surface, their golden bodies glistening in the bright sunlight. The people feed them bread crumbs.

Long ago as a small boy growing up in Santa Rosa, I saw these golden carp. I wrote a legend of the people who were turned into golden carp and the god who came to live with them. Now I see the man-swarm in the water, the same man-swarm I have seen in the rice fields of China, on the packed streets, in the train stations of Hangzhou, and in their midst I see a huge golden carp. This is as close as I came to saying that a god lives in our midst.

In the evening, we dine at a seven-course banquet given for us by the Chinese Sports Association. It is one of the best meals we have had. The food is delicate here, not harsh and greasy. We are served a red wine made of rice, slightly sweet. It is exquisite. I drink wine. I make a lot of toasts. We eat lotus seeds served in a sugared water. The lotus seeds are like soft kernels of hominy. The lotus is the plant of the Buddha. To eat lotus seed is to eat soul food—a delicacy we have not encountered before. It is like eating posole for Christmas in New Mexico—soul food. I eat two helpings.

After dinner, we wander around the grounds of the hotel, here called a "guest house for foreigners." We stumble into a ballroom where a dance is going on, fifty cents cover charge. The band reminds me of a Mexican conjunto—saxophone, accordion, drums, guitar, violin. In fact, the first melody we hear is like a Mexican ranchera. It is like being back home at a wedding dance or in some small village dance hall. Patricia and I waltz out onto the dance floor and do a fast ranchera, hips swinging to the good old ranchera tune. We are the only ones on the floor.

Later, we waltz. I am not a dancer, but in China, I can dance anything. Red rice wine rhythm. The Chinese do not dance much. Again, the Cultural Revolution hangs over us. A whole new generation must be taught to dance. What a pity. The surrender to the spirit of the dance is necessary for joy, for creativity, for renewal of the spirit. China! Learn to dance! Here, I will clap for you!

Alla en el rancho grande,
Alla donde yo vivía
Había una rancherita,
Que alegre me decia . . .

Too much red wine, but I am full of joy again. A Chicano singing in Spanish in Hangzhou. If there is one thing we could transport to China, I would take them our idea of fiesta: letting go, dancing, a good time. China, let your hair down. Sometimes I fear the Marxist doctrine is such a heavy load to carry. It needs a heavy infusion of our fiesta.

June 7

This morning it is raining, and we make our way in the cool, refreshing rain to visit a tea brigade. The commune is large, ten of the twelve brigades raise tea, the famous Longjing Tea. (The dragon-well tea.)

The brigade leader, a striking man, gives us an excellent lecture on the composition of the commune, a unit of government that is in the process of becoming something akin to a township. Unit, brigade, township, commune, ruled by a party unit, an economic or production unit, all overseen by an appointed governmental unit. It seems the politics of the commune, such as they are, are not so difficult to understand when broken down into small parts. The missing ingredients are free choice, votes, initiative.

We sit and drink the aromatic tea. Outside the rain falls. I think of home, I wish rain for my garden, I think of the wall I must build. A wall around my home, as China built the wall around her borders. Fear of foreign ghosts? Is that why we build walls?

The afternoon is still cloudy, but the fine mist only serves to enhance the green hills and stream that surround the Monastery of the Spirit's Retreat, a Buddhist temple. Here resides a giant statue of the Buddha and his four guardians. The most interesting statue is a giant rendering of the Goddess of Mercy standing on the head of a golden carp that comes out of the waters. Ming tells us that the Buddha, as a young boy, went to fifty-three masters, seeking the true path. All refused to teach him. The goddess took mercy and taught him. Looking up at her sculpture, I am reminded of altars I have seen in Mexican baroque churches. The Goddess of Mercy looks very much like la Virgen de Guadalupe standing on her moon. The babes in limbo surround the feet of the Virgin Mary, the fifty-three young Buddhas surround the Goddess of mercy. World religions meet at these archetypal points of reference. Intuitively, I make the sign of the cross on my forehead—the worshipers of the Buddha burn incense sticks and kowtow, clapping their hands and bowing to acknowledge the Buddha.

After our spiritual trip we take tea at Jade Stream, a lovely teahouse in the Botanical Gardens. What a treat it is to drink tea and eat a sweet, delicate pastry made of lotus roots. We order ice cream, the first we've had in weeks.

But the marvel of the teahouse is its small pool. It has two- or three-dozen large, golden carp swimming in it. We sit in wicker chairs and drink our tea and enjoy the graceful ballet of the golden fish. Yes, I have returned to the land of the golden carp, I have returned home. My pilgrimage is complete, and the time which now draws to a close in China is pleasant. Suddenly, right before me, the largest of the carp, a yellow fish well over three feet long, dives to the bottom of the pond and then comes up, leaping out of the water into the air, splashing the spray in a lunge of joy. Showing off. I like to think his jump is for me.

June 10

In the afternoon, I wander alone in the people's park. It is full of people. But still it is a respite from the packed streams of people in the streets. I love people, I need the security of their dense numbers, I need to feel with them, to become part of them. But I need to breathe, to assert myself. I was raised in the tradition of the independent Hispano, the rancheros and vaqueros who are part of my New Mexican community, and are known for their independence. Order creates anarchy in our hearts. Mao would have had a hard time organizing the Chicanos.

I seek solitude in the park. I watch families and their children, young lovers, the old sitting in the shade of towering trees. I smile at all. They smile at me. I wave. I am going home in a few days. Goodbye, they wave, we are glad to have had a Chicano in China.

Freedom to Publish – Unless
You're a Chicano

"All seem to be born equal," my grandfather said as he reflected on life,
"but some more equal than others."

"Freedom means to be able to move, to go where you want, to do what
you want," a university friend told me long ago when we were young
and idealistic.

"Look, the Man is the publisher, right. He will publish you or he won't.
Most likely he won't." This told to me by an old experienced writer.

These quotes somehow address the reality of the publishing world and
its treatment of Mexican American or Chicano writers in this country.
In other words, liberty and the pursuit of publication seem to be inalienable rights, unless you are a Chicano writer.

I know now that part of what my grandfather meant was that the
publishers who control the publishing industry in the U.S.A. have real
control over who is published and who isn't, who is equal and who is
"more equal."

We are all free to create literature, and under the most trying of times
and circumstances, Chicanos and other Hispanic writers have created a
writing renaissance within our lifetime. But since a writer writes to
publish, a writer must have access to publishers. Clearly, the Man (the
big publishers) has not been interested in Chicano literature.

Publishers, and the media in general, have the power to abridge the
civil rights of many writers. In the marketplace there is censorship by

---

Originally published as "Freedom to publish . . . unless you're a Chicano," in *Monte Vista Journal*, Monte Vista, Colo. (10 November 1982).

omission as well as by commission; therefore, the question persists: if any group in this country is denied access to the media, do we really have an enlightened media which is responsive to the civil rights of everybody in the society?

"An informed people will be a free people," Benito Juarez said. Because Hispanic writers have been denied access, we have been denied the right to inform the public and our communities through our literature.

There developed an alternative. In the 1960s and '70s, several Chicano publishing ventures were begun. These publishers provided access by publishing the works of a plethora of Chicano/a writers. In spite of many difficulties, a number of these publishers are still in business, and they are known and respected internationally.

So our community itself provided the alternative, and a part of our civil rights were restored. We joined the other small presses in this country which were being responsive to the ethnic, regional, and minority groups. The literary output grew, and the literature of the nation was enriched as new voices, never heard before, were published and circulated.

But the real problem wasn't solved. To have to provide an alternative in publishing simply means the system is still closed, and it means our work is not distributed as widely as one would want. It means the literature of many groups still remains unpublished. And the society suffers, because it is kept from knowing its true character. In other words, the civil rights of the entire society are abridged.

A society in which some are "more equal" than others is not a just society. Big publishers and big media can help in the formation of a just society, but they have to open up, provide access to all. That's a challenge for the future.

Letter to Chicano Youth

It is a pleasure to be with you today to celebrate this important national conference. I sense this will be one of those turning points in the history of our community. You are a new generation taking the future in your hands. This is a time not only for action, it is also a time for contemplation. There are historic dates which make us pause and review our accomplishments, and our faults. Nineteen ninety-two is such a date in the history of the people of the Americas and for our Chicano community. I am sure your discussions will focus on the meaning of this date and its implications for the future.

Around us we hear the voices of many of the long oppressed communities of this hemisphere, adding their song to the songline of the Americas. From these voices a new, truer history is being written, and what we learn from it will dictate our path into the future. You must listen to each other, respect each other, and reach a consensus which does not fractionalize and serve one vested interest, but a consensus that serves our community. You must act wisely if we are to insure that the future does not repeat the faults of the past.

What kind of future will you shape? If we assume our actions are guided by just and humanistic ideals, what are the ideals which guide your actions? What values have you gained from your families, your communities, and your education to guide you as you chart the course for this decade?

The task ahead of you is a momentous one. At the root of your work is the creation of a vision to serve our community. There is much to correct in the relationships which govern the communities of the Americas—much poverty, disease, and injustice to eliminate. There are

---

Address presented to the National Chicano Student Conference, Albuquerque, N.Mex. (11 April 1992).

the rivers and air to clean and Mother Earth to protect from constant ravage. There are new models of education to create and a technology to bend to humanistic endeavors.

The needs in our community are great, almost overwhelming. We need national leaders to give expression to our hopes. Leaders who understand our needs and express them in clear, positive terms. There are some among you who will become those leaders. So, I ask, what ideals will guide you into the twenty-first century? What is it you want to do with your life to make the Americas, and the world, a better place for all?

The rhetoric of the past holds few answers. We need a new vision which voices our aspirations. Those who preach only the rhetoric of hate and disgust cannot guide us. We need leaders who can put pettiness and envy out of their hearts and dedicate their energies to serving our community. We need men and women who have open hearts, a clear purpose of mind, and a vision which incorporates the diversity of our community.

As you discuss the issues facing your generation, speak what is true in your heart; do not be led by instincts you do not believe. Each time you subscribe to slogans you do not believe, you damage your own integrity, and you disgrace the teachings of our ancestors. Dare to stand up for your convictions, and let those ideals serve the common good. Seek a clarity of vision which can serve you and our community.

We are placing the future in your hands, as it was placed in our hands by our parents and grandparents. We have tried to be wise and not always succeeded. We have tried to keep their values and sometimes have fallen by the wayside. But we knew in our hearts the teachings of our viejitos, and we respected the traditions of our neighbors.

Where will you be ten years from now? Will you be able to say that you helped forge the ideals of your generation? Or will you follow the easy answers, the rhetoric of the past, the exclusionary tactics which divide instead of unite?

My life in writing has been a search for the ideals I could distill from my contemplations, my heritage, and my education. Clarity of vision is not easily arrived at, and too often it is easier to argue without having a clear statement of the purpose in mind. Sometimes it is too easy to say that virtue and compassion are our goals, when we are not virtuous or compassionate. It is too easy to separate people into groups and stereotype them. It is too easy to stop the process of communication and believe only you hold the correct answer.

In my life I have known despair and the loss of faith. In that crucible of experience, I had to find a new path, and for the path to lead to illumination it has to be good and true and beautiful. Those qualities of the spirit are not found in the rhetoric of an easy answer. I found those guiding principles not only in my heritage, but also in the teachings of world cultures. I listen to the chant of the Americas, and the songline I hear connects me to the world.

Dare to know yourself. Find the truth within. Love deeply and give of that love to others. Take time to contemplate the wonder of the earth and the universe. I know you want to change the world today, not tomorrow. You want to formulate action today. You want to start the journey right away. I only say first find the clarity within yourself to illuminate the path.

Become not only a truly liberated person and a servant of your community, but dare to become part of the songline of the world. When you do that you can truly reach out and touch others, help others, and join with others in common efforts.

Old divisions do not serve us. Your challenge is to write a new and clear vision in the pages of our history. With clarity of purpose we can face the future and make it blossom with new hope. We can correct old injustices. I wish for you that clarity of thought and purpose which will guide your actions.

Shaman of Words

Imagine a late October night in the llano of eastern New Mexico. The cold wind moans as it sweeps across the open plain. In the distance coyotes cry. An owl calls from a juniper tree. Overhead the Milky Way sparkles and swirls across a vast, dark sky.

A village dots the wide expanse of land. This is Pastura, New Mexico. The year is 1937. I am to arrive at one of the adobe homes tonight.

This is how it begins. A woman in labor. Outside the expectant father and his vaquero friends drinking wine, celebrating. None looks up to see the owl winging across the llano in the last light of dusk.

The llano is broken by arroyos and hills. The line separating earth from sky is barely visible. In this vacant land appear the lights of the village. The cross atop the Catholic church rises into the dark sky, a symbol of faith in the often times harsh land. At the edge of the village appears the dark water tank of the railroad station, once the hub of activity in this cattle and sheep country.

The village is a cluster of dim lights, a point of civilization in the dark expansion. Kerosene lamps, like faith, flicker in the adobe homes. Families gather around the kitchen tables; night is storytelling time. Children, hearing the piercing cry of the wind, draw close to their mothers. The mournful sound may be the cry of la Llorona, the woman who searches for the children she murdered. Or is it the cry of a disobedient daughter who danced with the devil and lost her sanity? Or is the cry of the woman in labor?

Every sound carries a story; every deed becomes a story.

"Cuentanos un cuento," the children beg. The ambiance is suddenly right for a story. The ghosts of the world outside are the same crea-

Originally published in *Genre: Forms of Discourse and Culture* 32, nos. 1 and 2 (Spring/Summer 1999): 15–26.

tures who inhabit the stories. Stories reveal the dark world of ghosts, witches, and other fantastic characters. All are familiar. In the confines of the story these characters reveal the terror that can stalk the land, settle in the heart.

There are many kinds of stories, and the storyteller selects one right for the moment. The cuentos reveal moral instruction, joy, humor, insight into human nature. Those who tell stories and those who listen have faith in the stories told, a faith akin to that they hold for the church, its mysteries and power.

One born in this ambiance is born into mythic time, a time when one strips away self-consciousness and communes with the transcendent power in the universe. The time of storytelling is like love or a mystical experience; it holds time in abeyance. It sheds light on the darkness. Those who listen give up their sense of self and enter into the story.

This naturalness inherent in the stories of my ancestors is the same throughout the world. Storytellers who related the great myths of the world knew how to create a story that kills time, expands time, makes time anew.

Yes, the time of storytelling re-creates mythic times, and I was born into that world. It was the world of my Nuevo Mexicano ancestors, the world of my family. My parents were born in Puerto de Luna; they knew both the Pecos River valley and the llano. They were colonists whose grandparents had left the Río Grande valley to settle the Llano Estacado. What sustained them?

Faith. A faith that has imbued the world of the Nuevo Mexicanos for centuries, a faith in the church, the earth, the seasons, and the mystery of creation. And they told stories. The trust they placed in stories was passed on to me.

Their time was filled with hard work—hard work and survival. But to sustain them there were the sacraments of the church, and there were the stories. They lived close to nature, and they understood the world of spirits. The world of spirits permeated not only the old cuentos their ancestors had brought from the Iberian peninsula, it was alive in their New Mexican experience. The world of man and nature was filled with a spiritual essence.

The storyteller's gift is my inheritance. The voice of the llaneros and the Pecos Valley people filled my young ears. I can hear them now. They taught me that stories create mythic time. Stories reveal our human nature and thus become powerful tools for insight and revelation. That's why my ancestors told stories. That's why I write.

Telling stories was natural in the everyday life of the people. It was ritual. It was also spontaneous. It was breath. Our elders didn't set aside time to tell stories. All phenomena were stories. Everything that occurred in daily life, dream, or memory was grist for stories. Even the nightly rosaries and novenas were stories. Custom, ritual, ceremony, the slaughter of animals, Saturday night dances, weddings, tragic deaths, windstorms, the whirlwinds the devil rode, people who could fly, people who turned into owls—everything was a story for the child born into that world.

There is a story of my birth.

"You were born with the umbilical cord tied around your neck," my mother said long after I was born.

Born that October night when the owls cried in the llano. Born that night in storytelling time. Born into the mythic time of storytelling. Born into that communion with the transcendent that is the essence of story. What a fortunate beginning!

"La Grande was there to help me. I don't know what I would have done without her," my mother continued.

Is it true? I ask myself. Was I born a hanged man? Or was the hanged man a story told that night? A family legend? What does it mean?

In the Tarot deck the Hanging Man card can be ominous. To be hanged is to be immobile, in a state of limbo. For a while the child being born is in a state of limbo. Does it struggle to be born or to remain in the womb? Was I near death at my birth? Or did I not want to leave the womb? I had become accustomed to its warmth and safety, and being born was coming into the world. Being born also implies coming into a "new consciousness." The voices of the storytellers drew me from the womb, drew me from one story into another.

What does it signify to be born a hanging man in mythic time, the time of storytelling? Was that the first sign that I should one day be a writer?

Here's another story.

"You were just beginning to crawl," my mother said many years later. "I sat you on a sheepskin on the floor. My family was there, and each of us placed different objects around you. Your father set down his saddle, because he wanted you to be a vaquero. I don't remember who put down a pencil and paper. Perhaps it was me, because I had always yearned for an education. I had a bright mind, but in those days girls remained at home. Only my brothers went to school. Anyway, you crawled to the pencil and paper."

This simple family rite proved to be prophetic. How could it be otherwise?

All Nuevo Mexicanos are storytellers. We are products of a rich oral tradition, a Mediterranean tradition, a New World tradition, hundreds of years of passing on knowledge through the ritual of storytelling. My time and place impressed the sacredness of a story into my blood. I was deeply affected by the stark beauty of the eastern New Mexico llano, land of my birth. The joy, magic, and mystery of growing up along the Pecos River is found in my early work. The voices of los antepasados, the song of the river and hills, and the hum of the earth permeate all my work.

I remember running home from school and hearing a voice call my name. I would turn and turn and cock my ear and wonder who or what was calling me. Was it la Llorona of the river? She haunted me and my childhood friends during those long summers when we played in the river bosque. When it got dark we heard her cry, heard her crashing through the brush, crying for the children she had murdered. She still haunts the edges of every story I write.

But mythic time is dying. We struggle to keep storytelling in the realm of the sacred, revealing the ghosts that haunt the heart, exorcising the terror. Once we were connected to nature. Once we knew how to cast out evil spirits. Once we were connected to the sacred. Now the circle of the story has been replaced by the flat images of television and the false myths of motion pictures.

Raised in Santa Rosa, New Mexico, I grew up in a Spanish-speaking home. I thought the whole world spoke Spanish. It was a struggle to learn English at school. But learn I did. In a changing world the story-teller grabs whatever magic he can find. Later, I was to include many of the experiences of those years in my first novel.

My family moved to Alburquerque, and I thrived in the barrio. With new friends I played baseball, basketball, rode bikes, met girls, got through junior high, and went to high school. Then tragedy struck. One summer swimming in an irrigation ditch, I dove in and fractured my neck. Floating in the water, unable to move a muscle, I was close to drowning. I lived through the near-death experience. I saw my soul rising in the air, looking back down on a reality I was leaving.

I tried to put part of that time of my life into the novel *Tortuga*. I tried to describe what it means to die and go to the underworld and return. Looking back on that time of extreme suffering, I understand how I came to be a shaman of words.

The days and nights of fever were a horror. I was visited by terrorizing demons in the form of spiders and insects that crawled down my throat. They were pills the nurse tried to get me to swallow, but in my nightmare everything became a spirit trying to destroy me. I was being eaten alive from inside, left with only the bones.

I do not wish to dwell on this time of pain and suffering; I thought I was done with it when I wrote *Tortuga*. But consider this. During that intense fever, I was strapped to a pulley. A strap went around my chin, with ropes up the pulley on the headboard. Weights pulled my neck straight. When that didn't work, the surgeon bore holes into my skull and inserted pins to hold the ropes.

Again, I was a hanging man. For days and nights I hung on those ropes, the weights pulling my neck and spine straight.

One goes through such experiences of pain, and if one survives, the old self is dead and a new self is born. The "Rudy" of my childhood was dead—died in nights of tortured fever while he hung on ropes. When I awoke and recognized the dawn, I had come into a new plane of life, a new consciousness. I recognized the physical change (I could barely move), but I did not yet recognize the journey I was beginning toward the new consciousness.

This happens in life. We are caught up in the ego and the flesh and recognize changes only at that level. I had to learn to walk again, and that was of primary importance. I did feel empty, but I didn't realize then the most important task in my life would be to fill the spiritual vacuum. Those who have been through traumatic changes in their lives understand this. The journey is toward the sacred, knowledge of the soul and its purpose, which doesn't come in one epiphany. We resist. We don't want to be chosen. We want to live as "ordinary" human beings live.

In the novel *Tortuga*, Tortuga resists becoming the new shaman of the blue guitar, that is, a poet of the people. He doesn't want to sing the songs of the world of spirits. He has had helping spirits come to him, but he doesn't yet understand how they can help him. Sonny Baca, my most recent hero, also resists leaving ordinary reality to learn the world of shamanic power.

When I was taken down from the ropes and the pulley, I was transported to a hospital in the middle of the southern New Mexico desert. Nearby, to the east, lay La Jornada del Muerto, a desert so dry it is called the Journey of the Dead. My Spanish and Mexican ancestors who had colonized New Mexico centuries earlier dreaded crossing this desert on their way to the cool northern New Mexico mountains. Everything returns in cycles. My stay in the hospital was my jornada del muerto. I had died. The journey into a new life was beginning.

I have learned that, in life, the environment often reflects the emptiness inside. Empty people sit alone in the darkness of their homes or in dreary bars to drink, to forget. Those who are blasted down to zero feel the vacuum inside, and the ordinary world they once enjoyed also turns to dust.

In the hospital filled with crippled children, the mystery of my transformation was to continue. I was encased in a body cast. The doctors saw me only as flesh and bones to be mended. I knew that if I was to survive, I had to depend on something other than the body cast. In that cocoon of plaster I was yet to suffer the long, hot summer, and though it provided safety, it also became my prison.

The hanging man had been lowered into a new reality, the time of amphibians. I became a turtle. Here is where I received my training. I acquired protecting guides; those who moved around me taught me how to deal with pain and suffering. My parents and family came and reminded me I could return to their world. I had not really died. They did not know their reality would never be the same for me.

For days and nights on end they offered prayers, visited the church, said rosaries, made promises to the saints. This faith has to impress even the most agnostic. Prayer is, after all, the breath of life. Prayer is song. Everyone needs a song. The shaman needs a song to sing as he journeys through hell.

Antonio hears the song of the river and la Llorona in *Bless Me, Ultima*. One hears Tortuga's shamanistic song in *Tortuga*. Sonny Baca is told to sing as he enters the world of his nagual, the world of his dream. The shaman of words can have many songs. Each poem or story or book becomes a song. Prayer and song are efficacious for healing. Books, too, have this power. Our stories use the pain and suffering of the characters in a transformative way.

Now the underworld is the world of my writing room. Here is heaven and hell. But I resisted becoming a writer, a shaman of words. What began as playful experimentation with poems and stories, when I was a young man, turned into a journey. The writer who has visited the underworld has to describe it. The more I write, the deeper I get into the world that has to do with our essence. Many a day I have emerged from my writing room, after taking my characters through their journeys, to complain to my wife: Why can't I be normal, like other people? Why me? Why do I have to be a writer, spending my life transporting characters into those depths? Is it madness? Or is it that once the gift is laid, we have no choice? One is doomed to become a shaman of words.

The hospital was full of stories. I learned each person was not only on a journey in and out of the hospital, but each was on a journey through life. What was the goal? Transformation into a new self. We were like snakes sloughing away the old skin, being born brilliant and new. I didn't know that yet. Remember, the process doesn't illuminate all at once. It is a slow and painful process.

I withdrew into the turtle shell. From its safety I could peer out at the world. Part of my world was centered on the reality of pain and suffering; the rest became a world of dreams. Nightmares. My life returned to haunt me, teasing me about my past. I struggled to free myself, to work, to break free of the cast. I did not want to be the new person I was becoming. I wanted to be the old me.

I write this to share with you how a person is transformed. If one goes through a traumatic experience then tries to return to the old way, he is fooling himself. One cannot visit the crucible of the underworld and return to the same path. If the truth and symbols revealed in the underworld are to make sense, a new person must be born. That is inherent in life—a series of transformations, a constant coming into a new consciousness. If we accept the new realities, the journey can be enlightening and miraculous.

I left the hospital, skinny as a board. The ember of light which was my essential self was so far buried in darkness it barely glowed. (As an aside: In one version of *Tortuga* a turquoise stone is placed into the wet plaster of paris as Tortuga's cast is formed. I finally didn't use that, but it is interesting to note that even during the process of writing the novel I recognized the crystal had to be embedded in Tortuga. The crystal would symbolize the new soul, the new power.)

Of course, my family and friends greeted me. Home was provided. But I felt different. I used to wander, as lamely as I could, the streets of 'Burque alone. Sometimes I hung out with another kid who had been in the hospital with me. We were different. No longer like the rest. A goddamned spirit of something had touched us, slammed us to the ground, nearly destroyed us, made us handicapped, ashamed of ourselves. Different. Nobody wants to be different. We cursed. Cursing God and the powers that be seemed an inherent early part of the process. Why me? I don't want to be different!

We looked for Mike, another kid who had been with us at the hospital. Mike was wiser. He seemed to know what we should be doing in the world of ordinary people. We didn't find him. We, each one of us, were on our own. Gimps. We met a few others like us, but the ordinary world just didn't seem to understand that we were throbbing with a new soul.

My mother was a curandera. Not in the sense that people seem to think. Not traditional, not practicing. She had the wisdom of broken bones and nerves most women seem to have. She massaged me back to life. It was a long process. Perhaps it is never done. The magic people with healing in their hearts and fingers will come to help. Many years later, my wife, Patricia, would do the same. Massage the tired limbs. We're still in the process together, trying to understand how the flesh drags us down. But the spirit cries for wonderful new transformations.

This is how we learn to love. With the human touch. Love is not abstract. It's about touch. Those who are curanderas in their own right come to touch, to massage away the pain and sickness of spirit. They give of themselves, they chase away the negative energy, all that residue of the underworld, and they begin to fill the emptiness left by the sorcerers of pain and suffering.

People continually ask me: Do you know any curanderas? Of course, I do. They're all around us. I live with one. I meet them every day. The personal time of transformation is reflected in the cosmic time of change in which we live. The healers are among us. Me—all I can do is write. A shaman of words.

I struggled to become whole. To be seen as whole. But I was still caught up in the flesh. I thought it was only my body that needed to be made whole again. The sacred was eluding me. I began not to believe in the faith of the church. The emptiness inside grew immense. It would take chapters to describe the loneliness of the young man struggling through high school. A struggle of human bondage. That would take many novels.

Then I became stronger and began to fit into a normal life, the regular life of friends and classmates. They only saw a skinny guy they went to school with. In my eyes I'm sure that owls flew, and in the blood swam turtles. Ah, well.

I graduated from high school. The subtle prejudices at work in the school system did little to encourage us Mexican American kids. I could keep up the grades, but where was I to go after graduation? I enrolled in a business school, and a life-affirming teacher helped me to learn, get jobs, keep busy. I worked around town, hung out with friends on weekends, went fishing, working my way toward normalcy. When you have been through extreme sickness, one of the false doctrines they teach you is to return to normalcy. That's nonsense.

We will never be the same again. We should learn instead to nurture the new person born within.

I felt that something was missing. I did very well at business school, but something else was missing. I was no longer meant to live in ordinary reality. Don't think this is boastful. It's just a true statement. If you've been there, you understand.

By pure chance—I don't even remember the motivation or circumstances, except that I was dissatisfied—I enrolled in the University of New Mexico, worked my way through, and in spite of hardships I persisted. But a longing, a reminiscing, told me I had moved out of mythic time; I had forgotten the stories of my ancestors. My way of life was not found in the textbooks I studied. There was no help to explore the realm I needed to explore. But then there were literature classes.

I fell in love with literature, with the study of ideas, and that saved me. In the literature of the world there were glimpses of the hell I had visited, the hell of Dante, Orpheus, the Scylla and Charybdis of Odysseus, the agony of poets I read. Others had suffered, others had been on the path, and they had written their experiences. So I began to write poems and stories. I tapped my creativity to liberate myself, to free myself of the shackles of aloneness. The high school and college curricula had never exposed me to the history and literature of my ancestors. Now I had a purpose: to write the stories of my community. I would return to mythic time and reveal its symbols in my stories.

That meant I had to reveal myself, reveal my journey toward knowledge. Go back to the beginning, the beginning that came with Ultima that night of my birth. Her hands. The milk of my mother. The rough scratch of my father's hands, the whiskey breath of the vaqueros, the poverty of the llano, the mystery of the universe at night. Oh, I knew something of the healers. They had come to heal my mother. They had been there at my birth.

Return to the time of my childhood. I began writing *Bless Me, Ultima*, a childhood novel, and then Ultima came to bless the work, to be the guide through my unconscious, to show me the way. What revelation! Hoorah! Words! I dared to speak! To write! About those common people of my homeland. El llano came alive. Puerto de Luna came alive. I dove into the lake, the unconscious. The shaman of words had found the door by which to return to the land of spirits. I could compose my soul anew!

In the beginning I wrote about the surface reality of life, the life of the 1940s in Santa Rosa, its people, customs, traditions, friends, events. When I dared to follow my helping guides, I found the world of spirits. I entered the world of the shaman, our curanderas, our healers. They had always been there, waiting for me. A new universe opened up as I pounded the key of an old Smith Corona portable typewriter my brother had left at home. I learned to travel across time, to fly like the old brujas and brujos used to fly, to bring lost spirits into the world.

I learned to use and interpret the symbols of my childhood dreams. I learned anew that I had once lived in storytelling time, sacred time, when la Llorona was real and not just a story, when all the characters of the stories told were real.

Returning to that time is not easy. It is a continuing effort. With each story I write, the hanging man is lowered again from an old awareness (the safety of the prior story) into a new consciousness. Every step is fraught with danger, and yet every word laid down on paper is a step toward a new illumination.

There is madness on the path, and I have known it as much as anyone. There is danger, the danger of remaining in the world of spirits. One can go too deep and face dangers, like the shaman who flies to the underworld in search of lost souls. One can be caught in the web of chaos and never return with the order one envisions. Delving into the subconscious is not Sunday sport. One needs a guide. I am fortunate. I have had many guides. The elders guide me. My parents guide me. My wife has been my guide. I pray to the ancestors, without them I am nothing. I thank those who guide me today, without them I am lost.

The most potent sickness in our world today is soul sickness. Perhaps it has always been so. The essence within is not integrated. It is shattered, searching here and there for focus. It strikes out in false directions, carrying the flesh with it, torturing the body. There is more need than ever for the medicine men and women who know about the soul, who know the shamanic journey to reintegrate the soul. The journey to the world of spirits.

For me writing is such a journey. The characters first come to me and tell me to write their story. They are floating and need a center: the story. They need the harmony and order of the story. With the character as guide, I set out into the subconscious to explore the true meaning of that character's life. As a young man, Ultima came to me and took me on that journey. I wrote not just a childhood story but one that explored the world of spirits. Some call that world witchcraft, but it is not. Even I used that term in the past, but that's because the revelation is long, and, early on, some of what was revealed to me was not clear. I am a slow learner.

It is not witchcraft. It is a world open to all of us. Many times it takes a traumatic illness to open the door to the journey. This is why I have talked about my stay in the hospital, not to seek pity or even understanding, but simply to let you know that was the beginning of my journey. From that experience I returned a changed man. That's obvious. Obvious to the flesh, not the spirit. What we make of pain and suffering, that traumatic shock that knocks us out of ordinary reality, is up to us.

Tortuga, I think, is a clear example of my journey. In that novel there are many guides for Tortuga. His stay in the underworld is concrete; his visitations by the spirits around him are quite clear. In the end he leaves the amphibian world and returns home, with his song, ready for the next step in his initiation. He does not yet know he must keep singing, that the song line must be expanded, that there are many stories to be told.

The story the shaman tells has a healing, reintegrating power. I do not heal people directly, I am not a curandero, nor do I take people on shamanic journeys. I write stories. I rely on the story. But my characters guide me—and therefore the reader—on a journey of reintegration. We all have some of the soul sickness within; we all seek the harmonizing power of prayer, love, meditation, exercise, right diet, religion, or philosophy. Or a story. The fewer stories we tell, hear, or read, the worse the soul sickness.

My characters then become my helpers, my guiding and protecting spirits. They lead me into depths unimagined. Of course, there is a conscious effort and the thrust to creativity, but for me all the energies are bound as one. And the theme of the shamanic journey is major. It is a way to knowledge, a journey toward the sacred.

Even in the recent Sonny Baca series, the theme is obvious. Sonny encounters problems in the ordinary world (kidnapped girls, the nuclear waste problem, the loss of culture), and he addresses those. But the guides around him, those who protect him and show him the way, know his real goal is to become a brujo (shaman). When people who know my work ask me if Sonny is like me, this means they see the overall theme is constant in my work. I write about a journey I have taken, a path I'm still traveling.

The theme reflects the writer. We write about human nature, revealing it for ourselves and for our readers, and the complexity of who we are leads us to explore specific areas. How I came to be in the world of the healer leads me to write more and more about it.

My work has limitations, as is obvious. It is bound by one writer, me, living in a specific culture, in a specific time and place. In fact, what I write is no longer a reflection of this specific place or culture. The theme is much wider, universal. It's not just about my culture, it's about the history of the world of spirits. Every culture that has ever existed has paid attention to this world. Today our scientific, technological world seems bent on destroying anything that smacks of the spiritual. We fight back. We tell myths. We write stories. We feel the presence of the transcendent in nature, in streams and mountains and sky, in trees and wind and lightning. We feel the essence in ourselves and understand that it has always been so.

I recognize my work as a writer is good because it has taken me on a journey of illumination. I have shared it with my readers. As I heal and reintegrate myself, I so wish this for others. I know the importance of order and harmony. And I have experienced chaos and its night of terror. A story and the storyteller fight against chaos.

Writing helps me to return to mythic time, the time of dreams. To re-create from depths of darkness the world of light. This is the role of the writer, the shaman of words. To dare to be born with each story into a new awareness.

PART TWO
Censorship

Take the Tortillas out of Your Poetry

In a recent lecture, "Is Nothing Sacred?," Salman Rushdie, one of the most censored authors of our time, talked about the importance of books. He grew up in a household in India where books were as sacred as bread. If anyone in the household dropped a piece of bread or a book, the person not only picked up the piece of bread or the book but also kissed the object by way of apologizing for clumsy disrespect.

He goes on to say that he had kissed many books before he had kissed a girl. Bread and books were for his household, and for many like his, food for the body and the soul. This image of kissing the book one has accidentally dropped made an impression on me. It speaks to the love and respect many people have for books.

I grew up in a small town in New Mexico, and we had very few books in our household. The first book I remember reading was my catechism book. Before I went to school to learn English, my mother taught me catechism in Spanish. I remember the questions and the answers I had to learn, and I remember the well-thumbed, frayed book that was sacred to me.

Growing up with few books in the house created in me a desire and need for books. When I started school, I remember visiting the one-room library of our town and standing in front of the dusty shelves lined with books. In reality, there were only a few shelves and not over a thousand books, but I wanted to read them all. There was food for my soul in the books, that much I realized.

As a child I listened to the stories of the people, the cuentos the old ones told. Those stories were my first contact with the magic of

Originally published in *Censored Books: Critical Viewpoints*, ed. Nicholas J. Karolides et al. (Metuchen, NJ: Scarecrow Press, 1993), 25–31; and reprinted in *The Anaya Reader* (New York: Warner Books, 1995), 385–95.

storytelling. These stories fed my imagination, and later, when I wrote books, I found the same sense of magic and mystery in writing.

In *Bless Me, Ultima*, my first novel, Antonio, my main character, who has just started to school, sees in books the power of the written word. He calls books the "magic of words."

For me, reading has always been a path toward liberation and fulfillment. To learn to read is to start down the road of liberation. It is a road that should be accessible to everyone. No one has the right to keep you from reading, and yet that is what is happening in many areas in this country today. There are those who think they know best what we should read. These censors are at work in all areas of our daily lives.

Censorship has affected me directly, and I have formed some ideas on this insidious activity, but fist, I want to give an example of censorship which recently affected a friend of mine. My friend is a Chicano poet and scholar, one of the finest I know. For some time I have been encouraging Chicano writers to apply for literary fellowships from the National Endowment for the Arts. A number of poets who use Spanish and English in their poetry applied but did not receive fellowships; they were so discouraged they did not reapply. This happened to my friend. He is an excellent poet—mature, intelligent—and he has an impressive academic background. He knew that when you apply for a fellowship you take your chances, so he did not give up after being turned down twice. He also knew—we all knew—that many of the panels that judged the manuscripts did not have readers who could read Spanish or bilingual manuscripts. In other words, the judges could not read the poetic language that expresses our reality. My friend rightfully deduced that his poetry was not receiving a fair reading.

"You know," he told me, "if they can't read my bilingual poetry, next time I apply I'm sending them only poems I write in English. My best poetry is bilingual, it reflects our reality, it's the way we speak, the way we are. But if I stand a better chance at getting a fellowship in English, I'll send that. But the poems I write only in English are really not my best work. It's just not me."

I was dismayed by my friend's conclusion. How he coped with the problem has tremendous cultural implications. It has implications that we may call self-imposed censorship. My friend was censoring his creativity in order to fit the imposed criteria. He sent in his poorer work because that was the work the panelists could read and, therefore, consider for reward.

My friend had concluded that if he took his language and culture out of his poetry, he stood a better chance of receiving a fellowship. He took out his native language, the poetic patois of our reality, the rich mixture of Spanish, English, pachuco, and street talk that we know so well. In other words, he took the tortillas out of his poetry, which is to say he took the soul out of his poetry. He still has not received a fellowship, and many of those other poets and writers I have encouraged to apply for the fellowships have quit trying. The national norm simply does not want to bother reading us.

I do not believe we should have to leave out the crucial elements of our language and culture to contribute to American literature, but, unfortunately, this is a conclusion I am forced to reach. I have been writing for a quarter century and have been a published author for eighteen years. As a writer, I was part of the Chicano Movement, which created a new literature in this country. We struggled to change the way the world looks at Mexican Americans by reflecting our reality in literature, and many eagerly sought our works, but the iron curtain of censorship was still there.

Where does censorship begin? What are the methods of commission or omission that censorship employs? I analyze my own experiences for answers. Many of my generation still recall and recount the incidents of censorship on the playgrounds of the schools when we were told to speak only English. Cultural censorship has been with us for a long time, and my friend's story suggests it is with us today.

If we leave out our tortillas—and by that I mean the language, history, cultural values, and themes of our literature—the very culture we're portraying will die. Publishing has often forced us to do just that. Trade publishers who control publishing in this country continue to have a very narrow view of the literature of this country. At a time when multicultural diversity is challenging the literary canon of this country, the major publishers still are barely now responding to the literary output of Chicano writers. After twenty-five years of contemporary Chicano literature, there are still only a few Chicano writers who publish with the big trade publishers. Thankfully, there appears to be a change in the air.

The alternative presses of the 1960s were created to contest the status quo. The views of ethnic writers, gay and lesbian writers, and women writers had been consistently censored out of the literary canon. Most of us grew up without ever seeing our identity reflected in the books we read; we knew that had to change.

Twenty years ago when Chicano writers began to create poetry and stories that reflected our contemporary reality, we were met with immediate hostility. The arbiters of literary acceptance instantly branded our works as too political. They complained it wasn't written in English. Does it speak to the universal reader? they continually asked. Of course the works of the Chicano and Chicana writers were universal, because their subject was the human condition. The problem was that, in the view of the keepers of the canon, the human condition portrayed in our literature was Chicano and the keepers knew nothing about us.

And, yes, it was political. All literature, especially poetry and fiction, challenges the status quo. Our literature introduced our history and heritage to American literature. There was a new rhythm, music, and cultural experience in our works and a view of an ethnic working class that performed the daily work, but was invisible to those in power. Yes, there was a political challenge in the work, it could be no other way. The country had to change, we insisted.

Many refused to listen. Censorship is fear clothed in the guise of misguided righteousness. Censorship is a tool of the powerful who don't want to share their power. Of course, our poetry and literature reflected to our communities our history and our right to exist as a distinct culture. Look at the plays of Luis Valdez and the changes they brought about in the agricultural fields of California. Look at the generation moved to pride and activism by Corky Gonzalez's poem "I am Joaquín." Even my "nonpolitical" novel, *Bless Me, Ultima*, has moved people to explore the roots of their agrarian, Mexicano way of life. And the healing work of Ultima, a curandera, illustrated to my generation some of our holistic, Native American inheritance.

Free at last! each of our works proclaimed. Every Chicano poem or story carried within it the cry of a desire for freedom and equality. That is what literature should do: liberate. But the status quo does not like liberation. It uses censorship as a tool. As I have suggested, in some cases, it is a thinly veiled censorship. Let me provide another example.

A few years ago, the editor of a major publishing firm asked me to submit a story for a middle school reader. Those readers have the power to shape how thousands of children think about Mexican Americans. The criteria were: "It can't have religion in it, it can't be mystical, it can't have Spanish in it." Everything that was in *Bless Me, Ultima* was rejected out of hand before the publisher would look at a manuscript. Needless to say, I didn't submit a story. Like my friend applying for the fellowship, I was censored before I got to first base.

In other cases, the censoring has been direct and brutal. On February 28, 1981, the Alburquerque morning newspaper carried a story about the burning of my novel *Bless Me, Ultima*. The book was banned from high school classes in Bloomfield, New Mexico, and a school board member was quoted as saying: "We took the books out and personally saw that they were burned."

Obviously, my novel did not meet the criteria of the status quo. Using a technique censors often use, they zoomed in on one detail of the novel, the so-called bad words in Spanish, and they used that excuse. Had they read the novel, they would have discovered that it is not about profanity. That was never the novel's intent. The novel was a reflection of my childhood, a view into the Nuevo Mexicano culture of a small town. I looked at values, I looked at folkways, I created heroic characters out of poor farmers. I wrote about old healing remedies used by the folk to cure physiological illness. I elevated what I found in my childhood, because that's the way I had experienced my childhood. Poverty and suffering did not overwhelm us, they made us stronger. My novel was my view of the human condition, and it reflected the Mexicanos of New Mexico because that was the community I knew.

What was its threat? I've asked myself over the years. Why did the censors burn *Bless Me, Ultima*? I concluded that those in power in the schools did not want a reflection of my way of life in the school. The country had not yet committed itself to cultural diversity. Fifteen million Chicanos were clamoring at the door, insisting that the schools also belonged to us, that we had a right to our literature in the schools, and the conservative opposition in power fought back by burning our books. These narrow-minded reactionaries are still fighting us.

The burning of my novel wasn't an isolated example. Every Chicano community in this country has a story of murals being attacked or erased, poets banned from schools, books being inaccessible to our students because they are systematically kept out of the accepted textbook lists. We know there are well-organized, well-funded groups in this country that threaten publishers if the editors publish the work of multicultural writers. The threat is simple but often persuasive. Books such groups don't like will not be adopted by the school district where they hold power.

The 1990 attack on the NEA by fundamentalist censors has created a national furor and discussion. Those of us who believe in the freedom of expression have spoken out against this infringement on our right to know. But as Chicanos who belong to a culture still existing on the margin of the mainstream society, and as a community that has struggled to be heard in this country, censorship is not new to us. We have lived with this kind of vicious attack on our freedoms all our lives.

For us, take your tortillas out of your poetry means take your history and way of life out of the poems and stories you create. That is what the censors who burned *Bless Me, Ultima* were telling me. Your literature is a threat to us; we will take it out of the classroom and burn it. We'll say it's the profanity we don't like, but what we really fear is the greater picture. Your view is a multicultural view of this country, and the status quo doesn't like that. We will not share our power.

The threat to keep us subservient did not abate. The English-Only movement continued the old censorship we had felt on the school playgrounds, but now the game had moved into the state legislatures. This threat continues to be used against our language, art, and literature.

The struggle for liberation continues. This summer a magazine from New York advertised for subscriptions. Here are quotes from their solicitation letter: "There is only one magazine that tells you what is right and what is wrong with our cultural life today." "Do you sometimes have the impression that our culture has fallen into the hands of the barbarians?" And, finally, "Are you apprehensive about what the politics of 'multiculturalism' is going to mean to the future of civilization?"

The editor is telling us that he knows what is right or wrong with cultural life, then goes on to call those that do not fit in his definition "barbarians." He then identifies the barbarians as those of us who come from the multicultural communities of this country. We are supposed to have no culture, and so they assign themselves the right to censor. This dangerous and misguided attack of the status quo on our creativity continues.

This type of censorship was focused against the National Endowment for the Arts in the halls of Congress in 1990. The censors of the far right attacked two or three funded projects because they objected to the content of the works. The censors assumed the right to keep these creative works away from all of us. Censors, I have concluded, are afraid of our liberation. Censorship is un-American, but the censor keeps telling you it's the American way.

Let me return to the theme of reading and books. Tortillas and poetry. They go hand in hand. Books nourish the spirit; bread nourishes our bodies. Our distinct cultures nourish each one of us, and as we know more and more about the art and literature of the different cultures, we become freer and freer. Art is a very human endeavor, and it contains within its process and the objects it produces a road to liberation. The liberation is significant not only to the individual artist, it is a revelation for the community. It is not we who are the barbarians, it is those who have one narrow view that, they are convinced, is the only right view. Multiculturalism is a reality in this country, and we will get beyond fear and censorship only when we know more about each other, not when we know less.

I don't know anyone who doesn't like to sample different ethnic foods, just as many of us enjoy sampling (eating) books from different areas of the world. I travel to foreign countries, and I know more about myself as I learn more about my fellow human beings. Censorship imposes itself in my path of knowledge, and that activity can be justified by no one.

The Censorship of Neglect

The theme of the 1991 convention of the National Council of Teachers of English (NCTE) in Seattle was the freedom to teach and to learn. In a country that is finally acknowledging its multicultural nature, the idea proved engaging. I want to examine this theme from my point of view as a Mexican American educator and writer.

I have taught English language and literature for twenty-five years in this country, and I know that we have not been free to teach. The literary history of this country has been shaped by forces far beyond the control of the classroom teacher. Our curriculum has been controlled by groups with a parochial view of what the curriculum should and should not include. These groups include teachers who hold narrow views of what literature should be, publishers who control what is printed, and politicians who defend their particular social and political interests. These groups represent the status quo and call themselves "universalists." For a long time these groups have told us they know what is universal in literature, and this has translated into a course of action which has kept the ethnic literatures of this country out of the curriculum.

The time for that narrow view to be exposed is now, and the time for us to take charge and implement into the curriculum the many literatures of this country is today.

For generations, freedom to learn has meant reading only the very narrow spectrum of literature proposed to us by the universalists. Most of us know there is no literature with a capital *L*. There are many

Originally published as "Free to Learn, Free to Teach," in *The English Journal*, 81, no. 5 (September 1992): 18–20; and reprinted as "The Censorship of Neglect" in *The Anaya Reader* (New York: Warner Books, 1995), 405–13.

literatures, and our country is rich with them. And yet most of us have succumbed to the pressures brought to bear by those in power.

Folk wisdom says, you can lead a horse to water, but you can't make it drink. You can lead students to books, but if the content doesn't engage them, they lose interest and soon become dropouts. My experience, and the experience of many teachers I know, has taught me that part of the cause for our alarming drop-out statistics is this narrow, circumscribed curriculum in language and literature. To reverse these deplorable drop-out statistics and to help create a positive self-image in our students, I firmly believe we need to present the literatures that reflect our true diversity.

The literature of the barrio, of the neighborhood, of the region, of the ethnic group, can be a useful tool of engagement, a way to put students in touch with their social reality. What is pertinent to our personal background is pertinent to our process of learning. And so if students are going to be truly free to learn, they must be exposed to stories that portray their history and image in a positive manner. They must be given the opportunity to read the literatures of the many different cultures of our own country.

That we are free to teach is a myth. We know every nation has a vested interest in perpetuating the myth of national unity and coherence. We know there is a social and political intent behind the concept of national unity. Those who hold political power in this country have used it to try to create a homogenous, monolithic curriculum. That intent betrays the many communities which compose this country, because it denies their histories.

This country cannot continue on this limited path and serve its people. Those in power can no longer be allowed to believe they are the sole possessors of the truth. I believe I represent, as a Chicano writer, part of that truth. Every educator represents part of that truth. We are tired of being told that we do not understand the needs of our youth because we belong to a particular ethnic group. We are told that because we are Mexican, Native, Black, or Asian American—or women—that somebody else has the right literature and language to describe our reality. Each of our communities has much to teach this country. Each barrio, each neighborhood, each region, men and women, all have a vested interest in education, and it's time we made that interest known.

We have not been free to teach. We have accepted the literature which is presented to us by publishers, those producers of books who have a direct link and a vested interest in the status quo. Big publishers have neglected or refused to publish the literature of minority communities of our country; their lack of social responsibility has created a narrow and paternalistic perspective of our society. The true picture of this country is not narrow: it is multidimensional; it reflects many communities, attitudes, languages, beliefs, and needs. Our fault, as teachers, is that we have accepted the view of those in charge: teacher training programs, publishers, politicians, and sectarian interests.

And yet we know better. We know one approach is not best for all; we know we have to incorporate the many voices of literature into the curriculum.

It is time to ask ourselves some tough questions. Exactly what literature are we teaching in classrooms? Who writes it? What social reality does it portray? Who packaged it for us? How much choice do we really have as teachers to step outside this mainstream packaging and choose books? Who provides the budget? Who calls the shots?

I raise this issue and try to analyze and understand it from my experience. I am a native son of the Mexican American community of New Mexico, a member of the broader Hispanic population of the country. When I published my first novel in the early seventies, I was part of the Chicano literary movement. We asked ourselves then the same questions we are still asking today.

We knew then that the desire to form a monolithic social reality which served those in power was very costly in human terms. We knew the oral and written literature of Native Americans had been neglected. It was never in the curriculum I studied. Even the better known African American writings have not been a consistent part of our undergraduate education. Chicano literature, in a country that has over fifteen million Mexican Americans, is still virtually unknown in the classroom.

Our community stretches from California to Texas, and into the Northwest and Midwest. But not one iota of our social reality, much less our aesthetic reality, is represented in the literature read in the schools.

Where is our freedom to teach? Who trained us, or brainwashed us, to the point that we cannot see fifteen million people? The teachers of this country cannot see—I mean that literally—the children of fifteen million people. That is how strong the censorship of neglect has been. That is why I say we have not been free to teach.

Living within the confines of a mainstream culture has caused me to look at this idea of cultural identity and self-identity. You have to ask yourselves the same question: how do your students create their self-image? Specifically, what role does the school and the curriculum play in the formation of identity? Literature is one of the most humanistic endeavors that has been used to reflect back to readers their own images. And yet until very recently the image, and therefore the history, of the Mexican American was missing from the spectrum of literature. Most teacher training programs and departments of English still refuse to admit the presence of the ethnic literatures of this country. Much of that training never teaches the diverse stories of the country, and so the teachers who go into the classroom are never really "free to teach."

Reading is the key to a liberated life. We must take action to wrest our freedom to teach from those forces that still don't acknowledge the existence of the multidimensional and multicultural realities of our country. We must infuse into the study of language and literature the stories of the many communities that compose our country.

The cost of having denied these many voices their rightful role in the study of language and literature has been enormous. The ethnic communities of this country have suffered the loss in human terms for many generations. We see the loss each day, and it hurts us. Now the loss is being felt in monetary terms by business and government agencies—and perhaps this is what will wake up this country. Our children who go into the world unprepared to deal with real-life experiences, our children lost to dope and prisons and those who suffer from poor images of themselves, are all a costly burden. Our ideal to be free to teach is based on our desire to enlighten humanity, our desire to contribute to a better world. Now, belatedly, those in power are waking up and seeing the devastation their universalist, colonialist approach has caused. Now they awaken and produce token changes in education, not because they are interested in freedom for the individual, but because they understand that an uneducated populace is not good for the business of the country.

Our diverse communities are rightfully demanding to be included in the curriculum of language and literature courses. This is perceived as a threat to those who want to keep the status quo, those who want to stay in power. There is a very strong element among writers and educators who insist that the ethnic writers of this country are not writing according to universalist guidelines that have been established. We, the people of the multiple communities of this country, no longer trust, nor do we believe, those who hold that view. We will no longer be demeaned and lose our students to that view. Our challenge is to incorporate into the curriculum all the voices of our country. Old worldviews have been crumbling since the advent of the twentieth century. Change and new views of reality must be acknowledged. And yet educators have resisted the formation of the new multidimensional world. Why?

Have we become the problem itself? Have we become the defenders of the status quo? Is it really we who have refused to see the reality of the African American experience, the Chicano world, the Asian American struggle, the woman's search for her own self-representation? Are we free to teach when we fear the social and aesthetic reality of other groups?

If you are teaching in a Mexican American community, it is your social responsibility to refuse to use the textbook that doesn't contain stories by Mexican American authors. If you teach Asian American children, refuse the textbook which doesn't portray their history and social reality. This kind of activism will free you to teach. If you don't refuse, you are part of the problem. But you don't have to be teaching in a Mexican American barrio to insist that the stories and social reality of that group be represented in your textbook. You shortchange your students and you misrepresent the true nature of their country if you don't introduce them to all the communities who have composed the history of this country. To deny your students a view into these different worlds is to deny them tools for the future.

The future is only going to get more complex. We need better and more educated answers to a plethora of issues which face us. The old, one-dimensional, narrow view of the world hasn't worked and will not work. It was kept in place by power brokers who sacrificed human potential. We cannot applaud the liberation the eastern European countries have recently achieved and still espouse a colonial mentality when it comes to teaching in this country. We cannot applaud the democratization of the Soviet Union if we still believe a monolithic, iron fist must rule our curriculum. Wake up, America. We are a diverse country. Let us be free to teach that diversity.

The Courage of Expression

Censorship is on the rise. We are witnessing it today, and its clearest, most pressing evidence comes from our schools, where a struggle is being waged over the books our young people will be allowed, or not allowed, to read.

Today's teachers, sensitively placed in the midst of the struggle, not only have to guide and influence the creative imagination of young people, they have to deal with many community and national pressures. We know from history that the forum of the classroom should be the place where all ideas can be discussed and debated, and yet teachers are feeling the new and present pressure of sectarian groups which are springing up everywhere. Bigotry is one of the pressures they face. A concerted movement is under way in this country to forge the people into one group which follows only one drummer. Special interest groups—often religiously motivated—are out to destroy the freedoms inherent in the forum of education. These groups propose that deviation from a preconceived norm is not to be allowed. These small groups, and they are small, fewer in power and number than we credit them to be, are mobilized to restrict the basic freedoms of expression that form the social and political contract of this nation. I say we must join together to resist the goals of these narrow-minded groups.

Literature is the reflection of humanistic thought. Teachers of literature must, because of our present time and circumstances, now make their commitment to the future of free thought. I suggest that this is the most pressing commitment they have to make in the decade of the 1980s.

Political or religiously motivated groups that try to exclude the litera-

Originally published in *Century: A Southwest Journal of Observation and Opinion* (2 December 1981): 16–18.

ture of any individual or group of people from the classroom also seek to stifle new and challenging thought. And history teaches us that when one group controls the thought of a people, that nation is bound to die a self-inflicted death.

We must recognize that an educational system is also a system of politics. The educational system of this country is entrusted to pass on the values of a society, and in that sense it is a conservative, closed system. But the same educational system is entrusted to pursue knowledge, and in that sense it is an open system. I am afraid that today we have the rise of powerful and narrow interest groups who want to close the system until it reflects only one narrow view of the world. We do not have at work a Moral Majority, but a Minimal Minority.

I could give countless examples of their force at work in our society. Teachers know there is a rise in the censorship of books—books branded as unfit for reading are pulled from library shelves and classrooms. In science the creationists' view is assailing the very idea of free inquiry. There are groups with money who use computerized mailing lists to mobilize communities against textbooks that do not fit their sectarian view of the world. And the threat is felt as educators comply with the wishes of such narrow groups. Publishers accept with resignation the threat of censored literature, and their capitulation to these groups means a watering down of free and challenging thought. Controversial subjects become taboo. Certain authors are excluded. And finally a narrow sectarian philosophy evolves that aligns itself with a particular moral view, and this fascist ideology quickly sets itself in place to use the schools for attaining its goals.

But not in New Mexico, you may say. Not here. News of censorship and book burning always reaches us from out there. Here, we are civilized people. We have learned to appreciate our diverse cultures. We practice the good life and believe that our shared cultural contexts make a richer and more interesting society for all.

I am not so sure. Book burning has come to our backyard. In February of this year, the *Albuquerque Journal* reported that in the New Mexico State Legislature a state senator, who is also a member of a board of education in this state, testified that she had personally seen to it that copies of *Bless Me, Ultima* were taken out of the high school of her district and burned. This was reported on February 28, 1981. On that day, George Orwell's *1984* arrived in New Mexico.

But what is even more frightening is that this same thing is happening in many localities throughout our country. There are numerous examples of special interest groups forcing schools or libraries to destroy or remove books. And an intimidated, liberal public stands quiet as these bigots and book burners have their way.

The burning of a book is a highly symbolic act. In my judgment, it is next only to the horror of burning human beings. It is a heinous act that has no place in a free society. A voice of concern and indignation should arise when such an act occurs. Teachers of literature, who value history and its literary birthright, should be the first publicly to condemn such an act. Their influence will be felt if they take a firm stance in opposing any group that would censor and burn books. I believe a society that allows books to be burned is a society that is afraid, and to be ruled by people who live in fear is to spread the contagion until there is truly no hope for the future.

To burn a book is an attempt to intimidate the very process of creativity and inquiry. History teaches us that those who would rule along their narrow doctrinaire lines first set out to destroy the literary works and thought and language of a people. If they are allowed to burn the work of one writer, to erase the history of one people from the face of the earth, then there is no turning back.

In New Mexico, in the Southwest, throughout this country, quite the opposite should be happening. I have served on national boards that deal with contemporary writing. I know there is a renewed interest in the writers of the regions and ethnic groups of this country. Women are writing more than ever, and we are grateful for their ideas and perceptions. People who were disenfranchised from access to literary production are now publishing works in alternative and small presses. The might of the big publishers is no longer equated with literary excellence. The minority and ethnic groups of this country have rich traditions to share with us if we but seek out their works.

In New Mexico we have a diversity of cultures. But all too often we have not sought out and we have not used the works of our own writers. We have been indoctrinated to believe that the regional perspective in literature demeans the literary work. What nonsense! The basis of the works of our writers is the imagination and the life of our people, and the works achieve universal qualities because of their portrayal of the human spirit.

This is true of many of the works by our own Southwest writers. It is time that all the schools of this state begin a sound program which presents the works of our writers, writers from all the ethnic groups that compose New Mexico. That program will not detract from a study of

American literature; rather it will be an integral part of the literature. Our writers have produced and are producing American literature. And the program can then rightly move to a national and world stage.

I said in a talk a few years ago in California that the coordinates of a true American literature have not yet come together. As long as we exclude the writings of any group of people who formed this country, then we still do not know American literature in its broadest sense. Let us begin here to introduce the writers of our own region and to build from there. That is the challenge today.

If I have one message, it is that we must not only be vigilant, it is that we must be involved. If we stand quietly aside and forsake our freedoms and the freedoms that the study of literature brings to us, then we become a part of the problem. Those who only look on while books are burned are as guilty as those who do the burning. Those who do not speak out for liberty and freedom of expression, for the dissemination of ideas, for the right for serious works of literature to be judged in the open forum of the classroom and the communities of this country help the enslaver forge the chains.

Right here in our state, in our communities, in our schools, all of us can help preserve the freedom of expression. We must not be afraid; we must not feel threatened. We can all help and sustain each other. And we know we are justified in our efforts, because our guiding motive is not the control of the minds of people, it is the enlarging and freeing of the minds and spirit of people.

Stand Up against Censorship Anywhere
It Occurs

I awoke the morning of February 28, 1981, to read in the *Albuquerque Journal* that the Bloomfield, New Mexico, School Board had ordered the burning of my novel, *Bless Me, Ultima*. A Bloomfield school board member, who is also a senator in the New Mexico legislature, was quoted in the paper as saying, "We took the books out and personally saw that they were burned."

Why would anyone in their right mind burn books? How did my novel threaten book burners? The book burning didn't make sense, but acts of censorship have never made sense. Even after the shock wore off I couldn't believe this act of desecration had occurred. Who were these self-appointed authorities who decide what literature we are to read in New Mexico?

Being raised poor in New Mexico has taught me the value of books. I grew up treasuring the few books I came across; I grew up believing my liberation was in books. If liberation is in books, did those who burned books oppose my liberation? I believe in the freedom of expression and the communication of ideas. Did they burn the book because it carried a reflection of my ethnic community? I couldn't believe that. New Mexico is a state where major cultural groups have interacted and lived in harmony. We respect the freedom of expression in art of all the cultural groups.

It was gratifying to me in February of 1981 when people stood up and expressed indignation about the book burning. These same people also stood up to those who wanted to impose textbook standards that would emasculate textbooks to the point of uselessness. The state already had an approved book list, and some politicians wanted to allow

Originally published in *Albuquerque Journal* (1 April 1990, B3).

in classrooms only those books which met their narrow standards. Did that mean books which didn't meet their standards were to be burned? Who are these self-appointed standard bearers of the state, I wondered. And why are they censoring my novel?

People from around the country wrote petitions protesting the book burning, but for me the shock of the event never wore off. I quickly learned, however, that what had happened to my novel was not an isolated instance. Censorship was on the rise in this country.

That same year I attended the National Writers Congress in New York and testified before a committee of writers and editors who were documenting and opposing acts of censorship in this country. I remember the long line of people waiting to testify spread from the room into the hall. We all had acts of violence to relate, acts of violence against our freedom of expression.

Why did they burn your book, people asked me. Someone doesn't like my message, I answered. The characters and images I used in my writing all came from my life in the Hispanic community. For the first time in our history a novel from our community was being widely read and accepted in the schools, and the reaction was to find excuses to burn it in Bloomfield. A very conservative element clearly wanted to dictate what students read in school. Someone did not want the voice of our Hispanic writers in the schoolrooms.

Books are a threat to some people. Books can be a threat to the status quo. Books bring ideas for change and challenge us. That's why people who see the world only in one image burn books. Books describe other possibilities and different thoughts, and books give people power. That's why we read, to taste and know the world of ideas. Books enlarge our experiences, acquainting us with the thoughts of others.

I don't have to convince serious thinking New Mexicans of the value of books. But I do want to emphasize that the burning of *Bless Me, Ultima* was an overt sign of a cancer within. In a society where books are burned or art is smashed, the cancer has surfaced.

In prior decades the ethnic communities of this country have insisted that power and responsibility be shared equally, and they have demanded that the books written by their authors belong in the schools. Finally an image of these communities was reflected in books which could be read in school. That was positive reinforcement in pride and identity for many students from these communities.

The multicultural voice of the country needed to be heard, but those who burned books were afraid. Convinced of the myth that this country was composed of a monolithic culture gave the book burners an excuse to silence other cultural communities. The acts of censorship could also be construed as acts of cultural suppression.

The making of art in all its varied aspects is the making of cultural artifacts. Art as a form of expression and communication reflects society, and that expression from all corners of our society rightly belongs in the classrooms as well as the ideas and artifacts of science and technology. But art contains the personal ideas and message of the artist, and those who guard narrow points of view don't like the multiplicity of ideas. We don't have to like all artistic endeavors, but we do have the responsibility to recognize that even in the most controversial piece of art or literature the artist renders a new perception of the world. We do not have the right to censor that expression.

Recently the National Endowment for the Arts, a federal agency that provides fellowships for artists, has been under attack by critics. Narrow-minded politicians want to take the freedom of expression away from the artist by dictating guidelines in accordance with their strict views. This is an act of censorship directed against the artists of our country. We know that censorship is impossible to administer fairly and that those who set themselves up as moral judges do not possess the truth. How dare they censor the expressions in art which may contain pieces of that truth we seek.

The creation of art must be free from exterior guidelines, because the artist probes perceptions of truth. Each artist is only one voice, but a totality of those voices creates understanding in our lives. Art contains a vision and truer understanding of our human experience. We can't afford to burn or destroy even the smallest detail reflected in the arts.

I don't believe that those who burned my book have the correct vision of life. In striking out, they sought to silence me, to burn images which presented another way of perceiving the truth. In a multicultural society the rights of all the voices need to be respected. If we live and work in a multicultural world, then our own cultural groups have something to teach us about the bigger world. You cannot burn the books of one group and expect democracy to work.

Now the cowardly act of art smashing and book burning has raised its ugly head again. In February 1990, the mural that Frederico Vigil painted at St. John's College in Santa Fe was vandalized and destroyed. The self-appointed censors are at it again.

Vigil's mural was commissioned in 1987 by the president of the college. The title of the fresco is *Santa Madre Tierra/Gente Mesclada*.

It depicts the history and tricultural heritage of Santa Fe. The images of the mural are indigenous to the Americas; they are rendered in a personal way by the artist. A vandal took a hammer and destroyed the images of the mural. Those images belonged as much to the college as to me and to our community. An act of violence has been committed again.

Images and symbols are powerful, they can liberate people. The person who took a hammer and smashed the painting was driven to destroy those images and symbols. They are a vision of truth which the vandals did not understand, and instead of learning from art the vandals proceeded to destroy it. Like the burning of *Bless Me, Ultima*, this occurred in a school setting, a university where understanding and learning are the goals, not fear and destruction.

It did not help matters when the newly appointed president at St. John's College said he found the mural "childish and offensive." The images in the mural are indigenous symbols common to our heritage as a "gente mesclada." Instead of understanding our heritage and its rich symbols, the new president found it "offensive." Shortly thereafter the vandals took the hammer and destroyed the wall.

Art should encourage discussion. The freedom of expression leads to more expression, and each view is safeguarded. That dialogue makes our lives dynamic and vital. None of us has the right to destroy the communication of another person. What is it the vandals had to fear from Vigil's mural? Why did they burn my novel in 1981?

In a multicultural setting, artists from each group must be free to interpret the world from their own perspective. They have a responsibility to do so. The other groups have the responsibility to respect those visions. We don't have to like the product, but neither do we have a right to destroy or censor it. Once we begin censoring and book burning, there is no end in sight. Those in charge will demand more and more power.

It's time all of us opposed these acts of censorship, whether they happen in New Mexico or in the halls of Congress where some want to dictate narrow guidelines of morality for the National Endowment for the Arts. Anywhere it occurs, we must stand against censorship. We must especially defend communities without political or economic power as they struggle to create their art and keep alive their cultural ways.

PART THREE
The Southwest

Landscape and Sense of Place

Mythical Dimensions/Political Reality

Many of us who live in the Southwest have developed a mythical dimension that enables us to relate to the land and its people. This dimension keeps us close to the land and its history. We value the indigenous myths that evolved on this continent. Now the tremendous economic changes that came with the Sunbelt boom that began in the 1960s have not only altered the landscape, they have altered the way people relate to the land and each other, and there is a danger of losing this dimension. Many of us are asking what happens when we lose our mythic relationship to the earth and allow only the political and economic forces to guide our way of life.

I take much of my identity from the values and tribal ways of the old Nuevo Mexicanos, from their legends and myths and from the earth, which they held sacred. In this essay I turn my attention to the processes of world politics and economics that are altering the Southwest so radically. The growth of the Sunbelt has altered our perception of our landscape—the personal, the environmental, and the mythic. The old communities, the tribes of the Southwest, have been scattered, and they have lost much of their power. If we do not take action now, that creative force of the people which has nourished us for centuries may be swept aside.

Originally published as "Mythical Dimensions/Political Realities," in *Arellano*, 6 (Winter 1993–1994): 12–13; reprinted as "Mythical Dimensions/Political Reality," in *Open Spaces, City Places: Contemporary Writers on the Changing Southwest*, ed. Judy Nolte Temple (Tucson: University of Arizona Press, 1994), 25–30; reprinted in *The Anaya Reader* (New York: Warner Books, 1995), 343–52; and reprinted in *The Multicultural Southwest: A Reader*, ed. A. Gabriel Meléndez et al. (Tucson: University of Arizona Press, 2001), 267–72.

Our future is at stake. We who value the earth as a creative force must renew our faith in the values of the old communities, the ceremonies of relationship, the dances and fiestas, the harmony in our way of life, and the mythic force we can tap to create beauty and peace. We must speak out clearly against the political and economic processes whose only goal is material gain.

It is the individual's relationship to the tribe and one's response to the elements and the cosmos that give shape to our inner consciousness. These relationships create meaning. They have shaped the Indian and Hispano Southwest, just as they have shaped part of the Anglo reality and myth. But the old communal relationships are changing as the new urban environments change our land. This diaspora that began in the 1940s has continued, the once stable villages and pueblos are emptied to create a marginalized people in the ghettos of the new urban centers.

Many of us no longer live in the landscape our parents knew. We no longer enjoy that direct relationship with nature which nurtured them. The Southwest has slowly changed, becoming an urban environment. We no longer live in the basic harmony that can exist between humanity and the earth. A new and materialistic order has become paramount in the land, and we have little control over this intrusion. By and large, the land that nurtured us is now in the hands of world markets and politics.

True, some of our neighbors survive in mountain villages and pueblos, on ranches and reservations. These folk remain an historical link to our mythic dimensions. They keep the values and communal relationship of our grandparents, and they struggle against the destructive development that characterized the past.

Urban Sunbelt population growth; renewed attention to the oil, gas, and mining industries; the construction of air bases and weapons laboratories; and a high-tech boom with its dream of a new economy are some of the elements of the politicizing process that our generation has seen become reality in the Southwest. The full force of that change has been felt in our generation as the New York and world money markets gained control over and exploited the resources of this land.

The signs of the web of the political world are all around us. Visit any of the large cities of the Southwest and you see unchecked growth, a plundering of land and water, and a lack of attention to the old traditional communities. Immense social disparity has been created overnight. We have lost control over our land. The crucial questions for us are these: Have we been defeated? Have we let go of our old values?

Because I am interested in and understand the power of literature, I have to ask what this means to writers from the Southwest. For some it means a retreat into formula: the cowboy and Indian story is still being churned out. Some writers armed with computers simply make that formula longer and more ponderous to read. For others the retreat means moving out of the city to the suburbs or, if possible, to the villages or the mountains. The Indian and Chicano way of life is idealized as some attempt to deal with the new engulfing economic and political reality. Some draw closer to the Indian and Hispanic communities, the old tribes of the land, seeking spiritual warmth from, and reconciliation with, these earth people. Others create new tribal centers: Zen centers, mosques, and monasteries in the desert, hippie communities. Some writers just drink and quarrel more, subconsciously surrendering to the old Western movie plot in their withdrawal.

In my lifetime I have seen this tremendous change come over the land. Most of my contemporaries and I left our Hispanic communities and became urban dwellers. The people, the earth, the water of the river and of the acequias (the irrigation canals), and the spiritual views of the tribal communities that once nurtured me are almost gone. The ball game has changed, and it is appropriate to use the ball-game metaphor, because the original game of la pelota in Mesoamerican history has a spiritual orientation, a deep meaning for the tribe. Now it is played for profit. In our most common ceremonies and rituals we see the change, we see the new view of the West.

Politicizing the Southwest has meant corraling people in the city. Reckless developers take the land for the false promise of the easy life, where homogenized goods and services can be delivered. Work in one's cornfield has become work for wages, wages which can never keep up with ever-spiraling taxation. The pueblo plaza or village post office where the community once gathered to conduct both business and ceremony has become chaotic urban sprawl. The center has been lost.

What does this mean to me—I who have now lived longer in the city than in the rural landscape of my grandparents, I who have seen this drastic change come to the land?

When I was writing *Bless Me, Ultima* in the early 1960s, I was still tied to the people and the earth of the Pecos River Valley, the small town of Santa Rosa, the villages of Puerto de Luna and Pastura. The mythic element infuses that novel because it is a reflection of the world I knew. Now the West has lost its natural state, and development after development sprawls across once empty desert. Growth and change are inevitable, but that which is guided only by a material goal is a corrosive element that has insidiously spread its influence over the land and the people. How can I write and not reflect the process?

Who has taken charge of our lives? We are now informed by television, the daily dose of news, the homogenous school system, and other communication media that are in the hands of the power manipulators. Many ancient ceremonies and dances are still intact along the Río Grande, but even the people who sustain these ceremonies are affected by the bingo parlors and quick cash. My city is hostage to those who control the flow of the river, and the quality of that water will continue to be affected by the chemical and nuclear waste it washes away. This reality must affect our writings.

The Chicanos, Indians, and old Anglos who worked the land are now a labor force to serve the industries that world economic and political systems impose on us. The time is disharmonious; no wonder we gather together to discuss the changing landscape and the changing human-scape. We know we have been manipulated, and in the resulting change we feel we have lost something important.

Our people have been lulled into believing that every person can get a piece of the action. We set up bingo games as we pray for rain, and we train our children to take care of tourists, even as they forget to care for the old ones. We begin to see the elemental landscape as a resource to be bought and sold. We do not dream the old dreams, we do not contemplate the gods, and less and less do we stand in front of the cosmos in humility. We begin to believe that we can change the very nature of things, and so we leave old connections behind, we forget the sacred places and become part of the new reality—a world reality tied to nerve centers in New York, Tokyo, London, and Hong Kong.

The old patterns of daily life are forgotten. The cyclical sense of time that once provided historical continuity and spiritual harmony is replaced by atomic beeps. The clock on the wall now marks the ceremonies we attend, ceremonies that have to do with the order of world politics. It is no wonder we feel we are being watched, our responses recorded. We are being used, and eventually we will be discarded.

But there is hope. The sensitive writer can still create meaningful forms that can be shared with the reader who is hungry for a mythic sensibility. We still have the materials and beliefs of our grandparents to work into poetry and fiction. Reflection in our writings need not become mired in paranoia. The old relationships of the mythic West need not be reduced to a formula. Technology may serve people: it need not be the new god. If we flee to the old communities in search of contact with the elemental landscape and a more harmonious view of things, we can return from that visit more committed to engaging the political process. We can still use the old myths of this hemisphere to shed light on our contemporary problems.

We, the writers, can still salvage elements of beauty for the future. We can help preserve the legends and myths of our land to rekindle the spirit of the old relationships. We can encourage the power of creativity that takes its strength from the elemental and mythic landscapes. The problems we face are not new: prior generations of Mesoamerica dealt with many of the same problems.

In exploring the legend of Quetzalcóatl while writing *The Lord of the Dawn*, I was astounded at the close parallels between the world of the ancient Toltecs of Tula and our own time. Then, as now, men of peace and understanding struggled against the militaristic and materialistic instinct of the society. Both the historical king and the deity known as Quetzalcóatl came to the Toltecs to bring learning in the arts, agriculture, and spiritual thought. Under the benign rule of the Quetzalcóatl, the Toltecs prospered. But much of their prosperity was taken by the warrior class to conduct war on the neighboring tribes. Toltec civilization rose to its classic apex, then fell.

In the end, Quetzalcóatl was banished from Tula. The materialists of the society, who waged war and conducted business only for profit, had their way. The deity who brought art, wisdom, and learning was banished, and the Toltec civilization fell. The influence of Quetzalcóatl was later felt in the civilizations of the Aztecs and Mayas, for every society seeks truth and the correct way to live.

Even now, the story of the Toltecs and Quetzalcóatl speaks to us across the centuries, warning us to respect our deep and fragile communal relationships within and among nations and our meaningful relationships with the earth.

The past is not dead; it lives in our hearts, as myth lives in our hearts. We need those most human qualities of the world myths to help guide us on our road today.

My novel *Alburquerque* addresses some these questions. The city where I live, like any other city in the Southwest, reflects the political processes that have permeated our land. The novel is about change, the change that has come during our lifetime. In it, some of the principal characters are driven by the desire to control the land and the water of the Río Grande. Others, members of the old tribes, take refuge in withdrawal in order to survive urban poverty. They withdraw to their circles of belief to wait out the storm.

We, the writers, cannot wait out the storm; we have to confront it. For us, the bedrock of beliefs of the old cultures provides our connection, our relationship. From that stance we must keep informing the public about the change that has come upon our land.

The battle is of epic proportions. We are in the midst of one of those times from which will emerge a new consciousness. The environment seems to reflect this struggle between evil and good; it cries out to us. We see the land scarred and polluted. The people of the old tribes cry out; we see them displaced and suffering. Even the elements of nature reflect the change: acid and toxic chemicals pollute the water; nuclear waste is buried in the bowels of the earth. These are the same signs the Toltecs saw hundreds of years ago as their society faced destruction.

We, too, face a measure of destruction. The goal of material acquisition and a homogeneous political process supporting that goal have taken hold, driving us deeper into the complex nature of materialism. Is it any wonder we look back to legend and myth for direction?

We are poised at the edge of a new time. We have the opportunity to look again into the nature of our hemisphere. We can see that the struggle for illumination is not easy. It was not easy for the Toltecs, and we know now that as they gave up their old knowledge and turned to materialism and material gain, they destroyed their society.

Will we preserve our old values or let them die? Will we rediscover our relationship to the earth? What of the communal relationships that are so fractured and split in our land? Is there time to bring peace and harmony to our tribal groups?

The first step in answering these questions is to realize that we have turned away from our inner nature and from our connection to the earth and old historical relationships. We have allowed a political and economic consciousness from without to take control. How we engage this consciousness not only describes us, but also will inform future generations of our values. Our writings will say where we stood when this drama of opposing forces came to be played out on our land.

A New Mexico Christmas

Christmas in New Mexico is unique. It is a time of celebration and a time of memories.

When I was a child, my mother's preparations for Christmas meant a week's work in the kitchen. Pots of posole would bubble on the stove, the plump tamales wrapped in their corn husks steamed in the pressure cooker. The aroma of these foods made from corn, the sacred food of the New World, pervaded the kitchen.

There were also desserts. Plates of empanadas made with fruit and sweetmeats were piled high. The anise and nutmeg fragrance of the biscochitos, the traditional sugar cookies, filled the house. These were just some of the Christmas foods prepared to celebrate Christ's birth.

It was my father's job to scour the countryside for a piñon tree. It was treasure trip for me as I accompanied him in search of the green tree that would grace our simple home. It would be decorated with an old and frayed string of lights, bright streamers of cloth my mother sewed. My sisters would add the store-bought icicles and the angel hair.

On Christmas Eve we hung our stockings on the stout branches of the tree. In the morning the stockings would be stuffed with hard candy, nuts, and fruit. There were always plenty of apples and dried fruit, the bounty of the harvest from the farms of my uncles in Puerto de Luna. Oranges were a favorite, but they were expensive, available only if my father was working.

Originally published as "Southwest Christmas: A Mosaic of Rituals Celebrates Spiritual, Community Renewal," in *Los Angeles Times* (27 December 1981): 4:3; and reprinted with revisions as "A New Mexico Christmas" in *The Anaya Reader* (New York: Warner Books, 1995), 283–92.

Christmas Eve meant bundling up at eleven o'clock at night to make the long trek into town to celebrate la Misa del Gallo, midnight Mass. The long walk into town was also a time for contemplation. Under the starry sky of the New Mexico llano, it was the family unit that made its way to church. My mother led, we followed close behind, my father came after us.

That walk rekindles memories of my childhood. The night was cold. Over us sparkled the mystery of the universe, the stars of the Milky Way. Once, long ago, one star lighted the way to Bethlehem. I learned then that to celebrate the religious spirit one had to be attentive. Each person could renew the spirit within, but each had to make an offering. My mother's offering was her belief in the birth of Christ, el Cristo. My father offered the green tree, the symbol of life everlasting, the tree of life itself. And we offered the long, cold walk to join the community of the Mass.

It is that individual and communal offering that cannot be packaged in the modern department store.

After Mass we hurried home. At two in the morning the cold of the llano had set in. Plumes of our breath filled the blue night. We hurried home, where my mother prepared hot chocolate and biscochitos. Then it was off to blissful sleep under warm covers.

In the morning we would awaken to search in the stockings and to open gifts—gifts we usually made ourselves for each other, because there was little money for store-bought gifts. If lucky I might receive a pair of gloves—that is, if the fingers were showing in the old pair. My sisters received clothing, curlers, and prized nylons—as bobby socks gave way to young womanhood.

Then I would run out to join my friends to visit the houses of our neighbors. Our shout was "¡Mis Crismes! ¡Mis Crismes!" We asked for and received the traditional gifts of Christmas, much as the trick–or–treaters do today on Halloween. Our flour sacks bulged with candy, nuts, and fruits when we returned home.

Later in the morning the family would start arriving, brothers from afar, aunts and uncles, and the entire potpourri of padrinos and madrinas, compadres and comadres, cousins, friends, the extended family.

For a child lost in the wonder of the celebration, everyone was a welcome sight. They all brought gifts. If the piñon season had been good that fall, someone would arrive with a gunnysack full of piñones, those sweet, little nuts we would crack and eat in front of the stove as we listened to the stories. Another might bring carne seca, jerky to be cooked with red chile from the ristra hanging in the pantry.

Perhaps someone had been working in Texas, and his truck would be loaded with oranges and ruby-red grapefruits, gifts from el Valle de Tejas where some went to make a living.

Then we would compare gifts, and my cousins would ask, "What did Santo Clos bring you?"

Our Santo Clos was the Santa Claus we knew at school, where we also decorated the classroom tree and acted in the annual Christmas play. Santo Clos, the stockings, and the Perry Como Christmas songs on the radio were the influence of the Anglo culture filtering into our way of life. The cultures were interacting, exchanging customs, and yet each group still retained its own ways, borrowing from each other and forming the mosaic of celebration that Christmas has come to be in New Mexico.

At the center of the celebration was the tree. For my father it was important to have it ready on December 21, the day of the winter solstice. This was indeed the tree of life, and its importance and the importance of the day were fixed in the religious nature of the Indians of New Mexico, as the importance of the day has been fixed since time immemorial in most of the cultures of the world. The shortest day of the year reminds us all that the sun has reached the end of its winter journey. It will return northward to renew the earth, but for one day it hangs in precarious balance.

Long ago on this day in ancient Mexico, and throughout the Americas, sacrifices were made in honor of the sun, the life giver. Incense was burned and sprigs of green were gathered. Ancient man understood his relation to the cosmos. For him the race of the sun was a mystery to be celebrated. One had to be attentive to the workings of the planets and stars, as one had to attend to the working of the spirit within.

I wonder how much of that awe we have lost today.

Our child's Christmas in New Mexico did not involve expensive toys. There were no malls beckoning with sales to distract the spirit and exhaust the mind. We gathered together to celebrate two ways of life, the Christian and the indigenous religious spirit that came to us through the traditions found in ancient Mexico. Our Christmas Day was not intent on football games, but on listening to the history of the families who came to visit. They brought many stories. The kitchen was warm and filled with good food, and after we ate we listened to the stories.

My child's Christmas was a celebration because it was a sharing. Out of that past I have evolved the rituals that are important for me to celebrate. I decorate with lights the piñon tree near the entrance to my home. I make sure it is lighted on the night of December 21. It also serves me well for Christmas.

There are other celebrations to share as the year draws to a close. When it is possible, I go to Jemez Pueblo on December 12, el Día de Nuestra Señora de Guadalupe. The Matachines dances at Jemez are among the most exquisite I have ever witnessed. The color of the earth is red, the hills are dotted with junipers and pines, and above the pueblo loom the dark Jemez Mountains. As one approaches, the pueblo appears serene and quiet, then one hears the violin of the fiddler. It is time to hurry to the plaza, where two brightly colored lines of dancers move to the music.

Each dancer wears an ornate, colorful corona, the headdress. The rattle of hollow gourds fills the air as the dancers move back and forth to the lively, repetitive strains of the fiddle. The drama is a mixture of a pueblo step and a polka, more Spanish than Indian. The Malinche, the little girl in white, symbolizing innocence, dances with the old Abuelo, the grandfather. Near her lurks the dancer dressed as El Toro. The presence of the bull frightens the children, for El Toro symbolizes evil.

This dance, brought by the Spaniards to the New World, is now performed both in the Hispano villages and in the Indian pueblos of New Mexico. It is a unique and enthralling way to start the season of renewal. An hour or two spent visiting with friends at Jemez and sitting in the winter sun while the dance drama unfolds can remind the most depressed that this community is still attentive to its spiritual needs.

All of the homes are open, strangers are fed. The tables are heaped high with posole, meat, chile dishes, tortillas, and Indian bread from the hornos, pies, and biscochitos. Imagine what a better life this would be if all the homes in the cities and suburbs enacted this noble sense of community.

Another experience not to be missed is the celebration at the Taos Pueblo on Christmas Day, but it could be any one of the other pueblos, because they are all celebrating. It is the end of a season, a time of dancing and singing. But in Taos at dusk on Christmas Eve the Mass is celebrated. After Mass the people come pouring out of the church in a winding line.

I was there one Christmas Eve when my friend Cruz pulled me into the procession to weave around the luminarias, stacks of crisscrossed piñon wood, bonfires lighting the way of the celebrants. And what are these luminarias but a symbol of everlasting light. The bonfires roaring into the night sky are a reflection on earth of the star that lights the way, the star that guided the shepherds to Bethlehem. The fires symbolize the renewal of the sun, and the renewal of the light within.

Those roaring fires at the pueblo rekindle the memory of the stars I contemplated as a child. The sweet perfume of the burning piñon rises into the dark, cold sky. So it is with the votive candles in the church. The smoke rises with its message for harmony and peace.

On Christmas Day the deer dance is performed, a dance both for the Taoseños and for their guests. One has to be attentive to brave the sharp cold of the winter morning. Then from the direction of the blue Taos Mountain, the cry of the deer is heard, and the frozen spectators stamp their feet and wait eagerly. The cold is numbing, but worth the effort. The deer dancers unite the elements of earth, sky, and community, symbolizing the deep, religious nature of the pueblo.

In Alburquerque, my home, there are other old and lasting rituals to be enacted. Even in the city the barrios preserve their traditions. Los Pastores, an old miracle play that originated in Spain, is a favorite. Many of the barrios and villages have their version of this nativity play. Some of the shepherds in the play represent a vice, and when Bartolo, the laziest of the group, is finally converted, the audience rejoices.

Las Posadas is another favorite miracle play. It is one of the oldest plays of the Western world continually reenacted in the New World. The story tells how Joseph and Mary sought an inn, a posada. Those who play the parts of Joseph and Mary go from home to home, seeking shelter for the night. They knock at the first door and are refused. The procession moves to another home, singing carols, until finally they are admitted at a designated home and all the guests are fed. There is singing and great rejoicing.

There is something beneath the ritual that must be the real message. Even when Las Posadas is not enacted as a play, the idea of welcoming the stranger to the feast persists. That is why so many people met in my mother's kitchen in those Christmases of long ago.

Time changes the customs in small ways; it does not dim the memory. Now the farolitos are not the stacks of piñon wood to be lighted, they are votive candles placed in paper sacks with sand at the bottom. When we were children, the brown paper bags from the grocery store were saved not only for sack lunches but so we would have enough sacks to use for the farolitos of Christmas.

The farolitos are a traditional New Mexico custom. Hundreds adorn homes, walkways, and street curbs. On a cold Christmas night, even the most humble home is transformed as the candles flicker and glow in the dark.

In a city like Alburquerque, caravans of tourists fill the streets in the evenings to view the symphony of light that glows to announce that in this home there is a posada. Neighborhoods become united as they gather in community effort to decorate their homes and streets. Candles and paper sacks are shared, even if today they are bought at the store. The children vie to light the candles, for the lighting of the farolitos is part of the child's sense of Christmas. More than one enterprising company is now making electric farolitos. Perhaps the important thing is that the lights continue to be lit.

In our memory we know that it is important to light the fire at the end of this season, whether the fire be the yule log or the luminarias of New Mexico. A fire shall light the way, just as the evergreen will remind us that life will renew itself.

Deep within the celebration of these customs there lies the flicker of hope. Christmas celebrates the birth of Christ, and it is also the celebration of the ending of the year, the cycle of the sun. Now the sun will return north and the days will grow longer, and those who were attentive to this mysterious spirit of renewal will be fulfilled.

The New World Man

My wife and I first traveled to Spain in the fall of 1980. We took an over-night train from Paris to Barcelona, journeyed through Andalucia and then on to Madrid. We returned home with wonderful memories of the Alhambra, Toledo, Madrid, El Escorial, and many other places we vis-ited. At the famous El Prado museum I fell under the spell of the genius of Goya, and the images of his prophetic vision are still with me. In 1988 when we returned to Spain, my trip was, in part, a pilgrimage to medi-tate again in the presence of Goya's work and to visit and contemplate the genius of Gaudi's inspiring church, La Sagrada Familia in Barcelona.

That return was made possible by my invitation to Barcelona to discuss my work at the Third International Conference on Hispanic Cultures of the United States; after that conference I attended a small gathering of Spanish scholars and professors from the University of New Mexico at La Fundación Xavier de Salas in Trujillo.

Spain was preparing for the celebration of its 1492–1992 quincenten-nial, and the conference was the beginning of a series intended to re-view the relationship of Spain with Hispanic America. We Nuevo Mexi-canos are part of that history: we speak the Spanish language. I prefer the term "Nuevo Mexicano" to describe my cultural heritage. My par-ents and my grandparents from the Puerto de Luna Valley of New Mex-ico spoke only Spanish, and as I honor my ancestors, I keep up their language and folkways. "Hispano" to me means using the Spanish lan-guage of my ancestors. The term "Latino" also connects me to other Spanish-speaking groups in this country and in Latin America.

The great majority of the Mexicanos of the Southwest are Indo-Hispanos, part of La Raza of the New World, the fruit of the Spanish

Originally published in *Before Columbus Review* 1, nos. 2–3 (Fall–Winter 1989): 3–4, 25–26.

father and the Indian mother. We take pride in our Hispanic heritage; that is, we know the history of the Spanish father, his language and his character. We also know that in this country it has been more seductive to identify with one's white, European ancestry. But the identification with that which is Spanish has often caused us to neglect our indigenous Native American roots, and thus we have not known and honored the heritage of our mother, the Indian mother of Mexico and the Southwest.

In world mythology there are few archetypal searches for the mother, perhaps because the mother is always evident; she is always there. In early religions she was the goddess of the earth, the provider. We forget that it is the mother who cultivates and in many ways creates our nature, both in an individual and in a communal sense.

For the Mexicanos of the Southwest, the symbolic mother is Malinche, who was the first Indian woman of Mexico to bear children fathered by a Spaniard. But the mother figure is more real than the symbolic Malinche; our mothers embody the archetype of the indigenous Indian mother of the Americas. If we are to truly know ourselves, it is her nature we must know. Why have we neglected that part of our history that was shaped by indigenous America?

I was born and raised in New Mexico, heir to the land of my Nuevo Mexicano ancestors, son of those Spanish and Mexicano colonists who settled the fertile Río Grande valley of New Mexico. My ancestors settled in the Atrisco land grant, across the river from present-day Alburquerque. I trace my family back a few generations, because the land grant has created a sense of communal belonging for the Anayas. But how do we relate to that Hispanic legacy that left the Peninsula in 1492 to implant itself in the New World? How do we relate to the peninsular consciousness of the people who crossed the Atlantic five hundred years ago to deposit their seed on the earth of the New World?

Located at the heart of what is now the Southwest United States, the people of Nuevo México have retained the essence of what it means to be Hispano, having preserved the Spanish language, the Catholic religion, and the folktales and folkways that came from Spain. Our ancestors imbued the history of Nuevo México with their particular worldview. For more than four centuries our Mexicano ancestors have lived in the isolated frontier of northernmost New Spain. But they did not survive and multiply in a vacuum; they survived and evolved because they intermarried and adopted many of the ways of the Indian pueblos. The Spanish character underwent change as it encountered the Native

Americans of the Southwest, and from that interaction and intermarriage a unique American mestizo was born.

We need to describe the totality of the worldview that was formed in what we now call the Southwest, understanding that we are heirs not only of the Spanish character but of our Native American nature as well. The Spanish character may be the aggressive, conquest-oriented part of our identity; the Native American nature is the more harmonious, earth-oriented side. We need to know both sides of our identity in order to know ourselves. We need to know the unique characteristics that have evolved from this union. To pay attention only to one side of our nature is to be less knowledgeable of self. If we are to fulfill our potential, it is important that we know the indigenous side of our history.

As I review my writings, I understand that it is the indigenous American perspective, or New World view, that is at the core of my search. I have explored the nature of my mother, not only the symbolic Indian mother but the real Indian mothers of the Americas. The blood that whispers my feelings about the essence of the earth and people of the Americas is the soul of my mother; it reveals the symbols and mythology of the New World, and that comprises the substratum of my writings.

During the Columbus quincentennial in 1992, a discourse will take place between Spain and its former colonies in the Americas. I wish to add a definition of my New World view to that discourse, hoping not only to share some of the findings of my personal literary quest, but also to encourage my community of raza to pay more attention to our multicultural and multiethnic history. We must know more of the synthesis of our Spanish and Indian natures, and know more of the multiple heritages of the Americas.

The Americas represent a wonderful experiment in the synthesis of divergent worldviews, and each one of us is a representative of that process. The illuminations of self that are revealed as we explore and understand our true natures can be one of the most rewarding experiences of our lives, for so much of the sensitive part of life is a search and understanding of the inner self. To define ourselves as we really are and not as others wish us to be allows us to become authentic, and that definition carries with it the potential of our humanism.

In the mid-sixteenth century, our Hispano and Mexicano ancestors begin to settle along the Río Grande of Nuevo México, bringing to the land a new language. They gave names to the land and its features. It is in the naming that one engages in the sacred; that is, by naming one creates a *sacred sense of time*, a historic sense of time. By engaging in naming, our ancestors imposed themselves on history and gave definition to history. The language used in that naming ceremony is our birthright.

I live in Alburquerque, a name that invokes some of the history of the Iberian Peninsula. In Spain, I spoke my Nuevo Mexicano Spanish, a language preserved and evolved by my ancestors in the mountains and valleys of New Mexico. But language changes with the passage of time and the vicissitudes of survival, and so I returned to Spain more proficient in English than in Spanish. All my novels and stories are written in English. While my parents' generation still communicated only in Spanish, my generation converses almost completely in English, a function of survival in the Anglo-Americano society. We struggle to retain the Spanish language, not only because it connects us to our brethren in Mexico and Latin America.

I returned to Spain to share with Spaniards the nature of my New World consciousness. At times I felt uncomfortable, believing I had to conform to the Spanish character, but the truth is that we who return to Spain no longer need to feel constrained to conform to the Spanish character. My generation of Hispanos, or Mexican Americans, liberated ourselves from that constraint by naming ourselves Chicanos. For us, using the word "Chicano" was our declaration of independence, the first step toward our true identity. By creating a Chicano consciousness, we created a process by which we rediscovered our history.

By naming ourselves Chicanos, we stamped an era with our communal identity; we reaffirmed our humanity by exploring and understanding the nature of our mothers, the indigenous American women. We took the word "Chicano" from "Mexicano," dropping the first syllable and keeping the "xicano." We are proud of that heritage even though we are not Mexican citizens, and although we are citizens of the United States, we are not Anglo-Americans. We have our own history rooted in this land. The word "Chicano" defined our *space in time*, that is, our history and identity. "Chicano" embraced our Native American heritage, an important element of our history.

Our first declaration of independence was from Anglo America; that is, we insisted on the right to our Indo-Hispano heritage. Now I believe the declaration has to go further. We have to insist on being the señores of our own time, to borrow a phrase from Miguel León-Portilla. To be the señores and señoras of our own time is to continue to create our definition and sense of destiny; it is a process of synthesis that embraces the many roots of La Raza.

This essay is a declaration of independence from a narrow view that has defined us *only* as Hispanos with only a Spanish heritage. The definition of our identity must be a New World definition. Such a definition should encompass the multiple roots and histories of the Americas; it should encompass the nature of the mothers whose soul provides the unique aesthetic and humanistic sensibility that defines us.

Language is at the essence of a culture, and we must remember that in Nuevo México, as in the rest of the New World, there existed pre-Columbian languages. The indigenous Indians had named their tribes, the rivers, the mountains, and the flora and fauna. They were the señores of their own time. The New World did not live in silence, awaiting the sound of European languages; thousands of years before 1492, it had its languages and it had participated in the sacred ceremony of naming. This is a fact that we must accept when we discuss our ethnicity, for not only was the Mexico of our indigenous ancestors peopled with Indians, the Río Grande valley, which became the home of our Hispano/Mexicano ancestors, also was thriving with many great Indian pueblos.

Language follows the urge of the blood: it moves with the adventurer to take root and be nourished by the colonist who tills the new soil. Languages mix, as does the blood, and so my gene pool is both Indian and peninsular. In reality, it has deeper and more interesting roots—roots I will never know. Knowing this allows me to honor las madres de las Américas. My journey has been that of a writer, and in my first novel it was the curandera Ultima, the indigenous woman who came to speak to me and share her secrets. She reflects the nature of La Virgen de Guadalupe, the indigenous mother born of the synthesis of Spanish virgin and Indian goddess. It is through Ultima that I began to discover myself. In my writings I have sought the true nature of the New World man, that person who is authentic to the New World view. I had only myself to encounter in the journey; I am the New World man I sought. I am an indigenous man taking his essence and perspective from the earth and people of the New World, from the earth that is my mother.

One of the most interesting questions we ask ourselves as human beings is about our identity. "Who am I?" We seek to know our roots, to know ourselves. When we encounter the taproots of our history, we feel authentic and able to identify self, family and community. Finding self should also mean finding humanity; declaring personal independence also means declaring that same independence for all individuals.

How did I begin this journey of self-knowledge? I listened to the cuentos of the old people, the stories of their history, and in retelling those stories and starting my own odyssey, I had to turn within. I had to know myself. Everyone does. The spiritual beliefs and mysticism of the Catholic church and the love of the earth were elements of my childhood, so I used those sources in my stories. The folkways of my community became the web of the fictions I create, for the elements of drama exist within the stories of the folk. Even today, when I feel I have outgrown some of the themes I explored as a young writer, I know my best writing still comes when I return to the essence of my Nuevo Mexicano culture.

But in all writing the depth of the universal element is that which allows us to communicate across national or ethnic boundaries, and so for me the most meaningful and revealing area to enter in search of the New World person was mythology. It is in myth that we find the truth in the heart, the truth of our place in time. Everyone can enter and explore his or her memory and discover there the symbols that speak to the personal and collective history. It is in this search that I found the legend of the golden carp and the other mythological symbols that permeate *Bless Me, Ultima* and my later work. I found universal, archetypal symbols, but these symbols were colored with a Native American hue. The earth, the elements, the sacred directions, the tree, the owl of the old curandera Ultima, the golden carp, the shaman as mentor or guide—all of these elements spoke to me of my New World nature. And it was Ultima, my Native American mother, who led the way and taught me to see.

My search continued. In *Heart of Aztlan* I reworked the myth of Aztlán, a legend that describes the place of origin of the Aztecs. I attempted to make that legend meaningful in contemporary context by exploring its possibilities as a Chicano homeland. In *Tortuga* I continued the search into the earth and totem animals, the search into the healing process of water and earth, as well as the art of writing itself. The writer may well be the new shaman for the old, displaced tribes of the Americas. In the novel *Tortuga,* I returned to the important revelations available to us in the nature of the mother, whether the mother was viewed as earth goddess or the feminine presence of the young girl who loves Tortuga.

I understand that many of my manitos, my Nuevo Mexicanos, often praise our Hispanic identity and shun the indigenous roots that have also nurtured our history. The young Chicano artists have changed part of that, and now I declare my independence of consciousness from the Iberian Peninsula. I have found that the symbolic content that best describes my nature comes from the people and earth of the Americas. So I declare, as an important step in the process of knowing myself, my independence. I see myself as a New World man, and I feel that definition is liberating and full of potential.

During this time of the Columbus quincentennial, it is important to look at the evolution of the consciousness of the Americas and to discern the unique worldviews that that evolution created. It is important for us and for Spain to look at the Americas and find, not an image of the Spanish character, but an image of our unique New World nature.

When I first traveled in Spain in 1980, I went into Andalucia. There in those wide expanses and mountains, which reminded me of New Mexico, I felt at home. But a person needs more than the landscape to feel connected; we need the deeper connection to the communal body.

The broad, political history of the independence of the Spanish colonies in the Americas is well known; now we must turn to an exploration of our personal and communal identity. That is what Chicano writers and artists have been doing since the cultural movement of the 1960s. The definition of Chicano culture must come from the multicultural perspective. Many streams of history define us and will continue to define us, for we are the synthesis that is the Americas.

Christ and Quetzalcóatl are not opposing spiritual figures; they fulfill the humanistic yearning toward harmonious resolution: harmony within, harmony with neighbors, harmony with the cosmos. The Virgin of Spanish Catholicism and the Aztec Tonantzin culminate in the powerful and all-loving Virgen de Guadalupe. And los santos of the Catholic Church, and those more personal saints of my mother's altar, merge with and share the sacred space of the kachinas of the Indian pueblos.

This metaphor, "Los santos son las kachinas," the saints are the kachinas, has become a guiding metaphor of synthesis for me. The Old World and the New World have become one in me. Perhaps it is this syncretic sensibility of harmony that is the ideal of New World character. The New World cultures accepted the spiritual manifestations of Catholicism; Christ and the saints entered the religious cosmology of Indian America. A new age of cultural and spiritual blending came to unite humanity's course in the Americas. It was an age born in suffering, but the very act of birth created the children who were heirs to a new worldview.

The New World view is syncretic and encompassing. It is one of the most humanistic views in the world, and yet it is a view not well known in the world. The pressure of political realities and negative views of the mestizo populations of the Americas have constrained the flowering of our nature. Still, that view of self-knowledge and harmony is carried in the heart of the New World person.

What is important to me as a writer is to find the words by which to describe myself and my relationship to others. I can now speak of my history and posit myself at the center of that history. I stand poised at the center of power, the knowing of myself, the heart and soul of the New World man alive in me.

This is a time of reflection for those of us who are the mestizos of the New World, and I believe the reflections in my writings and my attention to the myths and legends of Mesoamerica and the Río Grande help expand the definition of our Indo-Hispano heritage.

From Spain I brought back memories of the Alhambra where I felt my soul stir to Moorish rhythm, and in the paintings of Goya's dark period I saw his apocryphal vision of an era ending. At La Sagrada Família of Gaudi I bowed to genius, in the Valle de los Caídos I reflected on the Civil War—and on the wide expanses of Andalucia I thought of home. In all these places my memory stirred, and still I yearned for my home in Nuevo México, the mountains I know, the sacred places of my way of life. In that yearning the messages whispered their secret, it was time for me to declare my independence, time to center myself in the consciousness of the New World.

I was the New World man I had sought, with one foot in the glorious mestisaje of México and the other in the earth of the Indo-Hispanos of Nuevo México; my dreams are woven of New World earth and history. I could walk anywhere in the world and feel I was a citizen of the world, but it was Nuevo México that centered me; it was the indigenous soul of the Americas that held my secret.

It is important to know that the search for identity is not an esoteric search and not a divisive process. It is a way to reaffirm our humanity. We are all on this search; we all advocate justice, basic human rights, and the right of all to declare their independence of consciousness. We hope the spirit generated in Spain during the 1992 celebration addresses and encourages these basic rights.

History and the collective memory are vast. One delves into these powerful forces and finds that one is part of every other human being. I am proud of my New World heritage, but I know the tree of mankind is one, and I share my roots with every other person. It seems appropriate to end on the archetype of the tree. The tree, or the tree of life, is also a dominant symbol of the Americas, and its syncretic image combines the tree of Quetzalcóatl and the cross of Christ. My ancestors nourished the tree of life; now it is up to me to care for all it symbolizes.

Bendíceme, América

May the spirit of our ancestors watch over us as we enter the new century. May we walk in the path of beauty. Now it is our turn as poets and writers to take the breath of life, these words that are our gift, and bless the earth and people of the Americas. In the midst of the pain and the atrocities we commit on one another, in the enslavement of the worst oppression, we must remember the blessing. As long as we can draw breath to bless one another, we are still human.

Bendíceme, América. We ask the blessing of the earth, in return. O ravaged earth, O Eden we have trampled, O paradise we have filled with greed and hate and murder, bless us. Forests we have burned and llanos we have plowed, bless us. O sky we have polluted, bless us with your rain and kind breezes. It is the earth that nurtures us. Our mother, las Américas, bless us.

Let us resolve with this blessing that we will commit our hearts and souls to the earth and the people of these continents. To the guardian spirit of the Americas, to the grandfathers and all the deities of our people, to the sacred directions, we turn and ask for blessing. Center us in joy, in harmony, so we may act with purpose this day and during the difficult years ahead.

The history of the Americas tells us many things. We know that in 1492, the Old World met the New. And at once began the exploitation and colonization of these lands, which became a battleground for the souls and bodies of the Native Americans. We know, too, that the Euro-

Originally published in *Bendíceme, América: Latino Writers of the United States*, eds. Harold Augenbraum et al. (New York: The Mercantile Library of New York, 1993), 63–66; and reprinted in *The Anaya Reader* (New York: Warner Books, 1995), 429–34.

centric view has always been challenged by the indigenous cultures on which it was imposed—as it is being challenged today. And by those who have not had a voice in shaping their own destinies, the quincentennial is being celebrated as five hundred years of resistance. We, the many communities of the Americas, are the heirs of that long legacy. Today we must raise our voices to proclaim our various identities. We must demand an active role in determining the direction this hemisphere will take in our generation and in the future.

What should the quincentennial mean to us? There are fundamental issues facing the citizens of the Americas today: We must protect basic human rights. We must help formulate the hemisphere's economic policies. And we must champion the cause of democracy. We need to take part, as well, in the new age of technology and information and understand how this new age affects our children. And, yes, we need to protect the resources of the earth.

In this sector of the globe, a very small percentage of the population consumes the majority of the products, while many suffer in poverty. This year can be a time of activism during which all groups work at better understanding one another. The walls of separation must come down. The hermandad of the Americas must be proclaimed. Let us seek to establish fellowship and peace. Let us help instill a new pride in our children so they can face the coming millennium with confidence.

For five hundred years, another people's way of seeing the world became the dominant interpretation of history throughout North and South America. Indigenous histories were destroyed, and educational systems were remodeled on those of Europe. That Eurocentric view failed to portray the essence of our diverse civilizations. Now is the time for us to acknowledge and proclaim the true multicultural nature of the Americas—to listen to the many voices of the Americas.

Eduardo Galeano, in *The Book of Embraces*, reminds us of an African proverb: Until lions have their own historians, histories of the hunt will glorify the hunter. The hunters who wrote the histories of the Americas have glorified the European perspective. And, in the meantime, the chronicles of our peoples have been neglected, lost, even systematically obliterated. Now we must be the lions who rediscover right and redress the balance. Now we must restore and take pride in our own histories.

Each cultural group of the Americas must tell and write its stories and inform the world of its many accomplishments. One often hears that those who do not know their history are doomed to repeat it. Lest we subject our children to the oppression endured by their ancestors, we must teach them to be lions who are familiar with their past and who can wisely chart a course through the decades ahead.

Such knowledge will help foster a spirit of liberation. All of our communities have played a role in building the Americas, yet the efforts of many have not been acknowledged. When people recount their achievements, they create and inspire pride. That is why our children need to hear our voices. That is why our histories need to be read in the schools. Only in this way will our offspring be empowered to introduce a new vision of the Americas—one that transcends the offenses of the past.

At a gathering of writers in Managua, Nicaragua, during the summer of 1989, I heard Eduardo Galeano tell a story. A child is being born on an isolated ranch. By the time the doctor arrives, the mother is near death. It is a breech delivery, and the baby's body lies twisted in its mother's womb. The doctor does not think the child is alive, until its hand reaches out and grabs his fingers. The baby wants to live. And so the doctor goes to work and completes the delivery.

This, Galeano tells us, represents the birth of the Americas, a birth that took place in the midst of the cataclysm of 1492. Born into the exploitation, poverty, and pain of workers, that child nevertheless showed a tenacity for life. Against all odds, the Americas were born, survived, and became the mother we know.

From Tierra del Fuego to the Arctic Circle, our mother is known by many names, and she has herself given birth to many nations. Our mother, the Americas, has a history—or rather, many histories—which we are obliged to celebrate. And I am not speaking only of the past five hundred years, but also of the time before Columbus's crossing. For the roots of our own histories lie in those of the indigenous people of the Americas. Each of us can help write a new and complete account of our past. And the more we learn from one another, the more encompassing our vision of the future will become.

This willingness to learn the multicultural story of our land and cultures will help us deal with the real issues of life. As we know ourselves, we recognize our beauty. The old class and color distinctions must be eradicated. We cannot liberate another if we do not first liberate ourselves.

Many of the voices of the Americas have been repressed. But there is change in the air. New songs are being sung, new stories told. New battles for human decency are daily being fought. During our own time, writers from many oppressed nations have spoken out. Mothers have marched in the streets against unjust governments. They are the lions, pointing the way for us to follow. Together, then, let us take command of our destinies and make our voices heard.

Martineztown Builds Wall of Memories

Stories are preserved in the memory of a group, and as those accounts are told and retold the group is connected to its history. As long as the stories of a community are recited by elders, children learn about the traditions and cultural life of their ancestors.

But what happens when elders have a diminished role in the education of the young? What happens when there is a breakdown in this vital communication between generations? Will the heritage die? Can schools play a role in reflecting the cultural heritage of the neighborhood? These are crucial questions that Hispanic New Mexicans are asking. The same questions, no doubt, are being asked in communities around the country.

The problem of children not learning about their heritage is especially evident in our state's urban settings. In 1988, a personal desire to see this trend reversed led Albuquerque native Eileen Grevey to enroll her children in Longfellow Elementary School in Martineztown. The old school was demolished, but only after the community wrestled an agreement from the school board to build a new school on the same site. In the 1980s, Longfellow was converted into a magnet school with an emphasis on Spanish language usage throughout the curriculum and an improved fine arts program.

Martineztown, a stone's throw from downtown Albuquerque, not only saved Longfellow, but also created one of the most popular schools in the city. But even in this enriched educational setting, Grevey felt something could be added. She recorded her father's life story, and the experience was so gratifying she shared it with her classroom.

Grevey learned what many educators espouse: Children will grow in self-esteem if they experience a sense of their own history in a

---

Originally published in *New Mexico Magazine* (January 1992): 38–43.

school setting. To help the effort, she founded the Roots and Wings educational project. The project uses people of the barrio as resources. Their roots in the neighborhood are a treasure of experience the children should share. As children learn the importance of their heritage and grow in self-esteem, they sprout wings to carry them into the future.

A Roots and Wings committee of historians, authors, and community leaders was formed to develop concepts and to assist the project. All agree that an important ingredient would be community participation.

In its first year, Roots and Wings helped the school launch several intergenerational projects, including a bilingual school/community newspaper, herbal gardens, and arts and crafts projects. These activities united Martineztown elders with young students.

First Lady Barbara Bush, herself a strong advocate of enriched cultural literacy, came to Martineztown to help celebrate the Roots and Wings endeavor. Apple Computer provided the funds to sponsor five hundred Martineztown/Santa Barbara elders to attend a dinner given in the First Lady's honor.

It was a great start, but the net had to be cast wider if the neighborhood was to commit itself to the effort.

The people of the Martineztown/Santa Barbara neighborhood had the answer. Hanging on walls, sitting on altars, and hidden in old trunks were photographs of the past. Through the years people had treasured the pictures that documented fiestas, weddings, churches, dances, war, work, and family life. The photographs provided a pictorial history of the barrio, from the late nineteenth century when the community was established to the present.

Roots and Wings sponsored a drive to collect these photographs. Through a series of community meetings and events, the people were invited to lend their photographs for the exhibit and create a Memory Wall. The resulting photo montage would be a view into their history. The New Mexico Endowment for the Humanities helped fund the Memory Wall project. Roots and Wings turned to those on the committee who had the expertise and sensitivity to go into the neighborhood homes and gather the photographs.

Mary Davis and Kit Sargeant recorded an oral history of Albuquerque's North Valley. In 1986 the Albuquerque Museum published *Shining River, Precious Land,* their collection of interviews with North Valley residents. As they talked to elderly Hispanics in the valley, the viejitos commented with sadness that young people didn't know many of the old traditions. Feeling the pressure to assimilate, the young weren't learning Spanish.

It became evident that sharing was one of the values of the elderly. In the old days, everything was shared: food, fiestas, family joy, and tragedies. People came to the assistance of their neighbors, and the soul of the agricultural community was intact. Now, life in the North Valley is moving in a faster lane. New growth not only affects its geographic character, it also changes people. The very process of collecting oral histories rekindled the spirit of sharing. The memory and stories of people are again important.

In recent years, others have worked in the field of oral history in New Mexico. Academia, a nonprofit group, worked in the Dixon/ Embudo area in the 1970s. Academia collected el oro del barrio (the gold of the neighborhood) under the leadership of Estevan Arellano and Tomas Atencio.

In 1978, Martha Liebert helped revitalize the cultural heritage of the Sandoval County with her work. The collection of photographs she and co-workers have gathered is permanently housed in the Delavy House on the west side of the Río Grande in Bernalillo. This display, overseen by the Sandoval County Historical Society, is one of the most extensive of its kind. It is a model for others.

Recently additional photographic collections, depicting the Barelas and Los Padillas neighborhoods in Albuquerque, were gathered.

What is the history of the Martineztown/Santa Barbara barrio? Who were the people that first moved with the Martin family from Old Town? Legend tells us Old Town was getting rowdy, and a number of families moved to the foot of the sandhills near the present Mountain Road and Edith Boulevard. Old maps show a major acequia running through the community. The land was farmed, and homes were constructed from adobes made from the valley topsoil. Bernalillo Highway, a portion of the historic Camino Real, ran through the neighborhood.

Life was simple; men farmed, worked at the wool warehouses or at the sawmill and railroad shops. Women cared for their families.

Some women blazed new trails in education. Delphina Candelaria, a principal at Longfellow in the 1960s, devoted her life to education. Born in 1889, she taught in many New Mexico towns. "When I started teaching," she says, "they didn't employ married teachers. Married women should be home taking care of their children. I thought about marriage, but I wanted to go to college. Some girls' chief aim was to get married. Mine was to make a life for myself."

Today, Margaret Perea-Martínez, although married and raising a family, follows in Candelaria's footsteps. She is a program evaluator for Albuquerque Public Schools and an active community leader who has created a real presence in the barrio. The older leaders of the barrio respectfully listen when Perea-Martínez speaks.

One of the first suburbs of downtown Albuquerque, the Martinez-town/Santa Barbara area always has had a vital communal life with church activities often at the hub. Menaul School was founded by the Presbyterian Church as an Indian school in 1881. The Presbyterian church in the neighborhood was built in 1889, and the Roman Catholic San Ignacio Church was established in 1916. San Igancio conducts an annual fiesta in which many participate.

Eduardo Sandoval grew up in Martineztown. "It was heaven," he says of life at the turn of the century. "In those days there were no automobiles. You had to walk everywhere. But people came for the fiestas. People you didn't see for a whole year would show up. People used to dance up a storm. They used to be happy. In those days there was honesty. Consideration and respect."

Rose Saintz also remembers the vibrancy of life in Martineztown. She says if she had to do it again she would relive her childhood in the same way. "There was enough food," she remembers, "because everyone would borrow back and forth. I remember the fiestas. There would be a big tent, and everyone would dance and there would be rides."

Licho Martínez remembers the 1930s and working in his father's store. "There were eleven kids in my family. Martineztown was all adobe houses with outside toilets. We didn't know about bathrooms. We took a bath in a tub. We used to sleep outside in the summer. My mother would cook beans and chile—everybody shared. If someone killed a pig, everybody shared."

People's values shine through their memories; the photographic images on Memory Wall further enhance the history of the neighborhood.

Photographs taken during World War II show the drastic changes that occurred in the barrio. The men went to war and came back to face a new era. Another lasting change came with urban renewal in the 1960s. The Martineztown residents south of Lomas voted for a re-development project and new, modern homes were built.

Martineztown and Santa Barbara are essentially built like the old villages of northern New Mexico. The plots of land were long, running from the railroad to the irrigation ditch. The barrio was a village within the expanding city, then known as Albuquerque. Urban growth began to impinge on the neighborhood, and in the 1960s the Vietnam conflict came to wrench young men from their families.

The intent of the Memory Wall is to record as much of the history of the neighborhood as possible. The photographs will be mounted on panels and form a traveling exhibit that can be taken to schools, communities, and fiestas in Albuquerque and throughout the state. The panels then will become a permanent exhibit on the walls of the renovated Santa Barbara School.

Joe Herrera, a lifelong resident of the Santa Barbara barrio, was instrumental in the preservation of the school. Everywhere in the community one hears stories of leaders who have worked to make their community a better place to live. It is fitting that the school will serve as a community center for senior citizens. As poetic justice would have it, the photographs will come to rest in this new center for elders.

Projects like this renew people's curiosity about their history and roots and expand their aspirations for the future. Already a number of other communities from around the country have inquired about the project. New Mexicans aren't the only ones sensing the loss of heritage in our changing times.

This photographic essay will be one ingredient in the constant evolution of a neighborhood. The photographs and stories of the people will encourage everyone to value their history. The richness evident in their traditions is a heritage they can be proud to share with the world.

Memory Wall is a beginning that taps the roots of memory. New projects already are planned by groups in the barrio. To collect history is one thing, to use it to help your children move into the future is the real goal. The lasting recuerdos del pasado (remembrances of the past) are the stories the old people tell the children as they walk hand in hand through the streets of the barrio they call home.

Aztlán

A Homeland without Boundaries

The ceremony of naming, or of self-definition, is one of the most important acts a community performs. To particularize the group with a name is a fundamental step of awareness in the evolution of tribes as well as nations. The naming coalesces the history and values of the group, provides an identification necessary for its relationship to other groups or nations, and most important, the naming ceremony restores pride and infuses renewed energy which manifests itself in creative ways.

I have reflected often during the last fifteen years on the naming ceremony that took place in the southwestern United States when the Chicano community named Aztlán as its homeland in the late 1960s. This communal event and the new consciousness and consequent creative activity generated within the Chicano community during this period marked an important historical time for our people.

The naming ceremony creates a real sense of nation, for it fuses the spiritual and political aspirations of a group and provides a vision of the group's role in history. These aspirations are voiced by the artists who re-create the language and symbols which are used in the naming ceremony. The politicians of the group may describe political relationships and symbols, but it is the artist who gives deeper and long-lasting expression to a people's sense of nation and destiny. The artists, like the priests and shamans of other tribes, express spiritual awareness and potential, and it is the expression of the group's history, identity, and purpose that I label the naming ceremony. In the ancient world this expression of identity and purpose was contained in the epic; thus, we read Homer to understand the character of the Greeks.

Originally published in *Aztlán: Essays on the Chicano Homeland*, eds. Rudolfo A. Anaya and Francisco Lomelí (Albuquerque, N.Mex.: El Norte Publications/Academia, 1989), 230–41.

Various circumstances create the need for national or tribal definition and unity. The group may acquire cohesion and a feeling of nationhood in times of threat, whether the threat be physical (war) or a perceived loss of tribal unity. Group existence may also be threatened by assimilationist tendencies, which were a real threat experienced by the Chicano community in the 1960s. A time of adventure and conquest, or the alliance of political interests, may also bring nations to self-definition. Also, times of heightened spiritual awareness of the group's relationship to the gods create this sense of purpose and destiny in the community. Usually these times are marked by a renaissance in the arts, because the artists provide the symbols and metaphors that describe the spiritual relationship.

So it was for la raza, the Mexican American community of this country in the 1960s. This cultural group underwent an important change in their awareness of self, and that change brought about the need for self-definition. The naming ceremony not only helped to bond the group, it created a new vision of the group's potential.

Where did the Chicanos turn for the content needed in the naming ceremony? Quite naturally the community turned to its history and found many of its heroes in the recent Mexican Revolution. Some of us explored the deeper stratum of Mexican history, myth, and legend. It was in the mythology of the Aztecs that Chicano cultural nationalists found the myth of Aztlán. How did the content of that myth become part of the new consciousness of our community? That is the question which our philosophers have tackled from various perspectives, and it has been part of my preoccupation.

The naming ceremony, or redefinition of the group, occurred within the ranks of the Indo-Hispanos of the Southwest in the 1960s. Leaders within the Chicano community—educators, poets, writers, artists, activists—rose up against the majority presence of Anglo America to defend the right of the Hispanic community to exist as a national entity within the United States. Two crucial decisions were made during this period by these guardians of the culture: one was the naming of the Chicano community and the second was the declaration of Aztlán as the ancestral homeland. "Somos Chicanos," we are Chicanos, declared the leaders of the nationalistic movement, and thus christened the Mexican American community with a name which had ancient roots. By using this term, the Chicano community consciously and publicly acknowledged its Native American heritage, and thus opened new avenues of exploration by which we could more clearly define the mestizo who is the synthesis of European and Indian ancestry.

"Aztlán is our homeland" was the second declaration, and this assertion defined the "national" status for the group. Aztlán was the place of origin of the Aztecs of Mesoamerica, the place of the seven caves recorded in their legends. The Chicanos had returned to Native American legend to find the psychological and spiritual birthplace of their ancestors.

These declarations were of momentous historical significance. An identity and a homeland were designated once again on the northern borders of Hispanic America. The naming of Aztlán was a spontaneous act which took place throughout the Southwest, and the feat was given legitimacy in a meeting that was held in Denver in 1969 to draft El Plan Espiritual de Aztlán. The naming of the homeland created a Chicano spiritual awareness which reverberated throughout the Southwest, and the naming ceremony was reenacted wherever Chicanos met to discuss their common destiny. I believe that no other activity of the Chicano Movement was as important as this declaration. It is now time to explore why such an event took place and to examine closely the possibilities that were inherent in that event.

The threat to the Chicano community was most often defined by the leaders of the Chicano Movement of the 1960s as a political and economic threat, an exploitation of the Mexican American population. Finding solutions to economic and political exploitation was of paramount importance, but within the movement were also heard the voices of cultural nationalists who insisted that the definition of the homeland, Aztlán, and the reconstitution of the old tribal history and heritage were just as vital for the Chicano community. In fact, the two issues went hand in hand, and in retrospect we can see that the leaders of the two factions of the movement should have worked more closely together. The cultural nationalists created the symbol of national unity for the community; the political activists should have seen its potential and used the symbol to provide access into the mainstream political structure.

The context of the Chicano Movement was broad, and the struggles for definition of goals and leadership within the movement still need more historical analysis. I leave that review of the broader picture of the movement to other disciplines; my focus is the naming of Aztlán. What indeed took place when the Chicanos defined their homeland? Why had we returned to Aztec legend to name the homeland, and how did that return to legend create "rights (to homeland) by legend?" Would this "right by legend" be as powerful a binding force for Chicanos as "right by treaty"? We knew we could turn to the Treaty of Guadalupe Hidalgo, a historical treaty between nations, to define ourselves as Mexicans with certain rights within the borders of the United States, but that political definition had never been enough. A group defines itself not only politically, but also by its character, that is, its soul. To define ourselves, we turned to Native American legend, and there we found a meaningful part of our ethos.

My thoughts lead me to believe that the tribes of our species arrive at new stages of communal awareness as they evolve. During these historical moments of illumination, the group creates the context of its destiny in time, and so the group becomes master of its own time, or as Miguel León-Portilla, the renowned Mexican philosopher, would say, the group becomes the "señores of their own time." Did we indeed become the señores of our own time during the 1960s? Did we take charge of the time and create the epic literature which would define us?

Let us review the historical setting for the Indo-Hispanos of the Southwest when we celebrated the naming ceremony. It was a time when we saw our community assaulted by poverty and oppression; the denigrating effects of racism ate away at our pride and stamina. Assimilation, on the other hand, only raised false hopes for our people, so it was a time of crisis, a time that begged for the "señores of the communal time" to once again insist on our right to our values and history. If this didn't happen, our community was doomed to existence as a tourist commodity, admired for its quaint folkways but not taken seriously by the world of nations.

For too long the Indo-Hispano community had projected only its Spanish history and heritage, for that projection suited the powers that dealt with this community as a tourist commodity and as a community that could do service work for the society in power. That identity left out the reality of our mestizo heritage. Part of the movement's work was to revive our connection with our Indian past, and to seek a truer definition of that past. This meant reviving the history, myths, spiritual thought, legends, and symbols from Native America that were part of the Chicano's collective history. The search found the umbilical cord which led to Indian Mesoamerica and the Pueblos of the Río Grande; that is, in the act of declaring our identity and nationality, we acknowledged our Indian American parentage.

It was in Mesoamerica that we rediscovered the legend of Aztlán, a story of mythic proportions, rooted as it was in the tribal memory of the Aztecs. Why was the legend not readily available to us, say, in the legends of the Pueblos of the Río Grande? Perhaps it was, but by the middle of the twentieth century we as Hispanos were separated from the Pueblo Indian world of our ancestors. A color consciousness which has been such a negative element in the history of the Americas affected our own people, and, falling prey to the pressure, the large mestizo population moved to identify with that which was Hispanic. Indian thought, once accessible to our ancestors, was withdrawn to the inner circle of the Pueblo, and the myths of the Americas were revealed only to those of us who delved into the symbolic meanings in the collective memory.

In 1848 there was the continued sense of separation when the United States annexed what is now the Southwest from Mexico. Separation from roots created vulnerability, because our worldview was centered in community and its relationship to earth. Even in the endeavor of education, where democracy promised equality and access, we felt denied. Thus our search for Chicano roots led to Mesoamerica and Aztec legend, and there we found Aztlán—put another way, Aztlán was waiting for us.

In Aztlán, the legend said, the seven tribes emerged from the seven caves of a mountain, a descriptive and archetypal metaphor which expresses the coming into a new age of consciousness from a prior time. They left Aztlán because they had received the prophecy to migrate south in search of Tenochtitlan, there to establish their new civilization. How may we interpret this? Was this archetypal expulsion from the place of origin (Aztlán) like an expulsion from the Garden of Eden, the motif of an archetype in myth repeating itself? Or was leaving the place of origin a challenge to humanity, a challenge of evolution?

The ancestors of the Aztecs named their homeland Aztlán, and legend placed it north of Mexico. Aztlán was the place of origin, the sipapu, the Eden of those tribes. There they came to a new relationship with their god of war, Huitzilopochtli, and he promised to lead them in their migration out of Aztlán. This was spiritual yearning and evolution working hand in hand. They figuratively and literally emerged into the present world, their present time, and they became the señores of their own time. More literal interpretations have suggested the seven tribes were seven clans who broke the covenant of Aztlán and were expelled; I choose to interpret the legend in the context of world mythology.

Leaving the caves of Aztlán was paramount to being born, and with birth came suffering and the migration out of Aztlán to the land promised by their war god. Spiritual aspiration had moved them to form a new covenant with Huitzilopochtli which would sustain them during the long years of migration southward, eventually to found the civilization of Tenochtitlan, present day Mexico City.

The migration and quest of the original inhabitants of Aztlán can be viewed in the context of world mythology: like the Jews migration from Egypt in the time of their Exodus to settle in the promised land, the Aztecs migrated south to establish the new nation of Tenochtitlan. These elements of the saga are the stuff of great drama and tragedy. In 1521 Cortes and his Spaniards were to lay siege to the Aztec kingdom and destroy it. But good drama and tragedy rise from the archetypal content of myth, and the time of myth is continuous. For me, the most interesting element in that history is the often hidden fact that it was those Mesoamerican Indians who later journeyed up the Río Grande with the Spanish conquistadores; they were returning to their original homeland.

Chicano writers interested in the old legends which revealed our Native American past were drawn to the legend of Aztlán and its meaning. In it we saw a definition of our homeland from a Native American point of view, and we explored that area of history. What and where was the mythic Aztlán? Could the old legends of indigenous America serve a useful purpose in the Chicano Movement? Why did this legend of the indigenous homeland have such an influence on our thinking? We knew that the absorption of the Chicano into the mainstream American culture was occurring so quickly that unless we re-established the covenants of our ancestors, our culture was threatened with extinction. In fact, some suggested that the Chicano community should assimilate into the Anglo-American mainstream and forget its history and language. The concept of a bilingual, bicultural group within the United States was seen as a threat, and in many quarters that view is still held today. The time of crisis for our community demanded a new definition of national unity.

For me, part of the answer lies in an interpretation of human nature and its relationship to myth. Myth is our umbilical connection to the past, to the shared collective memory. After long years spent in the realm of imagination and creativity, I came to understand that many of the symbols which welled up from my subconscious were not learned, they were part of my ethos, symbols from the archetypal memory residing in the blood. Another question intrigued me: "What is our communal relationship with time?" The ancestors of the Aztecs had lived through a period of heightened awareness. Were we, the Chicanos, living through a similar period of time in the 1960s?

I believe the essence of the Chicano Movement was the naming ceremony I have described and the creation of a cultural nationalist consciousness that brought together our community. This coming together in the naming ceremony duplicated the earlier time in the history of our ancestors. Yes, there was a real Aztlán, but there was also the spiritual Aztlán, the place of the covenant with the gods, the psychological center of our Indian history. During the period of awareness, the collective soul of the group renewed itself through myth; it is what the tribes of humankind have done throughout history.

The communal activity was crucial to the scenario, for myth is a communal response to spiritual crisis. The new consciousness created in the 1960s was a psychological centering, and the possibility of being in touch with our real history was available to each individual. We had become the señores and the señoras of our own time in the ceremony of naming, and it is important to stress the role of the Chicana, for the women of our community played a pivotal role in creating the Movement. One only has to look at the literature of the period to read the celebration of Aztlán which we created.

We took a new look at the history of the Indo-Hispano community in the Southwest, a group whose tradition dated back to the sixteenth century and the entry of the Hispanos and Mexicanos into the pueblos of the Río Grande. A unique Indo-Hispano culture had evolved along the northern Río Grande, a product of the process of synthesis which was already at work in Mexico as the Old World and the New World met and merged. The most interesting development of that process was the evolution of the "New World person," the person in touch with the mythology of the Americas that I have explored in my writing.

The same synthesis would not take place when the Anglo-American came to the Southwest in the mid-nineteenth century. The Hispano and Anglo worlds remained apart, meeting to conduct business in an ethnic mosaic, but seldom creating a personal commingling. The genetic pools have not mixed in a significant way, and only in a small way is it occurring in contemporary times. Still, the issue of ethnicity is not static, and it is one we need to face creatively.

The established Indo-Hispano culture was based in the villages, but by the 1960s the community was largely an urban group, and so to reconstitute our history during this time of crisis some returned to the villages to look for origins. Another meaningful return was into the history of the Americas, where we examined our Indian roots, the soul of the Americas. There we found not only indigenous historical time, but mythical time which is continuous; that discovery was to have a tremendous impact on the healing of our social fabric. In Mesoamerica, we encountered the pre-Columbian thought of Mexico. That return to the legends and myths of the New World led the Chicano to Aztlán. In the process of returning to our myths and legends, we were not short-sighted idealists that thought the oppression our community suffered would disappear. We knew better, but our search was spiritual in nature, and our community desperately needed the reaffirmation. We had faith that by bringing to light our history, even the esoteric history of myth and legend, we could bring to fruition a cultural renaissance and create a new time of hermandad. That new era of brotherhood would not only unify us, it would unleash the creative potential of the Chicano community.

In the 1960s the same spiritual yearnings and crisis that had concerned the original inhabitants of Aztlán now concerned the Chicanos. A cycle of Chicano history was repeating itself. Our poets and writers became the leaders of the Chicano Movement, and as they brought to focus the aspirations of the people, they took upon themselves a role common to our culture, the role of older, wiser leaders or ancianos, the roles of those señores and señoras who dare to be aware of the burden of time and act to alleviate the burden for the communal good of the people. Needless to say, those same leaders would be criticized when the ambitious goals of the movement were not fully realized.

A new question arose: Would the promise of continuity and self-actualization inherent in our myths and legends bring with it the fruition of potential and freedom? Could we save our history and community from obliteration within the confines of Anglo America by reincorporating the old legends into our worldview? Some said no. Myth was ephemeral, it had no substance, it distorted reality. What the Chicanos needed was direct political mobilization, perhaps revolution. They did not need to arm themselves with ancient stories.

Those of us who saw the potential of myth as truth, or myth as self-knowledge, argued that it was indigenous America that held the taproot of our history; its mythology was the mirror by which to know ourselves. Chicanos had to experience a new awareness of self, just as our Native American ancestors had come to that new plane of consciousness eight centuries before in Aztlán, and coming to this knowledge of our historical continuity was a means toward community action.

Aztlán is real because myth is real, we argued. Aztlán was potential because it was a place of prophecy. Migrating groups of Asians, in the process of becoming indigenous Americans, had settled in Aztlán. There they evolved new levels of spiritual orientation to cosmos, earth, and community. Isn't this the process of spiritual and psychological evolution? Isn't this how our human potential evolves? So it happened to these tribes of Native Americans. Somewhere in the deserts and mountains of what we now call the Southwest, they created a covenant with their gods, and from there they moved south to Mexico to complete the prophecy.

Of course they did not arrive at full potential, no one ever does. They were still heir to human failure, but we know their later artistic achievements were of a grand scale. Even their warring society would incorporate the religion of peace of Quetzalcóatl. All of Mesoamerica and the tributaries as far north as Chaco and Mesa Verde were, I suspect, renewed during that era. A new age of spiritual illumination had come to the Americas, and the journey from Aztlán to Mexico was part of that tremendous change. From the Pueblos of the Río Grande to Mesoamerica and neighboring tribes, the people of the Americas were evolving into new realms of consciousness.

The need for a homeland is inherent in the collective memory of any group, it is a covenant with the tribal gods. The spiritual yearning for homeland is encompassing, but because the geography of the earth is limited, homelands rub against each other and create friction. We have not yet moved to a new consciousness where the earth truly becomes the homeland of everyone. Perhaps that is our next step in evolution, and perhaps there are already signs that this is happening. Do we, as heirs and inhabitants of Aztlán, dare to take this next step and consider our homeland without boundaries? Do we dare to reach out and encompass the true spiritual relationship inherent in homeland with every other group who dreams of homeland?

The Indo-Hispano of the Southwest was influenced by the spirituality of the pueblos of the Río Grande, even though the Catholic faith was imposed on the indigenous faith. There were elements of brutality in the Spanish conquest—this is documented—but the synthesis which was taking place in Mexico between the Old World and the New World was accelerated in Aztlán after the 1680 Pueblo Revolt. The Indo-Hispano religious sensibility was influenced by the Pueblos, and so respect for the earth became an important ingredient in the unique worldview being formed in Aztlán. The recognition of the Earth as mother (la sagrada tierra) permeated the spiritual life of the Hispanic villages, and the process of synthesis fused Spanish Catholicism with Native American thought. The clearest symbol of the process of syncretism was the merging of the Virgin Mary with the Indian Goddess (Tonantzin) to give form to the brown Madonna of Mexico, La Virgen de Guadalupe. Truly, an original blend of American spirituality was evolving.

What did all this mean to the real world of politics which the Chicano struggled to enter and influence in the 1960s? Unfortunately, the historical assessment made thus far weighs heavily on a materialistic interpretation. I am convinced that a history of that era and of our culture must take both the sacred and the profane into account. To understand our culture only through a materialistic account will not provide a true picture of the nature of our community. For me, the Chicano Movement succeeded because it changed part of our social and political role within the society, but also because it created a cultural renaissance in the Chicano community. The release of creative energy in which the artists defined self and community was the hallmark of the Movement. The spiritual energy which once filled the consciousness of the original inhabitants of Aztlán and propelled them south to Mexico to fulfill their destiny led us to proclaim our existence and found our nation.

A spirit of liberation swept over our people, releasing a chain reaction of new energy, initiative and originality. The Movement gave birth to the term Chicano, the bold new image born of Hispanic and Indian synthesis. To some extent that image penetrated the Anglo-American consciousness, and to some degree it moved onto a world stage. But the image was really for our community; the naming was to renew identity and awareness of our history. The changes wrought in the psyche of the Hispanos of the Southwest by the use of the word Chicano were enormous. True, some in our community resisted the naming and to this day do not identify with Chicano, but one cannot deny the positive benefits of reinvigorated pride, especially in artistic creativity, which swept across the land.

The true guardians of Aztlán have been the Río Grande Pueblo people, and the knowledge and love for their homeland has kept their spiritual thought alive in the face of overwhelming odds. They have kept themselves centered with the earth, and that has provided their communities a spiritual and psychological center. The Chicano, a new raza of the Americas, is heir to the same earth and a legacy of spiritual thought that can help center the individual. In a world so in need of ecological and spiritual awareness, which would allow us to save the earth and practice democratic principles of love and sharing, these ties to the earth and the care we must give to this area we call Aztlán still provide hope for our community. We have within us the inner resources to become new guardians of the earth and of peace.

We have seen the blossoming of this potential in our generation. Chicano art, music, and literature have gained a foothold and are shaping new perceptions. Within the arts lie reflections of our values, not only cultural trappings of the day-to-day world, but the old values which spring from our mythologies. Respect for the earth of Aztlán is one of these values, and if we are truly living in an era of a new consciousness, we must reach further into our human potential and consider Aztlán a homeland without boundaries.

This is a most difficult proposal—the idea that we can move beyond our ethnocentric boundaries, that we can envision the limitations of ethnicity even as we extol our self-pride. The argument of survival in our modern world seems to urge us toward the common center of our humanity. When we established our rights to the homeland of Aztlán, we understood that that right belongs to every group or nation, and we understood how we share in all the homelands of world mythology. The children of Aztlán are citizens of the world. We must move beyond the limitations of ethnicity to create a world without borders. Each community rising to its new level of awareness creates respect for self and for others, and we are in need of this awareness before we destroy the earth and each other.

An idealistic, utopian thought? Perhaps, but one we need to dare to consider. Those who deal in competition and the selfishness of the modern nation-state are in control, and they have falsely named competition and material gain as the true values of the world. Perhaps it's time to think of unity. Aztlán can become the nation that mediates between Anglo America and Latin America. We can be the leaders who propose human answers to the human problems of the Americas. The real problem of border regions when addressed from a world perspective should be dealt with in human terms, in terms of families and neighbors, not terms of profit or ideology. Unity and human potential should guide us, not market values and the gross national product. This, after all, is the challenge of our generation, to create a consciousness which fosters the flowering of the human spirit, not its exploitation. We need healing in our world community; it can start here.

This is the legacy of Aztlán: it is a place where seven tribes of humankind came to a new awareness of their potential, a new sensitivity in their relationship to earth and cosmos. Here those first inhabitants of Aztlán took their destiny into their own hands, they were born into a new prophecy, and they moved to complete it. Can we do less?

That illumination and leap of faith for those people did not make for perfection. History moves us toward perfection through small epiphanies. The tribes moved out of Aztlán as Adam and Eve moved out of Eden, to challenge the future and to fulfill their potential. Our nature moves us forward, groping for illumination, yearning for a truer knowledge of our spiritual and human relationships. We know within that we can create a more fulfilling and harmonious future. For me, this is the promise of Aztlán.

Sale of Atrisco Land Grant Means Loss of History, Tradition

Before my mother died she gave me three shares of stock in the Atrisco Land Grant. They were the shares my father had left with her before he died. These certificates of stock symbolize my legacy in this land grant established late in the seventeenth century by a grant from the king of Spain.

In 1967 the old Atrisco Land Grant was incorporated as a public corporation for its heirs. It is now known as the Westland Corporation. Recently, the directors have announced that they are planning to put the corporation up for sale. This would mean the highest bidder in Wall Street could purchase all that is left of the old Atrisco Land Grant.

Some shareholders of the Atrisco Land Grant have now acquired many shares and want to sell. Others of us, whether we own a few or many shares, are adamantly against the relinquishing of the last of this legacy. The land was not given to us by our ancestors to sell. The land was to be passed down to future generations to be used for the social good of the community.

I am an heir to that land which spans the West Mesa of Albuquerque from the Río Grande to the Río Puerco. It stretches from the village of Los Padillas in the south to the escarpment of the volcanoes to the north. Now approximately 49,000 acres are left of that old, immense grant.

The land encompassed by the grant is our historical legacy.

With Albuquerque expanding to the west, the Atrisco Land Grant holds within its boundaries some of the most valuable land in the Río Grande valley. The monetary value of the real estate is of primary importance to those who think in financial terms. That's not the kind of value that's important to me.

Originally published in *Albuquerque Journal* (3 January 1988): B3.

I am concerned about the value of the land in a historical sense. What did the land grant mean to the original Anayas who helped found la Merced de Atrisco? My parents told stories of my ancestors, Eugenio and Andres Anaya, who were involved in the original land-grant petition. They were men who came to settle the Río Grande long ago, to farm and raise their families.

They were Hispano settlers, Mexicanos with a long history in this river valley. They had a vision: to raise their families in peace with their neighbors, to be good people, and to care for the land which provided their sustenance.

They wrote part of their vision into their petition for the land grant. The land would be held in perpetuity. It would be held forever into the future so that their children and their children's children would always have a home. A place of belonging.

Those men and women took care to pass their cultural ways and traditions on to their children. They provided us with the most important gift, the gift of historical continuity. For all time we were to know what land we came from and what it means to us.

I am a native son of those farming families that settled along the river. They inspired honor, dignity, and respect because they honored the land.

Now some members of the board of directors of Westland Corporation want to sell the land. I feel a bitter anger when I hear this. How can anyone contemplate selling our culture and our history on Wall Street?

The old land grants of New Mexico, including the Atrisco Land Grant, were established for the good of the community, for the good of the settlers who would work the land. The land did not belong to a particular group of individuals. In fact, the land did not "belong" to anyone in the way we think of today when we own a title to a piece of land.

The land belonged to the community, it was cared for, it was the mother earth which nurtured us. It provided firewood, grass, and water for grazing animals. Over the centuries the people developed a spiritual attachment to the land.

Our community grew and thrived, and the people nourished the concept of la sagrada tierra. The land has its spiritual value because it nourishes us.

Sometime during the mid-nineteenth century, the Anayas moved to the eastern plain of New Mexico into the Pecos River Valley to farm. Places like Anton Chico, Puerto de Luna, Colonias, became new land grants. In 1937, I was born in that area, and my entire childhood was filled with stories of the old Merced de Atrisco. I loved the llano of New Mexico, and I wrote my first novel, *Bless Me, Ultima*, about that region. But our dreams were of returning to the original home of the Anayas.

I learned to revere the idea of the old land grant from my mother. She was a farmer's daughter, and she did everything she could to keep us connected to the land grant. Sometime in the 1940s, the Atrisco Land Grant was subdivided. My father was awarded a couple of lots on the West Mesa.

My mother struggled to keep that inheritance of land, but in the end the lots had to be sold to pay the taxes and debts. My mother regretted the day. I remember bitter arguments between my father and my mother. To her death she blamed him for letting go of the land. How bittersweet is the memory of her words: Hold on to the land.

We should have learned our lesson. If you subdivide the land grant or if you sell it and there is some gain, it will come at a high cost to our history and tradition. But it appears we did not learn a lesson, because now some are proposing to sell what is left of the land grant.

Within the present boundaries of the Atrisco Land Grant are some of the poorest barrios of Albuquerque. People in these South Valley communities need social services, education, medical clinics, day care for children, rest homes for the old. Let us use the fruits of our land to provide care to our community. The greatest leaders of a community are those that provide for progressive social change that helps the people, not those motivated by greed.

Why do I bother to keep my three shares? Because they are a thread to a historical continuity that I feel is important to preserve. If we cut ourselves off from our history and our land, we will lose an anchor to our culture.

The Pueblo Indians of New Mexico, who taught us so much about the land, believe the land is sacred. It is the mother which provides our nourishment. Can anyone imagine the Isleta Pueblo, our neighbors to the south, selling their pueblo land? No, because they know if they did in a few short years their way of life would be erased from the face of the earth.

I now live on the West Mesa, I live on the original lands of the old Merced de Atrisco. I bought the land for my home, it was not given to me. The pull of history has brought most of my family back to the original lands of the old grant. Or maybe we remember the stories of the old people, stories which admonished us to hold on to the land of our ancestors.

The value of my inheritance as represented by my shares means nothing to the stockbrokers of Wall Street. The value of my shares means everything to me. They are a thread I hold to my history. I would not give them up. I will not put my history and culture for sale on Wall Street.

The land will last forever. We must preserve that land which is left, because it is a symbol of our history and tradition, and because it can still be used to help the people.

As a historical footnote, in 2008 the land grant was sold to a developer in spite of courageous attempts to preempt it.

The Writer's Sense of Place

The luceros (those mysterious dancing stars that do their jitterbug before the sun rises) have finished their play, and now dawn is fingering her way over the Sandia Mountain, asking permission for her son to enter and hump the earth, the New Mexico desert-land, the llano, the river valley, and the sacred peaks of the Pueblo Indians. I sit at my typewriter in this mother-of-pearl dawn and muse over your questions. Do I as an artist, a writer, need the feeling of a place to sustain me and my work? The answer must be an emphatic "yes." My roots have always been firmly anchored to the soil of the southwest, and I have always been fiercely proud of this region I share with my people. My roots were planted here four hundred years ago when the Spaniards first came to the southwest, and before that they were nourished by the pre-Columbian thought and cultures of the indigenous people, the Native Americans. So I am very aware of region and place and the history they record. It is the elements and the people of the region which lent me the materials for my first novel, *Bless Me, Ultima*.

It seems to me that when we talk about the nourishment the writer receives from his environment and the extracting that he does as his imagination manipulates that milieu, we must stop taking a defensive position that somehow that literature that addresses itself to the region will lack the universality to sustain it as "true art." (Whatever that is.) This elitist, often academic, position is dangerous because it often drives young writers to an extreme in which they attempt to encompass more in their work than a natural response to their experience and region would dictate, all because they go tilting after universal truths

Originally published in *South Dakota Review* 13, no. 3 (Autumn 1975): 66–67.

that they hope the critic will say does not smack of their region. It is dangerous because they may begin to write to a norm that has nothing to do with the reality of a particular place or people. The manipulation of these national norms by a select group of people sets up a standard which does not necessarily reflect the reality of our varied country and its culturally different peoples. I think we have seen this happen in all the arts.

Of course great writing comes from a personal knowledge of a specific place and people! Literary history is full of genius which has reflected on its own back yard and abstracted out of there all of the universal elements necessary to tell the tales of mankind. I think those who argue against a regional perspective forget this and most often point to poorly done work as examples of the dangers of regionalism. The regional perspective fails only when the materials overpower the writer and he allows them to become more important than the human element behind them. Then writing enters the field of monograph. But to attribute this flaw *a priori* to the regional perspective is a grave error. Every writer attentive to the earth pulse and the human pulse of his place has accessible to him all the symbology, imagery, and archetypes necessary to touch the chords of his people and region on one level and of humanity in a deeper level.

Perhaps we are fortunate in the southwest to have at our disposal not only the land with which we have not yet lost touch, but also the many cultures whose art works are constantly before us. We can begin to feel the throb of the origins of Greek drama when we view the ceremonial Indian dances; we can begin to comprehend the latent power in the archetype by actually touching in the rock faces of our canyons the petroglyphs carved hundreds of years ago; we live daily with the people who own different consciousness and world views, and in the course of interaction we begin to find a way to cut through to the common core; and we have in our backyard the history and traditions of the civilizations of the indigenous Americans, so that the imagination is constantly in touch with the materials needed to reweave the new legends and stories.

I say, let us speak of regional literature and understand that this is not a limiting label but the fresh perspective from whence the writer sees his story. And sense of place or ambience is an important ingredient in literature, and I believe a most important ingredient in living. The task at hand now is to indulge our country in an exchange and sharing of these regional perspectives. I am sure this sharing will enrich us, and perhaps these perspectives will become the coordinates that will more closely plot a national spirit of consciousness.

Thank you for letting me share my thoughts with you during the early hours of this day. I know your project will engender some much needed discussion on this old debate, and that is good.

The Pueblo on the Mesa Revisited

Ladies and gentlemen, honored guests, friends of the University of New Mexico. It is an honor and a joy to be here to participate in this historic convocation.

One hundred years ago, the people of this community had a dream and from that dream rose the University of New Mexico, our pueblo on the mesa. One hundred years ago the university was established on this hill so that higher education would be available to the citizens of this territory.

Many dedicated people have nourished the hopes and plans of the founders since that first building was constructed, and the university has grown and prospered. It has provided an opportunity for an education not only for the citizens of the state and the region, but also has become an institution of higher learning respected around the world.

Today we revisit our pueblo on the mesa to celebrate the centennial of the founding of the university. Let us reflect on the role the university has played in our lives, and also let us plan for the important role the university must play in our challenging and sometimes uncertain future.

I first came up the hill from the barrios of this city to enroll as an undergraduate in 1958. Today I am a professor here. This university offered me the opportunity to develop my innate talents and abilities. The hunger I had for knowledge and ideas expressed in literature led me to become a writer. Today I pass on this knowledge to the young students who will be the writers of the future. I have, in one way or another, shared in almost a third of the university's hundred years.

The nature of a university is to safeguard the knowledge of the past and to explore and create a truer vision of our future. Now, more

Address originally presented to The University of New Mexico Centennial Convocation, Albuquerque, N.Mex. (20 October 1988).

than ever, the university serves as the intellectual and cultural center of our community, a place where new ideas and technologies are tested. In all areas of the humanities, sciences, law, medicine, education, and business, we represent the exemplary institution of higher learning in our region.

As we revisit our pueblo on the mesa during this centennial year, let us remember what this university has given each one of us and what is gives our community. We live in a complex world, and the role of the university is to shape the individuals who must live in and direct that world.

We live in the age of technology, a time of tremendous scientific advancement, but we see a decline in the study of the humanities. Advances in medicine allow us to live longer, yet around us our environment is being ruthlessly abused and illiteracy plagues thousands. The role of the university has never been more important, the role of our scholars never more crucial. We must acknowledge the forces detrimental to our multicultural society and conceive positive solutions for these problems. We must create harmony and reconciliation for our people.

This occasion is momentous. As we revisit our alma mater, it is important that we rededicate ourselves to that which is noble in our humanity. Let our convocation serve as a renewal in each one of us, and let our university be a shining example of a truly humanistic forum within the society.

Our university has before it the challenge of achieving greatness. We must support our teachers and their research, we must be innovative, and we must enter this second century of our university's history with vision and courage. Let us couple ingenuity with truth as we serve our students. Education still remains our hope, and it can be the hope of the dispossessed and the oppressed. We must fulfill the thirst for knowledge in all areas. We must create opportunities for women, minority groups, and the disabled. We must serve those who are changing careers and those who in later years still hunger to continue their education.

We are a center of learning in a unique place, in a unique time. Our cultural groups are a microcosm of the cultural groups of the world. And even as we envision the drastic changes that are coming in the next hundred years, we know that if we are to achieve our highest expectations, we must work together.

From those early beginnings of one building where teachers were trained, the university has grown to many colleges and schools. Hundreds of courses are taught by faculty from all over the world. We will continue to grow, and as we grow let us pledge ourselves to excellence and that which is good and true and just.

Let us walk together in the open space of our malls, past the pond, through our libraries and classrooms and laboratories, and remember the past and think of the future.

Let us resolve to keep the promise alive. Let us resolve that the gift of education which changed our lives at this community of learning shall be passed on to future generations.

The Writer's Landscape
Epiphany in Landscape

The barrio was a welcome place to drive into that afternoon. The summer afternoon air was thick with dust that rose from the feet of children playing and from the workers who trudged down the dusty streets. The dust swirled in clouds behind pachuco-laden cars, and it covered the sweating boys of the barrio who played baseball in the street. The dust settled over the towering elms and the house tops of Barelas, like a veil pulled by the golden fingers of the afternoon sun. . . . Jason listened. . . . Around him children called and ran to meet their fathers; neighbors visited across fences and paused in their small talk to turn and wave. . . . Smiles were in the soft air, and so was the fragrance of roasting chile verde and hot tortillas, supper for the hungry workers. The air was heavy with the damp smell of just-watered gardens, dirty with the bad smell of sewage that drifted up from the sewage plant in South Barelas, and acrid with the salty sweat-smell of the grimy workers from the railroad yard.

This selection from *Heart of Aztlan* illustrates my concern for conveying my sense of place and people to the reader. Although the passage strives to capture an actual barrio scene, it does not limit me or trap me into being only a recorder of an empirical reality. Quite the contrary, my interest in writing is to explore the magic in realism, and in that sense my immediate landscape and my relationship to my region is a point of reference, but a very important point because it is the "taking-off point." It is the place where imagination and the image-laden memory begin

Originally published in *Latin American Literary Review* 5, no. 10 (Spring–Summer 1977): 98–102.

their work. The three forces—place, imagination, and memory—are inextricably wound together in my work.

In speaking about landscape, I would prefer to use the Spanish words "la tierra," simply because it conveys a deeper relationship between me and my place, and it is this kinship to the environment which creates the metaphor and the epiphany available through landscape. On one pole of the metaphor stands man, on the other is the raw, majestic, and awe-inspiring landscape of the Southwest; the epiphany is the natural response to that landscape, a coming together of these two forces. And because I feel a close kinship with my environment, I feel constantly in touch with that epiphany, which opens me up to receive the power in my landscape. I don't believe a person can be born and raised in the Southwest and not be affected by the land. The landscape changes the man, and the man becomes his landscape. My earliest memories were molded by the forces in my landscape: sun, wind, rain, the llano, the river. All of these forces influenced the people who walked across my plane of vision. My vision was limited until I was taught to see the stark beauty that surrounded me. I was fortunate to meet a few, old ancianos who taught me to respond to my landscape and to see and experience the harmony that was inherent between me and my place.

So in *Bless Me, Ultima*, Antonio's eyes have to be opened by Ultima so that he can see for the first time the beauty of the llano and the valley, and he can begin to sense the latent energy in the landscape:

> She took my hand and I felt the power of a whirlwind sweep around me. Her eyes swept the surrounding hills and through them I saw for the first time the wild beauty of our hills and the magic of the green river. My nostrils quivered as I felt the song of the mockingbirds and the drone of the grasshoppers mingle with the pulse of the earth. The four directions of the llano met in me, and the white sun shone on my soul. The granules of sand at my feet and the sun and sky above me seemed to dissolve into one strange, complete being.

Antonio has described his first epiphany. He has opened himself to the power in the earth and he has been transformed, as we are all transformed when we feel the surge of energy that flows through our landscape. Whatever tension exists in the man/place metaphor dissolves in the harmony of the epiphany.

While growing up in Santa Rosa, New Mexico, I spent a great deal of time along the river. I came to know the river very well. A great deal of the time I tramped up and down the valley alone, and in those early formative years I was haunted by the soul of the river—the tremendous energy of the place that I later called the "presence of the river." That presence, which was the same power I felt on the open llano, touched my primal memory and allowed me to intuit the river spirits and the other essential symbols that were to become so important in my writing. It was those times when I surrendered myself to the surge of energy that I felt the potential of the epiphany.

The power of the earth is reflected in its landscape. And each of us defines our relationship to the energy of place according to our particular worldview. Energy flows from the earth, and as one learns how to receive that energy, one also learns how to give of one's energy to dissolve the polarity of metaphor and create the unity of epiphany. In *Heart of Aztlan,* Clemente Chávez seeks the strength that will help him become the leader of his people, and he remembers this energy of the llano:

Suddenly he stopped and remembered that there were certain spots of earth on the wide llano where he had once stood and felt the elation of flying. Yes, the power of the earth surged through him until he felt himself soaring over the landscape. . . . He had gone once to the old sheepherder they called el hombre volador, and he had asked the man if he could explain this strange feeling. The old man had laughed and said that the dark secrets of the earth were only for those who were willing to search to the very core and essence of their being.

And as time is also energy, it fuses the epiphany between man and place. When Clemente has learned how to respond, he can reach out and touch the heart of the earth, and his epiphany is described thusly:

Time stood still, and in that enduring moment he felt the rhythm of the heart of Aztlán beat to the measure of his own heart. Dreams and visions became reality, and reality was but the thin substance of myth and legends. A joyful power coursed from the dark womb-heart of the earth into his soul and, he cried out I AM AZTLÁN!

My heart is the heart of the earth!
I am the earth and I am the blue sky!
I am the water and I am the wind!
I walk in legends told today and turn and recreate the past.
I pause and give the future time to grow.
I am the image, and I am the living man!
I am the dream, I am the waking . . .

The pregnant power of the epiphany is described here. At that moment, time is infused with power. As man and woman at the peak of their love break the shell of solitude that holds them apart and in tension, man and place achieve a similar climax in the realization of this essential metaphor.

But how is this relationship useful to the writer? How does the power of the epiphany translate itself into the writer's task? My sense of place helps to define my center, and that center becomes the point of view from which I observe life. The discovery of place was very important to me, and very crucial to the writing of *Bless Me, Ultima* and *Heart of Aztlan*. My writing before that discovery was busy duplicating false models; it had no local flavor to it, weak characters, little story. So it was very important for me to realize that I didn't need to traverse the world suffering the slings and arrows of outrageous fortune to find the raw materials for my fictions; what I really needed to do was to stand still and discover my sense of place. From memory I recalled the epiphanies, and their power charged my imagination into recreating that universe where the stories could be played out. Now, in that lonely act of writing when I struggle with my craft, I aim to duplicate the power of the epiphany. The relationship I feel with the earth fuses with time and memory and imagination and creates the scenes, characters, images, symbols, and themes that are woven into the story. Sitting quietly behind the typewriter I evoke the epiphanies sleeping in memory, and the flood begins. The writer thrives on energy, and energy is what the epiphany rekindles. Characters awaken and move, they speak, and they bring with them their own landscapes, old impressions, joy and sadness, fortune and misfortune as they come to fill the writer's lonely room and to discuss the task at hand.

So the landscape of the southwest has been very important to me as a writer. Here time, or a sense of timelessness, permeates the earthfeatures, and it is that sense of timelessness that lends the vision to the epiphany. I have already likened both the spiritual and sensual aspects of the epiphany to a deeply shared human love. It is our ability to love and to make human connections that is necessary to our well being, and it is that feeling of strong love that envelops the epiphany. And just as the natural end of all art is to make us well and to cure our souls, so is our relationship to the earth and its power. I do not merely mean the awe and sense of good feeling that we experience in the face of grandeur and beauty in nature, I mean that there is an actual healing power which the epiphany of place provides. In *Heart of Aztlan*, Adelita, Clemente's wife, suggests this:

> "You see," she spoke earnestly to her daughters, "once there would have been the land to make him whole again. A man who met defeat could go out on the land, and the earth would make him well again. It might take weeks, or months, or years, but always the man who looked found himself in his earth and he was well again. . . . Well, things have changed, and your father, he is a man lost in a foreign land—"

These characters who have become separated from their land and sense of place become frustrated, alienated human beings. They lose their center, and most devastating, they lose their source of redemption. Does this separation also bode ill for the writer? Is the writer separated from his sense of place further estranged from the redemption in the epiphany? And if so, what is the vision of the world which he presents to guide us through our fragmented, often frightening, modern reality?

Memory has been a constant companion in my writing, and I found that it was the haunting beauty of those early epiphanies I learned to recall that triggered the latent images in memory. Some of the characters of memory were characters composed of river mud and water. Those that came from the llano were as restless as llano wind. I peered closely into their souls and discovered that they not only reflected their landscape but that they *were* my sense of place! The raw sensual beauty of my encounters with the presence of the river and the llano and the wind and rain and sun had become a part of me! All those times of haunting beauty and poignant sadness were stored in memory, and they could be aroused to energize and support the creative act! In my writing I became intensely aware of the process by which the landscape and its epiphanies had become incorporated into memory and how the same energy and emotion present at the actual epiphany could be used in writing! I felt I had found a natural reservoir that was as deep as I cared to explore.

Obviously this explains only a small part of the creative process that occurs in writing. The sources of energy that drain into the mental and emotional act of writing are bound up in other areas of this complex act. The characters themselves create their own energy and often clamor to write their own stories. The private writing place becomes a madhouse, and the writer a mere guide as to the course of the characters' lives.

The landscape can always expand. At this point in time I can choose whether or not to expand my landscape. In many ways I already have, but I find that which is honest to me and therefore to my writing comes from my deepest felt experiences, so I choose to stay at the center of the place which is providing me energy and whose energy is healing me, because the exploration into my world is a process through which I come to know myself and my earth better. For the moment, I am content to continue this exploration and to convey to my reader the center of my universe. It is our task as writers to convey our landscape to our readers and to work through the harmony of this essential metaphor. When the writer's sense of place and his sense of the landscape permeate his craft, then the reader will respond, and that response is the beginning of a new epiphany.

The Spirit of the Petroglyphs

One role of literature is to describe the importance of one's region to others. We know the Mississippi River through Mark Twain's novels, the eastern whaling culture by reading *Moby Dick*, the nature of our Southwest region and its natives by reading writers such as Frank Waters. Writers know that the environment shapes the people, but people also shape the environment.

At the close of the twentieth century we know too well how much we have changed the contours of the earth. Great forests have been decimated, the Amazon rain forest is going up in smoke, more and more of our water is polluted. Population growth and the ecology are issues we must face realistically.

World governments face this issue, but so do smaller eco-regions, communities whose character is shaped by the environment. In Alburquerque, New Mexico, our character is shaped by the Río Grande valley, the Sandia Mountains, the blue sky, and the petroglyphs of the West Mesa. We are struggling to preserve these environmental zones, because we know as we preserve them we safeguard the character of the place in which we live.

These environmental zones represent a special place we need and respect. We know that if we don't preserve these areas, their erosion will reflect negatively on our lives. Each area is deeply rooted in our lives. We have faith the river will always flow and its water irrigate our fields. We have faith the mountain will always be there, and the blue sky will provide the air we breathe and vistas for the body and spirit. The presence of nature informs our well being and provides a sense of harmony.

Originally published in *Voices from a Sacred Place: In Defense of Petroglyph National Monument*, ed. Verne Huser (March 1998), 11–13.

Creating the Petroglyph National Monument, like preserving the Río Grande bosque (forest) and limiting home building on the slope of the Sandias, was a social commitment we made to this environment. But it represents more than a social issue, it represents a deep belief we have in the importance of the environment in our lives.

In the case of the petroglyph area, the preservation of the site reminds us that history reveals layers of meaning. It is crucial to remember that long before Europeans came to this land the Native Americans of the region visited the area of these extinct volcanoes to conduct ceremonies of a very spiritual nature. The site acquired a sacred nature long before it was given monument status and, therefore, government protection.

It is difficult to convey to some people this idea of the divine in nature. And yet the religions and mythologies of the world are full of allusions to the divine nature of certain places. Greek mythology is full of references to sacred springs, mountain peaks, islands, or ocean coves. In our hurry to conquer the earth and bend its resources to our will, we have even forgotten the role nature plays in the spiritual affairs of humans. Even though we claim Greek mythology as part of the mythos of western civilization, when it comes to nature modern and postmodern societies have separated the sacred from the profane.

Here in the western United States we have already trampled much of the land. We refuse to acknowledge the sacred in the rivers, mountains, and desert. We refuse to accept the Native American view of the land and the one value the different tribes held in common: they treated the earth as mother. The earth's features were revered.

If we do not acknowledge this view, then we can go on devastating the earth. We tell ourselves we don't need regulations when we develop cities in the desert. We place our faith in progress, and we do not feel responsible for its consequences. If we need to cut a road through the petrogylphs, we say it is for progress, for more development, for faster traffic. We will find every excuse we can, as long as we do not have to accept the idea that the land is sacred.

I am proud of the efforts so many community people and government officials have made to preserve the Alburquerque environment. But more needs to be done, because the valley continues to attract people. We are growing, and our population has needs. Those needs have to be balanced with the efforts to safeguard our natural resources and the aesthetics of the place.

To preserve the spirit of our place we need to know the history of the place and people. We need to understand that for some of us the land holds this special sacred character. We need to preserve those shrines we set aside, shrines we now call national monuments, as the ancient Greeks preserved and revered their natural shrines. Our spirits expand when we view the natural beauty that surrounds us. We need to understand that as we demean the earth, we demean ourselves.

Perhaps we need to walk on the land itself, and let it fill us with its strength. The spirit of the place will whisper to us, and we will respond with acts of kindness, acts of preservation. Development and progress have their place in our community, but not at the expense of that which cannot be replaced. I am confident that once the intrinsic, spiritual value of our landscape is understood, the Petroglyph National Monument will be preserved in its entirety.

The Spirit of Place

The works of the writers collected between the covers of this book reflect diverse styles and content. The Southwest has always been a richly textured land when it comes to ethnic backgrounds, and yet few anthologies of the past have reflected this reality. This book, and the radio series on which it is based, is innovative in giving voice to the various communities of the region.

The writers included here infuse their stories with their own distinctive backgrounds. We write in English, yet our personal and cultural language is reflected in our stories. Here you will find the spirit of Navajo and Acoma chants, the homespun Spanish of the Nuevo Mexicano villages, the beat of African American street talk, and the voices of the older, established Anglo writers, and the newcomers. Collectively they reflect the reality of "el norte," the present-day southwest United States.

I once wrote that the true literature of this country would not be known until all the communities that comprise the nation are acknowledged. I feel the same way about the literature of this region. We, the writers, represent various and distinct communities. We are a border people, half in love with Mexico and half suspicious, half in love with the United States and half wondering if we belong. We live in a great space, separated by great mountains, harsh deserts, and the Río Grande. This book and the radio program that was the genesis of this collection help span those distances.

What do we mean by writing the Southwest? Are we describing surface or soul when we say a Southwest sensibility is reflected in our literature? For me, writing the Southwest means that the writers in this

Originally published as the foreword to *Writing the Southwest*, by David King Dunaway and Sara L. Spurgeon (New York: Plume, 1995), ix–xvi.

book have a special attachment to the people and the land of the region. I'd like to offer some ideas on that attachment.

Reflecting one's sense of place in one's stories has at times been construed as regionalism. Critics often take it upon themselves to decide for us what constitutes universal literature, and they have decided that allowing the sense of place to be an essential part of the story lessens it. I take the opposite view. By sense of place I mean the "spirit of the place," and I know that sensitive writers respond to that spirit as they write their stories. So for me the spirit of the place is an integral part of the story.

Writers from all regions have allowed the spirit of the place to permeate their works. When I sit down to read a southern writer, I understand I will encounter a set of historical, cultural, and language traditions that I *know* are the materials of the southern writer. Thus, the literature of each region reflects a tradition. That tradition is the spirit, the mythopoeia, of the place and its people. Each new generation of writers struggles to create a new way of telling the story of the people and the place, a new voice that will capture the time. But these new voices still continue to reflect the writer's deep sense of tradition.

Writers do have "a room of their own," meaning that the writer's place is the center of the universe for the writer. We in the Southwest know that every area is inhabited by the spirits of the place, so the story cannot be separated from the *spiritus loci*. The language, style, concerns, and perspectives are uniquely the writer's; and each story will add to the body of work from the region, but each work will also be guided by the spirit of the place, the soul of the community and the land.

A story from the prairie states should present the reader with the essence of the place and people. The writer fails us when the story *isn't* suffused with the spirit of the place. To read a story from New Mexico and one from Iowa and feel that either story could have taken place in either locale defeats the story. Even the most abstract and existential story has an essence of location, because writing must reflect the soul of the place. Even the story most separated from its *spiritus loci* reflects the essence of the place. The spirit of the place guides us, and we cannot help but honor it in our stories.

The spirit of the place precedes us, because the earth did not come to us, we came to the earth. The consciousness of the universe is infused in the earth, and we have come to learn from it. I think this is true for all regions of the earth.

Cities also have a sense of place, a spirit of the turf. I feel the spirit of people and place when I read the black, white, Jewish, and Nuyorican writers from New York. The traditions of the writer, the collective memory of the place help spark the writer's creativity. Writers infuse their stories with their language, tradition, food, music, tempo, and individual styles; they are driven by the spirit as they add to the communal history. Stories establish a tradition, even as they rework the materials of the past to create a new, contemporary voice. Stories are links in historical continuity.

Literary history grows in increments, and each region of this country plays a role in defining the literary inheritance. The specific history and persistence of spirit in each community dictate that there can be no one national epic. There are critics who hold up *Moby Dick* as the American novel that best describes us, and yet, from where I sit, *Moby Dick* is a regional novel. Its spirit is of New England, the ocean, and whaling as a way of life. It represents a worldview quite foreign to me, and quite foreign to the regions west of the Hudson River. This does not lessen its importance; the human struggle and conflict within the novel touch me. The novel captures not only the turmoil of its characters, it reveals the spirits of the place. Those same spirits lend their power to the overall essence of the work.

The argument that a regional novel cannot address universal human emotions is a specious argument. *Moby Dick* may be a regional novel, but its portrayal of the human condition is universal. Writing from a sense of place does not limit the exploration of universal human emotions that will resonate with readers. In fact, this is the challenge to the writer, to write from a sense of place and explore the human condition so deeply and profoundly that the work can touch the heart of any reader.

Sense of place does not merely mean that a writer uses the landscape of the place as background. It means that the spirit of the place affects and influences the characters by shaping their consciousness. We are all the products of our place and community, and while we may expand our horizons in any given lifetime and write about many places, we still reflect in our stories the *spiritus loci* that shaped our imagination. It is that shaping of the creative imagination that is the power of the place.

The mythos of a group is shaped by the place it occupies. The longer a particular group lives in a place, the more deeply attached the group is to that place. Elsewhere I have written that the very gods of the place rise from the features of the landscape. The deities of our place inhabit the earth, and our imagination resonates to their creative powers. The sensibility of the living force of the earth is ingrained in our psyche.

We see the process at work in Greek mythology. The ancient Greek gods rose from the mountains, oceans, storms, springs, and rivers; the god or goddess became the spirit of the place. As humans we are heir to the deities that rise from and walk in our region; those gods are the muses that influence the writer's creativity. The writer responds to the spirit of the place, and thus links the past to the present.

Historical continuity is a reality that anchors us. The human psyche needs this anchoring in the face of evolution. We change and grow and must adopt new archetypes to our original storehouse of symbols. That storehouse of images is necessary for coping with and interpreting the constant changes of evolution. Those primal images are our connection to human history, hieroglyphs of the spirit which help us transcend our daily life and feel connected to a purpose in the universe. The *spiritus loci*, therefore, is an evolutionary gift. The spirits of the place help us interpret the way; the spirits not only feed our creativity, they help us see our connection to the totality of life, and thus help keep us in harmony.

Our stories reflect on this mystery, and so there is a spiritual intent in the creating of a story, no matter how gross the subject matter. We are more than the scattered parts our stories portray; the intent of the story is to create meaning, to reflect a center. Writing is our communication with that spirit, a prayer asking that our community be spared the violence and evil that gravitate toward the sacred.

Throughout our time on earth, nature's forces have been harsh and chaotic. Violent storms, earthquakes, ghosts in the bush, the fear of night, and wildfires have plagued us. Our personal nature reflects the violence and evil abroad, and yet the spirits of the place remind us there are original archetypes of order and harmony. Spiritual evolution takes place in each new generation, and we reflect that in the stories we tell. Writing reflects that evolution, so we become what we compose. By writing stories we give order to the place we call home.

In today's often violent and cruel world, we need to probe the depths of our personal and communal souls, find some internal sense of harmony, and make it part of the vital energy of our stories. This is a responsibility handed down to us by the old storytellers who knew and communicated with the spirits of their place.

For me, a touchstone of good writing is that which transports me into the life of the characters. To be moved into the realm of the characters of the story means to feel the place, the food, music, language, and history of the characters' surroundings. Taken a step further, the power of literature is to transport the reader into the very core of the mythic and poetic world of the story.

Is the spirit of the place available to every writer? I am asked. If writers are the dream catchers, the story catchers of the place, and if writers are the sensitive shamans of the community, then they should be able to feel the pulse of the place and communicate it in story. Thus, writers who are newcomers to the Southwest can convey the sense of place as they are moved by the spirit. This collection includes some of those newcomers whose antennas respond to the region and its people and who are able to express the soul of the region.

Still, the gods of the place do not reveal themselves overnight. Evolution in a place marks the soul and the psyche of a group—that is, the spirit of the place leaves its imprint over generations. The myths of a community that have to do with the "coming into being" are the first stories of the group, and thus the earliest stories and traditions of the Southwest region belong to the Native American communities, those who first settled the region. Here covenants with the gods were formed; here ancestral voices still speak to us from across the span of time; here the landscape is still inhabited by spirits.

Myths, those stories that tell of our coming into being and learning to deal with our humanness, are powerful forces that shape the communal psyche. The myths of this region are the bedrock of belief, identity, tradition, and other cultural nuances of the first communal groups of the Southwest. The mythic stories feed not only our creativity, they also tell us that if we are to survive on this land we must listen to the stories of the place.

One theme explored in southwestern literature is the conflict we have created with the fragile earth of the region. The Southwest is an arid region; desert and formidable high mountains dominate. There is little arable land. As new groups enter the region, the amount of land each group can occupy becomes smaller. Cultural sharing and adopting used to occur; now we see more displacement taking place. Widespread development is shrinking the land base and the water available. This reality is an emergent theme in our literature.

The first Native American groups to inhabit the land were communal groups. Language and spiritual sensitivity kept them together, and kept them evolving stories from the first myths. The newer migrations into the Southwest brought not only different languages and religions, but a rugged individualism which stood in opposition to the communal spirit.

A second important theme in our literature segues from the first. Can the mythic individual of the Old West learn to survive in the communal circle, or will his needs destroy the spirit of the place that drew him there in the first place?

The newer arrivals to the Southwest must learn that to survive, the community must share land and water. The land, climate, and the indigenous people have taught the newcomers this simple lesson. We sense the reverence in the farming ways, in communal survival, and in the stories.

We are beginning to realize that the earth is a fragile planet. We call her Mother Earth. We say we are riding spaceship earth, and we have to take care of the ship. We call the earth Gaia, a living organism, and develop theories of the interrelationship of all things. But abstract statements like this don't move people to mend their ways. They don't mobilize people to act. Very few of us are actually working to save the Amazon rain forest, or the whales, or the ozone layer, or the Northwest forests. We go right on destroying regions for their resources. Our obsession with development is destroying the earth.

As the bumper sticker suggests, perhaps we need to think globally and act locally. The psyche is tuned to its intimate sense of place. From the intimate and regional, we can make universal statements. The desert we destroy here today will create droughts in Africa; the water we use from the aquifer will spell disaster in the Amazon.

One service the writers who are writing the Southwest are performing is alerting the people to the destruction of the place, their homes. The new information age is carrying our stories around the earth, and we also read stories from distant places. The communication creates a bond. The creative power of our spirits moves from our region to envelop the earth.

The literature of the Southwest forms part of the literary history of the United States. That it has not been included in the canon of literary history does not lessen its importance. Generation upon generation of natives from this region told stories around campfires, while hunting, at play, while building shelters, having babies, and otherwise carrying on the work of family and community. Generation upon generation passed down the stories of origin, the gods, the proper ceremonies and ritual, the relationship of the people to the spirit world. This is what the most profound meaning of sense of place describes: our relationship to the spirit of the earth.

Yet we do not really know our Native American inheritance. There are writers who are recording and building on the indigenous oral tradition and making it known. From their works we learn that we have not only destroyed each other, we have destroyed stories. The stories that carried the history and soul of the people were destroyed. Until we acknowledge the genocide of people and their stories, we cannot make peace with ourselves. This is what the new writers of the Southwest are doing. Making peace with our neighbors, making peace with the spirit of the place.

We must acknowledge the history and traditions that came before us. We must celebrate all of those stories of the ancestors, even as we celebrate each new poem or story told today.

There is a vigorous sense of experimentation going on in the style and language in the region. We are a multicultural, multilingual region. Here native languages mix with the high-tech languages of science. The language of the people of the villages, *los vecinos*, mixes with New Age lingo. The old dances for rain and harvest, prayer to the *santos* and the *kachinas* mix with the boom of the latest musical fashion. If we learn to listen to each other, maybe the country will learn to listen to its various communities.

Change is constant, and yet, beneath the flux, the old values resonate. Writers listen to the people and the place for inspiration. That listening is the catching of dreams, the catching of stories. The voices are the spirit, the ancestors, the hum of the earth itself. The writer who is in tune with those voices is truly blessed. The spirit has come to move the story. Writing is a participation and sharing in the place and the people. The writers in this book have listened. Now we invite you to listen as they share their stories of joy and tragedy, stories inspired by love and the spirit of the place.

Why I Love Tourists
Confessions of a Dharma Bum

I was born on the eastern llano of New Mexico—at just the right moment, so my mother said—a tourist from the great beyond. Just another guest on earth looking for his dharma nature. I discovered the core of my nature in the people of my region. But we also discover elements of our essential nature by traveling to other places, by meeting other people. To tour is to move beyond one's circle. So we're all tourists on earth, we go from here to there if only to just have a look.

But tourists and natives often clash, perhaps because the tourist cannot love the place as much as the native. We learn to love the land that nurtures us. We, the natives, become possessive about "our place." Westerners especially feel a great love toward this land that stretches north and south along the spine of the Rocky Mountains. I believe this sense of possessiveness about "our land" means we, the denizens of the West, are turning inward. We now truly understand that there's nowhere else to go, so we had better take care of what's left.

The open spaces of the West once allowed for great mobility, and so the nature of those who came here was more ample, more extroverted. Today the real and the mythic frontier have disappeared, so we seem to be growing more introverted. Maybe we just want to be left alone.

Change and the progress of technology are bothering us. Next to Alburquerque where I live, a city has been built around the Intel Corporation; the subdivisions spread across sand hills where once only coyotes and jackrabbits roamed. Along the Río Grande valley, subdivisions cover farming land. We know what overdevelopment of the land can do. We know we're running out of water, out of space, out of clean air to breathe.

Not previously published.

Westerners seem bound by one desire: to keep the land the way it was. Now the mega-cities are crowding us in. More and more people seem to be touring our turf. Are all those tourists looking for a place to settle? That's what bothers us. There are just too many tourists discovering and rediscovering the West. The tourist has become the "Other" to the westerner. I hear my New Mexican paisanos say: "Take their money, but let them go back where they came from. Please don't let them settle here."

Tourism is a very important segment of the western economy. Tourists bring bucks to grease Las Vegas, Disneyland, LA, Seattle, and San Francisco, bucks to oceanside resorts and Rocky Mountain ski slopes, bucks for boating and hunting and fishing. Tourism has become the West's clean industry. But deep inside we, the natives, know it's got its inherent problems.

Tourism affects our lives, we believe, because it affects not only the topography; it also affects the sacred. We believe there is a spirit in the land; we know we cannot trample the flesh of the earth and not affect its soul. Earth and spirit of the place go hand in hand. The transcendent has blessed this land, and we don't want it ruined, we don't want it destroyed. We have a covenant with the land, we have become the keepers of the land. No wonder so many dharma bums—those looking for their essential relationship to the earth—have crossed the West's rugged terrain looking for a home—not just a home with a majestic view, but a home rooted to a landscape that allows the true nature of the person to develop.

We have all been tourists at one time or another. We have traveled to distant places to entertain and rest the body and also to enlighten the spirit. The two are intertwined. We go looking for that revelation on the face of the Earth that speaks to the soul.

There are sensitive tourists, dharma bums who care about illuminating their nature and who appreciate the region and people they experience on their journey. There are some who respect the place and allow themselves to be changed by the people and region they visit. They return from the journey fulfilled, more aware of other cultures.

Then there are those who breeze through the place, accepting nothing of the local culture, learning little, complaining constantly, and leaving in their wake a kind of displacement. The natives take their money and are thankful when they're gone. Those travelers return home to complain about the food, the natives, and about the different lifestyles they encountered. They should never have left home. They did not travel to illuminate the spirit.

The land draws tourists to the West. They come to see the majestic mountains, arid deserts, the Pacific Ocean. Some come to experience our diverse cultural groups. Others come only to visit the cultural artifacts of the West: Las Vegas, Disneyland, LA, Silicon Valley, Hoover Dam. Those who experience only the artifacts miss the spirit we natives find imbued in the landscape. Those who deal *only* in artifacts miss the history and culture of the West's traditional communities. And so tourists also symbolize that tension between tradition and change, a change that in some places carries the weight of impending doom.

Have the traditionalists grown tired of sharing the spirit of the West? Are we tired of those who come and trample our sacred land? And is the West really one unified region? When we speak of tourism are we only talking about people visiting here from outside the West, or do we also speak of internal tourism? From Montana to New Mexico, we hear complaints about tourists from outside the region. In New Mexico, for example, we also complain about the Texans as tourists. Today I hear complaints about the nouveau riche Californians. Even Oregonians shrink from California tourists. "Please don't let them settle here," they whisper to each other.

The West was never one homogeneous region; it is not only the land of the pioneers and the cowboy of the western movies. The West is a grouping of micro-regions and cultural groups. Even the grandeur of the Rocky Mountains can't unify us, because there are too many different landscapes in the West, too many different indigenous histories. My home, the northern Río Grande, is such a micro-region, with its unique history and people. It is—and here I show my indigenous bias—one of the most interesting multicultural areas of the West.

The Spanish/Mexicano side of my ancestors were tourists who journeyed to this region in the late sixteenth century. Imagine the Pueblo Indians seeing the Spanish colonists coming up the Río Grande in 1598. I'm sure they shook their heads and said, "There goes the neighborhood." In many ways *it did go!* If anyone has suffered from tourists, it is the Native American communities.

But the tourists kept coming into the land of the pueblos. The first entradas were from south to north as Spanish speakers expanded north. In the nineteenth century the east-to-west migrations began. In a scene from my novel *Shaman Winter*, I describe Kearny marching into New

Mexico with the Army of the West in 1846. The Mexicanos in the crowd yell, "Why don't you go back where you came from!" "Go home, gringos!" "Hope they keep going right on to California." "We ought to pass a Spanish Only law if they stay."

Of course those "tourists" didn't go home. And they changed the West forever. Each group introduced a new overlay of culture. Each brought a new set of stories, their own history and mythology, to the West. Now the balance of what the land can hold has reached a critical point. Maybe we're uncertain about tourists because they represent the unknown. If the tourist decides to return to settle—and history teaches us that's the pattern—each one is a potential threat to the land; each one represents one more house to be built, more desert to be plowed up, more water to be consumed. They represent development in a fragile land already overdeveloped.

It's not just the growth in numbers we fear. We are convinced that outsiders know nothing of the nature of our relationship to the earth. This relationship defines our nature. I feel connected to la tierra de Nuevo México. This earth is all I know, it nourishes my soul, my humanity. The gods live in the earth, the sky, the clouds.

Growing up in eastern New Mexico, I felt the llano speak to me. The llano as brother, father, mother. Constant breezes caressed me, sang to me, whispered legends, stirred my memory. The Pecos River engulfed me with its bosque of alamos, river willows, Russian olives, thick brush. It sang a song of memory as it flowed south to empty into the Río Grande, from there into the Gulf of Mexico. Truly, time and the river sang in my heart.

This early attachment and sensibility to the land became love—love for the place and the people. The people molded me. The Hispano/Mexicanos of the llano were cattlemen and sheepmen who taught me a way of relating to the earth. The farmers from the Pecos River Valley initiated me into another relationship with nature: they planted my roots in that earth as they planted seeds. I saw the people struggle to make a living; I heard the stories they told. History and traditions were passed down, and everything related to the place and the people. Some of the teaching was unspoken; it was there in the silence of the llano, the faces of the people.

People told stories, joys and tragedies carried in the breezes. So I, too, became a storyteller. Listening to the people's story and then retelling the story relates one to the place. Will tourists who visit our land pause long enough to listen to our stories? The bones buried in the earth tell the story. Who will listen?

This spiritual connection to the land seems to describe the westerner. Even in the harshest weather and the longest drought, we stand in awe of the earth. Awe describes our relationship to the land. Perhaps tourists are simply people who don't stand still long enough to feel the immediacy of awe. They don't understand the intimacy of relationships woven into the people of the land.

As a child I felt this awe on the llano, along the river, on those hills which shaped my childhood. So the earth for me has a particular feel—it is the New Mexican landscape, the llano and Pecos River of childhood, the Río Grande and Sangre de Cristo Mountains of my later life, the desert which is always at the edge.

Still, we must be kind to tourists. It's part of our heritage to be kind to strangers. And we have all been tourists at one time or another. I, too, have been a tourist, a seeker who wanted to explore beyond the limits of my immediate environment.

One description of the Anglo-American culture has been its mobility. Anglo-Americans, we are told, are a restless lot. They couldn't just stay over there in the thirteen colonies; no, they had to go west. They love to quote the oft-repeated "Go west, young man, go west." So much a part of the history and mythology of this country is known from that western movement. Land—they smelled land, and gold and beaver pelts and gas and oil, all of which drew them west. So, Anglos are natural born tourists. Now they've even been to the moon. Maybe some people just take to touring better than others. Or perhaps there are times when mass migrations take place; need and adventure move entire populations.

The Indo-Hispanos of New Mexico have ancient roots in the land. Our European ancestors settled in the Hispano homeland along the northern Río Grande in 1598. Remember those Españoles coming up the Río Grande? They took to the land, became as indigenous and settled as their vecinos in the pueblos. Now wars, adventure, and extreme economic necessity have taken them beyond the homeland's frontier.

In this region Hispanics also claim tourist heroes. Cabeza de Vaca comes to mind. Shipwrecked on the coast of Texas, he set out on an odyssey that lasted seven or eight years. He is the Odysseus of the Southwest. Never mind that he was lost. Perhaps to be "lost" as a tourist is essential. Only thus can you enter fully into the place and the people. He was the first European tourist in Texas. Can you imagine the awe he experienced?

And he turned out to be a typical tourist. He went back to Mexico and spread the word. "Texas was great," Cabeza de Vaca told the Viceroy in Mexico City. "The streets are paved with gold. There are pueblos four or five stories high. And a strange animal called a buffalo roams the plains by the millions."

Other Spanish explorers quickly followed Cabeza de Vaca. Coronado came north. A tourist looking for gold and the fabled cities of Cibola. He found only Indian Pueblos, the original natives living in houses made of adobes. Accommodations in Native America weren't the best in the sixteenth century, so the Spanish tourists returned home, discouraged they hadn't found cities with streets paved with gold.

But the Spaniards were consummate note takers. They mapped the land, described it and the natives, and they sent letters to their neighbors back in Mexico. "You've got to see this place. La Nueva México is virgin land. Very little traffic, and the native arts and crafts are out of this world. I brought a clay pot for dos reales. I can sell it in Spain for twice that. In a few years the place will be spoiled. Come see it before it's gone."

Gone? That's what we fear. What if the spirit that attracted us here in the first place leaves?

Tourists do spoil things. The minute tourists discover a new place, they also bring their garbage with them. Some set up businesses to ship the clay pots back home, organizing the natives in ways the natives never wanted to be organized. Tourism leads to strange kinds of enterprises, some good, some not very humanistic.

But I didn't learn about tourism in the West by reading the Spanish explorer's notes. In my childhood we weren't taught the history of our land as it occurred from the colonizations that came to el norte from the south. We were only taught the history of the pioneers, the western movement. How many times did little Chicanitos in school have to sing "Oh My Darling, Clementine"?

The first tourists I encountered were in Santa Rosa, New Mexico, my hometown. On Route 66, right after World War II. It was the best of times; it was the worst of times. People were moving west, tourists in search of California. I remember one particular afternoon at a gas station where we went to fill our bike tires after goathead punctures. A car stopped. Dad, mom, son, and daughter. Blonde, blue-eyed gringos from the east. They usually didn't pay attention to the brown Mexicanitos gathered at the gas station. But this Ozzie and Harriet Nelson family did. They talked briefly to me.

"Where you from?" Ozzie asked.

"Here," I said.

"Just here?" he said, looking around.

"Yes." I had never considered anyplace other than just here. Here was home.

He wasn't too interested. "Oh," he said and went off to kick his car's tires.

"Where are *you* from?" I asked Harriet.

"Back east."

"Where are you going?" I asked.

"We're tourists," she answered. "We're going to California."

Heading west on Route 66, into the setting sun.

Imagine, I thought to myself. A family can travel to California as tourists. Just to go look. Look at what? The Pacific Ocean. I knew it from the maps at school.

I knew then I wanted to be a tourist.

I ran home and told my mother. "Mamá, I want to be a tourist."

Her mouth dropped. She stopped rolling tortillas and made the sign of the cross over me. "Where did you get that idea?"

I told her about the family I had just met.

"No, mijito," she said. "Only the Americanos can be tourists. Now go help Ultima with her herbs and get those crazy ideas out of your mind."

I went away saddened. Why was it a crazy idea to be a tourist? Was my mother telling me to beware of tourists?

"Why is it only the Americanos get to be tourists?" I asked Ultima. She knew the answer to almost any question that had to do with healing and sickness of the soul, but I could see that tourists puzzled her.

"They have cameras; they take pictures," she finally answered.

"What's wrong with that?"

"The spirit of who we are cannot be captured in the picture," she said. "When you go to a different place you can know it by taking a picture, or you can let the place seep into your blood. A real turista is one who allows the spirit of that place to enter."

She looked across the hills of the llano, then turned her gaze to the river. "The river is like a turista. The water moves, but yet the river remains constant. So to travel also means to go within. This place, or any place, can change you. You discover pieces of yourself when you go beyond your boundaries. Or you can stay in one place and learn the true nature of your soul."

I knew Ultima had never been a tourist. She only knew the few villages around Santa Rosa. But she was far wiser than anyone I knew. She had traveled within, and so she knew herself. She knew the land and its people.

Still I questioned her. "My tío Benito and his family are tourists, aren't they? They're always going to Colorado or Texas."

Again she shook her head. "They go to work in the beetfields of Colorado and to pick cotton in Texas. Poor people who go to work aren't turistas."

So, tourists didn't go to work. They just went to look, and maybe take pictures. What a life. I knew I *really* wanted to be a tourist.

"Who knows," Ultima said, "maybe someday you will travel beyond this river valley. You may even go to China."

China, I thought. On the round world globe at school it was directly across from Santa Rosa. One day I dug a hole in the schoolyard. "You better watch out, Rudy," the girls warned me. "You could fall through to China." They ran away laughing.

For a class project, I wrote away to cruise lines and did a report on cruise ships. They circled the globe. They went to Greece. Spain. Italy. They went to the Mediterranean world. "Maybe someday I will take a ship on the Mediterranean," I thought.

For another project, I made a sculpture of clay. The pyramids of Giza and the Sphinx. Set on a plasterboard with sand for the desert and twigs for palm trees. It was real to me. I got an *A*.

"What do you want to be when you grow up?" the teacher asked.

"I want to be a tourist," I said.

"Esta loco," the kids whispered.

Yes, to dream of travel in that time and place was to be a little crazy. I settled for books to bring distant places to me.

But I did go to China. In 1984, my wife and I and a small group of colleagues traveled through China. I saw wonders my ancestors of the Pecos River could only imagine. Beijing, Xian, the Yangtze River, the Great Wall. I got so much into the place and the people that at one point I felt transformed into a Chinese man. That's the kind of transformation the sensitive tourist looks for, becoming one with the place and people. If only for a short while. I have never written travel journals, but I did write one about China: *A Chicano in China*.

The memory of who I am stretches beyond the here and now. It resides in the archetypes, a biologic stream that is a strand into the past, to distant places and people. We sense the truth of images in stories and myths. And so we set out to test the memory. Was I related to China and its people? Was the Chinese dragon the Quetzalcóatl of the Aztecs? Was the god of nature, the golden carp I described in *Bless Me, Ultima,* related to the golden carp that thrive in Chinese lakes? Was the bronze turtle resting at temple entrances related to the boy called Tortuga in my novel by that name?

We travel to seek connections. What are the tourists who come west seeking? Is our job to take their money and be done with them, or should we educate them? Should they read our books and history before applying for visas to our sacred land?

Later in life I did cruise on the Mediterranean, from the Greek Isles through the Bosporus into magical Constantinople. From Spain—where I practiced my New Mexican Spanish in many a tapas bar—to Italy, down to Israel and into Egypt. Cruising the Nile, like a lowrider on Saturday night, I was transported into a past so deep and meaningful, I became Egyptian. I cut my hair like an Egyptian, wore the long robe, prayed at the temples, and entered into the worship. A tourist must also be a pilgrim.

I didn't participate in any revolutions like Lawrence of Arabia. I was a tourist. I knew my role and my limits. But even as tourists we can enter the history of the place. I would go back to the Nile at the drop of a tortilla. Now I consider my Río Grande a sister of the Nile. Long ago, Mediterranean people, my ancestors, came to the Río Grande, bringing their dreams. I am part of that dream that infused the land. I am part of all the dreams that have settled here.

How do we teach these connections to tourists who visit our Río Grande, or the Colorado River, or the Columbia? There are relationships of rivers. Those from the east bring knowledge of their Mississippi, their Ohio, their Hudson. They bring a knowledge of their place and history. How we connect to each other may show us how we can save the West, and save the world.

Still we fear that tourism has become just one more consumer item on the supermarket shelf. Tourists who come only to consume and don't connect their history to ours leave us empty.

Is there an answer to this topic of tourism in the West? The issue is complex. My tío Benito and his family who went as workers to Texas and Colorado weren't considered tourists, and yet they gave their work and sweat to the land. But they remained invisible. They worked the earth of the West, like prior groups have worked the western land, but they remained invisible.

The Mexicano workers who right now are constructing the history of the West through their work in the fields are not considered tourists. And yet they are lending their language, their music, and their food to enrich our region. The Pacific Rim has been connected to Asia for a long time, and that relationship continues to thrive in our time. The West now speaks Japanese, Chinese, and Korean.

Maybe the West is going through a new era. We are a vast and exciting region where new migrations of people are creating an exciting multicultural world, one that has very little in common with the older, conservative myth of the West. Perhaps the idea of the West as the promised land isn't dead; a new infusion of cultures continues, even as postmodern technology changes our landscape once again.

I am fascinated with the migrations of people. I have tried to emphasize this by saying some of those past migrations to the West were tourists. I don't mean to be flippant. We know most often it is necessity that moves groups of people. But migrations are a normal course of human events. Today, as in the past, it isn't only curiosity and available leisure time that creates the tourist. When people have to feed their families, they will migrate.

Our challenge is to be sensitive to those who migrate across the land. A lot of mistakes were made in the past by those too arrogant to appreciate the native ways. Clashes between the cultural groups of the West exploded into atrocities. That, too, is part of our history. To not repeat that waste is the challenge. The answer lies in how we educate ourselves and those tourists exploring our region. In this effort, major attention has to be paid to the migrant workers, those who put sweat and labor into the land but may not have the leisure time we normally associate with tourists. In many ways they know our region better than most of us, and many are settling into the land.

In Spanish we have a saying: Respeto al ajeno. Respect the other person's property, respect the foreigner. As we respect places and people in our travels, we expect to be respected by those who travel through our land. Respect can be taught. After all, we are on earth "only for a while" as the Aztec poet said. We are all dharma bums learning our true nature from the many communities of the West. Let us respect each other in the process.

PART FOUR
Culture and Art of the Southwest

Tribute to Paul Taylor

When Paul Taylor first came up the Río Grande of New Mexico, the natives knew he was a medieval scholar. Maybe it was because he was traveling with a raggedy group of pilgrims speaking Ye Olde English.

The Pueblo Indians and the native paisanos (Hispanic New Mexicans) looked at each other and shook their collective heads.

"Oh no," said one of the Chicanos, "here comes another group of pilgrims."

"Probably lost," his friend nodded.

The pilgrims *were* lost. They weren't on their way to Chimayó to visit the Santuario; no, these pilgrims were headed for Canterbury. The problem was the Wife of Bath insisted they take a right turn. She had heard that Latins make better lovers, so she wanted to check out the scene. The weary group landed in Aztlán, the Southwest United States, the homeland of the Chicanos.

"Ho, pilgrim, where headest thou?" the Pueblo man asked. "Might as well be friendly," he added.

The custom of Nuevo Mexicanos dictated that travelers be treated kindly. Especially pilgrims on the way to Canterbury.

Paul Taylor, wearing the funny rags Medievalists used to wear before they discovered deconstructionism, looked up. He appeared to be the leader of the group. The man named Chaucer, who was responsible for countless undergraduate students hating Ye Olde English, had long ago disappeared, tired of so many dissertations written about his epic poem.

"Hello to you, my good man," Paul replied. "We're lost and looking for Canterbury."

Oritinally published in slightly different form in *Multilingua: Journal of Cross-Cultural and Interlanguage Communication* 18, no. 2/3 (1999): 281–84.

"At least they're not looking for the Seven Cities of Cibola like the first group," one of the natives whispered.

"Oh, Canterbury." The Pueblo man nodded with a very serious look on his face. "You have to keep going west. Except it's now called California."

"California!" the Wife of Bath cried. "That's for me!" Picking up her skirt to expose rather fat ankles, she started west with the disgruntled pilgrims following.

Paul remained. "I've been to California. It's full of freeways, low-riders, and beautiful young people—all looking for movie roles. I like *this* place. What do you call it?"

A chorus of answers sang out:

"Earth of our origin."

"Land of the Anazasi."

"Cibola."

"La Nueva México."

"Aztlán."

"New Mexico, U.S.A."

Always the cosmopolitan pilgrim, who had seen much of the world, spoke many languages, and held a wide variety of jobs before he became a professor at the University of Geneva, Paul was intrigued.

"I love diversity," he beamed.

He came from Switzerland; it was easy to see why the brown-skinned Indians and Chicanos caught his attention.

"You need to wear a hat in this sun," I said, except I said it in Ye Olde English, and it made quite an impression on my beer-drinking buddies. The man's bald head was already getting red from the New Mexican sun.

"Thank you, dear friend," he replied. "What is your name?"

"I have many names," I replied. A trickster never gives his name right away. For all I knew, this pilgrim might also be a trickster. For one thing, how did a pilgrim to Canterbury get to New Mexico? You couldn't blame it all on the Wife of Bath's lust. But he did have a kind face, a radiating smile.

"What are they?" he asked.

"Antonia Marez Luna, Benjie aka Ben Chávez, Clemente, hijo de la chingada, hijo de la Llorona, Osiris, most recently Sonny Baca—"

At that moment this quiet, self-effacing man threw his arms around me and embraced me. He saw straight through me.

"Ah, Coyote, you're a writer in search of your characters?"

"Yes."

"And you write about the Chicanos of Aztlán and how they have been subjugated by the mainstream culture?"

"Well, yes, sort of . . . "

An elfish grin spread across his face. "Wonderful! I'll stay with you. This idea of liberation by third-world people interests me. I can see the dissertations my students will write . . ."

My Pueblo friends shrugged and left. The first thing I discovered about him is that he liked chile. Red hot chile. The hotter the better. We went to eat at Barelas Coffee House in my old barrio, and he covered everything with chile.

Mouthwatering tamales, posole, menudo, enchiladas, tacos, beans, rice, potatoes, meat, he covered everything with red chile and scooped it up with tortillas. When we ordered ice cream for dessert I wondered if he would splash chile on it too.

"You eat like a manito," I observed.

"We don't have anything like this in Switzerland," he kept saying, beads of sweat breaking out on his forehead.

I had been in Switzerland. Once. I couldn't remember eating hot chile there, so I sympathized with him. We have a saying in New Mexico: Food without chile is not food. I knew Europeans didn't understand this.

His second love was tequila. Before each meal we took a shot of tequila and sucked on salt and a lime. Then we would sometimes sing Mexican ballads and laugh a lot. Paul liked to have a good time. I think in his previous life he was Latino.

I looked across the table and tried to picture Paul as Latino. It was difficult. Times like this I doubted in past lives.

Still we drank tequila and ate hot Mexican food, discussed philosophy and Chicana/o literature, and the course of history. This man, I found, was not only a Medievalist, he was a Renaissance man. He knew the cultures and literature of many countries.

When he returned to Geneva, Paul quickly instituted a class to study Chicano literature. His students loved the stuff. They found Chicano history and identity to be fascinating. They began to write intriguing papers, and some came to visit New Mexico. Like Paul, they fell in love with the place.

Paul also tried to raise jalapeño peppers in his garden to flavor his food. But the climate didn't agree with the plants. Indian blue corn didn't make it either. Still, at the end of the term, Paul invited his students to his home. They tried their best to make tortillas, enchiladas, green chile stew. Even the tequila was difficult to find. I guess the Swiss haven't discovered this ancient Aztec remedy.

My wife and I got to know Paul's family. His wife Rose-Marie, and the children, Gareth and Aude. They are at the center of his life. When they first came to visit, Gareth and Aude were youngsters. Now they are grown and doing all sorts of interesting things. I'm sure they remember the blue skies of New Mexico, the Sandia Mountains, the people, and they will someday return to visit.

Last summer Paul returned to do some research, and we drove up to the Jemez Mountains to our cabin. We spent hours just sitting, looking at the red cliffs of our canyon, talking about literature. We sipped a little tequila.

Life is good when one sits with friends and enjoys the quiet passage of time. Paul's eclectic mind ranges through so many fascinating subjects. He spoke of his childhood, the artists he met in Paris, the jazz scene in New York, and I thought, "This man's life is a novel waiting to be written."

Maybe in retirement he'll turn his attention to fiction. He has done such an excellent job of branching into the field of Chicano literature that I'm sure he could write a novel if he chose to do so. But today it's Paul's scholarship we celebrate as he begins a new life. There are so many excellent books and articles he has published in his field. I've chosen to talk about his work in Chicana/o scholarship. He has widened the critical perspective of our work. By bringing to bear his background and worldview, he has enlarged the way we look at our literature. For this we are thankful.

I hope the University of Geneva doesn't let his efforts die. He has plowed the field and planted the first seeds; he has nurtured the work of excellent students, and thus we, the Chicanos of the U.S.A., have acquired a face, an identity, in his corner of the world. As our role in the world of letters grows, we depend on the pioneering work of scholars like Paul Taylor to introduce us to foreign countries. In Germany, France, Italy, and Spain, the study of literature continues to grow as more and more students find and read our literature. The view of life we offer the world is unique and important. Paul knows this, and so he has challenged his students to look at the U.S.A. not as a monolithic country with one history and one culture, but as a diverse country with many communities who have much to share.

The diversity we celebrate is one that Europe is coming to grips with. Switzerland, too, now must engage the world beyond the travel brochures. Your students will be far better citizens of the world if they listen to teachers like Paul Taylor. He challenges them to look at our diversity. I hope the study of our literature and culture continues when Paul leaves the university. Behind the tequila and hot Mexican food we have shared, there is a depth of history, art, and culture that has much to offer.

So become a pilgrim like Paul. Read our books, and who knows, maybe someday you too will come trudging up the Río Grande. With Paul as your guide you can't go wrong. And we'll be there to greet you, as we are always here to greet Paul and his family.

"Don't go to California, pilgrim. Let the Wife of Bath follow that path. There's an intriguing corner of the world here in Nuevo México. Paul has the maps and book. Follow him!"

Un abrazo fuerte, amigo.

Deep Roots
Or, We Have Been Here a Long Time

I think the idea for this issue is great. There is no doubt that this country needs to feel, sense, understand, acknowledge, and care about—I don't mean tolerate—the presence of Hispanics in this country. We get nowhere tolerating. We need to love one another!

The public knows about Mexico, through the movies or mariachi music, or through black legend materials that always make Pancho Villa a villain. We have to turn around these negative conceptions through education. So let's educate each other.

Our public also knows a little about Latin America through the novels in translation of the recent Latin American boom. But I find that the country knows very little about the Hispanic/Latino groups here. And this is our country. We have been here a long time. In the Southwest, we, the various communities of Mexican Americans, developed major industries; after a lot of exploration and shortfalls, we learned to live with the land and the Native Americans.

We became natives long ago and recently called ourselves Chicanos. So we have a history with all sorts of roots. Deep roots that date as far back as the European sixteenth-century entry into the lands north of Mexico. As far back as the Indian ancestors who taught us more than we can ever give credit for.

Now there are twenty million Hispanics, diverse groups even within our Spanish-speaking world, and the number is still growing. And still we are not known, felt, sensed, seen, acknowledged—unless it's in crime statistics or as a community that has to be constantly put in its place. English only. Proposition 187. Before that there were deportations, other abuses.

Originally published in *ANQ: A Quarterly Journal of Short Articles, Notes, and Reviews* 10, no. 2 (Spring 1997): 10–11.

The country will be wiser and healthier when it stops seeing us as the *Other* and sees us as integral to the land we have lived on for so long. Integral to the history our ancestors created, the stories they brought with them, told, the home life they honored, the faith of their religions, the myths of their many roots and the richness therein.

Perhaps the current wave of artistic production will awaken some. We will be seen for what we really are: human beings as simple and complex as anyone else. But why wait to be forced to *see* the many-colored Hispanos/Latinos who are now already neighbors? We invite everyone to look at the art, read the stories, smell and savor the food, dance to the music, understand and acknowledge that there are many Americas, many communities, not just one. Let us put the fear of each other aside. Don't just tolerate people, love people. All good flows from that.

The Magic of Words

A million volumes.

A magic number.

A million books to read, to look at, to hold in one's hand, to learn, to dream . . .

I have always known there were at least a million stars. In the summer evenings when I was a child, we, all the children of the neighborhood, sat outside under the stars and listened to the stories of the old ones, los viejitos. The stories of the old people taught us to wonder and imagine. Their adivinanzas induced the stirring of our first questioning, our early learning.

I remember my grandfather raising his hand and pointing to the swirl of the Milky Way, which swept over us. Then he would whisper his favorite riddle:

> Hay un hombre con tanto dinero
> Que no lo puede contar
> Una mujer con una sábana tan grande
> Que no la puede doblar.
> There is a man with so much money
> He cannot count it
> A woman with a bedspread so large
> She cannot fold it.

Originally published as "In Commemoration: One Million Volumes," in *A Million Stars: The Millionth Acquisition for the University of New Mexico General Library*, ed. Connie Capers Thorson (University of New Mexico General Library, 1981); and reprinted as "The Magic of Words" in *The Anaya Reader* (New York: Warner Books, 1995), 273–82.

We knew the million stars were the coins of the Lord, and the heavens were the bedspread of his mother, and in our minds the sky was a million miles wide. A hundred million. Infinite. Stuff for the imagination. And what was more important, the teachings of the old ones made us see that we were bound to the infinity of that cosmic dance of life which swept around us. Their teachings created in us a thirst for knowledge. Can this library with its million volumes bestow that same inspiration?

I was fortunate to have had those old and wise viejitos as guides into the world of nature and knowledge. They taught me with their stories, they taught me the magic of words. Now the words lie captured in ink, but the magic is still there, the power inherent in each volume. Now, with book in hand, we can participate in the wisdom of mankind.

Each person moves from innocence through rites of passage into the knowledge of the world, and so I entered the world of school in search of the magic in the words. The sounds were no longer the soft sounds of Spanish which my grandfather spoke, the words were in English, and with each new awareness came my first steps toward a million volumes. I, who was used to reading my oraciones en español while I sat in the kitchen and answered the litany to the slap of my mother's tortillas, I now stumbled from sound to word to groups of words, head throbbing, painfully aware that each new sound took me deeper into the maze of the new language. Oh, how I clutched the hands of my new guides then!

Learn, my mother encouraged me, learn. Be as wise as your grandfather. He could speak many languages. He could speak to the birds and the animals of the field.

Yes, I remember the cuentos of my grandfather, the stories of the people. Words are a way, he said; they hold joy, and they are a deadly power if misused. I clung to each syllable that lisped from his tobacco-stained lips. That was the winter the snow came, he would say, it piled high and we lost many sheep and cattle, and the trees groaned and broke with its weight. I looked across the llano and saw the raging blizzard, the awful destruction of that winter which was imbedded in our people's memory.

And the following summer, he would say, the grass of the llano grew so high we couldn't see the top of the sheep. And I would look and see what was once clean and pure and green. I could see a million sheep and the pastores caring for them, as I now care for the million words which pasture in my mind.

But a million books? How can we see a million books? I don't mean just the books lining the shelves here at the University of New Mexico Library, not just the fine worn covers, the intriguing titles. How can we see the worlds that lie waiting in each book? A million worlds. A million million worlds. And the beauty of it is that each world is related to the next, as was taught to us by the old ones. Perhaps it is easier for a child to see. Perhaps it is easier for a child to ask: How many stars are there in the sky? How many leaves in the trees of the river? How many blades of grass in the llano? How many dreams in a night of dreams?

So I worked my way into the world of books, but here is the paradox: a book at once quenches the thirst of the imagination and ignites new fires. I learned that when I visited the library of my childhood, the Santa Rosa library. It was only a dusty room in those days, a room sitting atop the town's fire department, which was comprised of one dilapidated fire truck used by the town's volunteers only in the direst emergencies. But in that small room I found my shelter and retreat. If there were a hundred books there we were fortunate, but to me there were a million volumes. I trembled in awe when I first entered that library, because I realized that if the books held as much magic as the words of the old ones, then indeed this was a room full of power.

Miss Pansy, the librarian, became my new guide. She fed me books as any mother would nurture her child. She brought me book after book, and I consumed them all. Saturday afternoon disappeared as the time of day dissolved into the time of distant worlds. In a world which occupied most of my other schoolmates with games, I took the time to read. I was a librarian's dream. My tattered library card was my ticket into the same worlds my grandfather had known, worlds of magic that fed the imagination.

Late in the afternoon, when I was satiated with reading, when I could no longer hold in my soul the characters that crowded there, I heard the call of the llano, the real world of my father's ranchito, the solid, warm world of my mother's kitchen. Then to the surprise and bewilderment of Miss Pansy, I would rush out and race down the streets of our town, books tucked under my shirt, in my pockets, clutched tightly to my breast. Mad with the insanity of books, I would cross the river to get home, shouting my crazy challenge even at la Llorona, and that poor spirit of so many frightening cuentos would wither and withdraw. She was no match for me.

Those of you who have felt the same exhilaration from reading—or from love—will know about what I'm speaking. Alas, the people of the town could only shake their heads and pity my mother. At least one of her sons was a bit touched. Perhaps they were right, for few will trade a snug reality to float on words to other worlds.

And now there are a million volumes for us to read here at the University of New Mexico Library. Books on every imaginable subject in every field, a history of the thought of the world that we must keep free of censorship, because we treasure our freedoms. It is the word "freedom" which eventually must reflect what this collection, or the collection of any library, is all about. We know that as we preserve and use the literature of all cultures, we preserve and regenerate our own. The old ones knew and taught me this. They eagerly read the few newspapers that were available. They kept their diaries, they wrote décimas and cuentos, and they survived on their oral stories and traditions.

Another time, another library. I entered Albuquerque High School Library prepared to study, because that's where we spent our study time. For better or for worse, I received my first contracts as a writer there. It was a place where budding lovers spent most of their time writing notes to each other, and when my friends who didn't have the gift of words found out I could turn a phrase, I quickly had all the business I could do. I wrote poetic love notes for a dime apiece and thus worked my way through high school. And there were fringe benefits, because the young women knew very well who was writing the sweet words, and many a heart I was supposed to capture for someone else fell in love with me. And so a library is also a place where love begins.

A library should be the heart of a city; with its storehouse of knowledge, it liberates, informs, teaches, and enthralls. A library indeed should be the cultural center of any city. Amidst the bustle of work and commerce, the great libraries of the world have provided a sanctuary where scholars and common man alike come to enlarge and clarify knowledge, to read and reflect in quiet solitude.

I knew a place like this. I spent many hours in the old library on Central Avenue and Edith Street. But my world was growing, and quite by accident I wandered up the hill to enroll in the University of New Mexico. And what a surprise lay in store for me. The libraries of my childhood paled in comparison to this new wealth of books housed in Zimmerman Library. Here there were stack after stack of books, and ample space and time to wander aimlessly in this labyrinth of new frontiers.

I had known the communal memory of my people through the newspapers and few books my grandfather read to me and through the rich oral tradition handed down by the old ones. Now I discovered the collective memory of all mankind at my fingertips. I had only to reach for the books which laid all history bare. Here I could converse with the writers from every culture on earth, old and new, and at the same time I began my personal odyssey, which would add a few books to the collection that in 1981 would come to house a million volumes.

Those were exciting times. Around me swirled the busy world of the university, in many respects an alien world. Like many fellow undergraduates, I sought refuge in the library. My haven during those student university years was the reading room of the west wing of the old library. There I found peace. The carved vigas decorating the ceiling, the solid wooden tables and chairs and the warm adobe color of the stucco were things with which I was familiar. There I felt comfortable. With books scattered around me I could read and doze and dream. I took my breaks in the warm sun of the portal, where I ate my tortilla sandwiches, which I carried in my brown paper bag. There, with friends, I sipped coffee as we talked of changing the world and exchanged idealistic dreams.

That is a rich and pleasant time in my memory. No matter how far across the world I find myself in the future, how deep in the creation of worlds with words, I shall keep the simple and poignant memories of those days. The sun reflected golden on the ocher walls, and the green pine trees and the blue spruce, sacred trees to our people, whispered in the breeze. I remembered my grandfather meeting with the old men of the village in the resolana of one of the men's homes, or against the wall of the church on Sundays, and I remembered the things they said. Later, alone, dreaming against the sun-warmed wall of the library, I continued that discourse in my mind.

Yes, the library is a place where people should gather. It is a place for research, reading, and for the quiet fomentation of ideas, but because it houses the collective memory of our race, it should also be a place where present issues are discussed and debated and researched in order for us to gain the knowledge and insight to create a better future. The library should be a warm place which reflects the needs and aspirations of the people.

The University of New Mexico Library didn't have a million volumes when I first haunted its corridors of stacks, but now these million volumes are available. The library has grown. Sometimes I get lost when I wander through it, and I cannot help but wonder if there are students around me who are also lost. Is there someone who will guide them through this storehouse of knowledge? A labyrinth can be a frightening place without a guide, and perhaps that is why I have written about some of the guides who took my hand and helped me. It is important to celebrate not only the acquisition of the millionth volume, but to rededicate ourselves to the service of our community which is an integral part of the history of this library. I am confident that the library will continue to grow and to be an example to other libraries. Service to the community is indeed our most important endeavor.

This millionth volume marks a momentous step in the process of growth of the University of New Mexico Library. This commemorative volume celebrates that step. In the wisest cultures of the world, entry into adulthood is a time of celebration; it is a time for dancing and thanksgiving. And that is what we, the staff of the library, the scholars of the university, the students, the friends, and the people from the community come to celebrate this year. We gather not only to celebrate growth, but also to note the excellence of archives in many fields, to acknowledge the change which has met the demands of the present and needs of the future, and to honor the service provided to all of the people who come here to read, to dream, to recreate.

So, let us celebrate this rite of passage. It is a time to flex our muscles and be proud. We have come a long way from the first collection, and we will continue to build. I would like to list the names of all the people who have worked to bring us to this moment, but since that is impossible, it is the intent of this personal essay to thank those people. This reminiscence through libraries I have known and dreamed in is a thanks to those librarians whose efforts helped to establish this library. In their spirit we will offer help to each person who comes through the doors of this library in that curious but inalienable right to search for knowledge.

At a Crossroads

What changes have come to the Hispanic community of New Mexico since statehood in 1912?

That intriguing question reminds me of a book of short stories by a fellow writer from Texas. In the first story from *Hay Plesha Lichans to di Flac*, Sául Sánchez describes the first day at school for Mexican American children. The bell rings and the Anglo teacher lines up the new first graders to recite the pledge of allegiance to the flag and country.

The teacher speaks English. To the kids from the barrio who have spoken Spanish all their lives, the pledge of allegiance sounds something like this (page 4):

> Ai plesha lichans to di flac, off june aires taste off America; an tu de reepablic for huish eet estans, guan nayshon, andar got, wits liverty and yastes for oll.

Needless to say, it was a difficult first day of school for the kids who knew no English. In many ways it was a sad day. They tried to fake the sounds; they wanted to belong. Belonging is what allegiance is all about. But at what price allegiance? I wonder how many Hispanos in New Mexico knew only Spanish in 1912, when the territory became a state? How many had to fake allegiance to the new legal language because they did not know it?

When I began school in Santa Rosa in 1944, thirty-two years after statehood, I could not speak a word of English. In Spanish I could pledge allegiance to the love of my family, to my community, and to my

Originally published in *New Mexico Magazine* (June 1987): 60–64; and reprinted in *The Anaya Reader* (New York: Warner Books, 1995), 331–41.

religion, but in English my pledge came out something like the pledge of the kids in the story. "Hay plesha lichens tu di flac . . ."

My first day at school was a sad and terrible time. I did not belong. Now I look back and ponder the winds of change that have swept over New Mexico since 1912.

I think of my grandfather Liborio Mares, a farmer in the Puerto de Luna Valley near Santa Rosa. For him life would go on much as it had before, uninterrupted except for the seasons. He held on to his land, his language, and his traditional lifestyle. It seems the great changes in his life, and ours, would come after World War II. But even before the war, perceptible changes crept into the Hispano villages. What were those changes? And, just as important, what are the values that would remain constant and pass into the collective memory of the people?

I remember my grandfather riding his carro de vestias to Santa Rosa to sell produce from his farm. Our grandfathers no longer ride their horse-drawn wagons from the farm to town to sell the produce of harvest; trucks now appear along the side of the road to sell corn, chile, vegetables. Beneath the surface of change we see the needs and age-old patterns of the people continue to define their cultural context.

Memory records history, that which is once stored lives on. The folkways live on. But what would the Hispano legacy gain in seventy-five years? What would it lose?

The most important change came as the Hispanos adopted the English language. The Nuevo Mexicanos were forced to learn the culture and language of the Anglo-American. The law of the United States became the law of the land, and one had to know some English or have a friend who spoke the language to file deeds to property, to buy a car or get an automobile license, to trade at the grocery store, to send the kids to school. These simple duties that we now take for grated required a major change in the daily lives of the Nuevo Mexicanos.

Other changes were discernible. At the soul of survival for the Hispano village was the earth and the sustenance it provides. The growing season in the northern mountains was short. Farmers had to sense changes in the weather and the earth. They irrigated with acequias, the irrigation ditch system that is a communal endeavor, engendering a faith that developed between the people and their earth. The patron saint of each village was taken out to bless the fields, and soon stories developed of the Santo Niño who nightly walked in the fields, guarding and blessing the crops.

It is in those simple ceremonies of daily life that we can best view the concepts we call cultural values. The story of the saint who watches the fields at night becomes part of the elements of faith: daily life, raising crops, raising children, tending the sick, church activities, and fiestas. Could that faith rooted in centuries of tradition survive?

World War II brought a decisive change in many aspects of Nuevo Mexicano culture. During that time, Hispanos left the rural life of the villages for the cities in unprecedented numbers. How did the new urban population relate to that faith that had allowed them to wed the elements of daily life with a more sacred order in the universe? We now plant gardens in our backyards, and we visit the villages to learn the old farming techniques. We look for ways to reconstitute the faith of our ancestors. The fact that we became an urban community was, without doubt, the most drastic change in our lifestyle.

In the mid-sixties, the sons and daughters of that mid-forties movement to the cities would look back in anger and realize they were losing many of their traditional ways. To renew their sense of identity, they created the most important artistic movement of our time, the Chicano Movement. The Chicano Movement really had its beginning in the struggle for the rights of workers and the civil rights of Mexican Americans everywhere, but the artistic arm of the movement has been very important in creating a Chicano consciousness.

The struggle of our community to exist and retain not only its cultural ways but also its soul has not been easy.

My father, who spoke only Spanish most of his life, went to basic training during World War I. I have a photograph of him in uniform, the American flag waving behind him. I wonder how he pledged allegiance to the flag, how he felt about the new state he was defending. He and some of his compadres went for basic training, some fought in Europe. They came back and returned to their old way of life. A generation later, my three older brothers went to World War II; when they came back, their way of life would never again be the same.

The paradox of change is that it brings with it positive and negative aspects. After the 1880s, the railroad would service the New Mexico mines. Entire communities left farming for mining. The mines paid wages, and in the changing lifestyle the question was not how much land and cattle or sheep a man had, but how many bucks he had in his pocket. A man with his week's wages in his pocket could feel as rich as the patrón, but even the age of the patrón was coming to an end.

It has been the migrations of people and the periods of active colonization, that have affected and changed this land along the Río Grande. The ancient migrations of the Native Americans into the Río Grande were first. In the latter part of the sixteenth century came the Spaniards and Mexicans from Mexico, and most recently the Anglo-Americans. Around the mid-nineteenth century, immediately after the United States war with Mexico, the movement of people into the Río Grande area accelerated. The old, traditional cultures of the valley continued their struggle for survival.

Today marks another time of rapid migration into the state and border region. The weather, the natural beauty, and warm winters continue to attract people. From Mexico, new workers arrive daily. The new arrivals and the old cultures must live side by side, as they have in the past. But if we do not seize this moment to understand and plan for change, future generations will be haunted by many of the old prejudices that separate communities.

There is a saying in Spanish: Each change brings a little good; each change brings a little bad. Today, seventy-five years after statehood, the mines have closed, and those who became miners are again displaced. Those who left the villages are without roots. Are the problems insurmountable for the continuation of the traditional Nuevo Mexicano culture? Can it survive as a growing, viable culture?

The answer probably lies in the family unit. Older, traditional communal allegiances to the village, church, or the patrón disappear as we became an urban culture, but the family unit survives. Beset with many of the new social problems that come with urban mobility and assimilation into the Anglo lifestyles and beset by the lack of educational opportunities, it is now largely in the family unit that the ceremonies and language of the traditional culture will be passed on.

American democracy and Anglo technology arrived, and all appears beneficial on the surface, yet we see the cost of allegiance beneath the social fabric. Nothing is for free, and change is always painful.

Another tremendous change has come in communications. Radio, the telephone, and television are connections to the outside world, and the outside world spoke English. I remember the telephone party lines of childhood and cranking the handle to get the operator. Las comadres could listen to the town's gossip, the mitote, by picking up the phone and listening to the party line; they didn't need to go visit. A facetious example, but one that illustrates that as the Nuevo Mexicanos adopted the English language and the American technology, changes in our lifestyle became very perceptible.

The slow pace of village communal life gathered momentum as cars and trucks filled the dusty streets. Neighbors no longer stopped to pass the time of day, they waved as they drove by. "Hi, how are you?" the kids called to their abuelos as they passed. I remember the first time I said "Hello" to a favorite uncle who came to visit. "¿Quién jálo?" he asked, his play on words reminding me I had changed my language when addressing him.

Respeto is a key value in our culture. Respect for the elders. We were bred on it as we are bred on tortillas and beans. Now we see signs of that respect and concern for the viejitos breaking down. That quality of respect for the elders in the culture is like faith in the earth, and like honor in the family, pride in community, and awe in the beauty and mystery of the universe. It's those important ingredients in our culture the family has to safeguard.

Changes initiated by usage of the new English language and technology hastened the breakdown of the traditional interrelatedness of the Hispano village. How people and ceremonies are interrelated is of prime importance in viewing small-town culture. The old Hispano villages were interdependent. Change meant a breakdown or readjustment of those relationships of mutual help and dependency. The ceremonies, traditions, relationships, and communal mutual help that were in place in 1912 are still there in some form seventy-five years later, but lack of jobs, education, mass media, and mobility, children leaving the villages and movement into the middle class have affected the last two generations. If those values we identify as part of our history are to be retained, they must be retained within each family. When we recognize the strength of those values, they can again play a role in the community.

Mobility came first in the form of the Model T Ford, as clear and radical a product of Anglo technology as there ever was. People moved to California to seek a new way of life, new opportunity. The young went to seek adventure, jobs, money, an education. Strangely enough, as there were more wages, there seemed to be less leisure time, or less time to pay attention to the allegiance to old relationships. Concern for the communal systems began to erode and, in places, to disappear. If you worked for wages, your responsibility was done at the end of the day. Churches and acequias fell into disrepair; families had less time for each other.

One can see the transformation in the ceremonies. At one time the bartering system was an important aspect of village life. Work and tools and talents were bartered for. You help me fix my roof, and I'll help you shoe your horses. Together we can plaster the church or the house of the viejitos. Helping and exchange of labor are still elements of Nuevo Mexicano life, but working a tight eight-hour day interferes with the ceremonies. Assimilation has its price.

Selling the land of the abuelos, the village land of the ancestors, was viewed with disapproval. Woven into centuries of tradition was the unspoken rule: the land cannot be sold. It is part of the heritage of the land grants, part of the heritage gained from the Indian view of the earth. To sell the land was to cut your roots, and a man without roots lacked identity. Families without a village lost their allegiance to place. Allegiance to the land is as important as allegiance to the family and to God.

I remember when my family left the town of my childhood, Santa Rosa. Leaving that place meant also leaving our connection to the farming community of Puerto de Luna, leaving the open llano of Pastura. It was a wretched experience. Sad. Part of our honor, pride, and history, elements important to the culture, was being left behind. Torn from the land of our birth, would we survive?

The land had been sold cheaply, and leaving the land was leaving the energy force and the blood source of the culture. The Hispanos became the new Okies as they moved west to the imagined land of milk and honey, as they moved to California. Recently I asked a cousin of mine who grew into manhood in the village of Puerto de Luna and who now lives in Albuquerque if he would ever return there. "No," he replied, "there is nothing there for me in the village of my childhood." Still, in his own way, in the urban environment, he lives in the old lifestyle, tending his garden and raising a few sheep. But there is no return.

Thomas Wolfe reflected on his South and saw similar changes take place. He put it best in *You Can't Go Home Again* when he said, "Oh, lost, and by the wind grieved . . ."

Now as the sons and daughters of the generation of the forties join the middle class, a greater change will take place. I teach their children in my university classes and find most don't speak Spanish, most do not know the ways or the history of the traditional culture. Now we will learn if the elements of that culture that took hundreds of years to evolve can survive in the middle class. Now there are more stratified groups within the Hispano community. There are the Hispano members of the middle class, living in cities, adopting more and more the way of the Anglo. There are the country cousins, those who held on to the land and still follow the folkways.

And there are the new workers from Mexico, who in future years will make their connection to the old legacy. These workers of the fields, the Mexicans seeking the opportunity of work, are the newest migration into the Río Grande. In a way, they continue the stream of migration that has always moved north and south along our border region, and a new time of transformation and change awaits them. As they renew elements of our Mexicano past, they play a positive role in our culture.

Today, reflecting on seventy-five years of statehood provides us an excellent vantage point. It is time to reflect. Without that reflection the pace of life and its tensions will increase, and it is a pity and a loss to move forward without knowing from whence we came.

Each of us changes in relationship to others. We grow and explore the world and experience love and joy and tragedy. Cultures are that way, always growing and changing. The Hispanos of Nuevo México have changed in response to their relationship to the Anglo culture, and to other cultural groups of the Río Grande region. The relationship to the Indian Pueblos of the Río Grande not only changed the culture centuries ago, it helped give it definition. The process of growth is constant and, yes, often painful.

For the Hispano community, the process of growth and change has been painful. But the turbulence of the surface change can be met if the values of the ancestors remain rooted to our memory—if our language, values, and ceremonies don't die. The surface is like the surface of the muddy waters of the Río Grande, sometimes turbulent, sometimes peaceful. But beneath lie the elements of water and earth, and the old principal elements of faith. To those we can always pledge our allegiance.

La Llorona, El Kookoóee, and Sexuality

In *Bless Me, Ultima*, my first novel, I looked at my childhood through the eyes of a novelist. In the process of writing the novel, I explored childhood experiences, dreams, folklore, mythology, and communal relationships that shaped me in my formative years. Writing became a process of self-exploration.

Why is childhood so important? During childhood one undergoes primal experiences, and one responds to experience directly and intuitively. The child occupies the space of first awareness, and thus the child is closer in spirit to the historical dawning of the first awareness of humankind on earth. The child is a storyteller who assigns roles; the child is a mythmaker.

I grew up on the banks of the Pecos River in eastern New Mexico, and as a child I spent a great deal of my free time along the river, and in the hills and lakes that surrounded the small town of Santa Rosa. In the 1940s the town was going through wrenching changes brought on by World War II, but it was still, in many ways, immersed in an ambience created by the first settlers of the valley generations before. For the Nuevo Mexicanos of the valley, the heritage was the Spanish language, the Catholic religion, and the old folkways preserved by the farmers from villages like Puerto de Luna, where my grandfather lived.

I am grateful for the cultural and natural environment in which I lived as a child, because the ambience provided me with a set of values that have served me all my life. Growing up along the river taught me that nature is indeed imbued with a spirit. One of my first awarenesses of this was the wailing cry I heard one afternoon along the river. My

Originally published in *Bilingual Review/La Revista Bilingüe* 17, no. 1 (January–April, 1992): 50–55; and reprinted in *The Anaya Reader* (New York: Warner Books, 1995), 415–28.

mother told me it was the spirit of la Llorona, the wailing woman of legend who wandered the river in search of her lost children. This fearful figure of our folktales was the first ghost in the bush that I encountered as a child.

Later, as I grew and expanded my territory, I made the journey with my boyhood friends to the Hidden Lakes. In the hills of the llano I felt the spirit of nature throb with life; I heard the voices on the wide plain and in the darker solitude of the lakes and river. Some of the ghosts were communal figures that were part of the Hispanic and Native American folktales. These characters from the folktales had names and personalities; they lived in the oral tradition. Others were more personal spirits which we as children created when we told stories; they were our ghosts, our childhood entry into mythmaking.

Because I grew up in a Catholic household, I was taught that life had a meaning. Later in life I began to understand that as we mature we question meaning, and we learn to construct new answers to the questions of life. Growing up in a Catholic family meant I spent a lot of time trying to understand the nature of God. The traditions of my ancestors and the church helped shape my knowledge as I grew into young manhood.

One of the most important rites of passage that children experience is the awareness of their sexuality. We are sexual creatures, and most of our identity is tied up with our sexuality. Sexuality was not discussed in our home or school, and in the religious arena it was only associated with sin. As I grew into young manhood there was no one to explain the new realm of sexual awareness. Many years later I realized that there were characters in the cultural stories that had a direct relation to sexuality. These folk characters were there to teach sexual taboos. To understand that important time in my life, I returned to childhood and analyzed the role of two such folk figures whose stories seem intricately tied to sexuality.

I hope to shed some light on childhood sexuality by looking at these two figures from our Nuevo Mexicano folklore, a folklore that is part of the wider Hispanic culture of las Américas. We know that if repressed or made a fearful thing by narrow rules, sexual awareness can be stifled. If the rites of passage into one's sexuality are understood, that understanding can enhance one's positive sense of identity.

Everything in the universe is related; we are all connected; from stardust to human flesh, we vibrate with the same elements of the universe. The web of life is infused by spirit, and each one of us has the power to use that creative energy to manifest our potential. This light that shines within can extend itself to others, and thus we very early learn that using the energy we have within, we can overcome the negative obstacles in our path.

In life we move from one level of awareness to the next, one identity to the next. Growing into the new levels of awareness in our journey is not just a function of aging, it also means growing in understanding. When there is a crisis of self-identity, we attempt to shed light on the passage. That struggle to know one's self is the crux of life.

The stories of the folk tradition helped me in that search, but I know now that my time to learn the truth embedded in the stories that dealt with sexuality was interrupted. With time the figures in the stories would have made sense, but at age seven I entered the Anglo-American school system and began to lose touch with the folk material of my culture. Long after, as a grown man, I had to return to the stories to understand what they had to teach me.

Some of the stories of the folk tradition told of the monsters that existed in the bush, and because I was to spend so much time in the hills, lakes, and river of my native town, I listened closely. It is in the bush that we encounter the darkness that assails our spirit. In the bush exist the monsters of our legends and myths, the ghosts of the communal stories. The spirits and monsters of the bush are creations of our minds, both the communal psyche and the personal. Awareness and coming to a new consciousness are steps toward maturity, and the stories can serve as guideposts.

For us Nuevo Mexicanos growing up in the Spanish-speaking villages, the cuentos of the folk tradition related the adventures of heroes who overcame the monsters, and through these stories it was possible to understand the role of the ghosts in the stories.

The historical role of the storyteller has been to characterize these monsters. We all have monsters to conquer, ghosts to confront in the bush. Today the bush has become the dangerous urban streets, the corporate boardroom, or the bedroom, but the folk stories have such a strong hold on the psyche that they serve us even in these new settings. When we understand the monsters within, we know ourselves better.

My childhood environment was a primal setting; it was the river and its bosque. There, under the canopy of the gigantic cottonwood, Russian olive, and tamarisk trees, I met my ghosts. I traveled deeper and deeper into the river darkness, always full of fear, because the presence of the monsters was palpable. My ghosts were real. The cry of the doves became the moan of la Llorona; the breeze shifting shadows in the dark paths where I walked could be the monstrous figure of el Coco, the boogeyman of our stories.

In the oral tradition of my folklore, la Llorona and el Coco, or Cucúi (Kookoóee, as I spell the name to fit the sound), were well known. I heard many stories about these two monsters, sitting by the warm stove of my mother in her safe kitchen when family or visitors told stories. And at the end of the stories the warning for us children was always the same: "Be good, be careful, or la Llorona will get you." "Don't stay out late at night or el Coco will get you." These two figures put fear in our hearts; the folk were warning us about something. Was it only about staying out late at night? Or was there a deeper meaning in the stories of these two figures?

Sometimes in the warm summer nights, the gang of boys I grew up with stayed out late in the hills or by the river, and we would build a fire and tell stories. We began to talk about women, or the young girls we knew at school, and we bragged about our newfound sexual powers. We told stories about witches and monsters, and the two favorite stories were about the well-known figures la Llorona and el Kookoóee.

When we left the warmth and safety of the fire, we had to walk home in the dark, which was full of sounds and shapes and lurking figures. Then someone would shout that he saw something move in the dark; any shadow could become one of the dreaded ghosts. "¡La Llorona!" was a cry of terror which turned our blood to ice. Oh, how we ran. I was safe only after I entered my home, the sanctuary that held the proper Christian fetishes to ward off the evil spirits of the night.

Sometimes I found myself alone in the dusk when I had to go down to the river to cut wild alfalfa for our milk cow. I would work fast and hard; I didn't want to be there when darkness engulfed the river. At that haunting time, the presence of the river came alive. The ghosts of the bush walked in the shadows. I felt fear, dread—real emotions that I had to understand and conquer. I had been warned: "Hurry home or la Llorona will get you!"

I did meet la Llorona, and I did meet el KooKoóee. There in the darkness of the bushes of my river, I met them more than once. The ghosts of the bush are real, whether we explain them as projections of our psyche or a creation of communal oral tradition; when you meet them in the dark and you are a child, you know they are real.

La Llorona, according to legend, had killed her children and drowned them in the river. There are hundreds of variations on the story, but the point is that she gave birth to illegitimate children. She broke a rule of the tribe. She was jilted or cast away by the man who fathered her children, and, in her rage at being used, she killed the children. Her penance was to wander the banks of the river looking for the children she drowned.

El Kookoóee was a masculine ghost, more nebulous, larger and more powerful, but as frightful as la Llorona. He was the father figure who warned the male child of the dangers inherent in sexual awareness and practices. A friend told me that when he was a child he was told to hurry back from the outhouse. "The Kookoóee will get you," was the warning. He was being warned not to take time to play with himself.

One ghost is feminine, the other masculine; both are there to warn the child not to indulge in sexual practices. I didn't know that then, I only knew I was aware of, and fascinated by, my new sexual world. Unfortunately, there was no one with whom to discuss my new feelings. Sex was sin, the priest at the church said. I sensed there was something in the story of la Llorona that would help me understand my change. I was drawn to la Llorona; I felt I had something to learn from her. She was, after all, a mother. Was I her child? How? What secret did she have to reveal to me?

Was she a product of the fear of sexuality of the elders of the tribe? Was she created to keep me from the sexual desires and fantasies that began to fill my world? They had made a monster out of her and banished her to the river, where I spent my time with my friends. After we swam, we rested naked on the warm sandbars and spun myth after sexual myth.

In the evenings when we played hide-and-seek with the neighborhood girls, the awareness of sexuality was overwhelming. We ran to hide with the girls, to be close for a moment and touch them. The girls whispered, "You're not supposed to touch, or that might make babies." Even kissing might make babies in that mysterious world of sex about which we knew so little. As the evening grew darker our parents called us in. "¡Cuidao! La Llorona anda cerca." La Llorona lurks nearby.

Now I know that those old men who condemned sexuality and insisted that we fear that natural part of our lives created the spirit of la Llorona. As a child I was on the brink of awareness that would shed light on my entry into young manhood. La Llorona and el Kookoóee were playing a part in my passage into sexual identity.

El Kookoóee was the father ghost, the old abuelo who rose up from the shadows. He was so powerful, I knew he could eat me alive, tear at my flesh, devour me. He sought my unquestioning obedience, he was a deity who allowed no transgressions. He was a reflection of the fathers of the village who warned me of sexual taboos. Perhaps it was more than masturbation the elders feared; the taboo of incest was also hidden in the warning.

Both folklore figures had a proper role to play, which was to teach me sexual taboos. Did they have to be so fearful? My guess is that most figures in the legends and mythology that are used to teach sexual taboos are fearful creatures. Their role is to frighten the young and to keep them within the fold of family, community, and religious dogma.

At each stage of life, we enter different awarenesses of our sexuality, and that sexuality is so closely tied to the energy that connects us to others that it is crucial to understand those new awakenings of body and soul. Understanding is liberation, and when I finally understood the meaning of those childhood ghosts, I understood myself better. But understanding did not come in one epiphany, it came over many years of searching—a search not yet complete.

My childhood was shaped by a worldview that has a long history in the valleys of New Mexico, but at age seven when I first attended school, I discovered a new universe. The society of the school knew nothing about my world, it knew nothing about la Llorona and el Kookoóee. They taught me about a gnome who lived under a bridge, a monster who would devour the Billy Goats Gruff if they dared to cross the bridge to greener meadows. (The figure of the goat is appropriate. It has come to be a symbol of sexuality or lust.) Of course I knew it was really la Llorona who lived under the bridge that I crossed every day on my way from my home on the hill into town. I heard the older kids whisper as we crossed the bridge. Lovers had spent a few moments under the bridge, by the banks of the river. The evidence of the night's passion for the high school students was there. They dared, I thought, to enter the world of sex in the very home of la Llorona and el Kookoóee. Weren't they afraid? Sex was supposed to be fearful.

Awakening into the world of sexuality was not easy; it was a fearful journey. The ghosts of the bush were there to warn us of our indiscretions, and the strict rules of the church were there to punish us. It was, after all, the patriarchal church that ostracized la Llorona for her sin.

In school I read the story of the Headless Horseman which Ichabod Crane met one fearful night. This Headless Horseman was like my Kookoóee, but the headless wonder was tame compared to el Coco. I knew about el Kookoóee, and what Ichabod experienced in one night I had already experienced many times. In my time of awakening sexuality, in that crucial time which was a crisis of identity, I had already met the taboo ghosts of my culture.

On the feminine side, the two characters I remember from school storybooks are Snow White and Cinderella. Both young girls were feared by the older, uglier stepmothers. Both young heroines are enslaved by the taboos of the older women. Both will eventually free themselves, and both stories have a happy ending. There is no happy ending to the story of la Llorona. She comes from a Catholic world, and breaking the taboo has finality to it. She is condemned to search for her children forever.

Was I, the boy coming into the awareness of my expanding sexual world, to be part of her condemnation? If I did not heed the warnings of my group, would I also become an outcast? The writer I was to become would question everything, and I would eventually break with some of the narrow ways of my community. I was destined to leave the strict, dogmatic teachings of the church.

My first sin was insignificant and natural; I broke a taboo in the youthful epiphany of masturbation. I became a confidant of la Llorona, and, like her, I had no one in whom to confide. We were both sinners, doomed to wander outside the proscribed rules.

During my elementary schooling, I realized the school was unaware of the centuries of oral tradition of my New Mexican culture. The school system didn't acknowledge the ghosts of the bush that I knew so well. The stories of la Llorona and el Kookoóee were never told in the classroom; there was no guide to lead us through our folktales. I was not helped to understand the meaning of my own world.

The schools did not deem important my oral tradition and the stories of my ancestors that came from that tradition. I worked my way through a graduate degree, and never did I hear the stories of my culture in the curriculum. The school was telling me that my folkways and stories were not important enough to be in the classroom. A very important part of my identity was never acknowledged.

Some will say there is no great loss at losing the stories of these ghosts in the bush I have described, but I insist they are crucial in the maintenance of culture. As these folk figures of the culture disappear, the culture that created them also is lost. And because el Kookoóee and la Llorona deal directly with the world of sexuality, they are not mere stories to frighten children, they are archetypal characters who speak forcefully about self-awareness and growth.

We need to bring the mythic characters of our folktales to the classroom. We need wise teachers to help the children understand their growth during their critical years. After all, the stories were created to teach values. The stories of la Llorona and el Kookoóee have much to teach us. In the reading circle a good teacher can lead the children into illuminating revelations about the role of these figures. Teaching can be an open process of revelation, not one that fears the intimate areas of growth. An open, accepting process is far better than one that favors fear and whispered interpretations.

We should learn the oral traditions of many tribes, of many places of the world. It was important for me to learn about the gnome and the Headless Horseman and Snow White and Cinderella, because the stories were a window into the culture that created the stories. The more stories I learned, the closer to the truth I got, the more liberated I became, the more I realized the common problems that beset all of us.

I understand that culture often disappears in small pieces. When the children no longer know la Llorona or el Kookoóee stories, a very important ingredient of our culture is lost, and we will be forced to look for those ingredients in foreign cultures. Part of my role as a writer is to rescue from anonymity those familiar figures of my tradition. I wrote a book, *The Legend of la Llorona*, a novella that describes, from my point of view, the trials and tribulations of the New World wailing woman, the Malinche of Mexico. In this love story, I not only looked into the motives of the lovers, Cortés and Malinche, but I also analyzed the political and cultural impact of the Old World conquest on the New World.

But what of the Kookoóee? Were the children learning about this boogeyman of our culture? Was one more element of our folk culture about to disappear? Was the old boogeyman already gone?

In the summer of 1990, I gathered together a group of Chicano artists in Alburquerque. I proposed to them that we build an effigy of el Kookoóee and burn it at a public fiesta. The artists responded to the idea enthusiastically. No one knew what el Kookoóee looked like, but given our creativity, we came up with sketches and began to build the sixteen-foot-high effigy. He had roosters' feet, some said, so that's what we put on him, and long arms with huge hands, and his head was big and round with red eyes and a green chile nose. His teeth were sharp, his fangs yellow and long. Matted hair full of weeds fell to his shoulders. He carried a large bag, so we decided to have each child write his or her fear on a piece of paper and put it in the bag. When the effigy was burned those fears would go up in smoke. The same cleansing effect stories have was duplicated in the burning of the effigy.

We drew together as a community to re-create one of our ghosts of the bush, the boogeyman of our childhood. We re-created el Kookoóee, told stories about him as we worked, and made sure the children understood the effigy and the stories of the old boogeyman. We re-created a cultural figure many thought was insignificant, and in so doing we understood the role of el Kookoóee better. A deep feeling of community evolved; we were no longer alienated artists working alone, we were a group with common roots.

When we burned the effigy one evening in October at a community festival in the South Valley of Alburquerque, over five hundred people attended. People gathered to look at the effigy, and they remembered stories they had heard as children. They began to tell the stories to their children.

The children were the winners. Unlike my generation's experience at school, they saw that the stories from their culture were worthy of artistic attention. As the sun set and the Kookoóee went up in flames, we realized that we had created a truly moving, communal experience. We had taken one character out of the stories of our childhood and rescued him from anonymity.

After the burning of the effigy, I began to look more closely at the role of this ghost of the bush in my childhood. El Kookoóee and la Llorona are not only connected to the awareness of sexuality; they resonate with many other meanings. But to understand those meanings we have to pass on the stories, we have to re-create the characters in our time, and we have to make the schools aware of their importance. For us, building and burning the effigy of el Kookoóee helped validate an element of our cultural ways. Nothing is too insignificant to revive and return to the community if we are to save our culture. We *can* rescue ourselves.

We still have much to teach this country, for we have a long history and many stories to tell. The stories from our tradition have much to tell us about the knowledge we need in our journey. We need to get our stories into the schools, as we need the stories of many different ways of life. We need to be more truthful and more sensitive with each other as we learn about the complexity that comes with growth. It is futile and wasteful to depend on only one set of stories to learn the truth. There are many stories, many paths, and they are available to us in our own land.

Luis Jiménez

View from La Frontera

Luis Jiménez [1940–2006], in his work, celebrates the vitality of life. This has been obvious from his early work up through today. Jiménez es un hijo de la frontera; he knows its people and the landscape. It is the transformation of those people into art that is his most important contribution to the art of this vast region between Mexico and the United States. He is fusing the Mexicano and the Anglo-American worlds.

Jiménez's creativity has been consistent, innovative, and experimental. The passion in his work exemplifies that deep search for an art that portrays the border region. He is the forerunner of a new generation of artists from this area, men and women who are proud of the land and the people and bent on creating an aesthetic that reflects la frontera. Much of the vitality and strength of Jiménez's work comes from this representation of the frontier that constantly defines who he is.

When I first viewed his early work, I knew this artist had something important to say to us. He represents not only a vision of the people of the Río Grande valley and the childhood influences of his El Paso, Texas, environment, but he also extends his view to the larger and lusty frontera. He has created a body of work that will outlast la muerte, that constant companion we see lurking in the soul of every piece.

A retrospective is a time to celebrate the artist and to appreciate the progress and impact of his creativity. It is an opportunity to absorb the artist's magic, the duende spirit of the desert. I have never been in front of a Jiménez piece when I did not smile. "Este vato esta bien loco" is a compliment we pay our artists when they reflect our sense of the world. What we call "locura" is the artist's unique vision and creativity, that which binds him to his roots, y gracias a dios, Jiménez has locura.

Originally published in *Southwest Art* (March 1994): 86–92.

He takes his inspiration and materials from his backyard, for he is aware that art springs from the place, not from abstract definitions. He opens new doors of perception, and what we see is an intimate portrait of our lives and the lives of our neighbors. Viewing his work is an encounter, a happening in which we come face to face with his locura, and it's not always pleasant, sometimes shocking, but never bland or dull.

Jiménez is an artist who creates a synthesis of vision, fusing the North American with the Mexicano, creating in the interplay the many faces of the new mestizos. There is a vision for the future in his fusion and syncretism.

Today the world focuses on borders, borders that divide and create conflicts and wars. On the border we can lose our humanity or regain it, and so for us the art of la frontera describes not only social and political reality, it carries the implication of hope. It is this sense of hope for an evolving world that we find in Jiménez.

The history of the Américas is full of much suffering and division, and that has been amply illustrated in its arts. The work of great Mexican muralists, to which Jiménez is heir, brutally depicts conflicts between the nations that share la frontera. Any border region can continue its age-old animosities, or it can be a bridge between different ways of living, an example to the world that where two cultures meet, peace and equality may exist. Jiménez is an artist who not only addresses those centuries of pain and division, but also uses his vision to bind. In his portraits of la frontera he captures two worlds and the multiplicity of worlds which those two create as they meet.

Jiménez achieves his syncretic view by utilizing undiluted, often garish colors (a legacy from his father's work in neon signage and the Mexican muralists) and fiberglass (the technology of the north). The myths of the Américas provide a basis for his work. Without that attention to the mythologies of the Américas, he might be just another pop artist constructing sculptures that sit in front of truck stops along the interstate. Jiménez's work is accessible, in the sense that it is popular, but it is also guided by his vision of history.

South of la frontera is the origin of one of the most compelling myths of the Américas: the story of Quetzalcóatl and all the stories which flow from that vast storehouse of legend and philosophy. As a Mexicano, Jiménez is heir to that wealth of knowledge. He taps the roots of Mesoamerican mythology. His brilliant colors are Mexicano colors—they are the plumes of the rainbow serpent. Legend tells us Quetzalcóatl promised to return to the Native people of Mexico. Jiménez shows us that the rebirth of the deity and the artistic impulse it symbolizes can take place in art.

His subject matter utilizes the popular images of the cultura del norte, and a large part of it is depicted and transformed in the rough-and-tumble world of la frontera. He is a son of *el norte*, and so he uses its materials and explores its emerging, popular myths. The tension—and attraction—of Jiménez's work is that he always creates within the space of his two worlds, the Mexicano and the Americano. He constantly shows us the irony of two forces that repel, while showing us glimpses of the synthesis he seeks.

This fusing of the poles of the divergent worldviews that meet in our region is also a path of knowledge, a way of knowing. Polarity is a way of perceiving, but it is limited because it keeps people apart. The natural inclination to protect one's history creates the world of us and them, *us* and the *Other*. Division engenders division, and each one of us comes to believe that he or she is the possessor of the true way of knowledge. This polarity has created a great chasm between the Américas, and it has often been used to create conflict that further polarizes. The artist is a guide between the poles, a mediator creating synthesis and thus a new way of perceiving through works of art.

Jiménez's style is gestural, dynamic, vital. His people of la frontera are muscular, hard, tough, always in action, almost grotesque in their reality. The women are "pura Mexicanas," women of high cheekbones, full hips, arrogant eyes—tattooed survivors of a hard life. Their faces are the faces of la frontera, and their sensuality reflects a gusto for life.

It is that sensuality which is a hallmark of Jiménez's work. While in O'Keeffe we find a southwestern exploration of our sexual natures in the curves of pistils, stamens, and the petals of flowers, in Jiménez we find it exploding from its proper nature, the bodies of men and women, the brute force of horses, even in the dynamic nature of the machine. The dynamo is perverted sexual energy, which the artist can't deny— we made it so he includes it in the myth of el norte.

Beneath the sensuality of the flesh lurks the figure of death, la muerte, a constant companion on the vast desert. Jiménez constantly pulls us back to the Mexicano view of death, reminding those in la cultura del norte that there are many ways to the truth, more than one door of perception. His men are men from la frontera: Mexicanos, Indians, Anglos or mestizos, as comfortable on horses as they are on motorcycles, ranch trucks, or lowrider cars. They are born of the desert earth and born of the machine, thus past and present merge in the work. The sexual overtones are everywhere. These are men who work hard, live hard, and often die young. The country-and-western ballad and the Mexicano corrido fuse in the work.

The Anglo women also have hard, tough faces, an energy that celebrates the vitality of life. You're not that different, Jiménez seems to say. Dance and make merry, because la muerte is always the partner. You are the woman at my side, in dance, at the rodeo, as my baby-doll chuca in the cantina or in my lowrider car, as mythic southwestern Statue of Liberty or giving birth to our children. Earth Mother and the reality of the woman of la frontera combine, and they have more in common than meets the eye.

In the works depicting the pachuco, Jiménez portrays the lowrider lifestyle, a reality from El Paso to Los Angeles. The socio-political message is clear. The descendents of Aztec princes, as Corky Gonzalez called them, now cruise the mean streets in customized cars. The pachuca becomes Tonantzin, in some works la Llorona. And always, Jiménez is pulling at the polarity. There is ambiguity and dissension, but it is not destructive—it is a door to enter.

Each sketch or lithograph or fiberglass sculpture carries the same message: The mythology of distinct worlds comes alive in the fusion that is art. The sod buster becomes a San Isidro from my perspective, reminding me of my ancestors who tilled the valley farmlands of New Mexico for centuries, drawing me closer to the experience of the settlers of the Midwest. The man on fire becomes a Quetzalcóatl, the machine man being born transports me back to Bellas Artes in Mexico City or other municipal buildings where I've stood in awe of the Mexican muralists. Each sculpture becomes a contemporary archaeological site, a place we visit as we would visit Tula, Teotihuacán, or Monte Alban.

I return to the Man on Fire sculpture because there I see our humanity on fire, each one of us burning in the meeting of two worlds on la frontera. The Man on Fire is the Christ of the desert, offering redemption, and he is also the plumed serpent, Quetzalcóatl. In every piece Jiménez pulls together the poles of experience and, most important, a way of seeing.

But in the end, each viewer brings his own mythology, emotions and aesthetics to the viewing—cada cabeza es un mundo—and one also brings one's needs to the viewing, the need to experience the piece of art and go away renewed. The experience of standing before the lithograph or walking around the sculpture is itself a metaphor: the viewer who is attentive to the message will go away a changed person.

Jiménez is accessible to his audience; he wants to communicate and will shock and dazzle us to do it. He has the intent and vision of a world artist. What else can we say? "Te aventates, bro." You did it. You were touched by the muses of the vast deserts around El Paso, and you held steady to your vision. Any artist who accomplishes that deserves our respect, un abrazo, and a whispered, "Te aventates."

A Celebration of Grandfathers

"Buenos días le de Dios, abuelo." "God give you a good day, grand-father." This is how I was taught as a child to greet my grandfather, or any grown person. It was a greeting of respect, a cultural value to be passed on from generation to generation, this respect for the old ones.

The old people I remember from my childhood were strong in their beliefs, and as we lived daily with them we learned a wise path of life to follow. They had something important to share with the young, and when they spoke the young listened. These old abuelos and abuelitas had worked the earth all their lives, and so they knew the value of nurturing, they knew the sensitivity of the earth. The daily struggle called for cooperation, and so every person contributed to the social fabric, and each person was respected for his contribution.

The old ones had looked deep into the web that connects all animate and inanimate forms of life, and they recognized the great design of the creation.

These ancianos from the cultures of the Río Grande, living side by side, sharing, growing together, they knew the rhythms and cycles of time, from the preparation of the earth in the spring to the digging of the acequias that brought the water to the dance of harvest in the fall. They shared good times and hard times. They helped each other through the epidemics and the personal tragedies, and they shared what little they had when the hot winds burned the land and no rain came. They learned that to survive one had to share in the process of life.

Hard workers all, they tilled the earth and farmed, ran the herds and spun wool, and carved their saints and their kachinas from cottonwood

Originally published in *New Mexico Magazine* (March 1983): 35–40, 50–51.

late in the winter nights. All worked with a deep faith that perplexes the modern mind.

Their faith shone in their eyes; it was in the strength of their grip, in the creases time wove into their faces. When they spoke, they spoke plainly and with few words, and they meant what they said. When they prayed, they went straight to the source of life. When there were good times, they knew how to dance in celebration and how to prepare the foods of the fiestas. All this they passed on to the young, so that a new generation would know what they had known, so the thread of life would not be broken.

Today we would say that the abuelitos lived authentic lives.

Newcomers to New Mexico often say that time seems to move slowly here. I think they mean they have come in contact with the inner strength of the people, a strength so solid it causes time itself to pause. Think of it. Think of the high, northern New Mexico villages, or the lonely ranches on the open llano. Think of the Indian pueblo which lies as solid as rock in the face of time. Remember the old people whose eyes seem like windows that peer into a distant past that makes an absurdity of our contemporary world. That is what one feels when one encounters the old ones and their land, a pausing of time.

We have all felt time stand still. We have all been in the presence of power, the knowledge of the old ones, the majestic peace of a mountain stream or an aspen grove or red buttes rising into blue sky. We have all felt the light of dusk permeate the earth and cause time to pause in its flow.

I felt this when first touched by the spirit of Ultima, the old curandera who appears in my first novel, *Bless Me, Ultima*. This is how the young Antonio describes what he feels:

> When she came the beauty of the llano unfolded before my eyes, and the gurgling waters of the river sang to the hum of the turning earth. The magical time of childhood stood still, and the pulse of the living earth pressed its mystery into my living blood. She took my hand, and the silent, magic powers she possessed made beauty from the raw, sun-baked llano, the green river valley, and the blue bowl which was the white sun's home. My bare feet felt the throbbing earth, and my body trembled with excitement. Time stood still.

At other times, in other places, when I have been privileged to be with the old ones, to learn, I have felt this inner reserve of strength upon which they draw. I have been held motionless and speechless by the power of curanderas. I have felt the same power when I hunted with Cruz, high on the Taos mountain, where it was more than the incredible beauty of the mountain bathed in morning light, more than the shining of the quivering aspen, but a connection with life, as if a shining strand of light connected the particular and the cosmic. That feeling is an epiphany of time, a standing still of time.

But not all of our old ones are curanderos or hunters on the mountain. My grandfather was a plain man, a farmer from Puerto de Luna on the Pecos River. He was probably a descendent of those people who spilled over the mountain from Taos, following the Pecos River in search of farmland. There in that river valley he settled and raised a large family.

Bearded and walrus-mustached, he stood five feet tall, but to me as a child he was a giant. I remember him most for his silence. In the summers my parents sent me to live with him on his farm, for I was to learn the ways of a farmer. My uncles also lived in that valley, the valley called Puerto de Luna, there where only the flow of the river and the whispering of the wind marked time. For me it was a magical place.

I remember once, while out hoeing the fields, I came upon an anthill, and before I knew it I was badly bitten. After he had covered my welts with the cool mud from the irrigation ditch, my grandfather calmly said: "Know where you stand." That is the way he spoke, in short phrases, to the point.

One very dry summer, the river dried to a trickle; there was no water for the fields. The young plants withered and died. In my sadness and with the impulse of youth I said, "I wish it would rain!" My grandfather touched me, looked up into the sky and whispered, "Pray for rain." In his language there was a difference. He felt connected to the cycles that brought the rain or kept it from us. His prayer was a meaningful action, because he was a participant with the forces that filled our world, he was not a bystander.

A young man died at the village one summer. A very tragic death. He was dragged by his horse. When he was found, I cried, for the boy was my friend. I did not understand why death had come to one so young. My grandfather took me aside and said, "Think of the death of the trees and the fields in the fall. The leaves fall, and everything rests, as if dead. But they bloom again in the spring. Death is only this small transformation in life."

These are the things I remember, these fleeting images, few words.

I remember him driving his horse-drawn wagon into Santa Rosa in the fall when he brought his harvest produce to sell in the town. What a tower of strength seemed to come in that small man huddled on the seat of the giant wagon. One click of his tongue and the horses obeyed, stopped or turned as he wished. He never raised his whip. How unlike today when so much teaching is done with loud words and threatening hands.

I would run to greet the wagon, and the wagon would stop. "Buenos días le de Dios, abuelo," I would say. This was the prescribed greeting of esteem and respect. Only after the greeting was given could we approach these venerable old people. "Buenos díos te de Dios, mí hijo," he would answer and smile, and then I could jump up on the wagon and sit at his side. Then I, too, became a king as I rode next to the old man who smelled of earth and sweat and the other deep aromas from the orchards and fields of Puerto de Luna.

We were all sons and daughters to him. But today the sons and daughters are breaking with the past, putting aside los abuelitos. The old values are threatened, and threatened most where it comes to these relationships with the old people. If we don't take the time to watch and feel the years of their final transformation, a part of our humanity will be lessened.

I grew up speaking Spanish, and, oh! how difficult it was to learn English. Sometimes I would give up and cry out that I couldn't learn. Then he would say, "Ten paciencia." Have patience. "Paciencia," a word with the strength of centuries, a word that said someday we would overcome. Paciencia—how soothing a word coming from this old man who could still sling hundred-pound bags over his shoulder, chop wood for hours on end, and hitch up his own horses and ride to town and back in one day.

"You have to learn the language of the Americanos," he said. "Me, I will live my last days in my valley. You will live in a new time, the time of the gringos."

A new time did come, a new time is here. How will we form it so it is fruitful? We need to know where we stand. We need to speak softly and respect others and to share what we have. We need to pray not for material gain, but for rain for the fields, for the sun to nurture growth, for nights in which we can sleep in peace, and for a harvest in which everyone can share. Simple lessons from a simple man. These lessons he learned from his past, which was as deep and strong as the currents of the river of life, a life that could be stronger than death.

He was a man; he died. Not in his valley, but nevertheless cared for by his sons and daughters and flocks of grandchildren. At the end, I would enter his room, which carried the smell of medications and Vicks, the faint pungent odor of urine and cigarette smoke. Gone were the aromas of the fields, the strength of his young manhood. Gone also was his patience. Small things bothered him; he shouted or turned sour when his expectations were not met. It was because he could not care for himself, because he was returning to that state of childhood, and all those wishes and desires were now wrapped in a crumbling old body.

"Ten paciencia," I once said to him, and he smiled. "I didn't know I would grow this old," he said. "Now I can't even roll my own cigarettes." I rolled a cigarette for him, placed it in his mouth and lit it. I asked him why he smoked, the doctor had said it was bad for him. "I like to see the smoke rise," he said. He would smoke and doze, and his quilt was spotted with little burns where the cigarettes dropped. One of us had to sit and watch to make sure a fire didn't start.

I would sit and look at him and remember what was said of him when he was a young man. He could mount a wild horse and break it, and he could ride as far as any man. He could dance all night at a dance, then work the acequia the following day. He helped neighbors, they helped him. He married, raised children. Small legends, the kind that make up everyman's life.

He was ninety-four when he died. Family, neighbors, and friends gathered; they all agreed he had led a rich life. I remembered the last years, the years he spent in bed. And as I remember now, I am reminded that it is too easy to romanticize old age. Sometimes we forget the pain of the transformation into old age; we forget the natural breaking down of the body. Not all go gently into the last years, some go crying and cursing, forgetting the names of those they loved the most, withdrawing into an internal anguish few of us can know. May we be granted the patience and care to deal with our ancianos.

For some time we haven't looked at these changes and needs of the old ones. The American image created by the mass media is an image of youth, not of old age. It is the beautiful and the young who are praised in this society. If analyzed carefully, we see that some damaging perceptions have crept into the way society views the old. In response to the old, the mass media have just created old people who act like the young. It is only the healthy, pink-cheeked, outgoing, older persons we are shown in the media. And they are always selling something, as if an entire generation of old people were salespeople in their lives.

Commercials show very lively old men, who must always be in excellent health according to the new myth, selling insurance policies or real estate as they are out golfing, older women selling coffee or toilet paper to those just married. Those images do not illustrate the real life of the old ones.

Real life takes into account the natural cycle of growth and change. My grandfather pointed to the leaves falling from the tree. So time brings with its transformation the often painful, wearing-down process. Vision blurs, health wanes; even the act of walking carries with it the painful reminder of the autumn of life. But this process is something to be faced, not something to be hidden away by false images. Yes, the old can be young at heart, but in their own way, with their own dignity. They do not have to copy the always-young image of the Hollywood star.

My grandfather wanted to return to his valley to die. But by then the families of the valley had left in search of a better future. It is only now that some of the grandchildren return to the valley, a revival. The new generation seeks its roots, that value of love for the land moves us to return to the place where our ancianos formed the culture.

I returned to Puerto de Luna last summer to join the community in a celebration of the founding of the church. I drove by my grandfather's home, my uncles' ranches, the neglected adobe washing down into the earth from whence it came. And I wondered, how might the values of my grandfather's generation live in our own? What can we retain to see us through these hard times? I was to become a farmer, and I became a writer. As I plow and plant my words, do I nurture as my grandfather did in his fields and orchards? The answers are not simple.

"They don't make men like that anymore," is a phrase we hear when one does honor to a man. I am glad I knew my grandfather. I am glad there are still times when I can see him in my dreams, hear him in my reverie. Sometimes I think I catch a whiff of that earthy aroma that was his smell, just as in lonely times sometimes I catch the fragrance of Ultima's herbs. Then I smile. How strong these people were to leave such a lasting impression.

So, as I would greet my abuelo long ago, it would help us all to greet the old ones we know with this kind and respectful greeting: "Buenos días le de Dios."

Introduction to *A Ceremony of Brotherhood*

Active revolt against oppressive government is not a new notion to the native people of the Americas. U.S. history books would have us believe that the eastern U.S. colonists' revolution for independence in 1776 is the hallmark of such a daring strike for freedom, but long before the Yankee revolution, prior revolts had been fought in many quarters of the newly colonized American hemisphere.

Although discussed in many works of history about the Southwest, the Pueblo Indian Revolt of 1680 deserves an even greater share of attention because of its significance. In that year, a confederation of nation-states (city-states, called pueblos by the Spanish settlers) rose up against the Spanish colonial government. Taking their cultural and historical destiny in their own hands, they drove out the Spanish rulers and what had come to be a harsh and cruel form of government. These native patriots who refused to be governed by an arbitrary colonial power created the Revolution of 1680. To those ancestors, and to all people who carry the vision of justice in their hearts, we dedicate this *Ceremony of Brotherhood*.

In that year of 1680, the land and survival of a native culture were at stake, and those who would oppress sought to turn the Españoles against the Pueblo Indians. But in spite of the tyrants, a group emerged from both cultures that had the wisdom to create a new harmony from both worlds' views. They learned to live together and to share the precious earth and water of the Río Grande valley and the mountains of Sangre de Cristo. These were the farmers—the common people of the land—from both cultures; they were the seekers after peace and

Originally published as the introduction to *A Ceremony of Brotherhood, 1680–1980*, by Rudolfo A. Anaya and Simon J. Ortiz (Albuquerque, N.Mex.: Academia, 1981), 2–3.

harmony. Together they created a living example of the ideal that simply said people from different cultures can live side by side in peace. They can learn from each other, they can share their ways, and they can create a better future.

It is as appropriate, then, to celebrate the 1680 Pueblo Indian Revolution, a three-hundred-year-old legacy, as it is appropriate to celebrate the Revolution of 1776. Both teach us that just men and women will never allow wanton and inhumane governments to rule them. This book celebrates that principle. It is the work of many people. It was conceived by representatives from both cultures who realized it was necessary to look at our past and invite contemporary artists and writers to rejoice in those aspects of our long and common history that have sustained the people.

Now, three hundred years later, the nation-states of the Pueblo Indians, the Españoles, the Mexicans, and all the blending of the mestizo culture they created are at peace along the Río Grande, having kept their own individuality, but adopting and using the best from each culture in shared respect. The languages are still alive, the ceremonies are still enacted, the folkways persist. And so we come together to celebrate a sharing and the right of cultural survival. For the brothers and sisters of all cultures who believe in freedom, we offer the stories and songs and art work in this book as a part of the new history, a recording which testifies that the race of the true warriors is still being run, the ceremonies of brotherhood are still being celebrated.

I would like to thank Consuelo and Tomás Atencio for their commitment to *A Ceremony of Brotherhood*.

Cuentos de los Antepasados
Spanning the Generations

In our culture there is a very deep relationship between the old people and the children. For us, los ancianos and los niños go hand in hand. In my own writing, it has been natural for me to use this special relationship of love and learning which takes place between an old person and a child.

For example, in *Bless Me, Ultima*, my first novel, the story revolves around the old curandera and the boy, and what Antonio learns from Ultima shapes his personality and his future. Likewise, in *Heart of Aztlan*, I created Crispín, the old poet of the barrio, and around him the younger men gathered to listen to his cuentos and learn from his experiences and knowledge.

Many of us, I am sure, grew up in households where ancianos lived with us as a natural part of la familia. I know that my childhood was more magical and mysterious and imaginative because of people like Ultima, and it was certainly enriched by my grandfather, who lived with us until he was ninety-four. He told marvelous cuentos and side-splitting chistes, and he teased my imagination with adivinanzas. I've promised myself that one of these days I'm going to write a book about my grandfather.

So what about these cuentos, or folktales, and the literary heritage of our antepasados? Are we to allow this wealth of oral tradition to die, or can we bring the wisdom and the perceptions about life that are incorporated in the cuentos into the lives of this young generation? That tradition forms a vital part of our culture and history; in it we can find the wisdom of the people, "el oro del barrio" as Tomás Atencio calls it. I

Address presented to the Seventh Annual Bilingual/Multicultural Education Regional Conference, Denver, Colo. (12 October 1978); and adapted for publication in *Agenda* 9, no. 1 (1979): 11–13.

believe that part of our heritage is relevant to us today and that it should be an integral part of the bilingual classroom.

The cuentos of los antepasados, and the contemporary cuento, which is still being generated today by the people, both carry messages that speak to our day-to-day existence. We should listen closely, and we should teach this new generation, which by and large will be an urban generation, to listen to the past.

The most interesting facet of our oral tradition is the most obvious one—that is, it is still being created and composed by the people as they go about their work and play. The Hispanic character loves the "sense of salsa" that is the seed of language, and so he constantly plays with it, whether it be to make love or war. I'll give you an example of a story I heard years ago that combines many elements of the cuento; it also incorporates a sense of our survival instinct in the face of a different culture.

I call this cuento "The Eliminator Is Broken," or "How to Succeed in a Minority Business."

Estos eran dos compadres—or we can start, Once upon a time there were two compadres. . . . You see, the cuento or story can be told either in English or Spanish, because most Chicanos are bilingual storytellers. Anyway, there were two compadres, one from Colorado and one from Nuevo México. And with all the Texans flooding to the mountains in the summer, they decided to take advantage of the business and set up a small café. So they renovated an old adobe house (they left the adobe exposed for local color), fixed the kitchen, hung up their sign, and waited for business. But the compadre from Colorado, who was the more timid of the two, grew a little worried.

"Oiga, compadre," he said, "I'm a little worried."

"Pues why, compadre?" his friend asked.

"What happens if we get a gringo customer? Our English ain't too good."

"My gosh, don't worry, compadre, I'll take care of it. I can handle it."

Ese compadre de Nuevo México era muy adelantao. A few minutes later their first customers arrived, a big three-hundred-pound Texan and his equally large wife. They waddled out of their big Cadillac and hurried in to order breakfast.

"Howdy y'all," the Texan says. "I'd like a couple of steaks smothered in onions, French fries, a tossed salad, a jug of coffee, and half a dozen scrambled eggs on the side."

"Me too," his wife nodded.

"Right away," the compadre who was waiting on them nodded. He felt good that he had been able to take down the order without any trouble, so he rushed to the kitchen to tell his friend the good news. "Look, I got the order without any problem." Then he added, "But they sure do eat funny, don't they?"

Meanwhile, the Texans, in a hurry to be on their way, decided to skip the eggs. So they called the compadre over and said, "Say, Pancho, we're in an awful big hurry, so could you just eliminate the eggs?"

Eliminate? Our compadre thought, uh-hum. He hadn't heard that word before, but he nodded and pretended to write down "eliminate the eggs." Then he turned and ran into the kitchen for help. "Compadre, we got problems. Now they want to eliminate the eggs! What does that mean?"

The compadre from New Mexico, el adelantao, said, "Don't worry, compadre, I'll take care of this. For me English is no problem." So he walked over to the Texan and his wife, drew himself up as high as he could, and in a cool, confident voice he said, "I'm sorry, friends, but today we can't eliminate the eggs. You see, the eliminator is broken."

There's a message here, a message of pride and adaptability. Perhaps the incident also tells us that the next time a school district decides to eliminate a bilingual program in one of our schools it's up to us to stand up as straight as our compadre and say, "Sorry, but there's not going to be any more elimination of bilingual programs. As of today the eliminator is broken!"

In fact, we should all be prepared to protest elimination and insist on a well-funded and planned effort to include bilingual/multicultural classes in the school curriculum where the need dictates! The only thing that should be eliminated is the idea that bilingual programs are compensatory and transitional in nature. It is not un-American to believe that the multicultural reality of this country should be reflected in every aspect of education, from kindergarten through twelfth grade and thereafter. Children today should not be denied the rich culture of their forefathers.

I trust that the process of cultural evolution preserves the best and the most beautiful aspects of culture, and so it is important that the schools not shut out our history and language.

We already know that the wisdom of los antepasados will survive, but in order to insure that this present generation is able to communicate across the gulf of time with los viejitos, we must encourage bilingual/multicultural classes; we must support the creation of more children's literature (a vastly ignored field to date), and we must insure that the indigenous languages and all their cultural ramifications find their way into the core curriculum of our schools.

I have been working on a project which interests me precisely because, in its final form, it will be one of these communications between the young and the old, and at the same time it will be a cross-cultural communication. I have been translating some of the cuentos in Juan B. Rael's monumental collection of folktales from southern Colorado and northern New Mexico. The folktales were collected in their original Spanish idiom, in the "patois of the native," como decimos alla en Barelas, and I am translating them into English. I am struck now, as I was when I was a child and heard many of these stories, by their deep knowledge of the human condition. They are bright, piercing commentaries on life. The language of the people is alive in them. And each one speaks across the centuries as to the conditions of our contemporary life.

Here is an example of the folk wisdom and the sense of justice that appears in one particular tale. It happened that a poet from New Mexico—keep in mind, this happened many years ago, before the most recent flowing of Chicano literature—by the name of Chicoria was invited to California to entertain two rich ranchers. When he arrived, the two ranchers sat down to eat, but they didn't have the good manners to invite Chicoria to sit and eat with them. So Chicoria decided it was up to him to point out their bad manners.

"You know," he began, "where I come from we use a different spoon for each mouthful we take."

The two ranchers were very impressed. What a unique culture that must be, they thought. What Chicoria didn't tell them was that each spoon was a piece of tortilla—cuchara de tortilla, it's called.

"And in our country," he continued, "the female goats all give birth to three kids at a time."

"But how can one goat feed three kids?" the ranchers asked.

"The same as you're doing now," Chicoria answered. "While two eat, the third one watches."

The ranchers realized their rudeness; they apologized and invited Chicoria to eat with them. We know that there are plenty of boards of education with the likes of the rich ranchers sitting at the table, and they're a well-fed bunch. So it's up to us to keep insisting that part of that public pie is rightfully ours. We're not going to sit and wait while everybody else gets their fair share; we demand ours too!

We must continue to insist that bilingualism not only serves to personally enhance the aesthetic part of our lives, but that it is one of the most useful economic and social tools available. Spanish, for example, ranks among the top five most used languages in the world, and that, coupled with the fact that we in the Southwest sit next door to Latin America—indeed are part of the progeny of the same forces that created the Latin American civilizations—is enough argument for the teaching of bilingual and multicultural classes in our schools.

But what about the children? What do they need? How can we get involved in their education? Because I am a writer and an educator, the one question I am most often asked is why we don't have more children's stories and literature. I suggest that we should have a national Chicano or Latino publisher sponsor a contest and award prizes to writers who would then be published in a special children's issue. We could even do it by grade levels. The point is to get established writers and younger writers interested in this field. And one hopes the interest by writers and publishers wouldn't stop there, but continue to mushroom.

I have tried my hand at writing for children. A few years ago I wrote a short story titled "Consuelo Goes to School." I also adapted it into the screenplay for the film *Promise for Tomorrow*. In it I used another one of the cuentos or chistes I had heard, and everyone loved it. The cuento is about two neighbors, a cat and a rat. The cat was a bilingual Chicano, but the rat was monolingual. The rat could only squeak in one language, and he insisted that was the American way.

One day the cat got fed up with listening to the rat's squeaking, so he decided to have him for supper. He chased the rat, but the rat ran into his hole. The cat tried to coax him out by calling him, "Meow, meow." But as long as the rat heard the meowing, he knew the cat was out there. "Oh no, I'm not going out," he said to himself. A short time passed, and then the rat heard a terrible noise and the loud barking of a dog. "Bow-wow! Woof! Woof!" "Ah," the rat said to himself, "now the dog has come and chased the cat away. It's safe to go out." But the minute he stepped out of his hole, the cat grabbed him and ate him. Then as the gato loco wiped his whiskers he said, "Ah, it's wonderful to be bilingual! Qué bueno es ser bilingüe."

Another question I am often asked is why I write in English. Spanish is my mother tongue, and I was raised in a completely Spanish-speaking environment. But when I went to school, there were no bilingual programs to sustain and build upon the native speaker's language; consequently, our reading and writing competency in our own language was not maintained. Now that I'm older and I recognize the value of language not only as a social means to communicate but as a creative tool, I am angry that the school did not help me maintain and develop the language which already was so natural to me. But a lot of us are in the same boat, and I think that is why we are such ardent supporters of bilingual education. We know that we shouldn't have to give up one language to acquire another. The gift of children is that given the right atmosphere they can learn so much!

So let's not have happen to his generation what happened to mine. Children deserve the full benefit of language study to live in this century and to deal with a rapidly shrinking and mobile world. School districts have to commit time, money, and personnel so that bilingual and multicultural programs are incorporated into the curriculum.

I would like to close with another cuento, and I want to emphasize again the importance of bringing this wealth of our old people into our homes and schoolrooms, so that it will not die, indeed, so that it will enrich our lives. In this story there is a mean daughter-in-law who doesn't like the old grandfather, her husband's father. The old man is too much trouble, she thinks, so she persuades her husband to move the old man to a room far away from the house. The room is very cold, and they often forget to feed the old man, so he suffers very much.

It so happens that one day the grandson visits his grandfather, and the old man tells the boy to bring him a blanket because he is very cold. The boy runs to the barn where he finds a nice, thick blanket. He takes the blanket to his father and tells him to cut it in two.

"But what's it for?" the father asks.

"It's for grandfather, so he won't be cold," the boy answers.

"Why don't you give him the entire blanket?" the father says.

"Oh no," his son answers, "I want to save the other half for you when you get old."

The father immediately realized he had been mistreating his own father, so he went and brought the old man into the house where he would be warm, and thereafter he visited him every day and saw to it that the old man was well taken care of. (Unfortunately, the story doesn't tell us what happened to the daughter-in-law, but I'm sure poetic justice took care of her.)

What the story does tell us is that it took the innocence and love of a child to point out the injustice being committed. It also tells us that we have often been treated like grandfather, restricted from our educational pursuits by this daughter-in-law culture that would keep us in the back room. But the children see. They see the injustice, and they ask questions. They want to know why their language and history are being denied to them.

We must be strong, like the father, to pursue the changes we know we have to make for ourselves and for the future. And the time for change is now. We must demand that the full benefits of education accrue to us, and that the fabric of the educational system be woven from the woof and warp of our own history and language! As long as society continues to place a value on a liberal education, then the schools of that society must incorporate the cultural values, the worldview and unique perspective, and the history of the indigenous people it purports to educate.

If it takes up this challenge, then this society will not only be a more just society, but it will insure itself a richer and more divergent history, and it will insure its own well being.

Curanderas/Women Warriors

"She's right," don Toto said and filled all the empty cups, "Concha used to know all the curanderas in the valley. And she could cure el mal ojo."

"Take an egg and place it on the person's forehead," Concha said, "or rub their stomach with it. Then break it open in a glass of water. You will see el mal. Most of the time it's just someone who looked at the baby too long," she continued. "You know, like when the baby is so cute and you adore it, you can pull out its alma. Make it sick. The spirit is strong, sabes. You can draw the soul of a person out—like when you fall in love, ese!" she kidded and poked Sonny with her elbow.

Draw the soul out, Sonny thought. El mal ojo actually comes from looking at the baby too closely, admiring it. His mother had told him stories of curing the evil eye. People, without knowing it, actually affected the young soul of the child.

"So you get out of harmony, como dicen los indios," Concha continued. "The person who puts the mal ojo has to spit on the baby's forehead. A lot of people think it's the spit that makes the baby well, but no, don't you see, honey, it's the breath. The breath is the soul, the breath gives back the soul to the baby. Makes it well. Ah, we used to have curanderas all over the valley who knew how to cure everything. Mujeres fuertes. They cured everyone, delivered babies, and—"

Here she paused and her bright, greenish eyes stared into Sonny's. "They fought el demonio. They were the only ones who fought the diablo. La gente doesn't realize it, but when the last of the old curanderas died, there was no one left to fight the brujas del

---

Not previously published.

diablo. Oh, there's a few here and there, these young women who want to learn, like Lorenza. Pero que saben? They don't know how strong evil is. Look around you, look at what's happening to la gente. The kids are crazy, and so are their parents. Dope, booze, violence. The diablo is loose, and there's no one to fight his brujas."

Don Eliseo and don Toto nodded.

"Oh, there's the medicine men in the pueblo," la Concha concluded. "But the people don't go there anymore. They go to the shopping malls, to the movies, but not to the right medicine."

This excerpt from *Zia Summer*, a novel I have just completed, reflects on the traditional role of the curanderas of the northern Río Grande, specifically New Mexico. If we assume there are many levels to the practice of curanderismo, then we have all seen them at work, because even the most simple remedies used by our mothers came from the large storehouse of the curandera's remedies and herbs.

When I got out of the hospital in 1954 after a serious accident, it was my mother who took on the role of sobadora, massage therapist. Her knowledge of bones and muscles brought life back to my limbs.

The coming of the Anglo-American doctor to Nuevo México diminished the role of the village curanderas. A more scientific view of the nature of illness and its causes became the dominant view, and the depth of knowledge that the curandera represented began to be lost. In the nineteen forties, when I observed their work as a child, the last of the old curanderas were still working, but most would be gone within twenty years. With their disappearance, the holistic view of medicine, which our ancestors practiced, would begin to disappear.

Some will argue that we lost nothing, that the western view of scientific medicine and its materialistic outlook was all we needed. I will not argue against the use of that medical technology; my argument is that in dealing with the deeper spiritual and emotional problems, the technology fails. The role of the curandera in addressing the needs of the spirit is still viable today.

What did the curandera represent to the community she served? Again, there are levels in which she worked. Perhaps she only knew the herbs and could make teas and poultices to heal. Perhaps she was also a sobadora who did massages. Perhaps she was a partera skilled in the delivery of babies.

But there are other levels, spiritual levels in which the curandera, like the shaman, worked. To understand this work we need to understand the worldview of the Río Grande valley. A component in our belief system has to do with the role of the soul, or spirit, and its illnesses. This component does not exist in the view of modern medicine, and it is quite different in its basis and in its practice from the view psychiatry holds.

For the sake of comparison, the curanderas who went deeper into the study of the soul were cognizant of the practice we generally call shamanism. Their role was to rescue the soul from the illness it suffered, and that illness was perceived as evil. Something had infiltrated the soul and was causing illness. I described this in the curing of the uncle in my novel *Bless Me, Ultima*.

The curing ceremony held some danger, and so these curanderas of the traditional culture were women warriors. As health-care workers, they understood and treated a wide array of psychological, emotional, and spiritual illnesses in the community. Their role was to correct the imbalances, to bring back harmony, as Concha says above.

Imagine a nation (or a community) without these health-care workers, these kind and knowledgeable folk psychiatrists who helped to restore harmony to those in trouble. That nation would be a nation out of kilter; its inhabitants would have no one to turn to in times of psychological and emotional stress.

That is what doña Concha reflects on in the above passage. The last of the curanderas, the warrior women, have died, and there is no one to turn to.

The Catholic church remains a place where the needs of the soul are addressed, but the church has a very dogmatic view that generally does not accept the teaching of shamanism; thus the work of the old curanderas, while they used many prayers of the church in their curing, was never acknowledged.

Quite frankly—and I realize this will invite some discussion—the church does not represent the indigenous worldview from which the curanderas of the New World took so much of their knowledge. The flight of the soul, the concept of the nagual and the infusion of a "bad" spirit into the soul of another are tenets of faith in curanderismo which the church has tried to erase.

The passing away of the curanderas coincides with the rise of antisocial behavior, the rise of violence and lack of respect for the elders in our community. In short, a general sense of disharmony has set in. How are we curing this disorientation? Concha says the parents are giving the kids money and cars, and so a car culture replaces the family culture. Leisure time is spent in video arcades, or watching television and movies. The element of love, love for oneself and for others, is not taught, and so the young think nothing of drive-by shootings.

We are a culture in transition, moving from the traditional way of life of our ancestors toward the mainstream culture, and as we do we trade off many of our values. We have traded the curandera for the doctor, without realizing that the two can work hand in hand. Those guides and mentors within the community to whom we once turned are gone. On the road of assimilation we have lost touch with the core of values and the healing which was our inheritance.

No one can predict the future, but without the return of those mentors, las curanderas, the warrior women who understand the nature of evil and its effect on the soul, we will not soon recuperate.

We need young men and women to apprentice in the healing art. We need training for curanderas, not for more data processors. We have filled downtown office buildings with secretaries, but we have not replaced the old curanderas.

It is not too late for young women and men to return to the traditional healing methods. This means studying modern medicine and getting degrees in nursing, massage therapy, organic use of herbs, and, at the same time, studying curanderismo. We can set up clinics where practitioners combine the old teachings and modern medicine, where they attend once again to the curing, not only of the flesh, but of the soul.

In some respects this is happening. A few Chicana registered nurses have studied with the curanderas, and in some hospitals doctors consult with the medicine men of the Navajos and the Pueblos. Healing ceremonies from the indigenous cultures are now being allowed in the hospitals by wise doctors who realize the healing of the patient involves the patients' faith and knowledge of what will make them well. Native Americans in some prisons are being allowed to construct their sweat lodges.

The souls of many nations are sick. We have only to see the world map of conflicts to sense the disharmony. We, too, reflect the same sickness. Disharmony, disorientation, being out of kilter. We are sick at heart. Those of us who grew up in the traditional Nuevo Mexicano culture now look back and see how much we have lost on the road of assimilation.

Perhaps our new curanderas and curanderos are the men and women working in the streets with disoriented youth. They are helping rescue the lost souls, but they need help. They need to study the traditional concepts and notions of healing. They need to know that at the basis of curanderismo is a worldview with roots in a healing process that evolved in the Americas and, in its most positive aspects, can assist in the curing.

I believe the folk, la gente, create and engender that which is good. The work of the curanderas was an important ingredient in our culture. Reacquainting ourselves with that way of knowledge will help restore the equilibrium we all seek in our troubled times.

Model Cities/Model Chicano/Norma Jean

Recently I attended the opening of the South Broadway Cultural Center, a magnificent building in one of our barrios in Alburquerque. This new community center has quite literally risen from the ashes of its prior incarnation. It had its origins as a model cities library.

I was told that this center is now the last remaining model cities library in the country. Can you imagine? LBJ and the vision of model cities, and now one city has kept the faith. Kept the dream alive.

That's what the model cities concept was, a dream. A desire to enhance society. A desire to create a model that everyone could emulate.

(This country has always had such aspirations. Remember Manifest Destiny? The conversion of the wilderness? The extinction of the buffalo?)

If you are in Alburquerque and tugged by nostalgia for the sixties, drop by the center. Of course you won't find the original storefront barrio library. It grew up. Everybody from the sixties grew up. In the sixties Norma Jean became Marilyn Monroe. In the sixties we lost our innocence.

My city also grew up. You won't recognize the rangy cow town of the sixties. Ah, but I have to remember, so *many* of you don't even know my city. When I mention I'm from Alburquerque, people smile: "Ah, yes, beautiful country. Desert, high mountains, and open skies. Very spiritual. I was there once. In Santa Fe. In Taos."

Never Alburquerque, the city I recently christened anew. Renamed. More correctly, gave back to the city its original name. I wrote a novel and gave it the name of my city, putting into the title the missing *R*.

Seventeen hundred six: La Villa de Alburquerque. A model villa on the Río Grande, with Mexicanos and Indians planting corn, chile, squash. A garden of Eden.

Not previously published.

In the early nineteenth century came the Anglo migration from the east, westward ever westward. The round adobe curves were squared. A new language flooded the land. New laws, fast-food joints, new needs and desires. As migrants are wont to do, the new Anglos influenced our Mexicano way of life.

A station master, it is said, in painting the sign for the new train stop, dropped the first R from the name of the city. Thus began the process of becoming a model city. But for what? For whom? Why?

Maybe you never heard of Alburquerque? Or assumed it was a place you had to pass through to get to Santa Fe. Perhaps you don't know what a model cities library is, or used to be. Model cities were a great social experiment in our country. Proclaimed by LBJ. Proclaimed by the politicos in Washington, DC.

Manifest Destiny. New Deal. New Frontier. History is full of such experiments. Men trying to remake the country in their own image. For my generation it was the Model Cities.

"A library," I once told a group of teachers, "should be the heart and soul of community. Every art and endeavor should gravitate around the library. Libraries can cure crime, youth violence, graffiti, acne, kids having kids, inertia."

They believed me. They cheered.

Everybody wants to believe in the "model." The archetype. The first beginning. Like it used to be. Before the Great Depression. Before the Great War. Before Stalin's pogroms. When we used to leave the front door open. Watch *Leave it to Beaver* on TV. Even before that. When the Blacks weren't uppity and there were no Chicano models.

"You are a model for your community," one teacher says to me. Her breath as toasty as yesterday's best seller. "Where are you from? Al-bur-quer-kee? I was there once. On my way to Santa Fe."

I am thinking of Norma Jean, and the new photographs just released. They were taken by X, the man who knew her when she was plain Norma Jean. He photographed her and helped bring about the young Norma Jean's transition into the model, Marilyn Monroe. The most photographed woman of our century.

He found her early, an archetype of the fifties, a virgin before the rough and tumble sixties, and he began photographing her, recording her growth, from bebopper to woman. And she, peering into the prints he offered, began to change. The image began to create the woman.

In Hollywood nothing is left alone. It is made to fit the film. In this world nothing is left alone. It is made to fit. A destructive desire.

X held the mirror for Norma Jean, and the girl said, "Yes, I can be that and more." Those who read our books hold up a mirror for us.

The past is always an age of innocence, then it goes sour. Men try to make it more than it is. The natives sometimes get in the way. Something in the blood drives us to be greater than the present. The natives sometimes have to be removed.

We can, we believe, create a Camelot. "I dream of things as they might be, and say why not." (Or something like that.)

Our barrios could be Camelot? Wow! And even Norma Jean could sneak into the White House. What immense possibilities!

We fell in love with Marilyn when we saw her first movies in the fifties. Who didn't? She not only awakened desire in us (anyone who rouses your hormones can do that), she was a model. We sensed the young Be-Bop-a-Lula in her! She came onto the screen and became available for our fantasies, daydreams, erupting sexual longing.

But through the flesh we saw the soul. We saw the model in her. We didn't want to lose our innocence even as we saw hers slip away.

"You are a model for the young children of your community. They love your books," another teacher says.

I have heard this from teachers since I published my first novel. There was no Chicano fiction then. We created it, following César Chávez's footsteps, he who was the model of what we could be. We created Chicano identity, and as we molded that "New World Chicano and Chicana" we became models.

Like Norma Jean, we were too young to become models. We still had a lot of learning to do. Nevertheless, we held up a mirror to our brown faces and proclaimed, "Aquí estamos!" It means, "We are here!" Usually followed by "And we will not leave!"

Ah, yes, the model. A Model Chicano. We hold up our models for emulation. We are surprised when they trip and fall, like Norma Jean fell. From innocence.

Maybe that's why we fell for Norma. She was vulnerable, as all young men and women are vulnerable. Is it that we set up models so we can throw tomatoes at them? Find our faults in them? Poor Bubba.

Never mind, plow ahead. Find that essence within! Build the model cities of the twentieth century!

Ganas we call desire in Spanish. We had the ganas to proclaim our identity even when the rest of the country wasn't listening, or didn't give a damn.

"Chicanos? What does it *really* mean?" one of the teachers asks me.

"Well, something like Mexican with an Indian mother, Spanish father, bilingual but speaking mostly English. We're Mexicans caught on this side of the river when the Manifest Destiny folks kicked the Mexican government out of the Southwest."

"Are you first generation?"

"Pues, some of us just got here, some are unto the umteenth generation. We're been here a long time. We're models. Like we're the first mestizos of the New World. Part European, part Indian."

"Oh, Hispanic?"

"God no! Don't let a Chicano hear you say that word!"

"Well, that's what the press calls you."

"Yeah, but what does the press know?"

They don't know that in the South Broadway area of Alburquerque a model cities library has risen. Like the phoenix, from the foundation of a storefront a model cities library springs, the new center. The dream lives on in one isolated corner.

The people wanted it. A few wise politicians helped.

"Is it a great responsibility, I mean, being a model for your people?"

"My people?"

"You know, the Chicanos."

I don't answer. I think it makes me vulnerable. Like Norma Jean.

Once they find the model, they think they've found everything there is to know. The essence. In the beginning was the word, and the word was knowledge. And the word became flesh. And the flesh became the model.

But we know it doesn't last forever and ever. Like Norma Jean didn't last. And there's only one model cities library left in the country. The dreams don't last. Those people who want to make things in their own image don't last. LBJ didn't last.

I won't last.

Is that true? That models don't last. That the ipso facto becomes de facto. That perhaps even the mathematical equations are changing as they curve around the extremities of space. That $E = mc^2$ won't last. That nothing lasts.

Or is it just the human model that doesn't last? Is the real model the soul?

I take some comfort. Norma Jean will last.

No she didn't. She became MM. Then she OD'd.

It's tough being a model. Like being a sex symbol. Things weigh you down. You have to give up smoking. Tell the kids to give up graffiti and join art classes. Question the value of rap music. Teachers call and want you to give lectures to their students.

"They're from your community. They're Chicanos. They need someone to look up to."

That's it! The model is held up and looked at. Examined. Photographed. Questioned. Quite often, depleted.

God, she was vulnerable. We sensed it. That was part of her appeal. Not just the sex, even though she filled out dreams. But in her eyes ("Yo! So whoze lookin' at her eyes!") we saw the vulnerability.

The model cannot live alone, even though the attention can drive one to the tower. The model must live with others. Perhaps that's why one model cities library survived in this country. It became a community.

Norma Jean. Well, she became Marilyn Monroe and died. Alone.

Chicano writers? Chicanas? The new models? More and more are revealing the myriad facets of identity. Thank the deities. We need them! If we don't record our history, it won't be recorded! Or the stationmaster will get the name wrong! Misspell it.

We have survived with the missing *R*. Now we put it back! Our writers grow in presence. Big east coast publishers come courting them. The country listens. Here and there teachers hold us up as models.

We smile and urge the kids to stay in school.

We delineate identity.

We create myth.

When the model becomes a myth, it enters the collective memory, the dream of the people. But you've got to be there, in the center of the whole enchilada! In the soul and in the flesh!

The people in Alburquerque saved the original model cities library! They cared. The people listen to the storytellers. They care.

If only Norma Jean had had a community of love, a cultural center where she could drop in. . . . Ah, we dream.

A Second Opinion

Graduates of the Medical Programs of the University of New Mexico, family members, distinguished guests and dedicated faculty members.

We are gathered here tonight to celebrate this passage which culminates years of dedication and hard work on the part of all of you.

I feel honored to be asked to speak at this 1982 Health Convocation. We are all honored to attend the graduation of these young medical professionals as they enter the service of mankind. What a momentous threshold! What a challenging journey begins tonight!

It is proper that we gather to pay you homage, to see you off. The tribes of the past and the nations of the present have always gathered to celebrate the rites of passage of their young heroes and heroines.

And at these tribal gatherings, the poet or the storyteller has always been present. It is the function of the storyteller to record the historic events of the community, to tell the stories of the past, and to look forward into the future.

I was invited to speak to you tonight because I am a storyteller. And, in your honor, I have written a story.

My story is called "A Second Opinion." For all of us, death is not only the second opinion, it is the final opinion. And only then do we know if we have used our life and our gifts wisely or unwisely.

Here, then, is my story: "A Second Opinion."

Once there was a young doctor who finished his studies at the university and went out into the world to practice. He shunned the villages and the countryside and went to a large city.

"Here I will build a fine practice," he thought to himself. "The entire world will recognize my skills as a healer."

Paper presented at the University of New Mexico Health Convocation (15 May 1982).

Soon he knew he had made the right choice. The inhabitants of the city were always sick, and they flocked to the young doctor.

One person who first came to the doctor was an insurance salesman. The insurance salesman said: "You are a bright, young doctor. Many will come to you to be cured. But you will be surprised how little they honor your profession. The smallest mistake you make and they will want your blood. I will sell you malpractice insurance in case a suit is brought against you."

The young doctor smiled. "I don't need insurance," he answered. "I have studied with the best doctors in the country. I am confident in my skills. I will make no mistakes. In fact, to prove the confidence I have in my training, I will collect a fee only from those patients I cure." So the insurance man went away.

A group of older, established doctors came to the young doctor. "It is best not to rock the boat," they politely reminded him. "There is unity in strength. Stick to our rules and regulations."

The young doctor agreed, but in his heart he had only one burning desire: to serve mankind, to cure the sick. He quickly had a thriving practice.

One of his first patients was a young woman who came to him and complained of a pain in her heart. "My heart is heavy and gives me great anguish," she said.

The young doctor, unschooled in the emotions of the heart, examined her with the most modern and wondrous machines he had purchased for his office. He could find no source of anguish; the machines recorded that she was healthy, so he pronounced her in good health and sent her on her way, prescribing a mild sedative so she could sleep at night.

Later, a young man came to see the doctor, complaining of a bitter taste in his mouth. The sour taste of bile rose from within and overwhelmed him. The doctor examined him carefully and prescribed medications. The young man took the medicine and found that, indeed, the taste in his mouth was now sweet.

A young poet came to the doctor and said, "I am blinded by what I see: I see much suffering and poverty; I see poor people go hungry, and their children are without clothes; I see the young without hope gather in the streets like packs of animals, and they prey upon their own kind and destroy each other; I see young girls sell their souls to the slavery of the false image of the image makers. I sing of these things, but no one listens, and my songs are full of sadness. Help me, doctor."

And the doctor, now far wiser than before, prescribed glasses that narrowed the vision, and the poet went away seeing only that which was before his feet. Because he could not see the ills of the society, he assumed they were gone.

The young people of the city heard of the famous doctor, and they went to him—their minds and souls ravaged by drugs. The doctor, full of sympathy for the young, worked deep into the night, and in his research he discovered a drug which would end their dependence on drugs.

The golden age of medicine blossomed. Each day saw the advent of a new invention or drug. The old scourges of mankind were conquered. The spark of life itself was touched and reworked to suit personal preferences. The life span of man on earth was increased by many years, and the old filled the streets and the parks, and the lonely houses where they lived in silence.

The art of healing became a strict science. At the disposal of the doctor were countless medications and machines which could peer into the darkest corner of a human cell. The patients came and went, countless faces full of pain and suffering. And with the tools of science, the doctor ministered to them all, but with all the technology available to him, sometimes weeks went by—months then years—and he didn't touch his patients with his hands. He had forgotten what one of his mentors had told him: that the real healing of the spirit comes from the human touch.

The doctor's practice grew. Around him grew a clinic. Many students came to study with the doctor, and he had many assistants to aid him in his work.

"He has grown old and wise," the people said of the doctor. "He is not a slave to the hubris which seems to infect so many of these learned men."

And it was true. The doctor was a humble man. Many patients came to him for a second opinion, and he took them under his care and did his best to cure them. He used the most advanced techniques and the miracle drugs of the time, and still the sick rooms filled with people full of dread and fear of life—a modern sickness which resisted the best care.

In his office and in the operating rooms of the great hospitals of the city, the doctor had much power over life and death, but out in the world the armies of great nations and the capability of nuclear holocaust threatened the very existence of life.

"That is the realm of the politician and the social scientist," the wise doctor said. "Who would treat my patients if I took up every social cause which afflicts mankind?"

Who indeed would treat the patients of the final reckoning? Who would speak to the doctor and hold out a hand of love, as one night, late in his life, he awakened from a restless sleep. He arose from his bed, and in the dimly lighted room he saw a form sitting near the window.

"Who are you?" the old doctor asked.

"I am death," the shadow replied. "You should know me."

"I've seen your work," the doctor said, "but I didn't know you could be so frightful. But what are you doing here, tonight. Who is dying?"

"I have come for you," death answered. "Your time has come."

"Me?" the doctor shuddered. "There must be some mistake. I'm not ill. And there is so much work to do. Yes, there is some mistake. I am not ready—"

"They all say that," death said and stood. "But I assure you, when I am sent there is no second opinion to be had. No, my coming is final; that's it."

"But one should have time to prepare," the doctor protested. "There should be some warning. I am planning a new clinic—I am doing new research—I am too busy to die."

"A modern complaint," death answered. "Everyone is too busy. And yet I must do my work. I agree, you have been busy. You have had many successful years, a large practice. You have grown wealthy beyond your expectations."

"I have lived well," said the doctor, "but I always have done the best I could to cure my patients."

"What became of your youthful promise?" Death asked. "Do you remember your promise to collect a fee only from those you cured?"

"That wasn't practical," the doctor answered. "It was one of those silly ideas of youth. I would have starved if I had kept my promise. Either that or I would have been the laughingstock of my colleagues. They exert a tremendous pressure, you know. No one can buck the system. That's the real world. So I learned to be practical. I adjusted my ideals to suit the real world. What else could I do? I didn't do anything wrong. Besides, you're not my judge. I don't have to listen to you."

"No, you don't," death agreed. "But this journey you are about to take involves eternity. Part of my job is to help you reflect on the past—to help you review your life."

"Don't I have time for anything else?" the doctor asked.

"There is no time left," death answered. "There are only these moments of reflection to consider what you did with your life. I will pass no judgment. Like you, I only do my work. I am a technician of sorts. I am very good at what I do. But I don't like to get mixed up with human matters. I don't like the emotions of the heart, the feeling of the spirit. Those human qualities are the most complex, the messiest to deal with. But you learned that early in your career, didn't you."

"Yes," the doctor agreed and bowed his head.

"Do you remember that young woman who came to you early in your career? She complained of a heavy heart. You examined her with the machines at your disposal, but you did not take the time to talk with her. If you had listened carefully, she would have confided in you and told you that the root of the pain in her heart came from a love affair which ended in a bitter and emotional parting between her and her lover. She didn't need medication, she needed to share her hurt with another human being. She needed to understand that the sad feelings of the heart can be projected into the body, and they are as powerful in making the person sick as any disease that has a physiological origin. You gave her a sedative, and she slept at night, but the pain within became nightmares. Because she could not understand her deep pain, she later took her own life."

"I didn't know," the doctor shook his head. "If I only had another chance to help her . . ."

"No," death answered. "That is the tragedy of life. We cannot undo it. What is done is done. We can only act at the moment. Only at the moment could she have been saved. And do you remember the young man who complained of the bitter taste in his mouth? Already you had placed your faith in the machines and drugs of the medical renaissance— a blossoming by the way, which you helped to create. The young man was full of anger. That was his sickness. He was out of work, he could not feed his family, he turned his frustrations on his wife. Someone to listen, a helping hand, perhaps only a little empathy would have saved that young man and his family."

"But I had no time," the doctor cried. "My office was full of the sick!"

"Ah, yes," death nodded. "No one can dispute that. But did you ever reflect on why so much of your time and energy was spent on treating the symptoms and not the causes? The young poet who came to you, he tried to make you see the problems of the society, the social ills that grew in the community as cancer grows in a body. You didn't listen. You didn't hear his songs. You grew more and more specialized. You had only the time to read in the narrow interests of your field. You did not listen to the sound of the storm around you."

"But I was good at what I did," the doctor responded angrily. "I could not be a good doctor and spend my time analyzing the social ills. Let the politicians take care of the society. They know what they're doing. And besides, you said you would not judge me."

"Forgive me," death said. "I do not mean to judge. Yes, you had your specialization. You were good at it. I only want to raise the question: 'Can your species remain human, and reach for all the best aspirations that being human means, if you remain locked in narrower and narrower fields of knowledge?' I have learned in my job that there is some interconnection in this grand design of life. Every action affects something else. Nothing is isolated. Did you think it possible that you could isolate yourself and still contribute to the betterment of that grand design?"

The doctor did not answer. A shudder passed through his body. He felt cold. It was the first time he had truly reflected on his life, and he did not like what he saw.

"It was an age of wonder in the field of medicine," death continued. "You beat me out of many years, but only years. In the end, my opinion is final. I take everyone. I cannot help but wonder if those extra years were worth the struggle. Yes, yes, I know the preservation of life is worth any struggle. You and your collegues gave long life to people. But did the quality of that life improve? I have seen the old dying of boredom. In silence. Alone. Ah well, the complexity you created is not your creation alone. Many have had a hand in it. I can only say I have noticed the neglect, the decay. The air is not as pure as it was, the waters of the rivers not as sweet. The earth itself is being poisoned. You use the atom to cure, and what is left over you discard. Who knows what it will burn tomorrow. Perhaps it's *the impulse to destroy* in mankind which should have concerned you."

"I am a man of medicine," the doctor answered. "I couldn't be all things to all people. I didn't have the time. How could I, one person, address myself or hope to cure that impulse for destruction? I am only one man, one person. I had my work to do . . ."

"As the old saying goes," death said, "the longest journey begins with the first step. One voice joining with many can change the course of mankind. But now, perhaps, it's too late. Every nation is armed to the teeth—the jaws of death grind away, as they say. The bombs are ready. A nuclear holocaust is perhaps just around the corner "

"You mean it is true . . . it will come?" the doctor asked.

"That I cannot say," death answered. "I cannot reveal the future."

"But what could I have done to prevent such a disaster?" the doctor asked.

"I have my own opinion," said death. "I think each time a single person gives up and believes there is nothing to be done, then that person has pushed the button of destruction. When enough people have given up, when enough buttons are pushed, then the dark force of destruction and chaos will have its way. Look around you. You see it everywhere. The apathy is clear. A few work to preserve the world, but the sad truth is that in the midst of the most sophisticated medical knowledge the world has ever known, we still do not know how to drive out that force of destruction that plagues mankind. In this society, to live for today has become the slogan. And as each of you humans separates yourself from the community of your brothers and sisters, so the final day of reckoning draws closer."

"I didn't know," the doctor cried, "I didn't know. There is so much I didn't do—so much to be done. I must begin now—"

"That is impossible," death answered. "Your time on earth is done. What you did, and what you didn't do, is now beside the point. There is no time left for you. You have been granted only this short time for reflection. Everyone is granted this time. It may comfort you to know that most people react as you have. Many, many are disappointed. They see what they could have done in life, and it is difficult to accept that it is too late to change their past. That is the tragedy. Even I am sometimes moved by this overwhelming human emotion. But my opinion is final. I cannot be swayed from my appointed task."

"I beg you," the doctor cried. "Give me one year, one month, one day. I will speak out. I will tell everyone what I have learned tonight. People will listen. I am a respected doctor. It is not too late to correct the mistakes. Please, give me only one day to finish the work I didn't do!"

Death shook its head. "No, it is impossible. This mysterious journey you are about to take has its own rules, laws that will never be known to you. Come now, take my hand. It is time."

The doctor felt his soul rise into the sky. Around him he saw the glitter of a million stars; he thought he heard someone whisper his name. Below him the earth was still and dark. Those he knew and loved slept warmly in their beds. For a moment he hungered for their company, to touch them, to speak to them. But it was too late. He turned and entered the eternal silence which awaited him.

This is the end of my story. It is the end of one doctor's story—a man who set out to serve mankind.

Tonight is the beginning of your work in medicine. I join with everyone here tonight in wishing you a good journey and every success.

PART FIVE
Literature of the Southwest

The Writer as Inocente

We have in New Mexican culture an oral tradition of a character called el inocente. Estevan Arellano has written a wonderful portrayal of the village inocente in *Inocencio:* "Ni pica ni escarda, pero siempre se come el mejor elote" (The innocent one neither plants nor hoes but always eats the best corn). We jokingly say of the inocente "que le faltan tuercas" (that he's missing some nuts and bolts). In the contemporary idiom, he is a person "whose elevator doesn't go all the way to the top floor." The inocente experiences life differently from ordinary people.

What does it mean to be inocente, and why do I feel that the writer must be an inocente? For me, the inocente is constantly in contact with the marvel, the beauty, and the mystery of life. So it seems that with the passage of time, I am each day more in awe of creation. The simplest experiences take on a marvelous aura that reveals a deeper reality. It is a reality I try to capture in my writings.

Where does it begin? It begins in childhood, in dreams, in memories, in the feeling that a divine spark animates the world and the cosmos. To be inocente means one feels a transcendent power working in our ordinary lives. The world is as much spiritual as it is material.

A large part of the life of a writer and of the inocente is lived in memory and dreams. I remember the river of my childhood as if it were yesterday. There I still hear voices, spirits moving at dusk—not only la Llorona, a spirit I really feared, but other powers. Powers of place. The river was alive, and it spoke. I tried to capture that experience in *Bless*

Originally published in *Mirage Magazine* 21 no. 3 (Spring 2003): 29–31, published by the University of New Mexico Alumni Association; and reprinted with adaptions in *World Literature Today* (January/April 2004): 41–42.

Me, Ultima, and some readers were surprised. "How can the river be alive?" they asked.

I thought everyone had heard the presence of the river speak, its natural soul revealed. I heard the groans of the giant cottonwoods, those ancient grandparents. The sky at sunset spoke volumes, not only of the weather but of the history of the people. The stones of the hills were as animated as the animals that roamed there.

"It's fantasy," some said. "It's real," I replied.

Now, today, so many years later, I feel not only the presence of nature's spirit, but I am surrounded by the lives of those who once walked on the hills I love in Alburquerque. The old people of the Tiguex pueblos, Mexican sheepherders who walked there long before there were buildings. Professors who taught at the University of New Mexico and are gone, students who studied there. They hover nearby. I am in Alburquerque not only as I am today, but as I was as a young man who matriculated at the university. I left something of my self here.

You see, everywhere we go we leave part of our souls. Everyone carries memories of the past, of places that were magical, of people we loved. Part of your soul is there with those people, in those places. The inocente understands this. The soul is not only in our bodies. It is everywhere we have been.

Each morning I look at the rising sun and give thanks. I offer a blessing at sunrise—I bless all of life. My wife and I sit over breakfast, and I am startled at the beauty of our relationship and how the very act of eating fills me with thanksgiving. The inocente is a person constantly saying, "Wow! Look at that!" "¡Mira!" Sun and clouds. Geese flying south. Apples hanging on a tree. Flowers going to seed. "¡Mira!"

Inocentes sense that divine spark that illuminates the simplest acts of the day. The inocentes know this intuitively, for that is how they live, that is how they are most alive.

I look at the faces of friends and see beauty. I see beneath the skin a psyche that shines with innocence. I smile. They say the inocente goes around with a silly smile on his face. For me, that smile is a sign of wonder. Let us practice going around with silly smiles on our faces. Let us slough away the pretense of what we should be and be who we truly are. Inocentes are on the road of life, friends to one another.

In our jardín, under the ramada in our backyard, Patricia and I sit in the afternoon sun, and each blade of grass shines with its unique character. Every flower sings its song. Clouds, like marvelous and gorgeous people, move across a transparent blue sky. I marvel at the beauty and diversity of life.

In light of these thoughts, I am still trying to process receiving the National Medal of Arts from President George W. Bush over a year ago. We flew to Washington, DC, for the ceremony. Patricia, our granddaughter Kristan, and I got on the plane and flew to the capital. Maybe I should write a story about our experiences. "An Inocente Goes to Washington."

They got us together in a room, and we met Johnny Cash. Yeah, I went up to him and said, "Hello, Mr. Johnny Cash. I'm Rudolfo Anaya from Alburquerque, and I want you to know I love your songs. New Mexicans love you. Here's my wife and granddaughter."

You see, that's an inocente talking. He talks to the good soul in those he meets. Some people say, "You didn't tell Johnny Cash that, did you? ¡Qué pendejo! Don't you have manners?"

What are manners to the inocente? We deal with the soul in the person, the daimon that drives us, the essence. Forget the formalities, go for the spirit. Tear down the fences that separate us. That's what the inocente teaches us.

And we met Kirk Douglas. And I said the same thing. "¿Cómo 'stá, don Kirk? What an honor. I like that movie you did with Burt Lancaster where at the end you plow the train into Mexico. I also liked *Spartacus*. Here's my wife and granddaughter. We love your movies."

The inocente, even though he is in pain and knows there is suffering and poverty in the world, smiles. He sees the quality of corresponding goodness in people. We all have that innocent quality. Inside. Deep in the soul.

And I told the president, "No nos estés fregando tanto. (Don't irritate us so much.) Lighten up. Take care of la gente pobre. Help the kids get an education." Pues, I really didn't say that, but the inocente in me thought it. The way I looked at him, he knew what I was thinking.

I was very civil to the first lady. She told me she had read *Bless Me, Ultima*. I said, "Thank you," and I thought to myself, there's hope for us humans.

I am always thinking. People from the past come to visit me. Those are the spirits of my ancestors. They are here with us. I speak to them and they to me.

What are the characters in our stories but spirits who want their stories told? Sometimes my characters are more real than real people.

And all my characters are inocentes at heart. All are learning that there are many secrets hidden in our souls. We have to bring them out. We should not be afraid to speak to each other as inocentes.

I know there are gente in the world who are muy cabrona. Somebody is always trying to get the better of somebody else. Tyrants of all sorts making people suffer the worst atrocities. But if we inocentes get together, we can be stronger than the bad guys. Let us practice that virtue of innocence in our souls. Let it shine. Let the power of place and all the spirits who inhabit a place make us strong. I think the medal they gave me in Washington, DC, is for all of us. Especially for the inocentes who have enriched my life.

My Heart, My Home

Books record the emotions of the soul. A good book inscribes itself in the heart, and we take it with us like a good companion.

In New Mexico, we are fortunate to have many writers writing about the diversity that is our state. It has always been so, for the people of New Mexico are steeped in storytelling. Oral tradition tells our history, and books record that tradition.

From the earliest Native American stories and myths, to the petroglyphs incised in boulders, to the commentaries of the first Spanish explorers, we have recorded history. Newer arrivals also write their experiences of their relationship to the place and the people.

My role as a writer began in listening to the oral tradition of my community. The people told cuentos, adivinanzas, chistes. Whenever visitors gathered at our home, they were served a meal by my mother, and they returned the hospitality by telling stories. Nobody went away hungry from our humble home, and everybody went away enriched by the stories they heard. Just as the hot tortillas we ate nourished the body, the stories we heard were food for the soul.

Tales of the daily life of the people of the Llano Estacado of eastern New Mexico, their joys and turmoils, became adventures of the human spirit that held me spellbound. The craft of storytelling was passed on through that gift we call imagination, perhaps passed on in our genes. It was my destiny to become a writer of those experiences of my community.

My apprenticeship as a writer was long and difficult, because the transformation of the oral tradition to the written word is not easy. The old bards never had to cope with typewriters or computers. But I was sustained by the power and magic in the word.

Originally published in *New Mexico Journey Magazine* (May/June 1997): 24.

Growing up in Santa Rosa on the eastern plain was an adventure. I spent all summer along the river with friends. We roamed far, fished, and gathered at night around campfires to listen to stories. In the dark the world of witches and boogeymen came alive. My imagination soared, for I believed every word.

In the fall we gathered for harvest at my grandfather's home in Puerto de Luna. Families reunited for la cosecha (the harvest). Sitting around, stringing chile ristras or paring apples, was really a time for storytelling. Late at night, the stories often turned to the supernatural, those occurrences that could not be easily explained. They were stories of men and women who had been bewitched, or those who had met the devil on some lonely road.

Winters were a time of rest, but also a time of struggle. I can still hear the blizzards that swept across the llano, feel the deep snow-drifts we broke on the way to school, see the icicles that hung like glistening spears. Around us, the ranchers my father knew came with tales of woe. Cattle and sheep froze, and hard times pressed down on everyone.

Each season had its stories. When I began to write my first novel, *Bless Me, Ultima*, I transferred those skills of the storyteller to the written word. And many of the stories I had heard as a child found their way into my novel.

The people of my childhood were fabulous, their experiences too vivid and meaningful not to be told. Life was difficult on the llano—ask anyone who has lived there. But there was a spirit of survival and generosity in the people that overcame the hard times. The llaneros shared what they had. *Vecinos* were not just the people next door, they were partners in life. My childhood friends became brothers and sisters. We respected the dignity of the elders and listened when they spoke.

But the real thrust of my novels was the belief in the power of the spirit. What did all these cuentos mean that told of people who could fly? What power did those curanderas have in healing the spirit?

In writing about la curandera Ultima, I began to explore the world-view of the people. I like not only to write a good story, but to explore in it the core of human nature. I have continued in that search I call a quest for knowledge.

After *Bless Me, Ultima*, I shifted to a more realistic, urban setting. In *Heart of Aztlan* and *Alburquerque*, I documented the migration of the rural communities to the larger urban centers. But even in the urban novels and my recent murder mysteries, *Zia Summer* and *Rio Grande Fall*, I write about the world of spirits.

A large part of our history was not written in books. It came in the voice of the person telling the story. The voice incorporated the spirit of the community.

Community is important to the old New Mexican tribes. We incorporate our sense of place and community in the stories we write. Personal angst lasts just so long, then it is connected to the community so the healing can begin. If one can identify shared beliefs, a history, a deeper mythopoetic sense, then one has strength.

I wish I had the space to list the writers of this region who share not only a good story with their readers, but a deeper sense of who we are. Our history. Each region within the state has these writers. Search them out, and you will discover the true diversity of our state. And I assure you, you will be a stronger person as you connect to the stories of our people.

Writing Burque

I've been exploring the soul of Burque since I first crash-landed here in 1952. So far I've written four novels (and I'm working on a fifth one) with an Alburquerque setting. In my second novel, *Heart of Aztlan*, the Barelas barrio was my turf. In the fifties, each barrio had a distinct identity, and so each neighborhood thought it was (rightly so) the soul of the city.

In the fifties, downtown was the heart of the city, a throbbing, bustling, hustling, thriving center. The space was intimate, from the El Rey Theatre to the YMCA at the railroad tracks, one could strut it with pride.

In 1992, the University of New Mexico Press published my novel *Alburquerque*. (I got the spelling right.) The novel leaves the barrio to capture a more sweeping picture of the city. What I found as the city's soul is its history. Migrations of different ethnic groups have placed their stamp on the city, but the original Pueblo Indian and Spanish/Mexican settlements remain at the core. So soul is the history, and history is what people make of their environment.

After the Anglo-American invasion of 1846, a new cultural element was added to the pot. The railroad and later the automobile were to change the course of events. One hundred years later, we still live with those consequences. By the 1930s, we were beginning to be punished for speaking Spanish on the school grounds.

How we use the land and water remain at the core of how we define ourselves. We're into a new immigration boom, new retirees, and

Originally published as "Writing Burque: Some of Albuquerque's Best Writers Write about Themselves, Their Craft, and the Soul of Our City" in *Weekly Alibi* (25 September–1 October 1996): 13–14.

development from the Sandias to the West Mesa sandhills. But do the newcomers know the history of the place?

Alburquerque is special. I live and work here because the valley is one of the enduring centers of spirituality in this country. The soul of the place is linked not only to the history of business and technology, but to its mythic past. Do we know that past?

Why do we feel at home here? After all, Phoenix, Denver, and Dallas have outdistanced Alburquerque in growth and in creature comforts. We stay rooted because we are rooted. We have learned to feel the rhythm of the earth, the songs, the dances, the tribal traditions that compose our mythopoetic world. We dance to the spirit of the place.

In *Zia Summer*, my first Sonny Baca murder mystery, I continued to explore the idea of soul. Personal soul, for sure, but still exploring the roots of the collective memory, the history. Ancestral values are important to us, and when we feel we're losing them, we feel disjointed. Sonny Baca's guide is don Eliseo, an old man in his eighties. He connects Sonny to his history. I think we need more teachers and leaders like don Eliseo.

In my new novel, *Rio Grande Fall*, I do find centers that nurture the spirit. There's Old Town, the Indian Pueblo Cultural Center, UNM, museums, barrio organizations, senior citizen centers, parks, schools, libraries, and so on. Like the barrios, these community organizations provide centers for stability. These new circles of influence help educate us and guide our lives as we enter the new age of Aquarius.

It's not just newer and newer technology we need, we need to feel grounded. The distinct parts of the city need to communicate with each other. There are a lot of social problems to address, lots of kids to save, but if we remain split, then we dilute the effort. Looking for the common spirit that unites us all is crucial. We are fortunate. We have a songline to guide us. Ancestral values and history. Let's listen to the teachings of the elders as we move into the twenty-first century.

Más Allá

When I was writing my first novel, *Bless Me, Ultima*, in the sixties, there were times I felt I wasn't getting anywhere. The space in which my novel was taking shape seemed to be a vacuum. I kept reading novels, looking for a guide, but the guides simply didn't tell me how to put my New Mexican soul into the story I was telling.

Everybody needs to find their voice, we are told. How could I find a voice which had been stifled for so long? My voice wasn't in other novels, nor in the books I read at the university. How does someone learn to speak? How could I learn to bare the soul of those characters who were clamoring to be heard?

Ultima, the healer, wasn't in the first drafts of my novel. She who becomes the powerful mentor and shaman for me and my protagonist was missing. She had no voice with which to speak. Generations of my Nuevo Mexicano community had had no voice.

One night Ultima came to me, and I was at that moment in just the right creative trance to receive her. She spoke. She told me her name, and told me I'd better get her in the novel, or the whole thing might never have soul. I remember the night very clearly, as one remembers a vivid dream. I remember how she was dressed, how she spoke, how she moved, the aroma of herbs clinging to her dress.

It is an awful thing to be without a soul. Without a voice. I listened to the old woman, and I realized that the collective wisdom of my community was in the old curandera. She spoke for the community, and she entered my novel. She came to give me my voice, the voice I could only find in that world which had nurtured me.

Originally published in *Hayden's Ferry Review*, 10 (Spring/Summer 1992): 76–77.

It was that night my novel came alive. It began to move "más allá," further on, from imitation to truth. At that moment I felt I could translate my Spanish-speaking world into English. I had found my voice! I was fortunate to have a communication from so strong a spiritual guide, fortunate to encounter the guide I needed.

Nobody can give us our voice; we have to find it. But when one is writing in a vacuum, one clutches for straws. When one writes from a different cultural perspective, one wonders who can help. A few, sensitive people can point the way, allude to the real strength of our stories, but the true voice comes from within. And really, isn't the writer only the conduit through which many voices speak? We, the Chicanos of the Southwest, were voiceless for generations, and now we are breaking the chains. Voice does break chains; voice is freedom.

Perhaps this is why so many writers become teachers. Somewhere, someplace, someone said, "*más allá.*" Look deeper. Look at your own soul, your own place. Find your voice. Now we try to pass on that simple secret.

The Genius of Patrociño Barela

Patrociño Barela is the patron saint of Nuevo Mexicano artists. This woodcarver from Taos influenced and changed forever the course of our artistic inheritance. But Barela does not belong only to the Mexicano/ Hispano community of the northern Río Grande, because like all great artists Barela transcends the bonds of ethnicity, time, and place. His work speaks to the world.

His bultos—the unique santos he carved—were briefly acknowledged early in his career. But fame was fleeting. The artistic establishment of the time did not fully recognize the genius of the man. It is our generation that is rediscovering the importance of this maestro and the lasting legacy he left us.

Look at his work! Feel the curves of the wood! Marvel at the organic forms that seem to rise from the earth itself! Every sculpture assures us the man was imbued with an imagination that transformed the art of his time. His creativity was driven by a spirit of the place, a transforming energy that drove Barela to enhance anew the aesthetic of our New Mexican heritage. In his work he bared his soul.

Patrociño Barela led a difficult life, and like many artists he overcame the obstacles in his path and persevered in portraying both the hope and agony of his soul. He could do no less. The tension in his work is revealed in sculptures that appear earthbound but are always aspiring to the heavens. This spiritual yearning of humanity is his constant theme.

Originally published in slightly different form as the introduction to *Spirit Ascendant: The Art and Life of Patrociño Barela*, eds. Edward Gonzales and David L. Witt (Santa Fe, N.Mex.: Red Crane Books, 1996), xv–xvii; and published in abbreviated form in the National Hispanic Cultural Center's 2008 Exhibition Catalog *Caminos Distintos: Patrociño Barela and Edward Gonzales in New Mexico*.

Each piece reflects our spiritual longing. Artists who have wrestled with their own creative imagination instantly recognize the universal implications in Barela's work. That is why we reach out to touch his santos, because we realize that each piece contains a message of love. We stand in awe of his work because each form speaks to our eternal quest for meaning.

There is also lunacy in his work. In Barela's life and work we feel the duende spirit of madness that can affect the artist. In Barela, the duende—or Barela's muse—was a call to carve not only the details of his daily life but to imbue each piece with his constant aspiration toward the spiritual. As tragic as the artist's life may have been, we honor the fruits of the labor he left behind.

There are many themes in the work of this man of genius. They include the playful, the picaro, and the innocence of the village inocente. Sex and irony. Especially irony, for the ironic twist abounds, creating a tension in every piece. Yes, we are supposed to smile at some of the sculptures, even laugh, perhaps ask ourselves, "Is he pulling my leg?" When you feel the duende in the work, you are truly in touch with the artist's intent.

Many elements constitute the Barela aesthetic, too many to list here, which is precisely why he is a man of genius. Genius does not follow a straight path. The tools and materials—a simple adze and pocket knife and wood to carve—may have remained constant, but his creativity knew no bounds. With these materials in his backyard shed, he portrayed the whole of our human experience from folly to sainthood.

Barela's tragedy was not that he drank, but that the underlying causes for his drinking reflect an age of transition in the cultural and social dynamics of New Mexico, an epoch that did not allow a man like Barela to fully explore and understand the value of his art. The artist records the currents of history that sweep over the land; most often he cannot control the forces. Barela lived in that time of displacement, recording the turmoil and change in the Hispano way of life. Times of great change call for great artists, and Barela responded. He recorded a personal and communal loss, while taking traditional santero art from a legacy of formalism into a twentieth-century art form as daring as any of his contemporaries in Europe.

Artists like Barela not only incorporate their daily struggle into their work, they are also prophetic. We have much to learn from this man. Across the sea the German expressionists were telling us an age of tortured humanity was at hand, and tragically it came to be. In many of Barela's pieces we see this same prophetic quality. His figures are haunted by the vices we are heir to. Like Frank Waters, his vecino in Taos, Barela acknowledges the clay that we are, but he also sees the transcendent spirit in every tree he carves. The Barela aesthetic is grounded firmly in a tension between flesh and soul and the possibility of essence. He carved away the excess and brought the santo to life. His art tells us what is possible, and so Barela had worlds to speak to us. Worlds to teach us.

I see many similarities between Barela and Gaudi. Barela's santos are organic earth forms, much like Gaudi's fanciful sculptures in La Sagrada Familia cathedral in Barcelona. A cathedral is a shrine for spiritual contemplation; we can meditate in front of Barela's carved figures as well. Each artist in his own way expresses the spiritual yearning of humanity.

Why has Barela been excluded from New Mexico art history? Why did early recognition in the 1930s and 1940s then go unnoticed for a lifetime? Why were those of us who sought the guiding spirits of creativity not able to find Barela in our art classes? These and many other questions are answered in previous scholarship, most notably in *Spirit Ascendant: The Art and Life of Patrociño Barela*, which offers guidance into the genius of Barela.

We owe Edward Gonzales and David L. Witt a debt of gratitude. *Spirit Ascendant* is the definitive study of Barela to date. It is safe to say they rescued the old master from anonymity and brought Barela's work out of obscurity and back into the public sphere, where it should have been these many years. Were it not for the Gonzales/Witt book, the same artistic establishment that once dismissed Barela would still be blind to the importance of this man in our cultural history. The 2008 exhibit at the National Hispanic Cultural Center, "Caminos Distintos: Patrociño Barela and Edward Gonzales in New Mexico," will also help to rectify part of the lack of attention Barela has suffered.

Barela knew intimately the tree as a universal symbol, and he cut into its heart to tell us stories. Barela was more than a santero; he was a man who dared to create new forms from an old inheritance. What more can we ask of a man?

The Silence of the Llano
Notes from the Author

The process by which a literary work is created intrigues us. Some readers feel that if we can understand something of that process, we might understand the very origin of the spark of creativity. A complete understanding of the writer's creative impulse will always elude us, but perhaps we can catch intimations of that creative drive as we read the individual notes and works of writers. In these notes I would like to share with the reader part of the process and the circumstances that went into the writing of the collection of stories *The Silence of the Llano*. This, I hope, will provide a broader setting for the stories and, at the same time, allow me to speak of my interests in the craft of writing.

My main objective in writing fiction during the last ten years was the creation and completion of the trilogy comprising three novels: *Bless Me, Ultima, Heart of Aztlan,* and *Tortuga.* However, during the course of those years, I also wrote a number of short stories. I have discussed the creation of the novels in various interviews and lectures; here I would like to share some observations and thoughts about my short stories.

The short story, when presented in the oral tradition, can be a simple but compelling form. It can also be made to move beyond its regional arena to engage language and form in the expression of a vision that reflects the writer's sense of life. A writer is an artisan who works with words, and so he must possess the language he uses. But he must also seek his inner voice; he must experiment with and use many variations

Originally published as "An Author's Reflections: *The Silence of the Llano*" in *Nuestro* (April 1983): 14–17; and reprinted with revisions as *"The Silence of the Llano*: Notes from the Author" in *MELUS* (Journal of the Society for the Study of Multi-ethnic Literature of the United States) 11, no. 4 (1984): 47–57.

of the craft; he must write toward the *truth inherent in the story*; and he must be keenly aware of style and form.

In these notes I would like to discuss each of the stories included in *The Silence of the Llano*. But first some background.

I was born on the high plains of eastern New Mexico, a land which drops from the Sangre de Cristo Mountains to form the Llano Estacado. I grew up along the Pecos River valley in a small town by the name of Santa Rosa. Once, this land belonged to the nomadic Indians; later, Spanish and Mexican settlers moved into the region from the Taos and Santa Fe area. Sometime during the mid-nineteenth century, Anglo-Americans began to fill the range land.

The history of this land and the different cultural ways of the people were depicted in many of the stories I heard as a child. Those people who moved in and out of my childhood came to tell stories, and it was the magic of their words and their deep, humble humanity that must have sparked my imagination. A writer must be a listener and an observer before he can be a writer.

I feel fortunate to have been born on the llano. The wild, nomadic vaquero was my father, sheepherders were my old abuelos, and a woman from the river valley was my mother; but in an extended family, all of the people I met while growing up nurtured me, and I had the need even then to put into words the magic I felt. The land was a mystical force, and so were the Hispanic people with their unique Mediterranean worldview, a value system formed in the Old World, infused by the Moorish and Jewish influence, and renewed in the Americas by the native religious spirit of the Indians. Those people and their view of the world have influenced me greatly, and so I often return to the llano for my inspiration. "The Place of the Swallows," "The Road to Platero," and "The Silence of the Llano" all draw from the land that I knew as a child.

There is something very positive to be said about a writer's sense of place, that is, that place he knows best, that place where his stance as a writer is most solid. "The Place of the Swallows" was one of the earliest stories I wrote, and it reflects my concern with the primary mystery of the river, water, birth, regeneration, and the subconscious. As a child I wandered up and down the river, sometimes alone, most often with the Chavez boys who were my closest neighbors. Adventures and escapades filled our days, but in addition to that, there was always for me the deep sense of the mystery of life that pulsed along the dark green river. Romantic? Perhaps, but I wouldn't trade that place of my childhood for any other.

"The Place of the Swallows" was a story written under the strong influence of *Bless Me, Ultima*. I used the group of young boys as a tribal group, and within the group the person who interested me the most was the storyteller. The story is really about the art of storytelling and the role and function of the storyteller within his tribe, his social group. The tribe of boys reflects mankind, but in the story they have moved away from the town and the neighboring farms to enter the river valley, and so in their game they undergo an atavistic metamorphosis and actually become the hunters of the cave. When they sit around the fire at the end of the day, they need the storyteller to recount their exploits. The storyteller records, in oral history and song, the entire history of the tribe, but as every writer discovers, it is also imperative that the storyteller be true to himself.

Was I—as I roamed the river valley with my childhood friends, moving back and forth between the civilized world of my Catholic heritage and the pagan truths that seemed so evident in the world of raw, primal nature—becoming the storyteller? I know the condition of childhood innocence has interested me intensely, for it was the innocent child in the novel *Bless Me, Ultima* who peered directly into the dark waters of the river and saw the primal (and therefore innocent) archetypes of the collective memory. The child is capable of becoming aware of and accepting the illumination of truth and beauty. The archetype, as a perfect symbol that communicates a truth, is obvious to the child. But the child can also see the ghosts of the past, the ghosts of the bush, the shadows of the cave which are a projection from within, and he is also aware of the demons we have created to haunt us since our first dawn on earth. Because the child is open to the presence of the primal mode, he is most in touch with the tribal memory and the truth latent in the archetypes, and this awareness can produce both fear and illumination.

As I have said, I was greatly influenced by the oral tradition of storytelling. The visits of neighbors or family were exciting and anticipated events. The visitor always brought a story. At night, after our supper, we would sit around the kitchen table, near the wood-burning stove to listen to stories. If it were summer, we would move outside to the cool evening air, and there would often be a special treat of a watermelon, cold from being in the icy water of the well all day, and the storytelling would begin. There is a special atmosphere which develops when a story is told. I feel an aura envelops the teller and his audience, and it is that same aura that now envelops me when I write, an aura that is a dimension of the time of the story. That is, the time that the story itself can create, a time that destroys strict, linear time and creates a continuous, cyclical time which is harmonious.

A storyteller is effective in his craft if his voice, style, delivery, and movements create this aura of time. It is more than just mood. The mood is the total feeling or intensity which the story creates, a total unity of atmosphere which tense then releases. But aura is mood plus time, it is the achievement of a story which completely engrosses the reader. Being in that time of the story changes the listener or the reader forever. Once one has lived in the magic moment which the words bring to life, once one has stepped into the reality of the story, one is never again the same. This is the power of the storyteller; he can create new visions of old realities. The aura of the story is the vibration of time and truth inherent in the new reality that the story creates. The young boy who is the storyteller in "The Place of the Swallows" learned that during the telling of his story.

In much of my writing I refer to the llano, the open plain country where I was raised and which I use as the setting for some of my stories. The llano is generally flat; arroyos and mesas dotted with piñon and juniper carve the land, and the muddy rivers move south to empty into the Río Grande. My forefathers moved there to raise sheep and cattle, ranches became haciendas and were given names, and some of those became small villages. Later the Texans came, hungry for land, and the two cultures which had already met in northern New Mexico and in the borderlands of Texas met on the Llano Estacado of New Mexico. There was the obvious shock and turmoil which is always present when two different cultures meet; sometimes there was a sharing, many times bloodshed. It was a time of change, and a time of heroes.

But it is people who are at the center of every story. I knew the vaqueros, the farmers, the people of the small villages. I listened, and their stories were a magic potion, a rendering of the everyday life where it was possible for small joys to lift us in exultation, where men and women I knew became heroes and heroines. Life could be made bigger than the sum of its parts when the storyteller spoke.

"The Road to Platero" and "The Silence of the Llano" are stories that obviously use the llano as a background, but allow me a short digression that I believe will shed some light on those stories. Some years ago while reading through old Mexican corridos, the ballads of the people, I came across the "Ballad of Delgadina." The story is about a man who falls in love with his daughter. He asks for her love, but she refuses, citing all the moral reasons why such a love cannot be. In a rage, he has his servants lock her in her room, and she is allowed to drink only saltwater until she changes her mind. By the time the father realizes his wrong, it is too late, she is dead. The ballad ends with the moral: Delgadina rests in heaven surrounded by angels; her father dies and receives the torment of hell. I took the outline of the story and wrote a drama I call "Rosa Linda."

I have been writing and revising that drama for a number of years, and so it is natural for the theme of the father-daughter relationship I am exploring in that drama to find its way into some of the stories I was writing at the same time. The theme begins to appear in "The Road to Platero." In a sense, the story is almost a warming-up exercise for the bigger and more challenging story in the play. This theme of incest is as old as mankind, and it has been the subject of many literary works, but the subject is still taboo, and it is a theme that is difficult to treat.

I like to use the term "the writer's stance" to describe or suggest the position the writer takes in relationship to the story—that is, the position and the distance of the writer in relation to the characters about whom he is writing. It is from that stance that the writer will relate the story. As the story develops, he may move into the story itself, his voice may decrease or intensify, as he wishes, but for the beginning writer sometimes a fixed, solid stance can help clarify the point of view. Because I like to use a first-person narrative, I often find myself too close to the story. In the first version of "The Road to Platero," the story was related in first person, and the narrator was the fetus in the womb of the woman. That's how I first thought out the story, and it was a unique and challenging view, but it compounded my problems. There was something surrealistic to the story, but it was too much for the story to carry.

At any rate, the story set out to create a mood, to intimate a set of circumstances that culminate in the story, so it didn't need much extraneous experimentation to achieve the mood. It was the "voice of the narrator" that would sketch out the village, the hot days in the llano as the women awaited the return of their men, the torture which men often inflict on women, and the hint of old relationships and murder. That "voice of the narrator" becomes the writer's stance—it becomes the story.

In the novel *Tortuga* the protagonist is a young man who is encased in a body cast; partially paralyzed, he cannot move about, and yet he relates the story. Other points of view are developed as we learn the stories of other patients in the hospital. Point of view, when confronted and used correctly, can make for unique style, but like time in a story, it can be fragmented, and beyond a certain point the unity of narration breaks down, and the very time the writer seeks to make continuous in the story becomes discontinuous. Some will argue that the thought process, dreams, and perhaps the neurosis of contemporary time all occur in discontinuous time, but I suggest that the mind seeks to give coherence and pattern to time in order to understand what thought and dream and neurosis have to reveal to us. To give in to discontinuous time is to give in to chaos.

Perhaps the fragmentation of time and of the soul are at the core of contemporary writing. As there is turmoil and unrest in the individual and in the world, the more reason for the story to become a new ordering of the mundane world. The laws of the cosmos are not out of kilter, and they have influenced our evolution as humans since the first day of creation. Deep within each one of us lies the integrated self that seeks unity and harmony, and stories are a way to reflect aspects of that search.

One of the most frequent questions a writer is asked is: "Where did you get the idea for your story?" The second most-asked question is: "Did it come from 'real' life?" I don't have a conclusive answer, but perhaps the writer is tuned in to some sensibility of life's vibrations that allows him or her to pick up a word, an idea, a character or theme, or an incident that strikes a chord in his subconscious. All of life, real or imagined, has the potential to be the spark that ignites the creative imagination.

Stories have come to me in dreams, while walking or watching television, from incidents in the past, from the people I meet every day, what they say and do, from memories moving into consciousness. Whatever suddenly rings with the tone and pitch that I have come to sense as a story is the "germ of the story." Once that small seed or germ is deposited, I have to write the story. Life provides us with the seed; the writer as artisan must give it form.

But a writer just doesn't sit and wait for the story to begin. One learns to think continuously about stories; in fact, one's thought process becomes that of reinterpreting life as story. I call this process "story-thinking." In my mind are the characters, dialogues, settings, and themes of many stories, of which only a very few will ever be written. "Story-thinking" is part of the creative process, the dialogue with the world. It is an exhilarating process.

One day I was telling my wife the story of a sixth-grade friend I had, and how he came up with the devilish idea of pasting small mirrors to the tips of our shoes so we could slip them under the girls' skirts and thereby solve the mystery of sex, a mystery that was bothering all of us about that time. I told her the story, and we laughed and suddenly I realized the idea was unique enough to be a written story. From that idea "The Apple Orchard" emerged, a story based on a real incident.

Perhaps the ending of "The Apple Orchard" stretches the reader's acceptance of what is believable. Even in fiction we have to deal with what is believable, by which we mean: given the total context of the story, how far can you stretch the pattern of consistency so that it fits a "realistic mode"? The reader will ask: Would a young teacher really do what this teacher does for Isador? This is not a "real" teacher; she is a character. Maybe we have never met a single teacher who would do what this teacher does, but within the context of the story, does it work? If I have convinced the reader that the story is not about sex but about love and beauty as they might be in a pure and sharing realm, then the ending works; it is believable. The young teacher is willing to give of her love and beauty (only at this time and place) so that Isador can progress in understanding love and beauty as forms that flower, grow to fruition, then change into the gnarled form of the winter branches. A friend of mine who read the story said, "I wish I had had a teacher like that when I was young." He meant how simple and courageous it would be to teach the beauty of the body in an honest and direct manner.

This story, "The Apple Orchard," is also the story of the artist. Isador represents the young artist. A number of my stories are concerned with the development of the artist, his rites of passage from innocence into adulthood, the vision of truth to be learned. Isador says at the end of the story that he has glimpsed a truth in beauty, but it is a fleeting thing. The important commitment he makes is to continue to explore truth and beauty. He has had his eyes opened for a moment; now it is up to him to learn to "see." Life and the universe are changing around him, and if he is to espouse a vision of truth on which to build the foundations of his world, he must keep in touch with life. The writer opens himself up and reveals his deepest secrets and feelings and thoughts. He is constantly open to the awesome mystery of life; he is exhilarated by its profound joys, and he feels the deep sorrows. One suffers less if one protects his inner self—if one shuts himself away from hurt—but I know few writers who can do this and write. The writer is an adventurer who is constantly exploring and observing the entire range of unpredictable human behavior and the constant unfolding of creation.

Now we come to that strange tale "The Village Which the Gods Painted Yellow." I was there in Uxmal, and when I returned I told parts of the story to my wife, and, later, I sat down one January day and wrote the story. I wrote the story in the first person because I was more or less convinced that I had experienced the story. I had met Gonzalo; I had been there; I had rambled alone around the magnificent ruins of Uxmal on that day of the winter solstice. So where did one reality leave off and a new one start? Is it possible that the writer can get too drawn into the story? This is a real concern of a writer. The story wasn't working because I was too close to it, I was too deep in it. How was I to extricate myself from being bound within the story? I changed to third person, created more distance between me and the story, and gave up the idea that the story had happened to me. I created Rosario, and the story became his. The story is not built around depth of character; it is built around an adventure and a theme. In the story, time and legend and the strength of belief are more important than the actual characters. For me, "The Village Which the Gods Painted Yellow" will always be a story that I entered too deeply.

I know I shall return to those ruins and to the other ancient cities of the Yucatán and Guatemala. There are very powerful places there, good vibrations for the person who is in search of truth. But one should not tamper with the power of the earth and the power of the people unless one is very committed and very strong. I do not wish to remain lost in the stories waiting there for me, and so I will walk lightly, armed with magic.

The Southwest, this place I call my home, a place called Aztlán in the legends of the ancient Aztecs, is the same kind of place, a place of power. Perhaps that is why it attracts so many writers and artists. Power flows through the land and the people, dimensions of reality quickly evaporate under our sun, the visions and the dreams compel as much as any other force.

"The Silence of the Llano" is a story that creates its own aura and ambiance. When I wrote that story I felt myself returning to the llano; I saw and felt it again as I knew it when I was young and growing up. The aura became very real for me. It became palpable. It is one of my longer stories, but I think it can maintain its mood for the reader.

The llano is a lonely place. One comes upon lonely, isolated ranch houses. Faces peer from behind parted curtains. How do these people live? What do the women feel? I had seen the face of the young girl in the story peer at me, so many times. I began the story in the oral tradition: "This man's name was Rafael . . ." This is the way an old storyteller from the llano might have begun a story as he sat around with his compañeros on a dark night in a sheep camp miles from the nearest village, with only the fire and the sound of words to give the hint of the human presence in the deep and dark of the lonely llano. That's how I wanted to tell this story—a story of a tormented man, a story of the cycles of time and the seasons which leave their imprint on the people.

One day the face of the young girl appeared again, and I sat down and wrote the story. It was as if over the years that young girl had been living in my memory, and suddenly she came with such force that I had to write the story. What if a girl were born without access to language, to the companionship of other women, what would her thoughts be like, what would she feel? If there ever was magic to the word, it is real magic to the girl in this story, as she lives in silence. The story is about silence, what it can do to people; it is about the sacredness of the word, spoken and unspoken, and it is also about the vast gulfs which can separate people when the word is not present between them.

What interested me greatly was the aura of the story. I wanted actually to move the reader into the llano, I wanted the reader to be at Rafael's side during the telling of the story. If every writer has a voice, a personal, internal rhythm and language which is unique to him as a storyteller, then *my* voice is what I hear in "The Silence of the Llano." Writing is a search for that voice.

The most recent story in the collection, "B. Traven Is Alive and Well in Cuernavaca," is a story which takes a number of experiences and incidents that happened over the course of a summer and brings them together as one story. Let me first say that I have been going to Mexico for many years, and most recently I have been going to Cuernavaca, to write and rest, and to communicate with the people and the earth of Mexico. I travel, wander through the mercados, visit ruins and museums, read, but mostly I just observe and listen. We have a dear friend in Cuernavaca, Ana Rosinski, to whom the Traven story should be dedicated, for if there was ever a woman with much power and a fascinating life, it is she. Anyway, one recent trip to Mexico turned out to be a nightmare of sorts, a journey in which we used every type of transportation imaginable and experienced the strangest incidents. A few months before the trip I had read B. Traven's *Macovio*. Then in

Cuernavaca I met a gardener, el jardinero, who loved to tell stories. We got along very well, always trying to outdo each other in the stories we told. All these separate incidents are not a story, but they began to clamor to be put into a story. During this time of germination, I am in a state of tension. I cannot share the story until the time is ripe. Nothing must touch the forming story. I think that is what the jardinero's treasure represents, the story in the subconscious of the writer. And it is the writer who must journey into that darkness to bring forth the final form, the truth of the story.

It was only after I finished writing the Traven story that I read the complete works of B. Traven and also read a biography of him. I was surprised to find how close I was to the man's character in the story. Actually, even if that revelation were not correct, it would make little difference to the story, because the story is not really about B. Traven. It is a story about a story being born. It also relates something of what I feel in Mexico.

The Traven story also relies on a series of events, or what is often called plot. In some cases the events begin to predict the development and ending of a story. As the events unfold, or as the lives of the characters change, the reader should enter the story and become part of the story. Then the story is dynamic and alive. If that doesn't happen, the story remains at one level. In the Traven story, the series of events, or the plot, which finally jell for me as the writer, are only the skeleton on which to hang the themes that the story develops about life.

Finally, I have included in this collection three excerpts from previously published novels. I think they illustrate how stories work (or are told) within stories. And the excerpts stand as stories within themselves. It may interest the reader to know that "The Christmas Play" from *Bless Me, Ultima* is actually a separate story I wrote as relief for the murder that is to follow that scene in the novel. Readers have liked its humor. Others have asked why there isn't more humor in my writing. The life of the Mexicano, the Chicanos of the United States, is full of wit, anecdotes, jokes—a rich picaresque word play—in short, a lively sense of life. When we gather together around the kitchen table, at weddings or funerals, at fiestas or community affairs, humor is an integral part of the occasion. Lack of humor in my work says more about my character than the character of the culture. In the face of a dominant and often oppressive culture, humor acquires aspects of cultural survival and resistance. We have our storehouse of jokes about the Anglo-American, as he has jokes about us. In the recent development of teatro in the last few years that humor has been used effectively, and a few Chicano fiction writers are also using it effectively. But I have been preoccupied with a worldview which is serious, and not much humor has found its way into my writing. Perhaps in the future I will attempt more humor, as I did in "The Christmas Play."

"El Velorio" is the wake scene from *Heart of Aztlan*. Velorios are an integral part of the Hispanic culture, but as the culture becomes more urbanized, velorios are seldom held. In the villages and barrios, however, they are still a part of the grief and outpouring of sentiment which comes with death. I think the scene is self-contained, as it explores a theme of life and the characters that revolve around a wake. This scene was written to honor the dead and the resador, the man who comes to pray and guide the departing soul and to guide the community of people who gather to perform one of the most human endeavors, the burying of the dead. The scene also allows me to combine the New World myth which I explore in much of my work with the Christian sense of death.

"Salomon's Story" is a story that Salomon tells in the novel *Tortuga;* as mentioned above, it is tied to "The Place of the Swallows" and some-day will be tied to an entire series of stories I want to write about this tribe of boys at the river. I hunted, during my younger years, with Cruz, an old man from Taos Pueblo. He taught me many things about the hunt. The deer is a brother, and if the hunt is not executed correctly, then the forces that balance life are disturbed. Not only the unwise hunter may be hurt, but the entire pueblo may suffer. Perhaps the same is true of writing: tell a story that is not true—not consistent with the internal working of one's worldview—and some may suffer. Of course I had hunted long before I met Cruz; along the river with the tribe of boys of the story; we roamed up and down the dark river valley in search of prey, driven by the instincts which told us we were hunters. But instinct and the dark blood in which it dwells must come to light. That is what Salomon is saying in his story: not only must the relationship with nature be in balance, but the internal balance of each person must be a goal, and the symbol for that is the light that must be shed on the history of the tribe and the individual.

The storyteller tells stories for the community as well as for himself. The story goes to the people to heal and re-establish balance and har-mony, but the process of the story is also working the same magic on the storyteller. He must be free and honest and a critic of things as they are, and so he must remain independent of the whims of groups. Re-member, the shaman, the curandero, the mediator do their work for the people, but they live alone. They embody the recluse of the society, but they accept their roles; they learn to live an independent existence. So the writer is the focus and the mirror of the community from which he takes his material, and yet he is apart from them. In the end the greater community is always humanity, and the individual has always been, at the same time, a single being within the community and a part of the whole.

Introduction to *Mi Abuela Fumaba Puros*

Those of us who enjoyed the stories in *Tierra Amarilla* have eagerly awaited this new collection by Sabine Ulibarrí. And the wait was worthwhile, for in many ways *Mi Abuela Fumaba Puros* is a continuation of the former collection. In this bilingual edition, Ulibarrí once again combines the artistry of our oral tradition (which he knows so well) with his personal approach to the idea of story. The transformation that occurs in *Mi Abuela Fumaba Puros* is strikingly original.

Utilizing the author/child point of view, he reveals the memorable experiences of the child to the reader. The child moves through a childhood filled with baroque characters, while the author casually comments on the rites of passage. The result is an interplay and a tension of time and memory, of child and man.

Ulibarrí is a talented storyteller, an expert in a tradition that the people of the Southwest have honed to perfection. In *Mi Abuela Fumaba Puros*, he addresses his readers as intimate friends, and invites us to travel with him to the world of Río Arriba, wherein he sketches his characters and the landscape with clear and precise images. He skillfully manipulates time, moving back and forth from the world of the narrator to the world of the child, drawing us deeper into that time and universe which he re-creates.

Life in rural, mountainous New Mexico is revealed in *Mi Abuela Fumaba Puros*. We rediscover the strong sense of daily life and tradition of the hardy pioneers of the land of Tierra Amarilla; we share their joys and tragedies and beliefs. Those who are sensitive to the culture of the Native American and the Hispanic Southwest will experience a mild

Originally published as the introduction to *Mi Abuela Fumaba Puros y Otros Cuentos de Tierra Amarilla*, by Sabine R. Ulibarrí (Berkeley, Calif.: Quinto Sol, 1977), 8–9.

shock of recognition in the stories of doña Matilde, the horseback ride with death, and the story of el Sanador.

These are stories we have heard before in one form or another, stories which provide intimations of a collective identity. In *My Grandma Smoked Cigars*, the personal perspective of the author blends with the elements from that vast storehouse of our culture to produce the story.

Ulibarrí lays bare the emotions of the people, and yet, throughout, there is a persistent vein of humor. La gente had an immense and ingenious repertoire of humorous stories to while away long winter evenings, and that sense of humor is reflected here. Some are ribald, paralleling the best of this form in world literature. Others are about playful jokes, given a New Mexico context. But throughout, there is the strength of love and sharing that characterizes the people of Ulibarrí's New Mexico.

His earlier book has already become a classic in its own right. Now, with its skillful characterization and artistry of storytelling, *Mi Abuela Fumaba Puros (My Grandma Smoked Cigars)* should join it as an equal partner.

Introduction to *Voces*

It is a pleasure to introduce this collection of prose and poetry by contemporary writers from the Nueveo Mexicano community. In this book the reader will recognize the works of familiar writers who are vital links in the oral and written traditions of the Nuevo Mexicano's literary history: writers such as Fray Angelico Chávez and Sabine Ulibarrí. However, if an anthology is to reflect a wide spectrum of a community's literary expression, it must also introduce to the public talented young writers. It is gratifying to see a new generation of Nuevo Mexicano writers developing and to have this opportunity to introduce them to the public.

It is also important to include in this anthology the works of Mexican writers who now live in New Mexico. The novels of Gustavo Sainz are well known in Mexico and throughout the world; they should be known here. These writers are representative of our Mexican heritage. The exchange of works between Mexicano and Nuevo Mexicano writers is a process that must be encouraged.

Our colonial ancestors brought their way of life, their religion, and their language up the Río Grande valley to establish the beginnings of Nuevo Mexicano culture over four hundred years ago. It was the daily as well as the poetic use of that faith and language that provided continuity and cohesion to the newly settled Mexicano/Hispano pueblos of Nuevo México. The Native American pueblos were already settled along the Río Grande. Their languages and their faith were an integral part of the area that the Spanish and Mexican settlers came to occupy. In

Originally published as the introduction to *Voces: An Anthology of Nuevo Mexicano Writers* (Albuquerque, N.Mex.: University of New Mexico Press, 1987), vii–ix.

the fields, in the daily life of the pueblos, in the kivas, their ceremonial ways and languages were crucial to the spiritual relationship they established with the earth and the cosmos.

The Anglo-Americans arrived in Nuevo México in the mid-nineteenth century, introducing yet another language to our land. We have all learned to utilize and share the languages of Nuevo México, even as we continue to preserve our distinct ways of life. The majority of the writers represented here use English, a reflection of the reality within which we live. At the same time, we applaud writers like Estevan Arellano and Erlinda González-Berry for continuing a tradition, creation of literary works in Spanish.

I believe we must pass on to the present generation a serious concern about learning to speak the native languages of the state. Traditions rest within the language. Nevertheless we realize we are compelled to learn English, not only to survive, but to develop completely our creative voices. Language is a tool we learn to utilize. We learn to use it to reflect on life, and that reflection becomes our history. We acknowledge that Nuevo Mexicano history and thought is inscribed in many languages, in an oral as well as a literary tradition.

These writers, through their stories and poems, represent the artistic expression of their community. Their voices introduce a new vision of life and literature; collectively, these writers introduce a new literary space which has at its core the nature of Nuevo Mexicano reality and fantasy. We continue not only in the tradition of the cuentistas and the poets of the Hispano villages, we recreate our own present space.

From my experience in writing, I have discovered that the most important concern for a writer is to identify and develop his most personal, intimate voice. That authentic voice within us tells the true stories and sings the songs. In any community that values creativity, this voice is encouraged and nurtured. The Nuevo Mexicanos have always appreciated their storytellers and the singers. The voice of the storyteller delighted and entertained; it also passed on history, values, traditions, ceremonies, and jokes as well as prayers.

Our community is evolving, changing, exploring its potential. Crucial to the development of our destiny and the definition of that destiny are the voices of the writers and poets. Thus it has been in all the cultures of the world, and so it is for our Nuevo Mexicano way of life. If we are to survive, we must explore our artistic expression, we must dare to share as well as borrow. So for our community I thank each writer represented here; each has dared to find and nurture his or her creative voice. This book assures us that the poetic voice of the Nuevo Mexicanos is alive and engaged in reflecting our reality.

Death in the Novel

One of the concerns I have encountered in my writing during the past few years has been the pervasiveness of death in my work. I don't suggest that I have just realized that death is a theme in my work or that I have been dealing with the death of a particular character, I mean to say that the actual writing of the story seems to draw me closer to an awareness of my own death. As I progress into the story, one of the most acute emotions which I experience is the sense of my own impending death lurking somewhere in the soul of the story. This sense of the reality of death has become so intense that I feel the nature of the experience is worth exploring.

Perhaps enough has been written about death in the novel, and the subject now rouses little interest. I can only say that this is a personal essay, and for me the exploration of the subject is imperative. If, as I create a story, I am also creating a real sense of my own death, then the subject is critical for me. I say the encounter of death in the soul of the story is a "real sense of death," because I have been near death in life. As a young man, an accident took me into the waiting arms of that time which is beyond death; I experienced the most acute epiphany; I felt death very close. Later, in exchanging ideas about death with others who have been close to death, I found our experiences have common elements.

Perhaps, since that experience as a young man, I have been trying to clarify the meaning of death. By reviewing my stories and my recent work, I come to the conclusion that death is an emotion, and like all emotions it has the power to transform us. Love, joy, hate, fear, and grief transform us, and we return (or should return) a better person from the experience of the emotions. Death also transforms us, but there is

---

Not previously published.

no return from the space of time that lies beyond the moment of the emotion. As we try to understand this great emotion of transformation, perhaps we can better understand our own humanity and our personal response to this shared emotion of the community of people.

To put the question in a more objective, critical manner, "Why is it that this awareness or emotion of death is such an integral part of my process of creativity?" I revel in the process of creativity; there is nothing I would rather do than to create stories with a soul. As the writer gives life, or as he encounters the soul of life in the story, then he must encounter the soul of death. Perhaps it's that simple, that in the story the old dualities of life and death, both the most powerful of the transforming emotions, meet; and the writer must intimately know both. Our stock-in-trade are the emotions of mankind.

So I revel in the creation of story. Why is it that sometimes when I sit to write, I am convinced that I will find my death in the next scene, the next chapter, the next turn of events in the lives of my characters? The feeling is at once frightening and exhilarating.

I have seen people die—good friends, family members—and I, in life, have experienced that edge of death, but I seem to have a more profound understanding of death when I'm writing. As in the very climax of lovemaking, a moment of epiphany when joy and the small death commingle, love and death in the novel have come to haunt me. Why? The answers are usually so simple one hurries to apologize. I indulge in the process of creativity—the process of writing the story with soul in it—because the process reveals something of my nature to me. I go in search of the emotions of the soul because they reveal my humanity, and the revelation in story form is something I can share with the reader.

In all my novels, I have had to bring death to characters I liked, characters who had shared intimate secrets of their lives with me. When I finished writing *Bless Me, Ultima*, the most difficult emotion I had to deal with was the death of Ultima. Before that I had to bring death to Florence, one of my favorite characters in the novel. Their deaths were a welling up of the emotions of death, a desire to look more clearly into the meaning of death, a need to understand. A writer cannot put aside those moments of great emotion in his work, and so the emotions grow and haunt him. As the writer moves more intimately into the soul of his story, he becomes heir, like his characters, to the emotion of death. I will discuss this more thoroughly when I talk of my new novel in progress.

Emotion transforms the soul, the heart, the person. We return from the experience of emotion a better person, a little wiser, a little more fulfilled. That is the power of all emotions, to wring us out and, in the transformation, to renew and fulfill us. That's what we deal with as writers, the presentation of emotions in the lives of the characters we create. But when we get to death, we arrive at the emotion from which there is no return. And if I as a writer am feeling each emotion I create, then, when I get to death, I am creating a danger, not only for the characters which must die, but for myself as well. I create danger in the soul of the story, for in the soul of the story lurks death.

Stories that succeed create danger, for the character, for the reader, and certainly for the author. If a story is written without a sense of danger, then it is a bland story, something we say subscribed to formula. But if we feel the sense of danger, then the story works. A writer has to take chances in encountering the danger within each story, and the greatest danger is to encounter the emotion of death.

A writer has to court danger—the brief illumination of the epiphany is not going to be given up to the lazy. Not in love and not in writing. Sitting behind the computer should be as dangerous work as any, because we are trying to describe the secrets of the emotions.

I write in the safety of my home; it is the center of my writing universe. On the surface, there is nothing dangerous about that. I am nearing fifty, a time to think of comfort and not about courting danger. But the courting of danger seems to be part of my life, or I subconsciously make it part of my life. I keep pushing, risking, challenging. I keep going to the edge to see if there are new revelations there for the story at hand. I am daily, behind my computer, courting danger, because I need it in my story. And if it's only in my imagination that I live dangerously, that's all right too, because it is in the heart where we feel emotions, it's there we have to learn to deal with life and then go on. The danger is within, and a writer who would reflect the reality of life has to probe emotions. That's the writer's work, to probe the emotions so his characters may, in each story, reveal a new facet of the complexity we call life. Death is a danger to probe, and yet it has revealed itself to me in my writing, not because I have been afraid, but because I have dared to taunt it out of the deep recesses of my soul; I have drawn out the emotion and dared it to reveal itself to me. If I dare to love, if I dare to live, I have learned, then, I must also dare death.

What conclusions do I draw from my years of writing—my desire to understand the emotions of people and to convert those lives into the characters of my stories? In this personal revelation, I can only suggest that death is an emotion of transformation, as are all emotions, and to have the story succeed I, as the writer, have to probe emotions. The soul of the story is also a soul energized by emotion, and in the soul of the story a danger lurks for all concerned. All emotions are capable of energizing the story—in making it worthwhile. Here I have been following the thread of death, not because I revel in thoughts of death, but because I see it as the emotion capable of producing the most tension for both the writer and the story. The tension the writer lives in, the danger he encounters in the story, should help illuminate the path for all who partake in the story.

In 1985 I wrote a story in Mexico. "The Gift" (published as "Jerónimo's Journey" in *The Man Who Could Fly*) is about the death of a young jardinero. Jerónimo is a character based on a real jardinero I know, a very good friend. I wrote the story after I returned home, and the deeper I got into the story, the more agitated I became. In the story, Jerónimo would die. But his death was so real and so forceful that death seemed to be in command. If the character in my story died, would the real flesh and blood Jerónimo also die? Would the creation of death in the story have power over Jerónimo's life in Cuernavaca? In a way, this is nothing new to those of you who know the power of brujeria. I as a writer/brujo was stirring a powerful potion, I was creating a powerful medicine, the medicine of magic, the story itself. How much power would it have across time and space? For days I wrestled with the question. I did not want to kill Jerónimo, but the story was taking its natural course. Death was working in the story. I finished the story and beat death by calling to Mexico. "How is Jerónimo?" I asked. "Jerónimo is fine, in perfect health," came Ana's reply.

I had not wished evil in the story. The point is I had looked closely at the face of death, and the emotion had overcome and entered me with its reality.

The second writing instance involves a novel I have been writing for the past four or five years. It is set in Alburquerque, and it tells the story of many characters from the point of view of the principal characters. I am one of the characters in the novel. I call myself "The Writer." As the story progresses, I lose my artistic distance, my objectivity, and begin to fall into the whirlpool of desire and emotion created by the characters. They suck me into the story. I begin to sense the danger inherent for me, because my arch enemy in the story is a man who has the power to destroy, and who will stop at nothing to destroy those who get in his way. In short, I began to understand how it is that death lurks in the novel, and how, as I become more involved in the emotions and desires of my characters, the more "character-like" I become, the more I, like them, am heir to the danger and the unexpected in the novel. In the novel, as in life, anyone can die at any time. And if you play the game of character in the novel, then the creative energy creating the growing, changing story can zap you at any time. No character is indispensable to the story.

How is writing, then, different from living? One doesn't choose to live consciously, that is, the majority of people alive are not choosing to live moment by moment. That great force of our collective and most natural imagination, which I call Nature—Nature with a capital N—is as creative as anything I know. Nature pushes hard, it doesn't want us to think about being alive, it wants only to reproduce and recreate for the total good of Nature. Nature abhors the thinker—the man or woman who thinks in the face of Nature begins to slow down the collective system. When Hamlet questions: "To be or not to be," Nature shudders. It wants him out producing children for tomorrow, not questioning the creative process.

But a writer chooses to create a world in his story, consciously, moment to moment. Living is not like writing for some of us. The moment I choose to consciously create a story, I have chosen to live danger-ously. I have no safe answers in the universe I create; I have to take my chances; I have to give part of my self-control over to a creative energy that may in the next chapter decide I am no longer needed for the purposes of the story. It may be that, in daring to think and create consciously, I am putting myself at odds with Nature, or the collective creative imagination. In other words, I am daring the gods, and the gods don't like puny poets entering their realm, certainly not if the writer attempts to explore the meaning of life and death. Consciously I dare death, because like the joys of life, it rounds out our inner world of emotion and desire. I want to feel what life is like, so I create a world in my story, but I also want to feel what death is like, so I tempt and taunt the feelings of that great and final awareness until I am so close I shud-der. How close can I go and still pull back. After all, I am still afraid. I want the truth and revelation of death, but for now I do not want to die. There are still many stories for me to write, exhilarating days of creation left in me.

Getting back to the Alburquerque novel I was describing: It has been a novel which has cost me in terms of stress, in terms of coming to grips with death in the novel. Writers pay for the work they choose to do in life. Our cost is the stress that comes from that exploration of the emotions, death being the costliest. In the novel, I don't die, I survive; I am here today. I journeyed into the soul of the story and came back with my personal vision, and part of that vision insists that the story must celebrate life, but it must also explore truthfully all of the emotions of life. Life is continuous transformation, and the last transformation is brought by death. How we respond emotionally to that experience describes our humanity. I'm still trying to write stories with an upbeat ending, though God knows it's difficult in our times. Facing death in the soul of the story forces me to come back from the journey not discouraged and in despair, but with hope. And what resonates today in my stories may be felt tomorrow in far and distant hearts.

When I finished the manuscript of the Alburquerque novel, I felt I had satisfied the desire to flirt with death, the same desire and emotion that must rule the afternoon of the bullfighter. My characters threatened me with death, the creative energy of the novel threatened me with annihilation. Survival is a crucial instinct to the Chicano novelist, it is an instinct all novelist have to develop. While writing the story, I survived as best as I could, but in order to survive I found I begin to separate myself from the other characters. "Leave me alone," I cried to my characters. You take care of yourselves as best you can; I need to live, I need to finish the story. I found a way to distance myself from the very holocaust I was creating. The shaman/brujo flying cannot afford mistakes, he has no parachute; behind the computer he is alone. But my instinct for survival bothered me. I wondered how much I had sacrificed for the story.

Recently I turned for respite to stories with more humor and sex in them, but I could not escape. This summer in Mexico an image I had had in me for years resurfaced, I sat down and wrote a play called "Death of a Writer."

In a matter of a week the play came to me; the writer is dead even before the curtain parts. The characters have their own emotions and desires to deal with. What does the death of a writer have to do with the reality of the survivors? Put another way, how does our life and work live beyond us? What dangerous exploration of the emotions did we undertake? How did we help light the way of darkness for our brethren? Did we explore love so others could see love through our eyes? Did we denounce injustice so others could clarify their understanding of justice? In the worlds we created, did we dare to taunt death so that all the other emotions and desires could become keener and more meaningful? Those questions bothered me as I wrote "Death of a Writer."

During the writing I kept asking myself: "Where are these characters coming from? What are they telling me?" I always knew I would write the story; years ago I had the idea of the writer who goes to read his work in a foreign city, then is invited from one party to another until he winds up with those who kill him. The writer is living dangerously; he is following the trail of his emotions, he is following the trail of the story, and he knows all along that one possible outcome is death. Perhaps he knows all along that the inevitable end is death. How many of us have not wandered the streets of distant cities and thought, perhaps around this corner is a story I seek, and in the story death is waiting? How many of us have not sat deep into the hours of writing, feeling the energy of the story developing, feeling the force of the characters growing, understanding that in the process of the story there is illumination, and the illumination can contain the spark of death?

In the play "Death of a Writer," the point is not so much that the writer died, but that he wrote dangerously. He dared to explore the energies which drive us toward love and joy and our eventual transformation in death? What's the value of the story? Any story. What right do we have to expect that others will pick up our books and read our creations if we do not explore emotions and desires, and in so doing we drive toward the last, great emotion, that sense of death in the story. A glimpse or a vision of the danger of death helps coalesce the other emotions; it helps build structure from chaos. This helps us understand that death is not as final as we would believe, but like any other emotion it can be a centering aspect of the self. And if the story helps in fulfilling and clarifying the emotions and desires of the reader, then it has communicated. The story helps us to learn that the emotions and desires of the blood need not be destructive, but that each emotion is a way of clarification in life. Fear not, the story should say to the reader—even as it makes him fear—if the writer lived through this, you can too. And both of you should be a little better for it.

Return to the Mountains

An eminent literary figure lived in our midst. That man has now passed on to merge with the ancestral spirits.

I wrote this essay in 1992 to commemorate the life and work of Frank Waters (1902–1992). I now offer it as an elegy for him.

I have been thinking of Frank Waters this summer. Since he and his wife, Barbara, took up winter residence in Tucson, I think of him as an eagle who moves south for the kinder winters of the Arizona desert, but he must return in the spring to the magic mountain of Taos. He must return to the hunting grounds he has known for so long. Only the mountain can mirror his weathered granite face, his soul.

Spring is a time of migration. Snow geese and sandhill cranes ascend from the Bosque del Apache where they have wintered, a sign of the return of life to the earth, one of the ceaseless cycles that Frank Waters taught us to see.

In spring, Grandfather Sun returns north, renewing fields and orchards, returning the essence of life to those who guard the druid spirit of fields and trees.

In the Jemez Mountains where my wife and I have a home in the Jemez Canyon, a place blessed by the spectacular beauty of the red cliffs, the peach and apple trees bloom in mid April. In late spring, I turn on the acequia water and think: "Almost time for Frank Waters to be migrating north to Taos."

Time for Frank and Barbara to come chugging up from Tucson in that cranky old Ford that has become an essential part of him.

Frank Waters wrote a story about the man who killed a deer. Before World War II and before the laboratories were built, when New Mexico

---

Not previously published.

was a more innocent place, Frank Waters wrote about that era. That novel has influenced every writer in the West.

Frank Waters's stories brought the cultural groups of the West together and taught us to see our relationships, good and bad, and he taught us to peer deep into the truths the Native Americans had been guarding for so long.

In *The Man Who Killed the Deer,* the new laws are already encroaching on the ancient traditions of the Taos Pueblo, changing the landscape and the people of the northern villages.

The novel is prophetic. It warned us the change coming was going to affect the ways our people hunted, gathered wood, watered our fields, and kept our ceremonies.

Ay Dios, we should have listened. Now I have written a short story, "Devil Deer." The story is about Cruz, a young man from one of the pueblos near the Jemez Mountains.

It is October, deer season, and Cruz goes hunting. He wants a big buck, so he wanders into forbidden territory. He enters through a hole in the fence that surrounds Los Alamos laboratory.

When he kills the deer, he discovers it is deformed, mutated. The deer has grown hair on its antlers, the tail is the tail of a donkey, the eyes are white stones mottled with blood. The brother of the forest has been changed by the forces of the laboratories.

Cruz carries the fetish of the bear in his leather bag. But the fetish has a crack in it, the medicine has a crack in it, and I worry about the meaning of the story. We know the poison of our technology is leaking down the mountain into the water and the grass. What are the old men saying in the pueblos? Will there be prayers to wash away the poison?

When Frank Waters wrote his novel, the time was still more innocent. But now the times are out of joint. Hunters return with strange stories of deformed deer they have seen.

Frank taught us to see the mountain, the deer, the birds, water, trees as living. He breathed in the teaching of our vecinos from Taos Pueblo and gave it to the world in his books.

But we have changed that pristine world of northern New Mexico. We are living at the end of an age, and we look desperately around for men like Frank Waters to point the way into the new cycle of time.

When I started teaching at the University of New Mexico in 1974, I taught a class on Frank Waters's works. I had just met Frank up in Taos, and I was as impressed by the man as by his novels. I gathered around me a group of students who knew and loved Frank's works, and for a semester we read and talked about his novels.

Every student in this state should know his work. The schools should insist that the history and literature of our region be part of the curriculum. Young people need to read and analyze our literature to better understand their own lives.

We need to take care of the earth, the air, the water. This is the enduring lesson in Frank's works, a lesson learned from his vecinos at Taos pueblo and the Nuevo Mexicanos of Arroyo Seco.

Men like Frank Waters and Cleofes Vigil from San Cristobal taught us a lot. The presence of Cleofes Vigil is still with us. The presence of Frank Waters is with us. These men from the Sangre de Cristo Mountains are the eagles and deer of the mountains.

The migrations of the spirit never end. Each spring I will await with prayers the return of Frank and Barbara. Ay Dios, the transformations occur. Todo se acaba, the old viejitos taught us. The soul remains. The signs remain. Let us be alert. Let us learn to see and listen.

PART SIX

Modern Ethnic Literature and Culture

What Good Is Literature in Our Time?

The millennium is just around the corner, and on a personal, world, and cosmic level we sense the movement of time as it enters a new era. We live in a time of transition, a time in which the human spirit can either be crushed or in which it can be transformed into a new level of consciousness. Because books incorporate time and history and, therefore, become signposts of our humanity, we sense an urgency to provide meaning and direction in our stories.

According to many prophecies an era of time is ending. Human history is being transformed. On the one hand postmodern history, by erasing our rituals and ceremonies, has forced us to enter a linear time, a time which promises no renewal, no rising from the ashes to a new awareness. We wonder if we can ever live again in the cycles of time that, though they ended, always held in their completion the promise of a new cycle. By time, of course, we mean not only the days accumulated on the calendar of history, but the spiritual evolution of humanity. Time and its consequences are incorporated into the human spirit; we are what we have created. Time has cosmic dimensions, but our concern here is more particular: life as we know it on the planet Earth.

For a linear-bound humanity, the coming into being of the new era will not be easy. Around the world we see the signs of disruption in the human spirit and in nature, and we appear helpless. The accumulation of wealth and violence seem to go hand in hand. We are burning forests for power—burning coal and gas and oil to go faster and faster, burning the rain forests far beyond their means to replenish. We live for the moment in a chaotic era we have created. Coming to the end of time may mean coming to the edge of that human-made chaos. The next

Originally published in *American Literary History* 10, no. 3 (Autumn 1998): 471–77.

step is crucial. But unlike archaic man and woman, we have lost touch with the rituals that once gave meaning to the crossing.

As writers, we need to address this depletion of spirit. We need to include social and environmental problems in our stories. If we do not engage the issues of our day, then what good is literature as we face the chaos that threatens to engulf us? Writers must provide a clear sense of meaning and direction in the stories we write. As postmodern humans we have lost the inherent sense of sacredness that literature once transmitted to us. This meaning is missing from life, and it is missing from much of our literature.

From the beginning of time, rock carvers worked to create a sense of meaning in their lives. Glyphs gave meaning to the gathering of seeds, the hunt, the gods, fertility, and the efficacy to stave off the ghosts in the bush. Scribes followed, recording in hieroglyphics the stories of their gods and creation, and thus they offered meaning even as eras of time ended. Knowing their myths of origin allowed those ancient people to understand that time ending meant moving into a new awareness. Those scribes understood the cycles of time the Earth is heir to.

I think of those ancestors from around the world, the writers who have recorded the end of their time in their stories and myths. Ages arrive and blossom to fruition, then they wither and die, but inscribed in rituals was the hope that something new would be born from death. Today we sense little of renewal in our art. We yearn for the written word to give meaning to our age.

We sense that between the prior cycle of time and the time being born, there is a space of transformation. In that space we can use history and art to complete the flourishing of a new consciousness. Themes in our literature must include a sense of this incredible age of transformation through which we are living. Conflicts and human emotions drive our stories, and we particularize those conflicts to character. But characters live in a context. Our context happens to be a time of great wrenching of the human spirit. To give meaning and direction to our time should be the task of every writer.

Literature and art have always provided direction. The great myths of the past teach that eternal return is possible for the individual and for the community. We have been constantly reborn, and each new awareness pushed us not only to be masters of new technologies but toward knowledge of the transcendent in our lives. Through initiatory rituals we connected ourselves to our earth origins; myths spoke of our heroes and of cosmic (transcendent) origins. We used to speak to the gods, and they provided direction. Can we do so today?

There are serious writers today who are describing the age of transformation in which we live. In many cases the descriptions are alarming, for any account of the depletion of our natural resources can only be alarming. What is more alarming is the depletion of our spiritual resources, the disrespect we show for human life, the widespread violence and use of drugs. To describe our age is to describe a loss of the center, a loss of harmony with nature, a desperate consumerism that seems to find hope only by consuming more and more. Is there hope, or have we capitulated to the forces of consumerism which are creating the good life for a very small percentage of the earth's population while the rest suffer?

During an age of transformation, chaos struggles to drag down the forces which provide meaning, harmony, and direction. We see this happening today, so we understand the context. We know what's going on in the world, if only subconsciously or subliminally, and that knowledge is internalized. We know what's going on, and as writers we either give in to chaos or we choose to use our literature as a guide to renew the earth and its people. All good literature has done this in the past.

It is the responsibility of writers to write stories that contain meaning and a sense of direction. The scribes, after all, have always been on the side of the gods and the telling of creation stories. How we came onto this earth compels us to write of our relationship to each other, to the earth, to the cosmos. Our bodies and spirit seek internal rhythm, balance and harmony. Living in an era of transformation, that time when human consciousness can crash or move to a higher plane, creates new dimensions of responsibility, especially in those of us who write. Or will history record that we, too, were swept up in the age of commercialism and consumerism to such an extent that we did not recognize the spirit of the time? We did not see the possibility of disaster or the possibility of rebirth.

The birth of the twenty-first century will be known (if history extends that far) as the blossoming of the age of information. We satisfied ourselves with dreams that technology could cure everything, as long as we got enough information. We indulged in the information age, but thought little of the value of the information we were getting. What was our role on earth? a few writers asked. Did we write about the waste and destruction around us? When violence swept around us and we lost our youth to drugs, did we write meaning and direction into our stories? Or were we too swept up in a cynical stance at the end of the century?

Some of us have found meaning and harmony within our own, smaller communities. Even as the world grows more global, we recognize a need to find direction in more intimate, particular communities. Communities we know. Perhaps it is in the particular region that one finds a truer relationship with community. It is in the particular community that one finds a sense of power and meaning. The global village, after all, is being created by forces far beyond the control of most of us. Falling back into the circle of our own communities may be the first step in saving the individual, and as we save the individual we hope to save the group. From the security of the place we recognize, we may be able to communicate across frontiers, the frontiers we only imagined had been erased by the World Wide Web.

So the creation of meaning within one's smaller, particular community may be a necessity for the individual to grow and be heard. It is there people speak to their ancestors and guard their knowledge. I find this sense of meaning and direction in the so-called third-world writers. Writers in the disfranchised communities of the world describe themselves with a strong voice, and at the same time they describe a sense of direction and meaning the rest of us can internalize.

Salman Rushdie's work, as complex as it is, comes to mind. So does Michael Ondaatje's recent novel, *The English Patient* (1992), whose powerful theme is really about the end of time we have created by building atomic/nuclear bombs. We find the spirit of history in the magical genius of a García Márquez. Writers from Latin America, China, Africa, and the third-world writers also come to mind. In our own country we learn more about the spirit of survival from the so-called ethnic, regional, and gender writers than from the old establishment, the so-called oligarchy of American intellectual life.

There is no one generation of writers in this country; perhaps there never was. Prior generations of writers have been defined by academics, and that process left many out. What we see happening at the end of our century in this country is the discovery of the voices of our distinct communities. We have discovered our diversity. Writers from the diverse communities of our country have insisted that literature can be created from the rich histories of their places, and small-press editors have brought their stories to light. The once voiceless communities have now spoken; in art, poetry, story, dance, and murals, the dispossessed have spoken. Our heritage is diverse, and so our literature is diverse. But there is more than just the acknowledgment of diversity at stake; there is a wonderful sense of discovery afoot. Why? Because it is the writers from our diverse communities who truly mirror the state of literature in our country, and it is in those writers that we find that sense of meaning and direction we so urgently need.

I am a product of this flowering of our literature in the 1960s; I am a writer from one of those communities. In the 1960s the Mexican American writers in this country created a literary movement. Much of it escaped notice by the editors and critics of the establishment. Initially we spoke and wrote only for our community, out of an impulse to give direction to our group, but the truth is, and the meaning of diversity is, that we wrote not only for ourselves, we spoke across frontiers. We breached gaps. Some heard us, in this country, around the world. Some began to ask: "Who are these Chicanos?" "What are they saying about meaning in their lives?" "How does the meaning in their lives affect mine?"

Meaning is the greatest gift we can give life. To help center the individual or the community is, for me, a primary reason for art. The purpose of the Chicano literary movement was to give meaning to our lives. Mexican American history in this country had been nearly lost. It was so neglected in the schools that generations of Chicanas/os began to believe they did not have a history or a literature. We were disconnected from the continuity of our history. The way of the ancestors was nearly lost.

What saved us from complete negation of self? How were we able in the sixties to create an artistic movement out of so many centuries of neglect? I think it is because our language and folkways had been kept alive at home, in the villages, in the barrios. There we existed within the familiar circle of the values of our ancestors. We heard the stories, we spoke Spanish to our parents, we kept the flame of our particular existence alive. A foreign world had encroached, and some of the meaning of our past was lost, but it was not completely erased.

This keeping of one's particular history is not a new phenomenon. It is the course of human events. It is not the flowering of communal histories that should alarm us, but their suppression. Even after centuries of suppression, the voices of all distinct histories will be heard. We would be wiser to honor those histories than to think we can forever erase the past of any community.

Many communities in this country found their voices in the sixties. A struggle for independence ensued not only in the Black community and with women's liberation, the struggle took place everywhere. We Mexican Americans in the Southwest United States called it the Chicano Movement. We created our voice and named it. While not as potent or long lasting as the Black Civil Rights Movement, it nevertheless helped to define us as we searched the archives of our folk for meaning.

Inscribed in the art of the Chicano Movement was an aesthetic that took its meaning from the people. Plays depicted the lives of the campesinos, the farmworkers. Murals depicted historical heroes, poets, artists, the daily life, and the Mexican warriors of the revolution. Chicana writers discovered Frida Kahlo and the Virgen de Guadalupe, because in such figures the feminine spirit was acknowledged and examined. They discovered their own feminism and how to give it voice in poetry and story. A revolution of liberation was made from that empowerment.

Chicana/o poetry used the real multilingual language of the street, the music and rhythm of a Spanish-speaking community that had learned English. Our poets mixed into it the Black American lexicon and swing, and the patois of the pachuco. The poetry of the Chicano Movement returned to the epic, using the personal search for identity and the overthrowing of oppression as its motifs. Epic poetry was written by poets who just yesterday had learned the power of the word. It spoke to the oppressed masses, as epic poetry should. A social, economic, and spiritual revolution sounded in the literature of the time. In an age of transformation, our writers did provide meaning and direction, and most potent was the unveiling of our spirit. A liberation from shackles is, after all, spiritual.

Novels and stories depicted our homes, communities, the folk. Suddenly our grandparents, neighbors, farmworkers, folk healers were the protagonists of our stories. In the early days of the movement, our community looked in the mirror of the work we had produced and applauded. They liked what they saw; they saw themselves. Those outside our community who read our poems and stories also took notice. The age of transformation was upon us, and one way to save ourselves was to become the protagonists in our art. That movement in various particular guises was happening around the world. That liberation of spirit is what characterizes the end of our century.

As we turned within we dealt not only with the oppression in our lives, we rediscovered our folklore and mythology. It flooded our art.

Mesoamerican mythology found its way back into our worldview as we searched for meaning. We found our Native American roots. We dug out indigenous myths and stories and the meaning they held, and we claimed them as part of our inheritance.

I worked with groups of writers from many communities in those days. What Chicanos and Chicanas were creating in the Southwest was happening elsewhere. Meeting the writers of this country was an education. These were not just the writers published by the Eastern publishers, but writers who sprang from the earth of their region, the people of their community. A diversity of voices was being heard in the United States, and it was great.

The literary history of the latter part of this century can no longer be written without taking into account this phenomenon of diversity. Whether or not the Chicana/o writers of this generation have made an impact on the larger intellectual community remains to be seen. The media still controls the image, and it still doesn't encourage a meaningful, vibrant role for Mexican American literature in the broader intellectual life of the country. A great deal of our contribution has been spread by small presses, through word of mouth, by one person handing another a book, by attending readings, by a network of seekers of knowledge. A slow process, but it has spread. It is perhaps, even in the age of the Internet, the way all liberating revolutions are spread. The contact is from one human to another.

How will history record our age of transformation? Will it be just one more cycle in the growth of trade and commerce? Will we use the technology of the Internet only to create consumers and label our progress only in terms of gross national product? Or will we be able to say that looking back at the end of our century we read in the works of writers a sense of the change, signposts for the road ahead? A warning that we had to repair the human spirit.

At the most extreme we can say we almost lost the way. We retreated into our specific communities so deeply we feared those not like us; we created the Others and blamed them for the problems of the world. We found the strength in the center of our community, then didn't share it across frontiers. We used ancestral wisdom only to empower ourselves.

I believe in a more positive vision. We can write that we entered our particular community to find the meaning and direction we needed in the face of a chaotic world. We entered our circle seeking ancestral meaning, and, centering ourselves in that inheritance, we found direction. We learned we could shape our destiny even in the era of transformation. We wrote that meaning and direction into our stories. The end of one cycle of time has within it the seed from which a new era will be born. We are that seed. Literature can have meaning in our time.

An American Chicano in
King Arthur's Court

A variety of voices comprises the literature of the Southwest. Writers from each of the cultural groups write from their particular perspective. Eventually these different perspectives will form the body of work we call Southwestern literature. I say eventually, because as of now the contemporary writings of the Chicano and Native American communities—while they are flourishing—have not yet been widely disseminated and have not yet made their final impact on the region.

It is understood that whenever cultural groups as different as the Anglo-American, Chicano, Native American, and others exist side by side, cultural sharing takes place; but also each group will develop a set of biases or stereotypes about the other groups. This is unfortunate, but it is a historical fact. The problem is compounded, of course, when one of the groups holds social, political, and economic power over the other groups. Then prejudices will affect in an adverse manner the members of the minority groups.

How do we make the literature of the Southwest a truly multicultural literature that informs the public about the variety of voices reflecting the cultures of the Southwest? Can our different literatures help to lessen the negative effect of cultural stereotypes?

I am an American Chicano, and I have titled my essay "An American Chicano in King Arthur's Court." For me, King Arthur's Court represents an archetypal time and experience in English memory, a memory that was brought to the American shores by English colonists. It is an

---

Originally presented as part of a lecture series for the Writers of the Purple Sage project, Tucson, Ariz. (October 1984); and subsequently published in revised form in *Old Southwest/New Southwest: Essays on a Region and Its Literature*, ed. Judy Nolte Lensink (Tucson, Ariz.: The Tucson Public Library, 1987), 112–18.

archetype that is very much alive. (Remember the Kennedy administration's reviving the dreams of Camelot?) King Arthur's Court represents a "foreign" archetype that is not indigenous to the Native American memory.

There is no judgmental value attached to what I have just said. King Arthur's Court has a right to exist in the communal memory of the British and the Anglo-Americans, and communal memory is a force that defines a group. The stories and legends surrounding King Arthur's Court are part of their history and identity. Camelot and King Arthur's Court are "real" forces inasmuch as they define part of the evolution of this group's eventual worldview.

In 1846, King Arthur's Court moved to what we now call the Southwest United States. During the war with Mexico, the United States forcefully took and then occupied Mexico's northern territories. In so doing, the United States acquired a large population of Native Americans and Mexicanos. What did it mean to the Mexicanos, those soon to be labeled Mexican Americans, when suddenly a very different social, economic, and political system was placed over them?

Historians have written about the economic and political castastrophe that occurred. I wish to explore the occupation from another angle. What happened when a different worldview with its particular archetypes was imposed over the communal memory of the Mexicanos? In the area of artistic impulse and creation, this element of the Anglo culture would cause as many problems for the Mexicanos, as did the new language and value system with which they now had to contend.

The Mexicanos of the Southwest had already spent centuries creating their own vision of the world by the time the Anglo-Americans arrived. Their worldview was principally Hispanic and Catholic, but it was also imbued with strains of belief from the Native American cultures. The culture was Hispanic in language, but in its soul and memory resided Western European thought, Greek mythology, and the Judeo-Christian mythology and religious thought; the thought and mythology of Indian Mexico and of the Pueblos of the Río Grande had already imbued the collective memory. The Mexicano of the north was, with few and isolated exceptions, a mestizo population. Therefore, its worldview was informed by the memory of the native cultures of the Southwest United States.

Since 1848, King Arthur's Court has been the social and legal authority in the Southwest. It has exercised its power—not always in a fair and judicious way. My concern here is to explore how the Anglo-American value system affected the artistic impulse of the Mexicano. Did it impede and stifle the creativity of the Mexicano, and if so, did it interfere in the Mexicano's self-identity and aesthetic?

The artistic impulse is an energy most intricately bound to the soul of the people. Art and literature reflect the cultural group, and in reflecting the group they deal not only with the surface reality but with that substratum of thought that is the group memory. The entire spectrum of history, language, soul, voice, and the symbols of the collective memory affect the writer. A writer becomes a prism to reflect those elements that are at the roots of the value system. We write to analyze the past, explore the present, and anticipate the future, and in so doing we utilize the collective memory of the group. We seek new vision and symbols to chart the future, and yet we are bound to mythologies and symbols of our past.

I remember when I started writing as a young man, fresh out of the university, my mind teeming with the great works I had read as a student. I was affected, as were most of my generation, by the poetry of Dylan Thomas, Eliot, Pound, Wallace Stevens. I had devoured the works of world authors, as well as the more contemporary Hemingway, Faulkner, Steinbeck, and Thomas Wolfe, and I felt I had learned a little about style and technique. I tried to imitate the work of those great writers, but that was not effective for the stories I had to tell. I made a simple discovery. I found I needed to write in *my* voice, of *my* characters, using *my* indigenous symbols. I needed to write about my culture, my history, and the collective experience of my cultural group. But I had not been prepared to explore *my* indigenous, American experience; all my education from first grade through a graduate degree had prepared me to understand King Arthur's Court. I discovered that the underlying worldview of King Arthur's Court could not serve to tell the stories about my communal group.

I suppose Ultima saved me. That strong, old curandera of my first novel, *Bless Me, Ultima,* came to me one night and pointed the way. Was she the anima, a woman of wisdom, the collective mothers of the past, or a reflection of the real curanderas I had seen do their work? I know she became a guide and mentor who was to lead me into the world of my Native American experience. "Write what you know," she said. "Do not fear to explore the workings of your soul, your dreams, your memory. Dive deep into the lake of your subconsciousness, your memory! Find the symbols, unlock the secrets! Learn who you really are! You can't be a writer of any merit if you don't know who you are!"

I took her kind and wise advice. I dove into the common memory, into the dark and hidden past which was a lake full of treasure. The symbols I discovered had very little to do with the symbols I knew from King Arthur's Court—they were new symbols, symbols I did not fully understand, but symbols that I was sure spoke of the indigenous American experience. The symbols and patterns I found connected me to the past, and that past was not only my Hispanic, Catholic heritage; that past was also Indian Mexico. I did what I had never been taught to do at the university. I explored myself and began to learn the workings of my soul. I was a reflection of that totality of the past which had worked for eons to produce me.

Each writer has to go through the process of liberating oneself and finding one's true stream of creative energy. For the Chicano writers of my generation it has been doubly difficult, because in our formative years we were not presented with the opportunity to study our culture, our history, our language.

My generation will receive at least some thanks from the future, if only because we dared to write from the perspective of our experience, our culture. Of course a steady stream of southwestern Hispanic writers had been producing works all along. Before and after 1846, poetry, novels and newspapers were produced, but those works were never part of the school curriculum. The oral tradition was alive and well, and its artistic impulse was invigorating to those of us lucky enough to grow up in its bounty. But by the 1960s the Hispanic culture had reached a crisis point. Not only were the old prejudices affecting us adversely, but the very core of the culture was under threat.

The Mexican American community needed economic and political justice in the 1960s. It also needed an artistic infusion of fresh, creative energy. We had to take a look at ourselves and understand the world-view that our ancestors had created. This is precisely what the Chicano Movement of the 1960s and '70s did. The Chicano Movement of those decades fought battles in the social, economic, and political arenas, and in the artistic camp. Taking up pen and paintbrushes, we found we could joust against King Arthur's knights and hold our own. In fact, we often did extremely well because we were on our soil, we knew the turf. Quite simply, what we were saying was that we wanted to assert our own rights, we wanted to define ourselves; we believed that our worldview was as important as any other in terms of sustaining the individual and the community.

We engaged actively in the large-scale production of creative literature. We insisted that the real definition of our community was in the arts, in poetry and stories. A wealth of works was produced that was labeled the Chicano Renaissance. The view of the writers working from within the Chicano community helped to dispel some of the old stereotypes and prejudices. We could think, we could write, we did honor parents and family, we did have a set of moral values, we were as rich and as complex a cultural group as any other group in the country, and so the old, one-dimensional stereotypes began to crumble.

We explained to the broader "mainstream" culture that we are American Chicanos; we are an inherently American, indigenous people. We are Hispanic from our European heritage, we are Native American from our American heritage. We are heirs to the mythologies and religions and philosophic thought of Western civilization, but we are also heirs to the mythologies, religions, and thought of the Américas. A renewed pride in our Native American heritage defined us.

Out of the Native American world flowed a rich mythology and symbology which the poets and writers began to tap and use. We confronted our mestizo heritage and proudly identified with this New World person. The idea of an original homeland, the concept of Aztlán, became a prevalent idea. The homeland was indigenous, it was recorded in Native American legend. For the Chicano consciousness of the 1960s it provided a psychological and spiritual center. One of the most positive aspects of the Chicano Movement was its definition of a Chicano consciousness. Spiritually and psychologically, Chicanos had found their center; they could define their universe with a set of symbols and metaphors that were inherent to the New World. We had tapped our Native American experience and recovered the important archetypal symbols of that history.

That consciousness, which was defined in the art, poetry, and stories of the Chicano writers, continues to exist not just as a historical phenomenon that happened in the sixties and seventies; it continues to define the Chicano collective memory today. The power of literature, the power of story and legend, is great. True, the Chicano Movement has waned in social action, but the renewed consciousness born in the literature of those decades survives in art, writing, history, and in the language and the oral tradition of the people. In a broader sense, its humanistic principles of brotherhood, its desire for justice, its positive cultural identification, its definition of historic values, and its concern for the oppressed continue to be guiding principles in the thought and conduct of American Chicanos. Chicano consciousness continues to center us, instruct us, guide us, and define us.

The evolution of Chicano consciousness created a new perspective in humanistic philosophy. It took nothing away from our European and Mexican heritage, it took nothing away from other Western influences; on the contrary, it expanded the worldview of the Américas. We are still involved in the struggle to define ourselves, to define our community. New labels appear, and each generation adds to the meaning of our history. Evolution is a slow process, and we should share in the process of identity, not allow the process to separate us.

Once a clear definition of Chicano consciousness has worked itself into the society, then we will not have to be so sensitive about the Edenic concept of King Arthur's Court. After all, we understand its right to exist as a mythology, we understand how it defines a particular group. The challenge for us, for the writers of the Southwest from all cultural groups, is to understand and accept those views that define groups and the individuals from all communities.

Part of our task is to keep reminding each other that each cultural community has an inherent right to its own definition, and so Aztlán defines us more accurately than Camelot. Hidalgo and Morelos and Zapata are as valuable as Washington, Jefferson, and Lincoln. The mythology of Mesoamerica is as interesting and informing as Greek mythology. Mexico's settlement of her northen colonies is as dramatic and challenging as the settlement of the thirteen United States colonies. As American Chicanos, we have a multilayered history on which to draw. To be complete individuals, we must draw on all the world traditions and beliefs, and we must continue to understand and strengthen our own heritage. We seek not to exclude, but to build our base as we develop a vision of the interrelated nature of the Américas. Our eventual goal is to incorporate the world into our understanding.

But in the span of world time, the Chicano community is a young community. It is still growing, still exploring, still defining itself. Our history has already made valuable contributions to American thought and growth, and we will continue to contribute. What we seek now, in our relationship to the broader society, is to eliminate the mindless prejudices that hamper our evolution, and to encourage people of good-will who do not fear a pluralistic society and who understand that the more a group of people define themselves in positive ways, the greater the contribution they make to humanity.

For over a century, American Chicanos have been influenced by the beliefs imposed by a King Arthur's Court scenario. We have learned the language, we have learned the rules of the game. We have adopted part of the cultural trappings of Arthur's Court, but we also insist on keeping true to our culture. The American Southwest is a big land, a unique land. It has room for many communities. It should have no room for the old, negative prejudices of the past. When we, each one of us, impede the fulfillment of any person's abilities and dreams, we impede our own humanity.

The Light-Green Perspective

I would like to discuss the role ethnic literatures of this country play in the curriculum of our schools, both at the secondary and the university level. The question I want to raise is this: Has the literature of our different ethnic groups penetrated the curriculum and therefore the literary heritage of the country, or are we still in the mode of the decade of the 1960s when one or two specialized courses in Black Literature or Chicano Literature or Native American Literature were tucked into a corner of the curriculum to satisfy the conscience of the educational community? I raise this question for a variety of reasons.

First, the demand of various ethnic groups in the 1960s to be reflected in the process of the educational community may have been satisfied in only a token way. Those of us who "grew up" in the sixties have the responsibility to analyze our role as teachers of literature and composition and to ask ourselves if we indeed do our work in a more open forum that truly reflects the variety of cultures in our country.

I raise this question to lead to the second point. "It's a small world!" More than ever we live in an age of interdependence. Groups within nations, as well as nations within the international arena, have moved into a fragile but exciting state of interdependency. The world is in a fluid state, and our most simple actions reverberate in far and distant places. That state of interdependency also applies to the study of literature. By adopting the literature of our different cultures and regions—including the literature of women, whose voices have comprised an important new entity during our generation—we can demonstrate to

Originally published as "The Light Green Perspective: An Essay Concerning Multi-Cultural American Literature," in *MELUS* (Journal of the Society for the Study of the Multi-Ethnic Literature of the United States) 11, no. 1 (Spring 1984): 27–32.

the world a model of interdependency which reflects the most worthy aspirations for humanism in the 1980s.

Education begins by teaching the student this rule: Know thyself. In our world we have to extend the rule to: Know thy neighbor and his world. In our complicated and technological society, I am afraid that both of these maxims could be subverted. In our rush to join the "computer generation," the new guiding principle might be: Know thy computer. In a real sense, it is technology that has created this new, interdependent world. Technology, science, the business world, the search for world resources and markets, tremendous innovations in transportation and communication, and a concern for our world ecology have all contributed to the shrinking of the world and to our new interdependent state.

Literature as art should bring us face to face with the interdependent, unifying characteristics of mankind, and yet there are forces which interfere with our goal to teach the various literatures of our country to our students. There are intermediate institutions that stand between us and our goal. How powerful is the role of these institutions? Allow me to illustrate this idea with a story I heard recently, a story which also explains my title for this essay, "The Light-Green Perspective." The story goes like this.

Somewhere in this country there is a bus driver whose task it is to deliver students to school each day. He takes his job seriously. The bus driver is the captain of the ship while the students are with him. The parents are happy to see their children board the bus each day. Someone, they feel, is in charge, and he is not raising hell for more pay, like the teachers.

But the kids on the bus have been fighting with each other. In the world of the bus, which represents our society, prejudice has reared its ugly head. The kids are calling each other names: Nigger! Spic! Redneck! Jew!

The name calling disturbs the bus driver. One day when the name-calling gets out of hand, he pulls the bus over to the curb and makes all the kids get out. He then lectures them on the evil of racial prejudice. He points out the contributions the different cultural groups have made to the country. Each group has contributed to the American society, he tells them, and our country is richer for the cultural diversity within its borders. Our system of justice is "color-blind," and each one of us should also be color-blind. Each group has a right to maintain its cultural ways and be proud of its heritage.

The children listen, and they agree. The driver is right. They have been behaving like adults, allowing prejudice to bring out the worst in their natures. What can they do to solve the problem?

"I have a solution," the driver suggests. "From now on let's all be Green. We will call ourselves the Greenies. We will all be equal."

The children agree. It seems like a good experiment to try. Okay, they say, we will all be Green.

"Good," the driver smiles. "Now line up to get back on the bus. The Light Greens first, please."

The children arrive at school. The Light Greens enter first. They read Light-Green stories. Once in a long while an adventurous teacher reads them a Dark Green story, but never in their entire schooling do they explore the whole range of Green. The children grow; the Light Greens go on to college and into the professions. Their perspective of life is Light-Green. They believe the experiment is working. When the world explodes in Iran, Beirut, Afghanistan, Grenada, Central America, and in the nuclear arms race, and in their own hometowns where some people desire to be other shades of green, the problems are viewed and acted upon only through the Light-Green perspective.

There is some analogy there to our society. The bus driver represents the intermediate institutions I alluded to earlier. These institutions play a real role in our understanding of the world, and these institutions also affect those of us who teach literature and writing. I want to discuss two of these institutions that help create the Light-Green perspective: the teachers training programs and publishers.

First, allow me to tell you that I am addressing this issue from my perspective as a writer and a teacher. As a writer, my perceptions were formed by my culture, which is Hispanic. I belong to a large ethnic group in this country, the Mexican Americans, and I choose to call myself Chicano. So I have not only been creating literature, I have been creating literature which has its own particular shade of green. And I have observed the role of literature in the curriculum all of my professional life. The phenomenon that most disturbs me is the lack of inclusion and study of the literature that writers like myself produce in standard literature and composition courses. In most cases, my work and the work of my contemporaries who are Black, Native American, Asian American and/or women, is still stuck away in specialized courses. Our work is not allowed to enter the mainstream study of literature, and that, I think, is a direct result of what I call the light-green perspective. If we are to attack the prejudice created by that light-green perspective, we must include the literature of all the cultural groups in the study of mainstream literature.

"Why?" I ask myself, "haven't the literary works of writers from specific regions and specific cultural groups penetrated the educational process?" I know that the curriculum does not represent the works of my Mexican American, Chicano fellow writers. I know that essays by Hispanic writers are not in the composition and writing books being proposed to publishers at this very moment. When the literary works are present, I find it is only a teacher of sensitivity and awareness who is interested in teaching those works of minority writers and who is interested in preparing her students for our interdependent world. Perhaps it is this teacher who dares to incorporate stories from other shades of green who will eventually change the system and make it more nearly equal, more interesting, and more representative of reality. My hope is with that teacher, because otherwise only token attention is paid to the diversity of writing in this country today.

When I review the role of teacher-training programs, it becomes quite clear that teacher preparation has not taken into account the broader literary streams of this country. The stricter definition of our literary heritage has, for the most part, left out those important tributaries which spring from specific regions and cultural groups. Those tributaries have not been explored or studied. Now a more active role has to be played by associations of teachers such as the NCTE [National Council of Teachers of English] and MLA [Modern Language Association]. I greatly admire and esteem those teachers out in the field who, largely with the use of their duplicating machines, are bringing the diverse writings of our country into the classroom to broaden the worldview of their students.

At the university level, the younger instructors are under tremendous pressure to "publish or perish." The profession may define the rules of the game, but the young scholar eventually needs to find a publisher. This brings me to the second of those intermediate institutions I want to discuss. Because publishers are intricately linked to the "publish or perish" rule, they wield great power. One de facto guideline that publishers adhere to affects us all, and it is that the books they publish must have national appeal in order to make a profit. It is a pernicious fact, but it is there, and at this point the numbers and profit game begins to get mixed up with quality, purpose, and the light-green perspective.

I live and teach in the Southwest, an area which has a large Hispanic and Native American population, the so-called ethnic groups, although the label "ethnic group" should be used with care. It is ironic at best to categorize the Native American Indians who were waiting on the shore when the rest of us landed as an "ethnic group." They are cultural groups, as are the Hispanics. In the area of teaching composition or writing, it still astounds me to see books that use the essays of various writers as models for students, but do not include essays by the writers of those cultural groups. One may argue that composition and grammar are a national concern which can be taught alike in the Northeast as in the Southwest. I would argue that the *content* in the essays used as models is an equally important reflection of the literary heritage, and students profit from finding in the curriculum something with which they can identify. A familiar essay with familiar content can provide a grounding and a knowledge which helps the educational process continue. But as long as writers from these important groups and regions are excluded from the contents of the books, we will continue to have only a light-green presentation of that which is worthy of study. As we turn our attention and support to that individual teacher in the classroom, perhaps we can also turn our attention to a regional perspective in the presentation of materials so that students can see their own world reflected in the curriculum.

Writers like myself and my contemporaries have little influence with the big publishers, and large and influential organizations such as NCTE and MLA seem not to be pressuring the publishers to correct their light-green perspective. In fact, the only concerted pressure on publishers today comes from the strict and narrow sectarian view of the Moral Majority and groups like the organization in Texas that directly aims to censor books and tie the hands of publishers. Those well-financed coalitions which seek to censor us into a more narrow view of our literary heritage become more of those intermediate institutions that oppose an equal voice for all in the curriculum and, in so doing, oppose the reality of an interdependent world. It is time that the cause for equal representation for all the cultural and regional writing in this country—and this would include the views of women who write—be championed in a positive and aggressive way by organizations such as the NCTE and MLA.

Granted, there are changes in the air. Just recently a major publisher asked my permission to reprint one of my essays in an eighth-grade reader. I hope soon to see composition books at all levels that include the essays of Hispanic writers as models. In the Southwest, it would seem natural to include models of writing that reflect in their content and presentation of ideas the Hispanic, the Native American, and the Cowboy culture, as well as the views of other groups that have helped to give form and character to the region. The entire border area has largely been ignored, not because writers are not using the border region in their works, but because that light-green perspective continues to ignore one of the most vital and interesting regions in our country. A generation of students will grow up not knowing the impact and contributions of the Mexican to the fabric of our life.

Discussions in our fields of interest, literature and writing, should also include a discussion of the heritage of those cultures that shape the literature. That discussion would be more holistic in its approach and more humanistic as it teaches the interdependence of groups. In literature courses, it seems imperative that more of the literature of our diverse cultural groups be included. This inclusion must reflect our ideal to prepare students for a new, interdependent world; it must not be only a token gesture. By including a broad spectrum of writers in the curriculum, we insist on eliminating prejudice and racial hatred. Our students have the right to know and understand all the shades of green, not just one. And we, as teachers, must be keenly aware of those intermediate institutions and groups that stand between the student and his right to know the diversity of the world, so that he can live in the interdependent world. In addition to the above points, I want to emphasize one other issue I consider most important. The inclusion of minority works not only would benefit the students from those groups who would have "identification interests," but it would also benefit children of *all* other groups in helping them to learn about the cultures of diverse people.

A more thorough discussion in groups such as the NCTE of the literature of our culture and regional groups is needed. And that discussion must have a sound rationale: altruistically the study of literature, on a more practical level, the rationale of the interdependent world we must all live in. Nothing could be more damaging to the future of education and to the American sense of fair play and equality than to espouse a system of tokenism, which in effect becomes one more de facto rule of the society. That will only perpetuate racism. We cannot waste the human potential and the creativity bound up not only in all the shades of green but in the spectrum of life. Not to explore that rainbow would be a terrible legacy to leave the future. To create a new order of respect and harmony among the cultural groups of this country and in the world is a worthy ideal. But it has to start with us. Sensitivity is the key. Sensitivity to an interdependent world, which is in a very real sense struggling for survival, is the key. From national groups such as the National Council of Teachers of English and the Modern Language Association, we seek and demand not only sensitivity to our multiethnic literary heritage, but active and aggressive action in correcting the light-green perspective. These organizations of national importance must take a role in redefining the literary heritage of this country. A new era of inquiry in this field should generate not only scholarly papers and symposiums on the topic, but methods by which to affect teacher training programs and the commercial publishing industry in this country.

"Still Invisible, Lord, Still Invisible"

One day my grandfather was called on urgent business to Alburquerque. He asked me if I wanted to go with him, and, of course, I said yes. I was a child, and for me, Highway 66, which cut through our small village, was a magical road. While herding our milk cow towards the river, I would often stop by the roadside and watch the cars which carried the gringos from the east as they sped by on their way to their vacations in California. In late summer I saw them return, sunburned and tired, and I envied them because they had traveled that magical road.

Now it was my turn. I was filled with excitement. I went everywhere with my grandfather, but never had we attempted such a long trip. "How will we get there, grandfather?" I asked. He smiled and said, "We stand by the highway, and one of these good turistas will give us a ride. We will be there in no time at all."

So I put my small hand in his brown, wrinkled hand, received my mother's kiss and benediction, then together my grandfather and I walked to the highway where we were to get a ride which would take us to the wondrous and faraway city of Alburquerque. Oh it was a day filled with excitement. It was also a day for learning a lesson.

We stood all day on the shoulder of the highway. My grandfather held up his hand and signaled each time a car approached, but the people from the east passed us by without so much as a look. We stood all day in the hot sun. By late afternoon we still didn't have the ride which we so urgently needed. I was very tired. I broke our silence and asked my grandfather, "Why don't they give us a ride?" He looked at the cars that sped by us and replied, "They don't see us, my son, they don't see us."

Originally published in *AMAE Journal* (Journal of the Association of Mexican American Educators) (1982–83): 35–41.

In this paper I will discuss ethnic cultures and their transformations, and in particular how those cultures are viewed by the mainstream, monolithic culture of this country. In addition I would like to talk about writers, like myself, who do not come out of traditions which were forged in the eastern United States, and most important, I want to analyze and reveal reasons why we have remained invisible to the critics of the mainstream culture.

It is often implied that writers in this country who are rooted in their ethnic cultures do not have the perspective to develop and expand their work on a universal level. Proponents of this critical view most often mean that those writers who do not denounce their cultural traditions and espouse the mainstream culture of this country are condemned to oblivion, to remain invisible. Such writers are called ethnic writers or regionalists. The message is clear—the keepers of the literary tradition of the mainstream culture continue to tell us that as long as we remain rooted to our cultures and its materials, we are voices which will not be heard outside our regions.

In the 1980s this argument sounds ludicrous; but unfortunately it is an attitude which those of us who are writers using the materials of identifiable ethnic cultures have encountered. Within the Chicano community—one group of the broader Hispanic community in this country, and a culture easily identifiable because of its language, history, and social traditions—a number of writers have been engaged in a vital literary movement for the past decade. It is a new movement, and yet it has its antecedents in both our oral and written literary traditions. It has a unique place in our history because it has oriented itself around a new attitude, the attitude of liberation inherent in the word "Chicano." It is a refreshing attitude, because the Chicano Movement is not only an artistic movement, but also a social and political movement. It is a movement of liberation, and, in the best sense of the word, it is a movement of renaissance. And yet except for some who know the culture intimately, very few non-Chicano critics have bothered to investigate and evaluate the literary production of the Chicano Movement of the late sixties and the seventies. Why is that? Exactly whose problem of perspective is this?

I cannot accept the argument that the problem is that of the Chicano writer. We have faced the reality of the mainstream culture of this country, we have been involved in many of its aspects, and we have lived with its image as a point of reference all of our lives. That cultural image, which for purposes of this paper I call the mainstream culture (to differentiate it from smaller ethnic cultures within its confines), is a conglomeration of peoples and cultures that began its "meltdown" in its self-forged cauldron in the eastern United States and that very early in its evolutionary history adapted the stance that the only good culture was its own culture. It moved westward, waving its manifest-destiny flag in the face of every ethnic culture it met, and demanded assimilation of those it didn't destroy.

That movement and its consequent evolution was a white, Anglo-Saxon dominated movement. Its literary history has not recorded the oral and written literatures of the Black, Native, and Mexican Americans.

Perspective requires at least two points of reference, and I submit that as Chicano writers we have a clear perspective of society and literature. We have both the materials and traditions of our own culture and those of the mainstream culture with which to work. Perhaps the problem of visibility and perspective is not ours, but one of the Anglo-American critic.

In spite of our history, and in spite of our current literary movement, mainstream critics, reviewers, scholars, and editors have refused to acknowledge our work. Why? I suggest that it is a peculiarity of the mainstream culture not to "see" those ethnic groups with histories and languages so firm and established that they refuse the "meltdown." When the mainstream culture opens its eyes and looks at the ethnic cultures that are thriving in spite of its negligence, it tends not to see the good and the beautiful, that is, the artistic production and the aesthetic nature of the group, but rather the negative aspects of the group. Hence the stereotypes that are so damaging to the members of that ethnic group.

If an ethnic group demands recognition, what does the mainstream culture ask in return? It asks the ethnic group to give up its identity and assimilate. Many ethnic groups have refused to pay the price and have paid the consequences. Today, Chicanos and other Hispanics in this country are refusing to pay the price. In a sense, we would rather remain invisible to the generalized representation that the mainstream makes of us, than give up the richness of life we find in our own cultural identity. For the writers, the choice has its penalties. We must depend upon our own small presses for publication, our work will not be reviewed by national review journals, and the sharing of our literature with the rest of the country will have to continue to depend on an underground movement. On the positive side, we retain our identity, we see ourselves in a historical setting, we read the ethnic writings of other groups in this country, and the sharing between the surviving ethnic groups in this country continues. What this country learns from our struggle will be most important to the survival of a diverse national literature.

I am confident that Chicano writers will continue to reflect in their work the particular perspective that their culture and contemporary society provide. The Hispanic community in this country will retain its language and its cultural traditions, and the writers will continue to use the elements of their culture as literary material. The writers will also continue to write both in English and Spanish, as they have in the past. In the case of the Chicanos, our ability to live in two different cultures will allow us a perspective which will be very valuable to us in both its practical and aesthetic sense. The fruits of this perspective could be a barometer that points to life in a multiethnic and multi-aesthetic world, a guide which can be immeasurably valuable to the dominant Anglo-American culture—if only it listens, if only it learns to see.

We know that traditions are transformed as they evolve. Cultures are not static entities. The particular ethnic culture which I represent is not the one in which my father lived. Change and transformation are a part of normal, healthy evolution. But change and progress must be evaluated carefully if a culture is to survive. One of the most interesting aspects of the Chicano Movement of the late sixties and the seventies was that it was a time of reevaluation. Many of the questions raised by the writers and activists of the movement put the brakes on the rush to join the Great Society, an interesting euphemism for the mainstream culture, which I have already described. The Chicanos in this country asked themselves: assimilation at what price? On the one hand there was the inclination to ask for our fair share of the American pie—a pie whose fruits were gathered by our workers, but whose taste was denied to us. We knew very well that equal access had been denied to us. On the other hand, we knew that if we plunged into the mainstream, we might drown and disappear, as other groups have disappeared. Like a bargain with the devil, we knew that once the deal was struck there was no turning back. It was dilemma: How could we achieve equal access into the institutions controlled by the mainstream culture and at the same time preserve our ethnic heritage?

So, for us, the sixties and seventies were years of a cultural revolution, one not yet documented in the journals and magazines of the mainstream culture. Some attention was paid to the revolution in the streets; the news media blew up the events it needed to fill its "ethnic minority news" quota for the time being, but they missed the revolution within. They missed the serious questions we were asking about our future.

What were those questions? Primarily, it was a call for liberation. We were asking ourselves who we were and where we were going. For answers we turned to our culture and to its values. We found that we had a long literary history, both from our Hispanic roots and our indigenous New World roots. We found we knew the earth that we had settled and the role that it had played in shaping our character. We found that we had indeed listened to the songs and myths of our Native American brothers, and a part of their blood and their worldview had commingled with ours. We found many answers in our hearts, in our souls.

These are certainly some of the questions that preoccupied me as I wrote in the sixties. For me, the materials and content for my novels lay in my culture, a particular New Mexican culture which had given me birth and nurtured me. That environment was one in which Spanish was spoken, not English. I was to learn English only when I went to school. As I grew, I was to learn and study and grow to love the literature of the Anglo-American tradition; but when I sat down to write, I had to return to my own culture to find the materials that were the content of my work. Most importantly, I had to return to my culture to find my voice. Although I never left my culture, I had to rediscover the rich and immense possibilities it had for me as a writer. In day-to-day reality or in the oldest and deepest myths, the material was there. It had always been there. It was waiting for me to give it meaning in my writing, and it was waiting to give me meaning. I rediscovered a part of myself in the process of writing—and what writing isn't the art of self-exploration?

Other Chicano writers dug into the culture and found similar materials at hand. There are too many to name, but surely the works of Tomás Rivera, Rolando Hinojosa, Miguel Méndez, Sabine Ulibarrí, to name only a few, are destined to endure. These writers produced some of the works of the seventies. Others were to follow. And when the novels and stories and poetry of the seventies were published, we saw that indeed we had tapped our own indigenous culture for the characters, the background, the drama, and the worldview that evolved in the literature. It was not the cauldron of the Great Society we had gone to; it was not the dominant and often overbearing Anglo-American world that we had found as fit subject for our works; it was our own culture. This is not a startling idea in the evolution of cultures and their artists; in fact it is quite natural. But it is of great importance to us, because it helped to turn the tide of assimilation that threatened to sweep over us. It should also be noted that the movement was not a nihilistic movement; that is, the right and necessity to exist on our own grounds did not fill us with the despair which other counterculture movements of the sixties and early seventies succumbed to. No, our history was too solid, our roots too deep in this continent. We will continue the struggle to obtain equal access in health, education, and well-being, but we will also continue to sing and paint and dance and act in our own voice.

The seventies were indeed a flourishing decade for Chicano literature. Major writers emerged. The fervor and excitement spread from our barrios into the universities. The artists were the literary arm of a movement which was creating part of our destiny. Chicano Studies and MECHA [Movimiento Estudiantil Chicano de Aztlán] organizations of students started up in colleges and universities. We were invited to read and share our thoughts and work with a new generation of Chicano students. The sad part of those vital years is that by and large we were only read in our own communities. Chicano clubs invited us to read on campuses; and when we read, we read largely to Chicano audiences. On reflection, this is a damning statement to make on the state of ethnic literature and the lack of attention it suffered even within the university communities. We learned very quickly after a decade of literary production, that even in the universities—whose goal it is to expose its students to the literature of all its people—even there we were still invisible.

Given that background, it is almost incomprehensible to understand how the second largest ethnic group in this country could be involved in a contemporary literary movement and not be recognized. In those ten years such major publications as the *New York Review of Books* have not reviewed the literature of the Chicano movement, and no major articles have appeared in such mass-appeal magazines as *Time* and *Newsweek*. Why?

It is important to note that during this decade an interesting phenomenon did occur—that within the same time span, the critics and reviewers leaped over the works of the Mexican Americans and other Hispanics in this country and rediscovered the writers of Mexico and Latin America. Dozens of reviews and articles on writers like Márquez and Fuentes appeared, and the works of these writers were quickly known to United States readers. Even Borges enjoyed a flurry of rediscovery. But these respected and gifted writers represent other cultures within the spectrum of Hispanic culture; they do not represent the reality or the consciousness of the Chicanos in this country. Why, then, did the critics and reviewers leap into Latin America in search of Hispanic works and refuse to deal with the literary production taking place within the Hispanic community in this country? That is a question of utmost importance.

It is a question that has many implications, certainly implications of importance to the past and future reception of the literature of minority and ethnic groups in this country. It is of particular significance to the Chicano writers who will continue to write in English and Spanish and who will continue to give a particular Hispanic focus to their works. After all, this culture is the oldest European culture in this hemisphere, and it has had a very close relationship to the Native Americans and their own narratives. The question is also important to the Native, Asian, and Black communities in this country and, I believe, to the women writers who have found their voices and demand to be heard.

When one analyzes this problem, one cannot escape the conclusion that there are deep-rooted racial biases at work. It is a problem that can and should be confronted openly and dealt with, perhaps, as the Black writers have dealt with it. It is a problem that points to the ignorance and short-sightedness of the manipulators of the culture in this country.

Reading, Mostly Novels

A good novel should excite us. It fills out our emotions and makes us more human, and at the same time it challenges us to think and to actively re-create our lives. A good story presents and engages us in a new world, and at the same time it comes clothed in the style that is the particular stamp of its author's craft. When both of these elements are in harmony, we have excellence. One of the touchstones I have used to judge literature is its total effect on me, that is, years after I read the work, how well do I remember it? What special power did it bring to me that still lingers? In short, how can I still point to its incorporation into my total self as I can point to all the other poignant experiences of life?

Using that as a guide, let me share with you the highlights of the reading I have done over the past year or so. The first novel which comes to mind is *The Jumbie Bird* by Ismith Khan, a southern Califas writer. The novel is an excellent portrayal of life in the Caribbean area, the story of a small boy growing up in a complex world. I found, while reading it, that Khan's people share many things in common with Chicanos. I really recommend it.

And what can I say about Fuentes's opus, *Terra Nostra*? I started it, put it down, started again, felt centuries of Catholicism weighing down on me—I couldn't finish it at one reading. It took me years to plow through Joyce's *Ulysses*. When one deals with masterpieces, one should return to them from time to time and savor them slowly. Too much at a time is liable to give one empache.

The Autumn of the Patriarch by Gabriel García Márquez? I felt subdued. Sheer genius. Pa' que decir más.

As I think back, it seems like I was on a round-the-world onda, pues porque no. Those of you experimentally inclined probably know the

Originally published in *Rayas* (May/June 1978): 4–5.

works of Robbe-Grillet. If you don't, start with *The Voyeur*—good mystery and scintillating style. I've also had time to go back to writers like Lagerkvist and Japanese author Kenzaburo Oe. Oe's four short novels in *Teach Us to Outgrow Our Madness* are powerful! And speaking of Japanese writers, John Okada's novel, *No-No Boy*, has just been reissued. It's the first novel ever written by an Asian American, and it's excellent. It's well written, develops strong characters, and provides a bitter and historic view into the terrible injustices committed on the Japanese Americans during World War II. There's a lot of writing going on in the Asian American communities in the northwest and west coast. Shawn Wong and Lawson Inanda, just to mention two of the most exciting young writers in the country, are writers we should follow.

And speaking of west coast writers, I think Ishmael Reed's *Flight to Canada* is excellent! Best he's done to date. Dripping with satire, he takes a new look at slavery and flights to freedom. Reed is a prime mover in the west coast in bringing formally isolated ethnic communities of writers and artists together. Great!

Closer to home, I was impressed by some of the young writers we read at Flor y Canto Quatro, writers who haven't published yet, but who are doing serious work. I have slowly been reading *Hechizospells* by Ricardo Sánchez and like the sense of humanity and sincerity I find behind each piece. And how about the poet of the year award going to Rafael Jesús González for *El Hacedor de Juegos/The Maker of Games*? He speaks from the heart with sharp imagery and dazzles us with his sense of craft and what he is willing to do with it.

I read a lot of the Chicano novels to teach them this past semester, and I came away with the feeling that we have a very solid body of work to look at. And it's only one level! I'm excited about the work that will be produced in the next few years. And how about the critica? Serious students seem to be discounting the criticism that is written from the hip and evaluates personalities instead of the works. The critics who seemed to help further the understanding of the entire body of Chicano literature and who are respected by the students were Joseph Sommers, Juan Bruce-Novoa, and Roberto Cantú. But like the literature itself, this field is growing every day. *The New Scholar* and *The Latin American Literary Review* have recent past issues devoted to criticism. *Minority Voices* is carrying more articles about Chicano literature. The future looks bright.